THE KIRYA SOLUTION

THE KIRYA SOLUTION

Christopher Harvey

iUniverse, Inc.
New York Lincoln Shanghai

The Kirya Solution

iUniverse, Inc.

For information address:
iUniverse, Inc.
2021 Pine Lake Road, Suite 100
Lincoln, NE 68512
www.iuniverse.com

ISBN: 0-595-28243-1

Printed in the United States of America

Acknowledgements

With any work of passion, there are those who have inspired, driven, criticized, or simply tolerated the creator throughout the long process. I would be doing a grave injustice to the message of this story if I did not let some of them know how very important their contributions were.

First, and most important, I must thank my wonderful wife. She has not only inspired my writing, but also answered my very dreams. She is my hero.

Phil S. and Harold P. for knowing honor and ignoring conventional wisdom at the peril of your own reputations. (Wait until you guys see my next book), Colonel Dave Tuthill for his priceless editorial feedback, Linda Bilbao for being such a great teammate, Lori Heunink for showing me how, and Mom for getting me started.

Finally I would like to thank the swift, silent, and deadly men of Marine Recon. Never in my life before, or since serving with them, have I found such a magnificent group of individuals. The trust, honor, sibling animosity, love, courage, and brotherhood built between these men is a treasure that never fades. While Americans sleep safely in their beds at night, Recon Marines are scouting the next battlefield. Never seen, yet somehow everywhere. This book is for them. Semper Fi.

If he that in the field is slain
Be in the bed of honour lain,
He that is beaten may be said
To lie in Honour's truckle-bed.

—Samuel Butler, *Hudibras* (pt. I, canto III, l. 1,047)

For Dana Jo

CHAPTER 1

The Rattle

Kingdom of Saudi Arabia
February, 1991

Cpl. Darrell House was a very unimpressive Marine, and not simply as a matter of appearance. The military-issue spectacles that rested near the tip of his nose out of sheer laziness on his part had smoked lenses to a factor of thickness that distorted his face, encircled with imitation tortoise-shell frames.

They were hideous.

House looked more like a Native-American version of Jerry Lewis than a Recon Marine.

It wasn't just his slovenly appearance that struck colleagues as a blemish to the polished image of the Corps, but his professional incompetence. He was given only the most menial tasks for the mission, and that was due to patent necessity.

For the next fifteen minutes, he only needed to stay awake at his post atop the police barracks and cast the occasional glance into the endless desert for any signs of movement. Unless he spotted one of the intermittent surrendering troops slowly approaching from the Iraqi side of the berm, his watch would pass in the routine bored anxiety of Observation Post Six and he could get some sleep.

Unfortunately for the Marine, his fundamental dearth of the self-discipline so cherished by the Corps was now dictating his fate. House made no effort to fight off the powerful sensation that cast over him like an evil spell, and let his eyes slowly close.

He was instantly asleep.

♦   ♦   ♦

As if the small band of Iraqi insurgents had been watching his every move, they slithered out of the trench where they had hidden and began slowly creeping towards the remote outpost. The desert sand beneath their feet was firm from the previous night's rains and they moved quickly.

The four men were conscripts who had agreed to the suicidal task under the threat that, if they refused, their families would be murdered upon the commanding officer's return to Iraq…not an uncommon incentive since the air war started.

Such motivation, combined with the abundant setting sunlight that shone from beneath the smoke-filled sky, practically insured that they would not succeed.

♦   ♦   ♦

"Pereda! What are you doing?" Gunnery Sergeant Corell barked from the opening of the small, subterranean domicile he'd dug near the base of the very building atop which Corporal House was now asleep at his post.

Lance Corporal Pereda's skinny frame jolted at the sound of Corell's voice.

"Head call, Gunny," the young Reconnaissance Marine said as he held up a roll of toilet tissue.

Though of Spanish decent, Pereda could have been a dead ringer for Mahatma Ghandi in manner as well as appearance. His glasses were not to Marine specification. The small, perfectly round lenses fit his face much more proportionately than did House's and added to his *Ghandiesque* countenance. The image Corell processed was the legendary Indian leader proudly brandishing a roll of Charmin.

Pereda had no idea what he'd said to make the gunny laugh.

"Well get back up there and help that idiot," Corell ordered as he regained his bearing.

Pereda was assigned to the rooftop with House for the duration of this observation shift and Corell did not trust the security of their position to his most inept Marine.

"Aye Gunny."

♦   ♦   ♦

Assuming the simple action of firing at the Marines on the building would fulfill their obligation and preserve their families at home, the Iraqi team began firing from over 900 meters, well beyond the effective accuracy of their AK-47s. With little more than a glance, they began spraying in the direction of the rooftop.

♦   ♦   ♦

Corporal House was roused awake by the rounds thumping the wall behind him on the rooftop. The confusing drunken fog of waking made it impossible for him to assess what was going on and his instinct was to stand up and raise the binoculars from around his neck. House stepped to the edge of the rooftop to see what was going on.

Before his eyes could focus the blurry image through the powerful Steiner binoculars, a single round from the Iraqi team pierced the beautifully mirrored, laser-deflective lens in front of his right eye.

It exited the back of the Marine's head cleanly, as if not slowing at all.

"Go!" Corell yelled at Pereda and Cpl. Felipe Rael.

Rael was a sniper assigned to Corell's recon team and slept much more lightly than did House. When the first Iraqi round flew overhead, Rael jumped from his bunker and ran for the rooftop cradling his M-40A1 sniper rifle. He was in remarkable physical shape and bounded up the stairwell of the five-story structure that had been gutted by an earlier Iraqi attack.

As he strode skyward in groups of three stairs, Rael heard the loud cracking of rounds into the Kuwait-facing façade of the building. He reached the roof and dove out onto his stomach.

The first thing Rael saw was House, there was no question he was dead.

Oddly enough, the image didn't stir rage in the elite operator. His was a business requiring complete focus and a chilling level of detachment. He crawled to the wall at the edge of the roof and slid the muzzle of his rifle over the top.

With the fluidity of a ballet dancer, Rael's muscular legs eased his lean frame slowly skyward to see over the edge through the scope.

"Humph," he grunted with a grin.

The Iraqis were too far to even see him, let alone target him effectively.

"Buh-bye," Rael whispered to himself as his fingers delicately came to rest on the scope and adjusted it to the distance he speculated through years of experience.

The Iraqi soldiers were lying prone in the middle of a vast expanse of desert. They had no cover, and apparently no support.

As rounds continued to impact around him in a random, chaotic pattern, Rael picked the Iraqi on the far right. He centered on the man's frightened face and squeezed the trigger.

Sniping for Rael was similar to golf in that once he fired a shot, a particular feel of the recoil and the sound of the shot told him that it was perfect. He had the next Iraqi lined up before the initial round practically decapitated the first soldier.

The second Iraqi suffered an identical fate and the remaining two stood in horror to flee, leaving their weapons behind.

They ran as if being pursued by the devil himself, but would never outrun the surgical lethality of the phantom recon Marine that had now targeted them.

The two Iraqis died less than twenty meters from their comrades.

Rael had managed to dispatch the four Iraqis before Corell and Pereda even made it to the rooftop. The silence that befell the post told the gunny that the situation was under control.

"Awe shit," he said simply as he looked at the single casualty they suffered.

"What was it?" he asked Rael, who was now standing erect.

"Four-man team," he turned and pointed out into the desert, "way the hell out there, I set up for nine-twenty."

"Poor bastard, they just got lucky," Corell said.

"His time to go," Rael said with no emotion in his voice.

Corell nodded, "well…load him up."

♦   ♦   ♦

"Whenever you're ready," Sergeant Ward said over the team intercom.

Cross was excited, this was the first time since he'd come to Saudi Arabia that he was able to employ his assigned weapon in a live fire exercise. His fingers pressed the gray leather tips of his Nomex flight gloves as his grip tightened around the wooden handles of the Browning M-2 .50 caliber machine gun. Both of his thumbs pushed down on the "butterfly", the twin trigger of the gun, so named because of its resemblance to the shape of a butterfly's wings.

As the first round lit off from the massive weapon, Cross jumped. It wasn't fear, but an unfamiliarity that comes with the static time away from the regular training that the operators of Second Reconnaissance Battalion endure every day.

Once the first high explosive, anti-tank round impacted the target area a kilometer away with a bright flash of phosphorous, Cross was fine. He settled in and loosed a volley of fifteen Armor-Piercing, Incendiary Tipped rounds. The substantial recoil of the weapon rocked the frame of the modified Humvee he was perched atop.

"Now that's what I'm talking about!" he yelled.

"Amen, brother." Ward replied.

Cpl. Len "Cross" Crossley continued firing at the stack of ammunition boxes the team had set in the distance, ripping them to shreds. With the wind in his face, the expended gunpowder mixed with the stale smell of the endless Arabian Desert.

He smiled.

The odor drove home the reality that he was in a war zone. The destiny he saw for himself since the age of ten was being played out. He was in a heaven that only warriors know, a blink away from combat with an enemy of America.

The rest of Team Three began firing their assigned weapons downrange. The effect was impressive. The six men that comprised the deep reconnaissance team projected the fire of an entire platoon of enemy soldiers. The small elite unit was formidable to say the least.

The sun was beginning to set, collecting extraordinary hues of red and purple only achievable with the aid of the exclusive composition of the infinite Arabian sand. The effect was not lost on Cross. The brilliant young Marine took a moment to appreciate the grandeur before the exercise was finished. He knew better than to mention his appreciation to the rest of the team though, they would never understand.

"Let's go," Ward ordered. They were almost out of training ammo anyway. "I got the lead."

As the team's two hummers turned to the north for the short trip back to the firebase, Cross saw the horizon ahead of them growing black.

It was the third day in what the guys had begun calling the "smoke cycle". Since the Iraqi Army set fire to over 600 of Kuwait's oil wells, the apocalyptic amount of smoke spewing forth into the atmosphere had become a slave to the prevailing winds. It just so happened that during the season of Shammal, which comprised the months of January and February, the winds switched direction every three days.

By nightfall the small firebase that constituted Second Recon Battalion's headquarters would be swallowed up by a darkness that the young corporal had never even imagined. The wind would shift just after dark as it had with clockwork regularity in recent weeks. With this change of direction, a black blanket would slowly devour the stars that filled the brilliant desert sky. The two contrasts were profound.

Growing up near Los Angeles, the flaxon-haired, blue-eyed surfer had never seen so many stars. He wondered if the medieval level of darkness associated with the smoke, on the other hand, had been experienced by anyone.

Cross's three exhilarating years in recon had served to sharpen his night vision to a level that he took for granted, but was very abnormal. His visual perception at night was twice as acute as that of an average person and this supernatural ability was universal throughout his team. Even on operations that took place on moonless nights, he could sense shapes and movements in the distance utilizing only the ambient light in the atmosphere.

When the darkness from the oil wells came, however, there was nothing. He had, on more than one occasion, even waved his hand in front of his face so closely that it brushed his nose and been able to see absolutely nothing. It was frightening even to the most weathered Marine. His next footstep could be off a 1000-foot cliff or into a sleeping company of Iraqis and he would never know. He knew the actual risk of either of these things was infinitesimal at best, but there is a tiny place somewhere in his mind that was never quite sure.

The absolute darkness did make for a somewhat restful sleep, however. As restful as could be expected when he knew that the bulk of the Iraqi Army was 10 miles away.

By the time the team reached the firebase, the solid wall of smoke looked to be about ten miles away, on the Kuwaiti border.

The hummers pulled to a stop next to the small two-man tents erected around several fighting holes. The small pyramids that reeked of stale, unwashed Marines and Korean War era canvas were the closest things the team would have to a home for the indefinite future.

"I'm going to the head," Cross told Ward as he jumped down from the rear deck of his vehicle.

Ward nodded, and Cross grabbed his own cherished roll of toilet tissue from inside his small tent.

As he walked towards the dugout latrines in the middle of the compound, Cross noticed the distant rumble of allied ordinance detonating over Kuwait. The sound excited him and promoted his misguided association between combat and glamour.

Kuwait, an involuntary grin crept across Cross's face at the thought.

Cross couldn't wait to get up there. Sitting under the sparse privacy netting, a thought occurred to him out of nowhere...*be careful what you wish for.*

The rogue tenet vanished amidst the unmistakable whirring of a circa 1950 Willy's jeep, a predecessor to the Humvee, growing in the distance. From the sound of the struggling little engine, the jeep was doing about as fast as it could. Cross's pulse quickened because he knew that there was only one person within a hundred miles driving one of these relics of wars gone by, his platoon commander.

Platoon Commander is normally a billet occupied by a commissioned officer, but Cross's was a gunnery sergeant. Gunny Corell was not due back from Observation Post Six for two more days, so Cross quickly gathered himself and exited the head. He began making his way to the Delta Company area while he poorly coordinated walking, buttoning his trousers, and cradling his rifle.

"You there! Marine!" the very heavily accented French-Canadian voice of Sergeant Major St. Pierre rang out from nowhere.

Before Cross could even look up to acknowledge the battalion sergeant major, he knew why he was being yelled at.

"Secure that flak jacket, dammit!" closely followed by his trademark saying, "someday you thank me for saving your life!"

"Yes, Sergeant Major!" Cross hollered with a veiled smile.

It would have been futile to plead his point, not that he would have. As a matter of respect for someone who had been in special operations since before he was born, Cross just shook his head, closed the front of his flak jacket, and continued towards the center of the compound.

As Gunny Corell's jeep was pulling to a stop next to the command tent, two corpsmen and the battalion medical officer stepped out to meet him.

Cross stopped several feet from the jeep.

The corpsmen heaved the poncho-laden body of a dead Marine out of the back of the jeep and scurried towards the BAS, or basic aid station. The sight caused every Marine in the area to freeze in their tracks. Corell looked directly at Cross.

"Crossley, grab your shit and get back over here. That's House in the bag," Corell gestured towards the corpsmen carrying House's body away. "I need you up there."

"Roger that, Gunny."

Cross started running towards the small tent he shared with his team leader.

"Cross!" the gunny yelled after him.

Cross turned, but kept running backwards, his adrenaline pumping like crazy.

"Yeah, Gunny!"

"Get updated freqs!"

Cross gave a thumbs-up and continued running, he was suddenly very scared.

Cross started grabbing the items he had methodically strewn around the front of his tent. He'd anticipated actually packing them into his rucksack sometime the following day. The ritual routine he followed before every mission was shot to hell, and now he was just stuffing the necessities into the ALICE pack. Absence of the time to pack properly meant that some things were going to have to stay behind and items were now thrown into the pack by order of operational necessity. Sgt. Ward walked over from another tent and saw Cross feverishly packing his things.

"What's up?" he asked.

"I gotta go up to OP Six."

"Now?"

"Yeah, House is dead."

"No shit?" Ward said, stunned.

Ward despised House for his ineptitude, but he was a fellow Marine and the enemy had taken him. As with siblings, Marines feel they are well within their right to ridicule each other, but no one else may so much as cast a dissatisfied glare in their direction.

"We still going up on our rotation?" Ward asked, wrongfully assuming Cross knew more than he did about the change in circumstances.

"I guess. This sucks." Cross snorted as he grabbed the last of his things.

He did not like the notion of being separated from his team, and he was scared. Having their team around was like having a security blanket to each of the members. Individually, they were vulnerable. As a team, they always stood a chance. He was also robbed of ample time to psychologically prepare for the mission. That was probably the most underrated aspect of mission preparation, but recon prided itself on its ability to adapt with little notice.

"Just don't get your ass shot off…and don't screw up." Ward made very little attempt at a goodbye.

He figured he would see him in two days anyway. The closest he got to exhibiting any real emotion was to give Cross a pinch of Copenhagen snuff from his own can. That gesture coming from Chris Ward equated to true love. Cross readily accepted, then heaved his ruck onto his shoulder.

"Later, bitch." Cross said as he turned to leave.

"Eat me, fag." Ward replied.

Cross flipped him off in the universal gesture of insult without a glance as he walked away. Marines have a unique way of showing affection, and the brotherly love they shared was thick in the air.

In reality, Cross was torn between the excitement of finally getting the hot mission he had always hoped for and the fear he felt at having to face the dragon without his closest family. That is what Team Three, Deep Reconnaissance Platoon was to him, and they would not be there to watch his back this time.

Ward, on the other hand, was envious that Cross would get there first. With accumulated combat experience comes respect in the Corps, and Cross would get it first. The worst part was that if Cross lived, he would rub it in—and Ward knew it. He smiled at the thought.

Conversely, if he died, Cross knew Ward would have to try to explain to his mother why he had not been there to protect him. The nervous corporal simply forced that thought from his head as he walked towards Gunny's jeep.

The executive officer of the battalion ducked out of the command tent just as Cross arrived with his gear.

"Well, it's nice to see you ain't dead too Gunny." The XO said jovially to the old recon war-horse.

His manner still suggested that he would like a detailed explanation.

"Yessir." The gunny grunted as he stuffed an entirely excess amount of snuff into his bottom lip.

Cross realized that the reason the major had not been aware of the OP team's status was that House had yet to establish communications with headquarters. That meant that there were recon teams in Kuwait operating with no support whatsoever. Cross's heart began pounding. This constituted a legitimate crisis.

The XO was standing with his hands on his hips. No one needed to remind him that Gunny Corell was one of the best, and if the mission had failed so far, it was most likely through no direct fault of his own. Corell grabbed his notebook and walked around the front of the jeep.

"House couldn't get shit done before he got dead, and no one else up there knows how to work a fucking radio." He said to the major.

The major let out a sigh as they went into the tent together.

The communications failure came as no particular surprise to Cross, who was still in shock that House had been selected to precede him on the battalion's first high-profile assignment. A mission that was sure to involve direct action against the Iraqis. OP Six was the radio relay sight for every recon team that was currently operating inside occupied Kuwait, and even the Iraqis knew it.

Corporal House was a stark, and fortunately rare, example of an unqualified Marine slipping through the cracks and accidentally being assigned to a Reconnaissance unit out of a need for a particular military occupational specialty.

House was a radio operator, a substandard one at that, who was assigned to fill a need for communicators in Second Recon Battalion. His inability to formulate rational thought was not even his own fault. He suffered from a significantly impaired IQ as a result of the fetal alcohol syndrome that was unfortunately commonplace in his hometown of Gallup, New Mexico. The fact that he had gotten into the Marine Corps with such a low grade of intellect was not very surprising, but his getting into one of the Corps' premier units was. The deep reconnaissance platoon considered it an oversight of criminal proportions.

Cross and Sergeant Ward had warned Gunny Corell of House's incompetence when he was first assigned to the team, but Corell insisted on evaluating him personally. Corell was under the delusion that he had a charitable, fostering nature. He was a great recon operator, a fact no one disputed, but he had grossly overrated his level of patience. Since Corell and House had not been gone for more than about twelve hours before the corporal was brought back dead, Cross felt it safe to assume that the evaluation had gone rather poorly.

Cross was completing the transcription of radio frequencies when Corell stomped out of the command tent. From the look on Gunny's face, it appeared that the commanding officer had not been as understanding about the communications lapse as had the XO.

"You have two hours from right now to establish comm or I'm just going to shoot you." The gunny said as he plopped in to the driver's side of the jeep.

His left foot came to rest directly on the starter button in the floorboard and the jeep choked to life. Cross saw that Gunny was not going to wait, so he lunged into the passenger seat with his ruck on his lap and grabbed hold of the dash to keep from being tossed out of the jeep. Corell wheeled it around and sped out of the compound.

The gunny was in markedly better spirits than he was when he arrived. He was confident that Cross would come through flawlessly, and he could earn back some of the ass that had just been bitten completely off by a certain lieutenant colonel.

♦   ♦   ♦

"Pardon, your Highness." Nasir Al-Hamal said when the ringing from the telephone on his desk finally irritated the prince.

He regretted not closing the door that led to his office.

Nasir stood and hastily walked out of the prince's palatial, even cavernous office to his own small niche, mindful to shut the door behind him. He would not have bothered with the call, but the distinctive ring was that of his private line. There were perhaps six people that had the number, and even his own wife was not among them. He felt compelled to take any calls on that line.

His office was a closet compared to that of his boss, Crown Prince Abdallah, but the mere prestige of Nasir's position far outweighed any need to better represent his status. Anyone granted an audience with the king's brother needed no reminders about the power of his closest lieutenant. All matters of security for the Kingdom of Saudi Arabia came across his desk on their way to the prince. Nasir pushed the flashing button on his telephone and picked it up.

"Yes?" he answered.

"I must see…" the caller began, but the roar of a jet taking off in the near background interrupted him.

The noise was so loud it overloaded the telephone and came across as a hideous hum. Nasir held the receiver away from his ear until the hum faded. The caller started over.

"I must see him as soon as possible. Can it be done?" the tense voice on the other end asked.

"Come, I will see what I can do," Nasir replied.

"I will be there in two hours."

He hung up the telephone. Nasir recognized the voice. It had been Colonel Wahid…an angry Colonel Wahid. He was one of the few people the prince insisted on fitting into his schedule no matter what. Nasir wondered how long it would be before Wahid called today. Colonel Wahid was very well connected and missed nothing. The prince knew that the latest troop movements would infuriate him and was anticipating the colonel's reaction. It was exactly the reaction the prince needed to motivate Wahid for a mission that addressed what he felt was a greater threat to the kingdom than the Iraqis.

◆   ◆   ◆

The strained whining of the jeep's little engine, combined with the lack of a windshield made conversation next to impossible. Cross had a thousand questions he wanted to ask, but the good gunny did not look like he was in quite the right mood to field a barrage of questions that would almost certainly be answered in short order.

In the dwindling twilight, Cross could barely make out the shadowy outlines of several small buildings in the distance. The wind had shifted right on schedule, and the sky ahead of them was giving way to pure black. The buildings were the only anomalies on a seamless horizon in all directions. Cross's mouth became very dry. He was conscious of these new, unexpected reactions to the stress of potential combat, and his inability to totally suppress them was frustrating.

"There it is!" the gunny yelled over the noise as he pointed to the small hamlet.

With that confirmation, Cross's heart began pounding.

God, I hope the gunny can't tell.

Little did he know that Corell really did not care whether he was scared or not. Corell drove with his knees momentarily as he retrieved his Copenhagen snuff can to reload his bottom lip. He offered the open can to Cross, who readily accepted. It had become ritual years ago. Anytime he got nervous, he turned to his old friend nicotine.

As they drew closer, Cross could make out the twenty-foot high dirt mound that had been erected along the entire length of the Saudi-Kuwaiti border in an attempt to stem the flow of illegal narcotics into the kingdom via Kuwait. It was called simply "the berm." The only breaks along its length were at border stations. Observation Post Six was located at one of these stations just west-northwest of Umm Gudair oilfield. The berm had been mentioned at all of the planning briefings, but Cross had never actually seen it. He found it exciting to behold.

Instead of a grease pencil stripe drawn on a map, the front line of this war was as clear as the nose on your face. A tangible barrier, beyond which were the bad guys.

Cool. He smiled at the thought.

Suddenly, Cross saw a powerful explosion about 100 meters away from the tallest building. The sight of it alone made him jump.

"What the hell was that?" he yelled.

Corell looked at him and couldn't help laughing. Cross was curled up in a ball around his ruck and had a look of sheer terror about him that was comical. He looked like the proverbial deer in the headlights.

"Arty!" the gunny yelled with a grin.

Oh shit, Cross thought.

He knew allied artillery would not be exploding that close to their position, a conclusion that narrowed the choices substantially.

"Idiots couldn't hit water if they fell out of a boat though!" Corell yelled with a gesture towards the shifting smoke from the impact.

If the comment was meant to comfort the young corporal, it failed miserably. As they pulled into what was more like a tiny town than a police station, Cross saw a mark-292 antenna erected on top of the largest building. The mast stood twenty feet from the roof and supported a transmitter assembly that was impossible to disguise. To Cross it looked like a big, ugly, green flower declaring their position to the Iraqis like a neon sign. Since the Iraqis appeared to be walking in artillery on the building, it was obvious that they had seen it long ago.

"What's with the two-niner-two?" Cross had to know why Gunny had opted to be so non-tactical.

"I did that. That fucking retard House couldn't do any better."

The jeep pulled to a stop on the side of the building opposite from the berm.

"Where's the team?" Cross asked.

"Up topside." the gunny pointed up.

Cross could not believe that a super secret recon team was parked atop the tallest building for fifty miles underneath a massive, green, GI radio antenna while it was obvious someone one the other side of the berm was using them as an artillery practice target. He desperately wanted some answers.

Boom! Another round impacted about two hundred meters away this time.

The concussion scared the hell out of Cross, who dropped between the jeep and the building. Gunny Corell did not even wince. He just grabbed his rucksack and headed for a series of bunkers dug out in the courtyard adjacent to the building.

"C'mon!" he yelled at Cross.

Cross grabbed his things and quickly ran after Corell like a lost schoolboy. The whole experience seemed like a perverse dream. This was nothing like what he had pictured combat to be. Corell threw his pack into one of the small bunkers.

"Throw your shit in my hooch," he told Cross as he started for the entrance to the building.

Cross lugged his own pack into the hole and again ran to catch up to the gunny, making sure not to drop his field-expedient antenna bag. He called it his "goodie bag," and was seldom without it.

It had become almost completely dark, and Cross began to feel the fear that came with it. He looked timidly up at the building and noticed the chunks of mortar that had been blasted from the light blue paint. They walked into the battle-ravaged building and sought out the stairwell. The interior of the building was in shambles.

On January 29, Iraqi forces charged across the Saudi Arabian border into the town of Khafji. Saddam Hussein declared that with the offensive, the ground war had started and would soon end with the victorious Iraqi Army crushing the Americans. While the world watched the battle of Khafji unfold on CNN, an identical, yet unpublicized assault occurred at the tiny outpost that housed OP Six.

A small team from Second Air Naval Gunfire Liaison Company, or ANGLICO, had been caught by surprise while they manned the observation post. They managed to successfully escape the town to the relative safety of an American armor column that was approaching from the south to counter the incursion. Their haste had caused them to egress without destroying sensitive cryptographic equipment and code books.

Although the invading army did not last long at the hands of the Americans, they recovered the cryptographic assets and compromised all of the information. This particular battle never made the news, and for good reason. Unbeknownst to Cross and the rest of the battalion, this compromise of sensitive materials pushed back the allied ground invasion by three weeks. The oversight had gotten ANGLICO reassigned, and recon took over at OP Six.

Being this much closer to the front, Cross noticed that the rumble from the allied bombing was much more pronounced. He experienced the same hollow feeling in his ears from the rumble that he heard during earthquakes as a child. The rumble absorbed all of the surrounding natural sounds.

What disturbed him so much was that this rumble never completely faded, even though it constantly varied in intensity. The whole building creaked from the seismic activity. As the rumbles ebbed, Cross heard a strange noise trail off behind it, then a brief instant of total silence before the rumble began again in earnest.

The footsteps of the two Marines echoed throughout the building as they climbed the stairs. It was haunting. Another artillery concussion caused Cross to drop to a knee in order to maintain his balance.

"That's a little more like it," Corell quipped.

He was actually impressed that the Iraqi gunner had hit close to the building. Cross heard a large metal door two flights above them open with a loud bang. It was closely followed by the sound of someone running down the stairs. Within seconds, the Marine who had left the roof came into view.

"Screw this Gunny, I'm going to the hooch." Lance Corporal Jimmy Fallon told Corell.

It was clear that he had had enough of close calls. He was another Marine that had been sent to recon on loan from a communications unit and was really not suited for this.

"The hell you are. You ain't doin' a damn thing until we get comm," the gunny replied as he pushed past Fallon. "Get your scared little ass back topside."

"C'mon Gunny," whined Fallon.

That caused Corell to turn.

He grinned and leaned towards Fallon until his face was an inch from the scared lance corporal.

"You get your ass back up there before I throw you over the berm as a peace offering," he growled.

Fallon had nothing to say, and Cross was disgusted by the Marine's cowardly whining. Cross pushed past him and followed Corell up to the roof. Lance Corporal Juan Pereda and Rael, the sniper, were on the rooftop. Rael was peering through an early version of a DIM 36 thermal targeting sight at the darkening northern horizon.

The DIM 36 was developed as part of the sighting system for light armored vehicles, but it could also be mounted on a tripod for individual use. Its only drawbacks were the heavy weight and short battery life. Battery life for this particular one was not a problem since Corell had dismantled the battery pack and adapted it for use with a gas-powered generator he stole from regimental headquarters. It was not a classified optical system, so packing it out in the event of an emergency was not a necessary option. The generator quietly sputtered away on the ground below with a bright orange, extensively reengineered extension cord leading up the side of the building to the DIM 36.

The roof of the building had not turned out to be such a bad place after all, Cross thought. The walls of the building continued four feet above the surface of the roof, giving the Marines adequate cover from small arms fire and any shrapnel from the impacting artillery. He was beginning to think that the Gunny really did know what he was doing, contrary to his initial impression. Were an artillery round to impact them directly, their choice of position would be of very little consequence.

"Any time there, Crossley," Corell derailed his train of thought.

"I'm on it, Gunny." Cross snapped back to the task at hand.

For some reason, the M292 antenna was not allowing the team to transmit. Cross surmised that the silicon content of the sand played havoc with radio transmissions. He quickly figured out that he would only be able to cover the required distance with a little help, so he went to work on an alternative. He grabbed his frequency sheet to make sure that the AN/PRC-77 radio they were using was set correctly for today. He then untied the top of his small, black bag and retrieved a bundle of radio wire.

"Why don't you have an MX-2020?" he offered to the three Marines surrounding him to watch his work.

"They're issued out to all the teams. There aren't any left." Corell said.

"Nice." Cross continued working.

"Yeah, no shit."

Cross fished around in his blouse pocket for something to write with and retrieved a dull pencil. He didn't notice that the other Marines on the roof were scrutinizing him, trying to figure out just what he was doing.

"Nine thirty-six…nine thirty-six." Cross began mumbling.

Pereda and Corell both recognized the number from their classes on field expedient antennae. Nine thirty-six was the constant used in the formula for calculating the length of a full-wave antenna, and Cross was repeating it so he would not forget. Fallon had no idea what the significance of the number was, and he was from a communications unit.

"What are you doing?" Fallon was terrible at concealing his ignorance, and this was just a small example.

"Shut up, dumb ass," Corell snapped. "Watch and learn."

Fallon did not take any real offense to the retort. Marines were not known for their sensitivity, nor did they want to be. He fully accepted that he was, in fact, a dumb ass in the face of any analytical thought and he was just fine with that. Corell did some calculations in his head and concluded that Cross was endeavoring in the wrong direction.

"That won't work," he began. "It's too far of a shot for a longwire, the sand will absorb it."

Cross did not look up from the calculations he was drawing on the roof.

"Trust me, Gunny, I know this shit."

Cpl. Rael smiled from behind the Dim-36. He had known Cross for years, and knew he was the best.

Corell was impressed with the kid's confidence and had become curious for his own knowledge. He was the consummate recon Marine, always eager to learn new tricks of the trade.

"OK, hotshot, then school me," Corell ordered.

"Heard of NVIS?" Cross asked.

"Niv-who?"

"Near Vertical Incidence Skywave."

NVIS is a radio wave propagation tool that had been around for some time, but the average Marine communicator usually never bothered to further their learning and master the skill. Fallon was living proof.

"Near what?" Fallon asked.

"Near Vertical Incidence Skywave," Cross repeated. "You bounce the radio waves off the ionosphere down to wherever you want to talk."

"No shit?" Corell said.

He was now a willing pupil and found this interesting.

"No shit. I can bounce a comm shot into a pickle barrel at a hundred miles." Cross lied right through his teeth.

He had never done it before, but had seen it work and knew he could replicate the experiment. It was one of his better abilities.

"This oughta be interesting," Corell conceded. Cross continued his calculations. He had always struggled at mathematics, so calculating lengths and angles with an audience was very trying.

Foom.

Cross did not recognize the distant hollow sound as coming from an American-built, Iraqi-owned 105mm Howitzer firing. One thing he knew immediately was that whatever it was, it made a bad sound. He'd heard artillery fire before, but never in his direction. The sound was significantly different.

"On the way," Rael said simply.

"Oh shit, shit, shit." Fallon ran to the stairwell and jumped down a flight of stairs.

Cross looked up at Corell in the dim red glow from his flashlight as if to ask what to do.

"Well, let's get this thing up," Corell told him.

It was as if he had not heard the incoming round. Pereda seemed totally unaffected as well. They were desensitized to it. Cross took the hint and got back to his calculations. He heard a deep humming noise that was slowly growing louder. It seemed like the shell was taking forever to reach them, and he just knew it was going to land right on his head. He looked up just as the sound reached the climax of its crescendo and immediately before it impacted 300 meters to their east. The flash silhouetted Corell as Cross dropped to his belly, covering his head. Pereda ducked also.

Corell had not so much as blinked.

"C'mon...we're burnin' daylight," Corell said in the darkness as chunks of soil and gravel rained down on the group.

Cross could not believe it. Gunny was certifiable.

He shook off the shock and continued to work. When he was sure of the numbers, he shot an azimuth to Battalion Headquarters with his compass, measured and cut the correct length of wire, then strung the homemade antenna up on the large roof in the direction of the firebase. He then stretched a length of wire underneath the antenna to act as a counterpoise, or reflector to amplify the power of the signal. Without it, a portion of the signal would be absorbed by the roof's material. When the antenna was hooked up, he listened for a moment to see what the reception was like.

There was nothing.

Oh, no. Cross thought he had done something wrong, or that it just was not as easy as it looked.

He checked the team's call sign, and keyed the handset.

"Mike-two-Charlie, this is Yankee-three-Foxtrot, radio check, over."

After a brief silence, the ear piece squawked so loudly that Corell and Pereda heard it.

"Three-Foxtrot, this is Two-Charlie, authenticate whiskey-zulu, over," the voice on the other end said.

"Grrr." Cross fumbled through his pockets in search of his AKAC encryption sheets.

He knew better than to think headquarters would not ask him to authenticate his identification, especially since they had not heard from OP Six in days.

Pereda had his sheets out, and quickly handed them to Cross. "Here."

"I authenticate Hotel, over." he told the Marine on the other end.

"Roger that, I have you five-by-five, how me, over?"

"I have you same, out." Cross grinned.

The transmission was crystal clear. He handed the handset to Corell with a smile. It had taken one hour, including travel time and Corell was genuinely impressed. Cross had successfully completed in fifteen minutes what had taken House three days to fail.

"Alright, you lucky prick." Corell attempted to burst Cross's bubble to no avail.

The handset squawked again.

"Three-Foxtrot, do you have SITREP on Delta-one and Delta-two, over?"

Corell looked inquisitively at Pereda.

In Corell's absence, it had been Pereda's job to cover the radios in the hope that the two teams operating in Kuwait would not get into any trouble. If they had, they would have been on their own since OP Six was unable to relay messages to Headquarters.

"They're good to go." Pereda assured him.

Corell keyed the mike.

"Both teams are fine. Next comm window is zero-two."

Gunny Corell sometimes dispensed with communications formalities.

"Roger that. Two-Charlie out."

Corell put the handset down and looked at Pereda.

"Now that's how you get comm," he said.

They all breathed a sigh of relief knowing that the current crisis had passed.

♦   ♦   ♦

Crown Prince Abdallah despised Americans and everything western, a sentiment shared by a majority of his countrymen. His brother, King Fahd, found the Americans a useful commodity on the other hand, especially when it came to the defense of the kingdom. No one but the king knew for sure, but the royal family understood that since the 1979 fundamentalist uprising in Mecca, King Fahd felt that the monarchy was vulnerable.

A group of armed Muslim extremists had taken over the Grand Mosque by force and held it for 10 days. The event not only showed that there was sedition within the kingdom, but that it was strong enough to secure the defining icon of Saudi Arabia. The symbolism alone was enough to stir the king. His allegiance to the United States is widely believed to have evolved from a deal he struck after the uprising to secure the protection of the monarchy. The deal offers the full resources of the US Armed Forces to reverse any coup against the house of Fahd within seventy-two hours. That allegiance had brought them here now, the prince was certain.

The current situation had Abdallah very uncomfortable, but he was not about to publicly disagree with the king. King Fahd realized the gains to be made by allying with the Americans and balanced his commitment to Islam with the opportunities the west presented. This approach had not only brought protection, but great wealth and power as well.

Saudi Arabia was the most powerful and influential country in the region not only because it housed the two great mosques of Islam at Mecca and Medina; it had become so with the help and energy demands of the United States and its allies. The king had shown a great ability to achieve all of this without betraying his religious obligations in any way and still maintained the kingdom to high Islamic standards.

To this end, he had put Abdallah in charge of the Tribal National Guard. The National Guard was an ultra-conservative branch of the Royal Saudi Ground Forces. This paramilitary organization was Abdallah's tool for monitoring western influence within the kingdom and rooting it out. When the American generals came to the kingdom at the request of the king, the National Guard had fallen under their command as well. This fact did not sit well with the prince.

Late the previous night, the remainder of his companies had been moved to within ten miles of the front. Many of his officers saw this as a calculated move on the part of the Americans to place the National Guard directly in the path of an attacking Iraqi army. It appeared to be a convenient way of eradicating the conservative body from presenting a hurdle to American control of the country.

There were even those who adopted the radical view that the move was a way to destroy the National Guard as part of a permanent occupation and conquest of the kingdom. Colonel Wahid was one of these. He was absolutely convinced that the presence of the United States Army was part of a larger plan to take over the kingdom—if not to take over, then at the very least to establish a permanent presence here.

As he walked down the passageway to the prince's office, he mentally went over the issues he wanted to discuss. He wanted to be firm, but not insult the prince. Certainly, he thought, the prince had not completely bought into the king's naïve position towards the Americans.

Or had he? He had to choose his words carefully.

"How are you today, my friend?" Wahid said to the prince's assistant.

"Very well, you may go right in." Nasir gestured toward the open door leading into the side of Abdallah's huge office. As Colonel Wahid walked into the office, the prince looked up from a notebook he was scribbling in. Nasir closed the door behind him. Wahid came to attention and saluted. The prince motioned him to sit down.

"Thank you, your highness, but I'd like to stand."

It was a slight breach of protocol to brush off the prince this way, and Abdallah sensed the Colonel's anxiety.

"I had nothing to do with it, Colonel, if that is your issue."

"Yes, your highness, it is," Wahid replied.

"Well, sit down Colonel."

Wahid was not about to symbolically press his position twice. That would be an outright insult. Something no one would do to the prince, especially if he is also a friend. The Colonel took a seat and allowed himself to be a bit more at ease.

"The order came from the king," Prince Abdallah told his favorite colonel.

The issue was no longer up for debate, regardless of the colonel's theories behind it.

"What now?" Wahid asked.

It seemed as if all the cards had been played out and the only missing element was an Iraqi invasion.

"Be vigilant, Colonel. His Highness believes that we may also be brought great honor by leading the kingdom to victory."

The prince did his best to dispel Wahid's concerns even if they reflected his own.

Wahid was not convinced.

"There is something deeper, I know it."

"Then, Colonel, you are in the perfect position to identify it aren't you?"

"What do you mean, Highness?" Wahid asked.

"Our mutual friend is still pressing his point from Jeddah. I, of course, have to officially tell you that any contact with him is strictly forbidden."

"Yes?"

"But you have some time on your hands right now, and I trust you to make decisions on your own."

Wahid knew that any contact he had with their mutual friend would have to be kept from the prince for his highness to maintain plausible deniability. The influence of the Americans had even silenced the one voice of reason that existed in the prince. Wahid was on his own.

◆   ◆   ◆

Cross still had not relaxed enough to sit in the metal folding chair next to him on the roof. Gunny Corell had, in the days before Cross's arrival, set up quite a little office on their perch. He and the other Marines manning the post had rooted around the gutted buildings to assess any resources left behind by the Iraqis and had found the chair. They also found a small folding card table and even a slate chalkboard. The chalkboard leaned against the north roof wall where it could be quickly referenced. The call signs and frequencies of every team operating in Kuwait were written on the chalkboard as well as the frequencies for fire support, extract, and medivac, should they be needed.

Sitting next to the chalkboard was a large wet towel that could erase the information with one swipe. Things had been happening very fast, and this system eliminated the need to search for the information in the pockets of uniforms. Corell had always believed in smarter versus harder. If any task could be done more easily, yet remain tactical, Gunny had figured it out.

The team's radio sat on the table, still hooked up to the NVIS antenna Cross had built. It had worked without fail all night, and Cross had refused to rotate out of his watch monitoring the radios. The latest session of Iraqi "Artillery for Idiots," as they had taken to calling the daily bombardment, had stopped for the night and the last few hours had been relatively quiet. Cross leaned against the wall in front of the radio table and stared at the most enormous column of flame he had ever seen. He wasn't sure exactly how far away it was, but judging from the slow, lumbering way the fire lapped at the sky, it must be pretty far. It was somewhere in the middle of the Umm Gudair oilfield, no doubt.

The thick layer of smoke overhead, combined with the miles of orange-glowing sand beneath it, was something out of a biblical nightmare. The entire town was bathed in a flickering shade of orange, and the blanket of black descending upon it looked like death.

"Eerie, isn't it?" Lance Corporal Pereda's thick Spanish accent almost startled Cross. "It looks like something out of Dante."

Cross was taken aback by the comment. A Marine versed in the classics was a rare commodity indeed.

"Yeah." Cross rubbed his eyes. He had not blinked in several minutes. "It is."

"Alpha-two-Victor, this is Delta-two, radio check, over."

The handset clipped to Cross's load bearing equipment came to life. Cross looked at his watch. They were right on time. He grabbed the handset and keyed up.

"Delta-two, roger that."

"Two-Victor, Delta-one, radio check," the second team checked in.

"Delta-one, roger."

Cross was relieved, knowing that the communications were still working and that the teams were safe.

He finally sat down in the chair and felt his remaining stores of energy leave his body. The door leading from the stairwell onto the roof opened, and a sleepy Lance Corporal Fallon staggered out.

"This sucks," he observed.

"Quit your sniveling, Fallon," Cross told him. "Where's Gunny?"

"On his way up," Fallon said with a yawn.

"Nothing going on, both teams just reported in," Cross advised his relief although he was not planning on leaving.

Gunny Corell came onto the roof looking about as well as to be expected for two in the morning. He grabbed his Copenhagen can and stuffed about four finger's worth into his bottom lip.

He held out the can for Cross.

"Anything going on?" he asked before the snuff had packed into his lip.

A significant amount fell out onto his chest and sprayed onto Cross with every word. Cross had gotten used to it weeks ago and found it amusing. It had become the gunny's trademark. Cross took a pinch for himself.

"Nah, Gunny."

"All quiet on the northern front, huh?" Corell replied in one of his attempts at humor.

"Yeah, something like that," Cross said as he sat down in the chair for the first time all night.

"Go get some rack time," Corell told Cross.

Corell could tell Cross was running out of gas.

"I'm alright Gunny."

"That wasn't a request."

"C'mon Corporal Crossley," Pereda said as he grabbed Cross by the arm and helped him out of the chair.

Much to Cross's surprise, he actually needed the help. They grabbed their rifles and headed downstairs.

"You know, you can call me Cross," he told Pereda.

"I didn't want to be improper in front of the Gunny," Pereda said in perfect English.

"I guarantee you Gunny doesn't give a shit."

"Very well."

Cross laughed. The kid was just too well mannered to be a jarhead. Cross followed Pereda to retrieve their sleeping bags. It was his first night here, and he did not know the routine. Pereda picked up on the fact.

"We've been sleeping over there, keeps the rain off."

Pereda pointed to a concrete slab underneath an overhang. Rain normally was not an issue in the Arabian Desert, but the smoke from the oil wells was in such volume that it produced pyrocumulus clouds that developed into their own weather systems. They would often condense enough to drop heavy, black rain on the landscape. All of the Marines that had been into Kuwait or far enough into northern Saudi Arabia to be rained on were covered in a dark, greasy film.

The two Marines laid out their bags on the slab, next to a lightly snoring Cpl. Rael. Cross sat down on an adjacent curb since he did not yet feel like sleeping. It became very quiet, and he again noticed the rumble from the bombing. It was then that he noticed the rattle. The oscillation of the earth from the detonations was enough to rattle the broken windows throughout the town in perfect synchronicity. The larger the bomb or the more closely it exploded to OP Six, the louder the town would rattle.

What haunted Cross was not so much that the whole town rattled, but that the whole town rattled as one. It was genuinely frightening, and a phenomenon he would remember for the rest of his life with stunning clarity.

"Jesus, that's weird," he observed as his head slowly turned to view the panorama.

"This whole God-forsaken place is weird." Pereda seemed wary of the place.

"This is not the place I would want to die." he said as he looked up and around the skeleton of a town.

"Why not? What's the difference?" Cross asked.

He never believed Death was particular about location when it arrived.

"Even God has abandoned this place. I want him to find me."

The observation sent a chill up Cross's spine.

"Well, I guess we have to get the hell out of here in one piece then." Cross assured him with his best attempt at a comforting, confident grin.

He noticed Pereda pull his Walkman from a small bag and regretted forgetting his own in the haste to leave headquarters.

"What do you listen to?" he asked the lance corporal, who at one rank below him was actually eight years his senior.

"Opera." Pereda told him.

"Oh, I love opera," Cross admitted.

Pereda assumed the Corporal was just humoring him. That, or making fun of him. Cross had never told anyone in the Corps his deepest, darkest secret. He had been a young violin virtuoso as a child, but had given it up years ago. He'd never lost his love of classical music though. He realized upon meeting him that Pereda was not your average Marine. The Spaniard was refined and educated, the two scarcest qualities in the enlisted Marine Corps.

"Here, she's new. The most amazing mezzo-soprano I've ever heard." Pereda handed the Walkman to Cross.

While he unraveled the cord to the headphones, he asked Pereda a question that had been bothering him since they met.

"Why on Earth did you enlist in the Marine Corps?"

"I'm from Spain. I've only lived here for two years and I owe it to my new country." he continued, "It's just what you do."

Cross was impressed to see someone who actually appreciated what America was. He had long ago tired of seeing Americans take for granted a freedom that most of the world does not believe exists.

"In a perfect world, maybe. Where do you live now?" Cross asked.

"New York City." Pereda told him.

"No shit? Where?"

"Manhattan."

"You like it there?" Cross asked.

The idea of New York had never really appealed to him. He got enough of urban sprawl in L.A.

"I love it. It's the greatest place on Earth."

Pereda closed his eyes, imagining the bright lights and the smells of his relatively new home.

"If you say so."

Cross pushed the play button on the Walkman and proceeded to hear this rising mezzo-soprano star from Rome belt out *Se tu m'ami*. She was the most magnificent singing talent he had ever heard. For a few brief minutes, the world around Cross transformed from an imposing hell of fear, fire, and smoke into pure heaven. Pereda saw the emotion in Cross's face and realized that he was indeed an opera lover. It seemed strange to both of them that they were able to discover a common appreciation for fine culture in such a forbidding place. War had an odd way of uniting the most drastic contrasts.

"Wow," Cross said, "she's awesome."

He was not as current on the American opera scene as he would like to have been, but the life he had chosen for himself was not one that necessarily encouraged the pursuit.

"She's not very well know over here, my cousin sent it to me from Europe," Pereda told him.

No matter where a Marine is on the globe, *here* means the United States.

"Her name is Cecilia Bartoli."

"She'll be huge, I bet," Cross said as he handed the Walkman back to Pereda, "thanks."

"My pleasure," Pereda said with a respectful nod.

Fellow Marines usually chided Pereda for attempting to push culture their way. He loved to show the rest of these barbarians that, although he would face any foe beside them, he was still slightly above them from a Darwinian perspective. They played the game back and forth. Pereda put on his headphones and curled up in his issue mummy-style sleeping bag for the night, escaping to his own small paradise.

The excitement of the past twenty-four hours was beginning to exact a toll on Cross, and he was getting very tired. He noticed the rattle of the town grow more pronounced from a particularly large detonation in the distance. The sound brought the rattle as a whole back into his consciousness. The constant rumble of the earth and the *chuk chuk* of the broken windows were the only sounds he heard. He dismissed it and assumed he would just get used to it, so he grabbed his bag and climbed in for some much-needed rest. As he attempted to tune out the rattle, it crept more deeply into his thoughts. It beat out a tempo reminiscent of a horror movie score. The intensity would vary, but the sound was the same, and he was not going to tune it out.

Cross sat up, looked out at the abandoned town in the orange glow of the radiating fires, and listened to the rattle. He tried for a moment to make light of it by picturing a young, scantily-clad Jamie Lee Curtis running from one of the abandoned buildings with a serial killer in tow, but the sound was too real.

It was horrifying.

There was no one to speak on its behalf, so the remote outpost spoke for itself. It rattled out its message of death to anyone who would listen.

To Cross, it was pure evil.

No forces on Earth alone could combine in such a perfect composite to exude such suffering. There were other powers at work much greater than that.

The thought of death had never before bothered him, but Pereda was right, God *had* forgotten about that place. Cross didn't want to die there either.

CHAPTER 2

"Baby Milk Plant"

"Come on, come on, *come on*," Dr. Mike Stanford mumbled with guarded optimism as he nervously chewed the remaining yellow paint off a number two pencil.

As the message popped up in an error window on his computer screen, he spat the pencil onto his desk.

"Damn."

There was no one in the control room within earshot to hear him voice his frustration, so he made no attempt to subdue it. The repugnant sight of the saliva-soaked cedar core of the pencil provoked him to throw it into the waste-basket under his desk…yet another victim of his frustration.

From his desk at the NASA Goddard Space Flight Center in Greenbelt, Maryland, he had been very anxiously awaiting an endless string of coded photographic information from the Hubble Space Telescope to arrive at his computer. The data would assure him that the photos he had tasked had indeed been processed. That information would then be automatically sent to the Space Telescope Science Institute in Baltimore and returned to him as breathtaking images of a storm on the surface of Saturn. Having the raw tracking data sent to his terminal simply assured him that the data had in fact arrived.

Today, rather than the dependable flow of information he was used to getting from Hubble via a series of Tracking and Data Relay Satellite Spacecraft, he received a message that the TDRSS had been preempted by a higher priority user. He'd been grappling with this problem since September and had only been receiving about a quarter of the requested data from Hubble. There really was no one to complain to about the issue though.

There was only one object in orbit that could override the telescope: the Lacrosse 1 imaging radar satellite.

Designated 1988-106B 19671, Lacrosse belonged to the National Reconnaissance Office and was under the direct control of the CIA, which answered to the President of the United States. There was nothing Dr. Stanford could do, so he simply submitted the instructions to Hubble for the fourth time in the last thirty-six hours, and swore to the empty office.

◆   ◆   ◆

Lacrosse 1 had just made a pass over the Kuwaiti Theater of Operations and used the TDRSS to relay its own information to Area 58. Officially known as The Defense Communications Electronics Evaluation Testing Activity and commonly referred to as the "Ground Station," Area 58 sat at the corner of Telegraph Road and Beulah Street on Fort Belvoir, Virginia. From there, the encrypted digital signal traveled to building 213 at the National Photographic Interpretation Center in Washington, D.C.

Since the Iraqi invasion of Kuwait in August, analysts at the NPIC had been working eighteen-hour shifts to assess the thousands of images that came into the office not only from Lacrosse 1, but from three Kennan KH-11s orbiting as well.

Lieutenant Junior Grade Michael Roch was one of the overworked analysts at NPIC, but the long hours of coffee and terrible food had not reduced his keen ability to discern the smallest details contained within a half-meter resolution satellite photo.

He just received an image from Lacrosse 1 with a swath that included the Al Wafra oilfield. The prevailing winds caused the area to be obscured by smoke, rendering it invisible to the KH-11s, and he had been eagerly awaiting the data from Lacrosse 1, since his area of analysis included the oilfield and its surrounding area.

Lacrosse 1 gathers images using synthetic aperture radar which can see through the smoke. By transmitting about 1500 high bandwidth microwave signals per second at a specific ground area, it generates images that are almost as clear as the photographs gathered by the KH-11s. The signals reflect off of ground targets and are collected by Lacrosse. Lacrosse constantly stores the information and repeats the process.

The returned signals are combined in an effect that produces results only normally accomplished through the use of an enormous antenna, the radar equivalent of a photographic aperture. The aperture synthesized by Lacrosse would equate to an antenna so large it would be impossible to orbit.

The data is then Doppler-shifted through very powerful land-based software to adjust for the velocity of the satellite relative to the ground target. The resultant images are crystal-clear representations of all ground anomalies to a resolution of better than one meter.

Lieutenant JG Roch needed the Lacrosse images to update the last known position of the Iraqi 5th and 14th Infantry Divisions. The last viable KH-11 images had shown them firmly entrenched in an agricultural area Northwest of the oilfield, but that was almost 48 hours ago. Anything could have happened since then.

He first pulled up the image on his desktop to give it a quick once-over while it printed in large scale on a nearby photographic printer. He scrolled the image around and immediately noticed that most of the regiment was on the move to the west.

"Hey, Captain Bryant?" he called to the senior watch officer at NPIC, who just happened to be standing two tables away poring over another set of prints.

The captain immediately walked over to Roch.

"This is the SARs pass over Al Wafra. Look like they're pulling up stakes to you?" he asked the Captain for verification of his assessment.

"They've got scouts doing Recon over here," Roch told him as he pointed to three vehicles west of the oilfield.

"Oh yeah," Bryant said.

The verification was more a matter of protocol than necessity. It was obvious to both of these experienced analysts that the unit was preparing for a move. Captain Bryant looked around the photo and something caught his eye. There was a large truck on the road from Mina Abd Allah approaching Al Wafra that was entirely out of place. The hair on the back of Bryant's neck stood straight up as if he had just found the Holy Grail. Bryant pulled a pen from his breast pocket and pointed it at the top of the screen.

"Enlarge that," Bryant ordered as he circled the truck with the tip of his shiny silver pen.

Roch quickly adjusted the image on his computer to where the vehicle was centered on the screen. The truck appeared much brighter than any of the other vehicles in the photo. This effect was caused by more radar energy being reflected back to Lacrosse.

The truck was painted bright white.

Not even the Iraqis were normally so tactically unsound this close to the front.

"What does that look like to you?" Bryant pointed to a large box on the front of the trailer.

"Refrigeration unit," Roch confirmed as he turned and locked eyes with Bryant.

Without another word, Captain Bryant picked up the secure telephone next to Roch's table and dialed directly to the Iraq Task Force in the CIA headquarters building at Langley, Virginia.

The line Bryant called was actually located in the Near East Division of the CIA on the sixth floor. The needs of the war had expanded the headcount of the task force from 10 to 150 agents and necessitated taking over most of the Near East Division's offices.

"Warren," stated the agent who answered matter-of-factly.

"Is Sheffield in there? This is Captain Bryant."

"One sec, Captain," Bryant heard agent Warren's hand cup the mouthpiece momentarily, then release to the sound of chatter in the background.

"Sheffield, what can I do for you Captain."

It was obvious he was very busy, but Bryant never called with anything trivial. By contacting Sheffield, he was in essence bypassing the normal channels of dissemination.

"Mike, I think I found your truck," Sheffield's face flushed.

This was huge.

"Send it over."

❖   ❖   ❖

Sergeant Zarife squinted through the choking black smoke and could barely make out two headlights emerging about 200 meters up the road as he leaned just far enough from the bunker entrance to convince an unlikely passing superior that he was actually diligent in his sentry duties. His guard station was directly between two of the rising plumes and afforded about that much visibility in each direction along the main supply route from Mina Abd Allah.

Today, anyway, he and his fellow conscript were just breathing the peripheral sludge from the air, and it was not even noticeable. The black film lining the inside of their lungs had desensitized them to smoke inhalation in the same way smoking two packs of cigarettes a day does over time. The effects of sitting in this hell would not materialize for years. As the truck grew closer, he noticed that it wasn't an ordinary military transport.

"Galeb, come here," he ordered his partner up from his seat on the floor of the shelter as he grabbed his rifle.

The subordinate soldier was surprised by the order. They had not seen a vehicle for two days, and none of those coming before that had required both men to inspect.

As the soldiers loped up to the roadway in their smelly, oil-soaked, olive drab uniforms, they heard the whine of the truck's brakes slowing it at the sight of them. Zarife held up his hand ordering the truck to stop. Before it had come to a halt, an Iraqi colonel in fresh utilities who was obviously not an imposter stepped out of the passenger's side and yelled to the sergeant.

"Out of the way, idiot! We must pass!"

"Yes, Sir!" Zarife yelled to the colonel while he back-stepped off the road-way.

His fellow sentry backed away to the other side. The colonel re-mounted the big white truck and it began pulling away. As it passed, Zarife read the English writing on the side of the truck. He knew enough to know what it read, as did the young Corporal Galeb, standing on the other side of the road.

When the truck passed, both men were directly across the roadway from one another. Their looks of utter confusion caused both to chuckle. If that colonel only knew how stupid he looked barreling through the desert in a big white truck that said "Baby Milk Plant" on it.

◆   ◆   ◆

Mike Sheffield had compiled most of the research on Project 600 personally and had convinced the Joint Chiefs of Staff that it warranted target assignment for destruction, and it had been destroyed on February 3rd by four GBU-17 laser-guided bombs.

The very idea of what Project 600 represented was frightening to anyone who had clearance to know about it, and Sheffield wanted any fruits of the project's labor wiped from the earth.

Project 600 was a significant satellite program of the Iraqi biological warfare program located at Abu Ghurayb near Baghdad. It was established during the early years of the Iran-Iraq War under the direction of the Al Hazen Ibn Al Haytham Institute located in Al Salman. Al-Salman was the epicenter of Iraqi chemical and biological warfare.

The institute commissioned the French construction company Sodetg to build a milk processing plant near the veterinary college at Abu Ghurayb, about twenty kilometers west of Baghdad on Highway 10. From the very onset of construction, however, the plant only vaguely resembled a facility for such a benign use.

Control of Project 600 was taken over by the Aqaba Establishment, the government administrative body of Project 400 located south of Baghdad, in 1989. As soon as the initial construction was completed, the French workers left and were quickly replaced by Iraqi chemical and biological warfare troops under the command of a Ba'ath Colonel named Faa'du. The colonel was the military commander of the facility and regulated all matters of security. He answered directly to Brigadier General Abdel' Fatah, code-named Mahmud by the CIA and head of the Aqaba Establishment program.

The actual director of the project and owner of all creative control was the head researcher, a German microbiologist named Klaus Meinholtz. Both he and his wife, Pauline, had been recruited by the Aqaba Establishment while on the faculty of the Cellular Biology department at the University of Hamburg.

It was nothing as noble as political ideology that convinced the couple to abandon their tenure, but rather an obscene amount of money. Unfortunately for the Aqaba Establishment, they were profoundly naïve in the ways of international espionage or military operational security and made little effort to blend in with the Iraqis.

Pauline worked her way through Medical School, and was a very Westernized, liberal woman. The Islamic position on women in Iraq disgusted her, and she refused to be legislated by what she considered arcane religious laws. She felt she had worked too hard to be oppressed by a religion that was not her own. What she failed to understand was that a beautiful woman walking around in a bright red skirt would draw unneeded attention to a project that violated international law.

Descriptions of she and her husband quickly reached CIA agents working in Iraq, and before long the agency was able to identify them both. This immediately confirmed suspicions that the facility was not being used for the production of infant formula as the Iraqis had publicly claimed.

Access to the plant was strictly regulated. A barbed-wire perimeter fence was erected just inside an eight-foot dirt berm. The narrow road leading to the constantly manned security gate from Highway 10 had eight ninety-degree turns necessitated by concrete traffic barriers.

One particularly inept move from a security standpoint was the placing of the pens for research animals in an open area near the northwest corner of the facility. To no one's knowledge had animals ever been required in the production of infant formula—a fact that did not elude photoreconnaissance analysts for even a moment. All of these measures drew attention to the project from the CIA. There was no need for such security around a civilian facility.

These factors caused the CIA to increase its monitoring of the facility. Had the Iraqis left the building unguarded and not introduced such a strong military presence, it is likely that the project would have gone unnoticed. It had become apparent since the onset of the war, however, that the Iraqis were tactically clueless. In an effort to protect a closely guarded state secret, they had essentially alerted everyone in the western world as to its whereabouts and purpose.

Activity at the facility was relatively insignificant for the first several years of the plant's operation. The bulk of the research and development was being conducted under the supervision of Dr. Meinholtz in a U-shaped building nearby that housed a veterinary medicine plant. During this time, the Meinholtzes successfully developed weapon-deliverable strains of dry form anthrax spores and botulinum toxin.

The US suspected that the infant formula plant was being used as a storage facility until around 1988 when activity at the site began to increase.

The plant was then officially listed by the CIA and the Defense Intelligence Agency as a suspected biological warfare production facility. Agents were able to confirm the installation of twelve high-capacity industrial fermenters imported from Italy, as well as the installation of high-particulate air filters in the ventilation system. It was at this point that Mahmud ordered attempts at camouflaging the facility as a legitimate factory.

Five Mercedes refrigeration trucks were brought into the facility with the words: "Baby Milk Plant" stenciled along the sides in English. There was even a press tour arranged to highlight the exterior of the facility and showcase its legitimacy. This backfired on Mahmud when products carrying an American brand name were shown on TV. The American company denied having ever dealt with the Iraqis and discounted their claims. It had been a poorly planned public relations nightmare, and the CIA had taken the cue to turn up the heat.

♦   ♦   ♦

Reconnaissance imagery in all of its forms had been vital to every aspect of the gulf crisis since the first southern movements of the Iraqi Army early in 1990. Images presented personally to King Fahad by the US Secretary of Defense showing Iraqi troops massing on the kingdom's northern frontier after the invasion of Kuwait had been the deciding factor in allowing US involvement. The images had been presented within hours of their collection and even as Saddam Hussein gave his word to the international community that he had no plans to invade, their validity could not be brought into question.

The only fact more damaging to the Iraqis throughout the course of the conflict than imagery was the fact that they could not get an aircraft off the ground without it being summarily destroyed by coalition fighters.

In any conflict, there are tactical imperfections. As skilled as the US had been carrying out the opening air onslaught, no one could have known that the truck from Abu Ghurayb had gotten away. Just as someone could emerge unscratched from a bomb-leveled building, so too had the truck escaped the destructive totality of the allied air umbrella.

The unwavering confidence of the military leadership in Riyadh had not clouded the skepticism of Mike Sheffield. He had combed over the damage assessment images of project 600 time and time again and was still not convinced that they had gotten everything.

"Colonel Hampton, this is Mike Sheffield in Langley," he began cordially as he fixated on the bright anomalous rectangle within the image of Al Wafra.

It had taken a full twelve minutes of relaying through the intricate network of secured telephone lines and satellite links to get through to Hampton. Colonel Hampton was the assistant tactical planning officer in Riyadh who had overseen the targeting of Abu Ghurayb.

"Oh, I only have a minute Mr. Sheffield, what can I do for you?"

The bombing of the Baby Milk Plant had been a feather in Colonel Hampton's cap, one that would look very nice when he came up for selection to Brigadier General. He had heard about Sheffield's skepticism and was not very pleased with being deflated by an agency spook. He viewed Sheffield's vigil for the phantom missing truck as an insult.

"I want to send you something to get your opinion."

"OK, I can't say for sure when I'll get a chance to look at it," the colonel brushed him off. "We're pretty busy around here, there's a war on."

OK, you smart-assed prick, Sheffield thought, but he held his tongue.

He was setting Hampton up to soil himself and that was revenge enough.

"I think you'll want to look at this right now, Colonel."

Hampton was surprised at Sheffield's tone. He didn't care for the little worm, but he had never asked for anything with such urgency.

"OK, I'll give it look. Send it."

"It's on the way," Sheffield assured him, "Call me back at AV23642."

"Right."

Hampton hung up first, sending a very direct message that he did not appreciate the inconvenience. After Sheffield faxed the image to Hampton, he sat back down and leaned back in the plush leather office chair of the Assistant Director, wishing it were his own. He took a deep, confident breath and enjoyed the brief break. It lasted exactly three minutes and forty-five seconds, ending abruptly with the ringing phone.

"Sheffield," he answered.

"I've been around long enough to know when I'm wrong, Sheffield," Hampton immediately diffused any animosity between the two men.

"Nice piece of work you got here. Now what do we do about it."

"Well, I've been wondering exactly that. It's right on top of Second Marine Division down there."

"Do you know if it's Anthrax, or Botox?" Hampton asked.

It would make a very distinct difference in how the threat was to be dealt with.

"No, I don't," Sheffield told him.

"See if you can find out for me…quickly. This just moved to the top of the list."

"Yessir," Sheffield assured him, although he doubted that he'd be able to find out.

Hampton knew that the Second Marine Division was preparing to breech the berm and head directly for the position of the truck. There were enough Reconnaissance teams operating in the area that it did not matter much which way the wind was blowing, the threat of whatever was in the truck was too great to just bomb it.

Colonel Hampton was sufficiently perplexed with the issue that he felt it necessary to invoke his analytical crutch, a half-smoked and raggedly chewed

Have-a-Tampa cigar that had been resting stoically in the top drawer of his desk.

In a single fluid motion that waxed of William Holden, he stuffed the gnarled end into his mouth, began chewing on it and went directly for a light without looking. Never averting his stare from the picture sitting on his desk, he withdrew a Turkish matchbox from his shirt pocket and lit the cigar.

The flame at the end of the stale roll of tobacco jumped with every puff as it came to life. Hampton shook the match to extinguish it and tossed the spent stick into the ashtray atop his desk. He took a long pull and leaned back in his chair. As he sat within the thick shroud of fine cigar smoke combined with his own thoughts, Sheffield's obsession with the truck quickly consumed him and became his own.

♦   ♦   ♦

Sergeant John Foy passed his tongue along the outside of his maxillary row of teeth and noticed that they had the texture of wet sandpaper. He figured the feeling must be accompanied by the ungodly stench of rampant halitosis, but he had grown used to it over the last four days. He turned the small knob beneath his AN/PVS-5 night vision goggles and they whirred to life.

Honeycomb-patterned green light assaulted his eyes and jolted his nervous system back from the blissful exhaustion that was overtaking his body and mind.

As the Hummer he was riding in crawled along, he scanned the horizon for the other element of his team. He spotted them about 500 meters to the south, just before they drove behind one of the last burning oil wells in the southwest corner of Umm Gudair oilfield.

The minefield laid out by the Iraqi Army ran just south of the oilfield and Second Recon Battalion's mission was to map out lanes of passage through the minefield for the advancing Second Marine Division when the ground war commenced. Foy laughed as he recalled the intelligence briefings for the mission. Saddam had touted far and wide that he had erected an impenetrable barrier of death and destruction the entire length of his Army's front line.

Foy was told to expect thousands of land mines, miles of tank traps entwined with barbed wire, countless trenches ablaze with burning oil, and the unwavering resistance of the Iraqi fighting man. What he and his team found instead was miles of empty desert pock-marked by the occasional poorly concealed land mine.

"There's some," Foy said over the team radio frequency.

"Roger that, I see 'em," his assistant Team leader in the other vehicle, Corporal Sean Doran, replied.

Foy smiled. The most profound symbol he had seen to indicate that the Iraqi Army was entirely unprepared and out of their league was their method of employment for the M-21 anti-tank mine. Rather than use the mine's intrinsic pressure trigger which allows the entire mine to be buried invisibly beneath the sand, the Iraqis armed the mines with M607 fuses and tilt-rod triggers. Tilt-rods are designed for use within concealing vegetation since they stick out of the ground a full half-meter to contact the leading edge of an advancing vehicle. In the Arabian Desert, they simply served as convenient minefield indicators.

"Three-Alpha, you got enough streamer?" Foy said to his assistant over the radio with a chuckle.

"If not, we will distribute shit paper, over," Doran murmured in his best Drill Instructor voice.

Foy permitted himself to laugh aloud. Their mission had metamorphosed from one of sneaking around the desert waiting for a fight to tying markers around tilt-rods sticking out of the sand from here to the horizon.

They were up against rank amateurs.

Foy knew by the poor engineering and apparent lack of training that most of Iraq's southern army had to be conscripts with no clue about warfighting.

Within the next twenty-four hours, Foy's team would be back at the firebase getting some rest and would be replaced by a fresh team. He could not wait to pass along the intelligence he had gathered to alleviate the anxiety on the rest of the battalion, all of whom were sure they were going to die before the ground offensive even started.

◆   ◆   ◆

Several kilometers away at OP Six, Gunny Corell stared out in the direction of Sgt. Foy's recon team as he monitored their communications. The grin on his grimy old face pierced the desert darkness.

◆   ◆   ◆

"The default assessment has to be the worst-case, Anthrax," Colonel Hampton told the small group of very powerful officers gathered in a small conference room at the US CENTCOM forward headquarters in Riyadh.

They had no way of knowing for certain whether the truck might contain botulinum toxin, which was produced at Abu Ghurayb, or Anthrax, which may have been stored there for the arming of weapons.

"Obviously if we could confirm that it's Botox, we would just put it on the sortie list."

As he looked at the faces around the table, he could tell that they all understood the stakes. The combined analytical power in the room had to determine an appropriate military response to the threat posed by the truck and that depended greatly upon what was in it. Botulinum toxin is one of the deadliest substances in the world, but is very fragile. It would become inert shortly after exposure to air and sunlight, which would be easily facilitated by bombing the truck from a safe altitude. Anthrax, on the other hand is a stubborn, resilient substance that can be carried by the wind and infect people for days.

"What's the forecast look like?" Major General Malcolm Scott decided to ask about what Hampton should have touched on by now, but Hampton was still waiting for the weather liaison officer to arrive with the latest reports.

"I had to get a WLO with clearance. He's on the way now," Hampton told him.

This topic was incredibly sensitive, and it was not ordinary for a weather officer to have top secret clearance. As if on cue, an Air Force captain was let in the room by one of the military policemen outside the door. Everyone in the room looked at the young major.

"Good timing Major Tovar, go ahead," Hampton ordered.

"Yes, Sir," the major cleared his throat.

He was not nervous from the display of brass facing him, but was a bit embarrassed by his tardiness. He passed a stack of papers to General Hampton. Hampton saw that they were computer-generated weather maps and passed the stack around after taking one for himself.

"There is a low pressure area moving in from the north that will be over Al Wafra within the next twelve to sixteen hours."

Tovar allowed everyone to reference the grainy maps he had passed out before continuing.

"It will essentially remove the inversion and allow pyrocumulous caps in excess of 40,000 feet," that raised some eyebrows. "An ideal vehicle for distribution."

"Thank you, Major," Hampton told him.

Tovar took the cue that he was no longer needed and left the room.

"We're going to have to send someone in there," Colonel Brentley Denson, the lowest ranking man in the room announced.

He was representing the Marine Corps at the meeting since the threat was in their area of responsibility. The tension in the room became palpable as the men realized in turn that the only way they were going to deal with this threat was through containment. That meant a ground unit.

"Unfortunately, the Colonel is right, we have to secure it," Hampton said. "but all of our SOCOM assets are in isolation or already staging."

They all had sufficient clearance that they were currently involved in the planning of the allied ground offensive just days away. All special operations units were tasked in preparation of the invasion. Denson cleared his own throat before offering his humble solution.

"General, may I make a suggestion?" he said as he pensively rolled a pen around in his fingertips.

"That's why we're here, Colonel," Hampton told him.

"We've already got Recon Teams in there prepping the breech, they're familiar with the area and they're good." he pressed his advantage, "I think they could handle it. They're direct-action capable."

Hampton mulled over the offer briefly, then turned to Major General Dewey Hadlock who was present representing US Special Operations Command, SOCOM.

"Don't you have anyone, Dewey?" Hampton asked the General.

"Yes, Sir, I've got the Zulu team; they're trained for this. I've also got a pararescue team on TRAP duty with two Pave-Lows at King Khalid that we could use for insertion. I think this is big enough that the Bear will give us some latitude."

Zulu team was Special Forces Operational Detachment (Zulu). They specialized in nuclear, biological, and chemical warfare. The Bear was the Commander-in-Chief of US Central Command, CINCCENT. Any deviation from the plans already set in motion would have to be cleared through him. Colonel Denson felt his chance to showcase the Corps' premier fighting force threatened by SOCOM's willingness to take over the operation.

Not only that, but he knew that if Army Special Forces took the mission, Second Marine Division would be left oblivious as to its success. The Marine's subsequent advance through Al Wafra could unknowingly expose them to biological warfare agents. The Colonel spoke up.

"We're already in the area," he said with confidence. "We can take care of this."

General Hampton had already made up his mind to let Recon have the mission, but he wanted them to be well supported.

"I want Zulu to go also. Get the commanders on the horn and let's do this thing. This is MARCENT's AO, so Colonel Denson has the ball"

There were no objections to assigning the mission to the Marine Corps Central Command. General Hampton looked at his watch.

"I'm going to clear it with the Bear. You have two hours."

❖   ❖   ❖

Colonel Wahid arrived at a block of flats at Eskan Village on Riyadh Airbase ready for some rest after racking his brain over the prince's mission. In the morning, he would begin tracking down some American officers with whom he had trained. He wanted to get an immediate feel for what the infidels had in mind when their services were no longer needed for the defense of the kingdom.

He grabbed a black leather attaché from the back of his Mercedes sedan and started up the sidewalk to his assigned quarters. He would be waking up his family when he called, but he needed to hear his youngest son's voice. He had seven children living at his home in Jeddah by two wives, the youngest being three years old.

He could mentally conjure up the sound of his sweet little voice and it made him forget about the stresses that consumed him. Little Rhafji was his motivation. All he needed in the whole world was Allah and his boy. With them at his side, he would find paradise.

Colonel Wahid opened the door to the small apartment and flicked on the light. His first step into the modest room nearly rested upon an unmarked envelope on the floor. He looked outside the door in both directions as if to see someone in waiting, but saw no one in the darkness of the blacked-out airbase. He went back into the room and closed the door.

He tossed the attaché onto the small, hideously green colored couch in the sitting area and picked up the envelope. The tan envelope was dirty and worn on the edges. It appeared to have traveled some distance to reach him, but there was nothing to indicate from where it had come. He opened it to find a handwritten note. His natural instinct was to look at the signature and he saw that it had simply been signed *Muta'*. He read the note:

My brother, Allah the merciful be with you, Allah is the one and only God. My warriors stand ready to serve the kingdom and to destroy the infidel invaders. I will contact you when the time has come.

Wahid's heart began pounding. He knew that the resources Yafai could bring to bear were enormous, and a war with the Americans was coming. His mind began racing again and he knew he would not sleep for a while, so he began his task of tracking down the names of his American army contacts. He grabbed the attaché and moved to the table where he could spread papers out, and forgot entirely about calling his son in Jeddah.

CHAPTER 3

The Arab Solution

Muta' Yafai stared at the rising Arabian sun as he strolled silently across the courtyard of his palace on the outskirts of the port city of Jeddah. His compound was a palace by western standards, but considered subdued on the scale of opulence for Saudi Arabia, especially for a man from such a prolific family.

He looked down and gently kicked a stone with the tip of his sandal in a universal, almost involuntary sign of reflection. His ever-present entourage of bodyguards shadowed him from an unobtrusive distance along the surrounding walkways.

Yafai not only shared Wahid's anxiety about what was sure to come, he also harbored contempt for the way he had been treated at the hands of his homeland. Yafai and Faisal Wahid shared a common passion for Islam that was forged in their youth and tempered in conflict. Both Wahid's father and the powerful Mohammed Awad Yafai raised their children in a strict Muslim environment. Mohammed Yafai worked tirelessly in the construction business until he had built the largest construction company in the Middle East. He had vast wealth and influence throughout the kingdom, particularly with the royal family.

Every year, Mohammed Yafai opened his house up to Muslim pilgrims fulfilling their obligation of Hajj, the journey to Mecca, and his fifty children continued the tradition even after his death. During the Hajj of 1978, while Muta' was pursuing a degree in Public Administration, he convinced Wahid, his classmate, to stay at the Yafai palace.

During his stay, Muta' introduced Wahid to two Afghan pilgrims who told stories of Soviet pressure on their sacred religion and the infighting of the Muslim tribes. He spoke of the guidance of Rabbani and Sayyaf, two Muslim scholars who had taken up the cause of uniting Afghanistan. The purity of the holy struggle touched both of the young men, and they longed to travel north and join the conflict.

Wahid was already committed to the Royal Saudi Ground Forces to answer his calling as a defender of the kingdom, but Muta' was merely waiting for a catalyst. In December of that same year, it came in the form of the Soviet invasion. He went to Afghanistan a few months later and contacted Rabbani and Sayyaf. They had been elevated within the ranks of Mujahedeen freedom fighters in a very short amount of time and passionately urged Muta' to join their cause.

Yafai saw the breadth of their struggle and had discovered the meaning of his life, so he returned to Saudi Arabia to rally support for the resistance. He was moderately successful and returned to Afghanistan at the head of several thousand men augmented by millions of dollars of the Yafai Corporation's construction equipment. This gesture of support quickly provided him with the reputation he would need to ascend the ranks of the Mujahedeen.

He quietly studied the military tactics of the Soviets and the capabilities of the Afghan defenders. CIA non-official cover officers supplied him with weapons and military doctrine. He took the practical lessons of the war and those taught from a distance by his friend Wahid to formulate unusual but devastatingly effective tactics.

His tactical genius would come to fruition at the 1985 Battle of Jaji Pass. It was the first engagement in which the Soviet Army suffered significant casualties and was the very beginning of what would become a bitter, drawn-out end for the invading forces. Muta' capitalized on the momentum it caused and dealt blow after blow to the Soviets. It surprised the whole world when the powerful Soviet Army withdrew from Afghanistan in 1989, having been bitterly defeated by a rag-tag band of mountain tribesman. Vastly understated was the influence the United States had on the war's outcome.

Yafai was riding high upon a wave of victory when he returned to Saudi Arabia in 1989. While there, he gave lectures to eager audiences about his experiences in the war with the Soviet Union. He also spoke out about the direction of Saddam Hussein and predicted that within a year Iraq would attempt to gain control of the Islamic world by invading the Gulf States, including the Kingdom of Saudi Arabia.

King Fahd had no choice but to placate Saddam at the time because he was in good standing with the regime, so he issued a censure of Yafai and restricted his travel out of the kingdom. The censure failed to alter Yafai's theorizing and he wrote a letter to the king in its wake volunteering his advice should Iraq indeed invade.

In October of the next year Saddam invaded the small emirate of Kuwait and swiftly poised his army to invade Saudi Arabia. Yafai saw this as a fulfilled prophecy that would convince King Fahd of his providence. He wrote another letter to the king outlining his tactics for the defense of the kingdom through the exclusive use of Arab warriors and prepared himself to carry out the plan.

While the "Arab solution" was taken into consideration by the king and vehemently supported by Crown Prince Abdallah, the lack of immediate response concerned Yafai. He was afraid that he might not be selected to lead a glorious Muslim army in the defense of Islam's holiest sites.

Yafai's face flushed and his hands balled behind his back as the most distressing moment of his life came rushing back to him.

The day he learned that the Americans were coming.

He kicked another rock, much harder this time.

Yafai loathed being within the same borders as the infidel army and continued speaking publicly in support of an Arab solution upon the arrival of the Americans. Immediately thereafter, he rallied support through fundamentalist Muslim scholars, convincing one senior cleric to publish a fatwa ordering Arabs to travel to Afghanistan for training. Four thousand Arabs followed the holy declaration and made the journey, much to the dismay of King Fahd and the American leadership.

King Fahd further restricted Yafai's travel to within Jeddah and put him under the surveillance of Saudi Intelligence. This also failed to quiet Yafai, so on the advice of the Americans, King Fahd ordered Prince Abdallah to raid his home. Colonel Wahid tipped off Yafai, who left his residence an hour before the raid by the National Guard. Yafai was no less infuriated by the symbolic strike at him then if he had been present.

Yafai was not allowed to travel back to Afghanistan where he hoped to continue planning for a Muslim defense of the kingdom. He hoped that Allah would guide the king and make him realize what a mistake he had made. He simply waited for word from Wahid: proof that the Americans had plans other than the defense of Saudi Arabia, or a sign that he could present to the Custodian of the Two Sacred Mosques that would cause him to expel the infidels. He would be patient, and trust in Allah not to prolong his torment.

❦   ❦   ❦

The faint, distant rumble of approaching Humvees was enough to rouse Cross from the two hours of light sleep he was able to manage after the shelling had stopped. The ominous rattle of the tiny outpost wouldn't allow him to sleep any more deeply. In the mental fog he felt prior to emerging into a state of full wakefulness, he was swept by an exaggerated sense of excitement similar to that caused by a loud alarm clock jolting him awake.

His adrenal glands instinctively began overproducing the hormone. It was not from surprise, though, but from knowing that the Humvees carried *his* team for their turn in the rotation at OP six.

Cross quickly scampered out of his mummy bag fully dressed and began to roll it up. He couldn't wait to share his experiences of the last few nights with his friends. As Cross stuffed the mummy bag into his ALICE pack, he began to discern the approaching sound of more than two Hummers. This piqued his curiosity, so he grabbed his M-16 and walked around the small platform he had slept on to get a view of the road leading into OP Six. He saw a drifting cloud of tan dust being kicked up from the approaching vehicles.

The wind was blowing just hard enough to move the plume from the lead vehicle out of the way to reveal the second. Beyond that, Cross could only tell that there were others, but not how many. He looked up to see Gunny Corell staring south from the top of the building through the binoculars that had become a permanent fixture around his neck.

"Four! They're ours!" Gunny yelled down from the roof.

No one besides teams from Second Recon were supposed to come to OP six, but they had seen their share of unannounced guests in the last week. It was comforting to know for sure who was approaching from their flank.

The lead Hummer slowed as it entered the town and Cross could make out the filthy, oil-stained faced of Lance Corporal Kenny "Danno" Daniels peering over the top of the M-2 50-caliber machine gun mounted on the rear deck of the truck. Cross waved his hand in the air to draw Daniels' attention from the nervous scan the gunner was conducting of the alien outpost.

Daniels kicked the driver, LCPL Rueben Roybal, in the shoulder and pointed to Cross. Roybal drove right up to the beleaguered Corporal and pulled to a stop. The other vehicles pulled in line with the first as their worn-out brakes ground them to a halt.

Cross recognized the other team in the second set of vehicles; it was Sgt. Richard Little's Team Two. Sgt. Ward climbed out of the passenger seat of Roybal's Hummer and met Cross at the front of the truck. He took off his goggles to reveal the crusted, grimy oil mark left around the perimeter of his eyes.

"You look like shit," Ward observed as he pulled out a can of Copenhagen and offered it to his wayward assistant.

"You seen a mirror lately, dumbass?" Cross replied as he took the can.

"Gunny around? We're not staying," Ward said with obvious excitement in his voice.

He looked around at the remains of the small town and was taken aback by the total devastation that had reduced it to rubble.

"Topside, what do you mean we ain't staying?" Cross asked.

"Littledick's team has the rotation, we're going in."

Going in only meant one thing…Kuwait.

Cross's heart began beating faster, and he smiled. This was what it was all about, and they had prayed for an incursion mission. Gunny Corell came around the corner of the building to greet the arriving relief.

"Gentlemen, welcome to our illustrious shithole," he announced with typical swagger and a vain attempt at eloquence.

"Hey Gunny, Little's team is your relief, we're going in to finish up for Foy," Ward informed him.

"So I guess you'll be wanting my Comm God then," the comment flattered Cross.

"Yeah, I guess we have to take him," Ward said sarcastically.

"Alright. Cross, take Little up topside and brief him on the setup."

"Roger that Gunny."

By then, Little had walked over from his Hummer to get in on the tail end of the conversation. He followed Cross into the building that would be his home for the next three days.

◆   ◆   ◆

Wahid would be on the road for most of the day, but that option was more appealing and, by far, more discreet than arranging for a flight out of Riyadh to King Khalid Military City. Nothing took off within the theater without AWACS seeing it.

The Mercedes he drove belonged to the Royal Saudi Ground Forces and would simply blend into the heavy volume of military traffic that clogged the sparse highways within the Kingdom. He didn't want to draw undue attention while he positioned himself closer to the pulse of the Coalition leadership. Besides, the drive would give him further time to organize his thoughts and plan for the mission that lay ahead.

He reached over to the passenger seat and pulled a piece of paper from the pouch on the outside of his attaché. He had listed the names of several American and Saudi officers on it, as well as that of his cousin, Marwan who was a doctor of emergency medicine at the hospital in KKMC. He would drop in to see him before tracking down the other men on the list. The visit would allow Wahid to exorcise some of the demons that he felt for neglecting his family obligations.

◆   ◆   ◆

Buried beneath the ancient sands of the Hakirya District in central Tel Aviv lies the nerve center for the Israeli Ministry of Defense in times of conflict. The "Bor," as the Wartime Military Command Center is called, lies underground within the confines of the Kirya complex, Israel's answer to the Pentagon.

The effects of fatigue and the radiant heat of a room full of arguing military officers overcame Colonel Mordechi Urit. He leaned forward and poured a drink of water from the stainless steel pitcher found between he and his old friend Major General Elon Yaakobi, Chief of Staff of the Israeli Defense Forces. They were all tired and frustrated.

The people of Israel had been forced to sit through fourteen unanswered Scud attacks and had grown furious. Israel had historically dealt with assaults on their sovereignty swiftly and with very decisive ferocity. This time they had listened to the Americans and uncharacteristically sat on their hands while Saddam's rockets terrorized innocent civilians.

"The time has come, gentlemen. The Patriots are not doing the job you promised," Major General Yitzhak Ya'avi, head of the Israeli Air Force, stated with a succinctness that had come with 34 years of just such meetings. "Yes, they hit the incoming missiles, and that would be great if they were attacking somewhere small and remote, like Beersheba, but here the pieces still fall on the city." He concluded, "If you can't hunt them down, we certainly will."

Brigadier General Thomas Samuelson with US Central Command responded respectfully. At this point, it wouldn't take much for the Israelis to blow off the Coalition and do their own thing.

"General, no one has put into question how hard you could hit Baghdad, but, again, the President has asked that you give us time to fulfill the UN resolution."

"And no one has put into question the fact that you can do just that, General, but Israel will not be an idle victim. We will do what is necessary to answer these attacks."

At least the Israelis had displayed the common courtesy to show the US their hand before they played it, but General Samuelson still had not called the bet. He was told before he even entered the meeting that the Israelis were arming a flight of F-16 Fighting Falcons at Lod Airbase east of the city. He was on orders to give the Chiefs of Staff every opportunity to back down once again. He had done his best, but it was time to lay down the cards.

"General, your jets won't make it past Jordan," Samuelson delivered the sentence like ice-cold steel and the room fell completely silent.

After several tense seconds for the words to sink in, General Yaakobi spoke.

"Just what exactly are you saying, General?"

"We will engage any aircraft that enters the theater without proper IFF codes."

All military aircraft transmit a coded Identify Friend or Foe radio signal that identifies them to the Airborne Warning and Control System, or AWACS.

The codes are classified so that US warplanes can immediately identify whether the aircraft is the enemy, in which case the plane can then be targeted from 100 miles away and blown from the sky. General Yaakobi leaned back in his chair.

"I don't suppose you have any intention of providing them either," Yaakobi said.

"I'm afraid not, General."

"You're serious?" He asked the stoic American

"Absolutely."

General Yaakobi looked at Major General Ya'avi, and with a slight lift of his head, silently relented. Ya'avi immediately picked up the phone embedded in the table in front of him and called off the attack.

"Let's take a small break, gentlemen," General Yaakobi said as he rose from his seat.

He turned and walked out of the room, followed by several of his officers. The rest of the men in the room who had been seated at the table stood and milled around with their respective countrymen.

General Samuelson walked around the table to Colonel Urit, who was talking to an IDF Captain. The Captain looked over Urit's shoulder, cueing the senior man to the American General's approach. Colonel Urit turned around and walked to meet his old friend away from the others.

"How are you, Motta?" the General asked.

"How do you think?"

"I know," Samuelson conceded, but they both knew that business could come on company time.

"How's Dana?" General Samuelson asked.

"Too much like her father."

"What, mean and stubborn?"

"Watch yourself, General, you are on my turf," both men smiled just enough to acknowledge the deep friendship they both shared, but not enough for anyone else in the room to notice. The issues at hand were indeed very serious, but men of action never knew anything greater, or more important than a brother-in-arms. The military affairs of the evening would play themselves out at the table and now was a time for catching up with an old friend. They were able to remove themselves from the fray of the evening and drift to a time when they were young and fearless. When the only things that mattered were making it to morning formation on the chains at Airborne School, trying to look a little better and a little less hungover than the enlisted men in the class.

The American general looked at his old friend and saw that even though he had once been one of the greatest soldiers in the IDF, Motta was beginning to show some wear. The colonel's dark eyes seemed more distant, and his waistline a bit softer than it had just a few years ago. He looked to Samuelson to be a gentle older man ready to settle down and play with grandkids that were sure to come soon enough.

"You ever going to retire?" Samuelson asked his Israeli comrade.

"I thought about it, but I would be bored to death. I wouldn't know what to do with myself."

Colonel Urit looked at the floor, unconsciously revealing his deeply hidden feelings of shame.

"I'm not going anywhere soon."

He should have been a General long ago and both men knew it. He was a distinguished Army officer who had been decorated for valor, but was forever haunted by the unfair association drawn between him and the most disgraceful event in the life of the adolescent country.

He had sacrificed his entire career out of a loyalty that few could understand, but it was that lesson in loyalty that endeared Colonel Urit to anyone who knew him. Samuelson quickly changed the subject.

"Why don't you come see me and Angela in Virginia. I've been meaning to take some leave time. We could go fishing or something. She misses you, so do the kids. Well, they're teenagers now, but they still miss you."

The gesture made the Colonel feel better. It had been almost nine years since he had seen General Samuelson's beautiful family. They were going through US Army Ranger School together a week after they both completed Airborne School and in the extreme mental and physical demands of the course had formed a friendship that is only really understood by those who have suffered in such a way. They had depended on each other under inhuman levels of duress and found a trust that would never falter. When the three-month ordeal was over, their families had spent a week together at the Samuelson Ranch in the rural Virginia hills.

"Thanks, Tom."

Colonel Urit genuinely appreciated the gesture, but they both knew that it would not be the same without Kitra. She had been the light in Colonel Urit's life since they were married at the age of seventeen. She died of complications during a miscarriage four years ago and would have left his life completely empty were it not for their beautiful daughter, Dana. General Yaakobi walked back into the room with his retinue of officers.

"Let's conclude, if you please General Samuelson," he said as he sat in his chair.

"Of course, General," Samuelson said.

With a nod to his old friend, he returned to his end of the table.

◆   ◆   ◆

Cross was still in disbelief as he scanned the horizon for any sign of life. He wasn't being particular simply because any life he saw on this side of the berm would be the enemy. His perception was made razor sharp by the fear that was attempting to gain complete control over his exhausted body. The barrel of the M-2 he had taken over from Danno followed his sweeping gaze in the hope that he would get the drop on an enemy soldier that appeared out of the gray haze of smoke and dust to surprise him.

"Radio check," Ward said with tactical brevity over the net.

Cross reached up and keyed the switch strapped to the middle of his chest that activated the microphone pressed against his bottom lip.

"Roger" was all he replied.

He took a deep breath and clenched his teeth to fight back the fear. Every fiber of his being was tuned into its natural flight instinct and yet he was pressing forward, into the mouth of the dragon, into certain death by uncertain means, and he loved every minute of it. He again pictured what he must look like right now to people back home. Blazing through the desert atop his Hummer, wielding the massive gun in search of an enemy on his own ground.

This is so cool, he thought as a smile crept across his face.

He was intoxicated with the bliss of ignorance to the pain and fury that invariably accompanied battle. He had no way of knowing that the fortuitous hand of fate had placed his team closest to Al Wafra oilfield among the rest of the Battalion and thus had altered the course of his young life forever.

The dark blanket of smoke that hung overhead suddenly reflected a bright flash just beyond a slight rise in the topography northwest of their position.

"All stop," Ward said on the radio, but they had already frozen at the sight of the flash and sound of the accompanying report.

"What was that?" Ward asked.

Cross's element of the team was closer to the source of the flash than his.

"Dunno," Cross caught himself whispering into the radio.

He was not sure how far away it was and his instinctive reaction was to treat it like an enemy standing a foot away. Everyone in the team had frozen and was analyzing a course of action when the radio came to life.

"Hollywood, this is Actual, we've got incoming from somewhere near your pos. You see anything?" Gunny Corell asked, dispensing with normal radio protocol.

The flash they had seen was from the elusive 155mm Howitzer that had been shooting at OP Six for the last week. Team Three had wandered right on top of it undetected.

"Roger that, Actual, stand by," Cross whispered as he dropped down from the vehicle and crouched next to it, not wanting to move an inch knowing the Iraqis were so close.

Danno and the driver, Lance Corporal Mike Huffman, grabbed their weapons and joined him. The team had been following what meager low areas they could find which had allowed them to remain out of view of the apparent artillery emplacement.

"Alpha, you copy?" He asked Ward.

"Roger, we're on the way," Ward told him.

His own Hummer crept toward Cross, making sure to keep the high ground between them and the Iraqis.

"Huff, you cover," Cross whispered with a nod for Danno to follow him.

He reached back to his fanny pack and began pulling out a desert guille suit to use as camouflage. The thick burlap fabric of the suit had been sprayed with aerosol glue and affixed with a layer of sand. Danno did the same. As soon Cross draped the suit over his head and made the necessary adjustments, he dropped to his belly and began low crawling towards the crest of the dune that was the only thing keeping them out of sight. Danno closely followed.

The concealing suits made them nearly invisible on the desert floor. Cross found it more difficult to pull his slithering body through the sand the closer he came to the top of the rise. He unconsciously wished for his body to become smaller and smaller, to become one with the sand. The thought of peeking over the top mortified him. He crept with an agonizing caution until he saw the elevated muzzle of the Howitzer about 400 meters away. He was swept with a wave of relief now that he was sure he had some distance on his side.

Cross leaned forward until he could see the whole area. Just as Gunny Corell had surmised, the suspect artillery piece was a self-propelled M109, one of many items sold to the lesser of two evils by the US during the Iran-Iraq war. It sat in the middle of a primary oil field service road and was surrounded by two half-ton trucks that carried additional support personnel and equipment.

Cross slowly pulled out his binoculars to get an exact picture of what they were dealing with as Danno crawled into place alongside him without a sound. Cross counted twelve people total, two of whom appeared to be officers by the look of their uniforms. They appeared also to be readying the gun to fire again. He moved slowly over the landscape, making mental note of everything.

He was just completing his preliminary observation when Ward and Ayala came slithering up. Ward took out his own binoculars to get a better look while Cross slid down, out of sight, to retrieve his map and Global Positioning System receiver. One close look at the map, and he had pinpointed what he thought were the positions of both his team and the Iraqi gun. He placed a small dot on the map where he thought Team Three was located, next to the only two contour lines on the entire sheet. Reading the grid lines on the nearly featureless topographic map, he wrote down the six-digit coordinates of the dot and turned on the GPS receiver. Ward backed down the draw and joined him.

Without a word, Cross showed him the map and pointed along the draw. He then looked up and pointed to the small rise they were on. Ward nodded his acknowledgment. Cross held up the GPS receiver and waited for it to acquire satellite signals. Within five seconds, it displayed signals from four satellites, enough to pinpoint their location to within one meter. With the turn of a knob, Cross set the readout to correspond to the map sheet they were working off of and six digits appeared that matched identically those that Cross had written on the map. Both men looked at each other and smiled. Cross made the necessary adjustments in his head and wrote down the coordinates for the Iraqi gun.

Boom! The concussion from the Howitzer firing made both of them jump. Cross keyed up his mike.

"Gunny, you have incoming, over," He whispered.

"Roger that, you have a pos. yet?" A frustrated Corell replied.

"Roger that, we're switching to the fire support freq. now."

"I will too, out."

Cross pulled out his notepad and flipped it to the frequency list. He handed it to Ward and pointed to the third entry, which was simply marked "FS." He then rolled over so that Ward could dial in the frequency on his back-mounted radio. Ward tapped Cross on the shoulder when he was done.

"Tango-two-whiskey, this is delta-one-delta, adjust fire, over."

After a brief silence, Cross repeated the call, but again received no answer.

"Papa-six, you read?" He called Gunny Corell on the fire support net.

"Five-by-five, one-Delta," then the Gunny called the fire support unit himself.

"Tango-two-whiskey, this is Oscar-Papa-Six, did you copy fire mission traffic, over?" Cross radio crackled with the faint reply

"Negative."

"Roger, break, One-Delta, I'm gonna have to relay for you." Corell told Cross.

"645234, troops and artillery in the open, danger close, how copy?"

"I copy 645234, troops and arty in open, danger close."

One of the few times the Gunny followed radio procedure to the letter was when real rounds were about to fly.

"That's affirmative. We are four zero zero mikes at 170, over," Cross gave the Gunny Team Three's position from the target.

Being within 500 meters made them dangerously close for the 155mm guns that would be firing at their request. Now the Fire Direction Center could enter their position into the computer to keep friendly fire from hitting them.

Hopefully, Cross thought.

Corell relayed the message to the FDC and waited.

The anticipation of bringing firepower to bear on a live target made the wait excruciating for both Corell and Cross. The poor reception Team Three was getting made the FDC's response come across as little more than a hiss. When it was through, Corell came on.

"On the way."

"Roger," Cross replied.

Cross hissed at the others to get their attention and they turned to face him with sloth-like deliberation to minimize the perception of movement. Cross put his hand on his head, signaling that they had rounds inbound. With every second that passed, the team's collective heart rate increased. The 72 seconds the rocket-assisted marker round was in flight seemed like an hour. A faint crackle in his ear startled Cross.

"Splash," the young voice of the FDC communicator said simply, alerting Cross to the imminent impact.

A moment later, the team heard a loud pop overhead, immediately followed by the eerie white fingers of burning white phosphorous emerging directly over the heads of the unsuspecting Iraqis.

"Fire for effect, over," Cross said into the mouthpiece with a grin.

Corell relayed the order to the FDC twice to make sure they got it. The marker couldn't have been more accurately targeted and the Marine artillery unit was about to unleash twelve guns on the exact same point. Unfortunately for the enemy troops scrambling to start their vehicles and get away, these rounds wouldn't be relatively benign markers. Cross knew the Iraqis would never make it.

Cross again got the attention of his team and pointed to his eyes with the index and middle fingers of his right hand then pointed in the direction of the target. All four of the team members got as low as they could and positioned themselves to witness the carnage.

When death arrived for the weary Iraqi conscripts, it would be more devastating than any of the young Recon Marines expected. The incoming rounds were 155mm Dual-Purpose Improved Conventional munitions each carrying a mixture of 88 M-42 and M-46 grenades. Each individual grenade radiated shrapnel with such force that it penetrated 2-and-a-half inches of armor, and there were 1056 of them about to blanket the target.

"Splash."

Cross had barely digested the words when the entire world exploded in a rapid series of brilliant flashes. The soldiers that had been caught out in the open were ripped to pieces by the bomblets. Cross saw nothing but body parts and the pink mist of vaporized blood where people had been. The ones who had made it into the trucks had died just as immediately, the steel and canvas failing to even slow the fusillade of razor-sharp projectiles. The howitzer itself remained relatively intact, but Cross could see that a tread had separated, immobilizing the unit.

"Papa-Six, maximum order, target destroyed."

"Roger that, nice work," the Gunny replied.

Ward and Cross observed the target for a few more moments before determining that no one had made it to the safety of the armored gun hull. Within two minutes, Team Three had retreated to the Hummers and vanished into the desert without any sign of ever having been there.

CHAPTER 4

Fate

Colonel Urit left the Kirya feeling slightly emasculated by the outcome of the meetings with the US representatives. As the innocuous black military sedan he was riding in turned North on Derech Petach Tikva towards the Ayalon River, he slapped the folder he was leafing through onto the seat next to him and stared out at the streets of suburban Tel Aviv. The rhythmical passing of orange street lights calmed him somewhat.

"Everything alright, Colonel?" his driver and bodyguard, Mikael asked with a glance in the rearview mirror.

"Hmph, yeah Mikael."

Colonel Urit was not in a very conversational mood. Normally he didn't mind discussing issues with the young IDF lieutenant and was slightly embarrassed that his mood was so easily noticed.

The streets he gazed upon were eerily devoid of life.

It had been determined that as many as forty percent of the residents of the city left by nightfall to the safety of price gouged hotels or relative's homes in order to avoid the Scud attacks that had become commonplace. The mayor of Tel Aviv, Shlomo "Chich" Lahat, had taken to calling the nightly emigrants deserters for showing a lack of solidarity. Colonel Urit did not fault them for staying away. Perhaps, he thought, if they stayed far enough away they would not react to the lack of action on the part of Israel.

It was shameful for them to sit idly by and serve as a passive target. The Americans had even convinced the Knesset that it was in their best interest to stay uninvolved. This certainly wasn't the Israel he had always represented.

Over the years, Colonel Urit had grown used to striking viscously against threats to Israel's sovereignty. It had been five days since eight Iraqi Scuds hit Tel Aviv, and still Israel had done nothing. Motta sat back in his seat and reflected.

The one most influential event in his life came rushing to him like a flood of warm water. He had been a captain once, seemingly centuries ago, and in 1976 while serving under a brilliant American-born officer, he traveled 2200 miles in the middle of the night to strike vengeance deep into the heart of Palestinian terror.

The officer was Lt. Col. Yonatan Netanyahu. The place was Entebbe, Uganda.

Four terrorists representing the Popular Front for the Liberation of Palestine had tried, like Hussein, to hold Israel a hostage of violence. Their method was the hijacking of Air France flight 139 en route to Paris from Athens with 246 passengers on board, most of whom were Israeli. They made their way to Entebbe, Uganda where they enjoyed the protection of Ugandan Dictator Idi Amin and his Army, well out of the operational radius of the Israeli Defense Forces.

All hostages but those holding Israeli passports were released making it clear to the world that this was a crime against Israel. Lt. Col. "Yoni" Netanyahu led an assault force of eighty-six officers and men from then Captain Urit's Paratrooper Division of the IDF and the Golani Infantry Brigade to Entebbe.

Their ingenious act of stubborn resistance to terrorism would be one of Israel's finest hours and forever a model for Special Operations Forces worldwide. The members of Operation Thunderball assaulted the old terminal building at Entebbe International Airport where the hostages and the aircrew were being held. Within ninety minutes the assault team had rescued 103 hostages and killed all but one of the terrorists.

As the Israeli teams were evacuating to the awaiting C-130 Hercules transports, the surviving terrorist fired a single shot from the control tower striking Yoni Netanyahu in the back. A young Captain Urit had helped carry Yoni to the awaiting aircraft as medics worked in vain to save his life.

That was how Israel was supposed to deal with threats against its people. Yoni Netanyahu had not died gloriously as a hero of Israel so that his homeland could leave its safety in the hands of American Patriot missile batteries.

"Politics," the colonel snubbed.

The sedating effect of the street lights had lost its influence on the colonel.

He was not a politician, he was a warrior. In the deepest recesses of his mind, he questioned the value of any alliance that would cause Israel to be victimized. If he had things his way, he would risk the consequences and bomb Baghdad to the ground. He grumbled again as the car crossed the river and turned onto Derekh Jabotinsky near the Diamond Exchange.

◆   ◆   ◆

Cross thought he was hearing things, but realized that the faint beeping noise was coming from the Digital Communications Terminal in his radio pack. Just as he realized what the sound was, he heard Gunny Corell's voice over the radio.

"One Delta, you have flash traffic to your DCT, over." Cross tapped Danno on the shoulder with his foot.

"Hold up," he said just loud enough to be heard over the sound of the Hummer.

Danno came to a stop.

"Roger that," Cross replied on the radio. "You get that, Ward?"

"Roger."

Ward was already on his way over. The only thing that headquarters would be sending on the DCT was a fragmentary order. That is the military term for a drastic, usually unwelcome change of plans.

Cross dug the DCT out of the pack and pulled open the canvas cover that protected the small screen. The terminal stored and decompressed burst radio transmissions into a pre-programmed format. He unfolded the sides of the cover and attached them to Velcro strips framing the screen to conceal the display. Cross pushed the receive button and the very detailed operation order began scrolling down the rows of tiny red LED lights that comprised the screen.

As he read the details of the mission drawn up by General Hampton and his advisors, Cross began holding his breath. He couldn't believe what he was reading. Finally he took a deep breath.

"Holy shit," he exhaled.

The day had just worsened dramatically.

♦   ♦   ♦

Claxons blared throughout Tel Aviv. Colonel Urit could clearly hear them through the bulletproof glass of the military sedan.

"Mikael, stop!"

The young lieutenant pulled over immediately, just east of the diamond exchange.

"Mask!" the colonel ordered, fumbling through his bag for the gas mask he refused to wear on his hip.

Lieutenant Perrin's mask was where it was supposed to be. The men slid their masks over their heads in a drill that had become all too routine.

"I should keep this damn thing on, sir."

"Yes, I know," Urit grumbled.

Flashes from the Patriot missile batteries east of Ramat Gan startled Colonel Urit. He leaned forward so he could see the departing missiles draw brilliant white streaks into the sky. The realization that Patriots do not fire at hunches swept over him in a sudden rush of forgotten, yet familiar excitement.

He knew that there were Scuds inbound to Tel Aviv.

His fears were confirmed when he saw the fiery orange dissipating plume of a Scud passing clear of the outbound Patriots. It appeared to be coming directly for them.

"My God!" Colonel Urit sighed as he dove into the rear floorboard of the car and braced himself.

Mikael ducked under the dash. The single Scud impacted with a deafening explosion just two blocks away from where the sedan sat. The blast wave cracked the windshield as it sent the front of the vehicle several feet into the air. The car settled back down with a deafening jolt. Colonel Urit hit his chin on the rear door handle, causing him to bite through his bottom lip. The taste of blood only served to feed his anger as he clambered out of the floorboard. His bodyguard leapt over the front seats to check on his charge.

"Sir, are you hurt?" he asked as he patted the colonel For injuries.

"I'm fine!, I'm fine!" the colonel responded as he pushed Mikael's hands away.

As he rose, Colonel Urit looked over the front seat towards the impact site where an orange glow and billowing smoke marked disaster. The neighborhood was densely populated with high-rise apartments that didn't typically react well to explosions.

"Get us over there, hurry!"

"Yes, sir."

Lieutenant Perrin restarted the stalled car and drove towards the impact site. The shock had damaged the steering and he found it a struggle to keep the car moving in a straight line.

"Faster, Mikael!"

The younger officer mashed down on the accelerator and turned left onto Remez Street. Colonel Urit could see ambulances coming from a distance and armed civilians running in the direction of the blast.

◆   ◆   ◆

The air raid sirens had finally roused Habbas al-Razzaz from a very deep sleep. As his apartment shuddered from the impact of the missile, he jumped from his bed and threw open the blinds. He could see the smoke rising from across Abba Hillel Street and immediately switched into reporter mode. He worked for a freelance Arab Press weekly called the Al-Sha'b as the Tel-Aviv department. He was not a staff member of the department, but solely comprised the entire department. He was the writer, photographer, and editor for all stories pertaining to the Arab world coming out of Tel-Aviv.

Along with a majority of the other Arab writers in the city, he tried his best to word reports of Scud impacts in such a subtle way that they could get by Israeli censors while still offering valuable targeting information to the Iraqis. The more fundamentalist Arabs in the region saw the Gulf War as an opportunity to strike crippling blows to Israel and secretly hoped for success to that end through Saddam Hussein.

Habbas put on his gas mask and grabbed his camera case as he left. The bag was always at the ready with any equipment he needed to cover a breaking story, and judging by the proximity of the blast he saw from the window, he would be the first one on the scene. He ran out of the building and got into his tiny car to drive to the blast site a few blocks away.

◆   ◆   ◆

"Thank God," Colonel Urit observed.

The Scud had impacted the middle of the street adjacent to an empty lot. The open area had absorbed the brunt of the explosion, but many of the buildings surrounding the new crater had received substantial damage.

"There...go there!" Urit ordered his driver.

The corner flats on the first three floors of a 14-story apartment building were missing. They were on the North end of a large crater. It appeared to be the only substantial damage from the Scud.

The sedan slid to a stop at the South end of the crater as Colonel Urit jumped out. He and Mikael ran along the sidewalk around the crater as people began filing out of the buildings surrounding the impact site. Colonel Urit ran across the street to the building missing the corner.

All of the lights on the block had been knocked out, but the adrenaline coursing through his veins combined with the dull glow of the fading fires provided ample light. He climbed over a crumpled pile of concrete and down into a first floor apartment.

He saw the upper half of a young girl, perhaps nine years old, protruding from underneath a dresser that was partially covered by rubble from the collapsed floors. The colonel scrambled down to the beautiful young girl.

She was an exact image of his daughter at that age and his heart suddenly ached. There was a pool of blood beneath the dresser. The tiny girl looked badly injured and he knew he had to get her out quickly if she stood a chance of survival.

A piece of concrete fell from the edge of the ceiling. The building had become unstable and Urit knew they had to move with haste.

"Lieutenant, here!"

The young wide-eyed lieutenant dashed over the rubble and came to Urit's aid. The two quickly began removing huge blocks of concrete from atop of the girl with the exaggerated strength that accompanies fear. They both knew the shifting weight must be very painful for the girl, yet she didn't speak nor cry. Colonel Urit wasn't sure whether she was dying, or just incredibly brave.

"You'll be out soon little one," he reassured her.

"It hurts," she moaned in Hebrew, the words caused the tears to finally come.

It broke his heart to hear her gentle voice. Through the sweat beading up on the Mikael's face, the colonel saw tears in the huge officer's eyes.

Their pace quickened.

They had removed about half of the concrete from atop the dresser and were running out of time. Though Colonel Urit was a large, muscular man, Mikael was much larger. In fact, he was massive. Urit thought the younger officer might be able to lift the weight off of the child.

"Can you lift it?" the colonel asked.

"I think so," Mikael squatted down with his back to the dresser and slid his hands underneath.

Colonel Urit squirmed his hands under the girl's back and grasped her under her outstretched arms.

"Now!" the colonel ordered.

Erupting with a yell from deep within, Mikael began lifting the enormous weight. When it had been lifted a few inches, Colonel Urit began sliding the girl out. Her leg caught on something.

"Higher!"

With a final burst of strength, Mikael's quaking legs extended the few more inches necessary to get the girl free. Colonel Urit slid her the rest of the way out of her concrete tomb.

"O.K." he exhaled.

The dresser came down with a crash and collapsed from the weight of the concrete atop it.

"Let's go."

Colonel Urit scooped the girl up into his dusty arms. She was covered in abrasions and it appeared that both of her legs were badly broken. Mikael climbed out ahead of them.

A piece of concrete the size of a golf ball hit the colonel in the head. He looked up to see the ceiling collapsing in on him. His brain processed the image quickly enough for him to realize that he would never make it.

At the last instant, he heaved the girl forward as hard as he could. She landed painfully on the far side of the crest of the rubble pile, and clear of the falling mass of concrete and steel.

It would have been futile for the colonel to resist. The weight was incredible. He had never felt anything like it. The mass pushed him to the ground in the blink of an eye and all of the breath left his body as he impacted the uneven rubble below him.

Instant darkness shrouded him.

When he felt the cessation of movement, he tried to breathe, but it was nearly impossible with the weight now on top of him. The fact that he was able to breathe at all reassured him that he was not dead yet, but the pain accompanying his labored breathing was extraordinary. He knew his body as well as anyone, and something was badly wrong.

◆   ◆   ◆

Al-Razzaz had arrived just as Colonel Urit dashed into the building and the journalist got pictures of the entire episode. He now possessed pictures of a senior IDF officer being crushed to death by a falling building. Knowing how sensitive the photos would be, he started to panic. He needed to act fast, so in a very subtle movement he rewound the roll in his camera. He had only taken about eight shots on the 24-exposure roll, so it only took a few seconds.

He ducked around the corner of an adjacent building and quickly removed the film, stuffing it down the front of his pants until the roll was resting next to his crotch. He pulled a fresh roll from the bag and popped it into the back of the camera. He began emerging from the alleyway just as he closed the camera. He hadn't yet looked up when he heard the voice of an Israeli policeman.

"You there, give me that camera," the armed officer shouted at Habbas.

"For what reason?" the reporter barked, feigning self-defense.

"Quiet!" the officer snatched the camera from the Arab's hands and opened the back, exposing the small strip of film that had yet to engage the winding spool.

"Here," the Israeli handed the camera back to Habbas, at the same time pocketing the roll of film. "Now clear the area, there is nothing more to see."

Habbas was so nervous, he did not know how much farther to press his position to erase any suspicion the police officer might have. He backed away and walked to his car.

◆   ◆   ◆

Dana Urit had been doing research into the early morning hours at Tel Aviv University when the sirens went off. Feelings of inconvenience had replaced those of fear when the "all clear" had sounded. She emerged from the library basement, removed her gas mask, and neatly put it in the pouch she wore around her tiny waist.

Colonel Urit's only daughter honestly did not think that even Saddam would be insane enough to actually use chemical weapons. If he did, Israel would nuke Baghdad back to the days of Mesopotamia. She dusted off the jeans her father had brought back from training in the U.S. and walked over to the stairs.

She looked at her watch.

The Scud alert had broken the momentum in her research, so she decided to go home and get some sleep. She went upstairs and left the library.

As she descended the stairs leading to the street, she noticed a small crowed gathered around a TV at Café Ephriam. Curiosity got the best of her and she wandered over in hopes of catching a glimpse of the news. She figured reports of the Scud alert would be all that could gather a crowd at this early hour.

♦   ♦   ♦

Colonel Urit heard the dull vibrations of people yelling through the rubble that entombed him. He knew that he must not be buried too deep. Mikael was working like a man possessed. His bloody hands frantically removed enormous blocks of concrete from atop his principle. Devoutly loyal to his chosen profession, he would not accept the death of someone he was charged with protecting. That equated to failure, which was not an option to the lieutenant.

"Faster! Hurry!" he shouted at the growing mass of volunteers attempting to locate the colonel.

Some of them had arrived in time to witness the rescuing of the girl.

Where is he? Mikael stood exactly where he was prior to the roof collapsing. He thought they would have reached him by now.

♦   ♦   ♦

Dana strained to see over the small crowd.

Damn. She was again frustrated by her size. She was a mere five feet, five inches tall on her tiptoes. So she settled for listened to the rumblings between the curious onlookers as she nervously chewed at the small scar on her upper lip.

She never knew that she possessed such a strange habit, but her father did. He had, after all, felt responsible since she got the blemish while he taught her to ride a bicycle. Whenever she did it, he always smiled, and she never knew why.

"What is it?" she asked the back of a man's head.

"A Scud got through and hit an apartment building." he said without turning his head. "Some people are trapped."

"Where did…" she stopped herself.

Being a reserve lieutenant in the IDF, she knew better.

The location of Scud impacts was never mentioned in the press for fear that the Iraqis would be able to improve their targeting data. She pushed forward to get a view of the small TV. She settled into a small niche in the crowd and sat her cumbersome book bag on the ground at her feet.

♦   ♦   ♦

The colonel noted a slight change in his visual perception. *Light,* he thought.

The rescuers had reached him.

"That's him! That's him!" the lieutenant shouted when he saw the unearthed epaulette of his boss.

He quickly extrapolated from its position where the colonel's head should be. He threw debris back between his legs like a dog digging a hole until he saw the colonel's black, blood-matted hair. He exposed the rest of the colonel's head to the night air. When enough rubble had been cleared, he saw a puff of gray dust emerge from under the colonel's head.

"He's still alive!"

♦   ♦   ♦

"My God, they found someone in that mess," the anonymous woman's disclosure urged Dana closer to the front of the crowd.

Finally, Dana thought.

She stuck her head between two men and had a clear view of what appeared to be a member of the IDF pulling someone from the remains of an apartment building.

Wait a minute.

Another rescuer came into the distant camera shot and Dana was able to gauge the size of the officer.

It was Mikael.

Although the camera crews had been kept at a distance that made identification of the rescuers impossible, she had no doubt.

Lieutenant Perrin had protected her father since his assignment at IDF Headquarters.

They must have stopped to help, but where is father?

She fumbled through endless mental scenarios in a vain attempt to calm herself. She knew better.

Her instincts told her the horrible truth.

She saw the improvised team of rescuers pull the man from beneath the debris. She ran as fast as she could, leaving her books behind.

◆   ◆   ◆

"Colonel, hold on!"

Mikael ran alongside the stretcher that carried Urit to a waiting ambulance.

The colonel tried to nod, but found it too painful. It was a struggle just to breathe. The pain was overwhelming. He wanted to sleep to escape it, but knew he may not wake. He felt his life slipping away.

"Fight Colonel! Fight!" Those were the last words Colonel Urit heard as his stretcher was slid into the ambulance and he lost consciousness.

◆   ◆   ◆

Dana knew that the closest facility to handle severe injuries was Ichilov Hospital. She prayed that she had been mistaken, but knew she had not. She had seen her father lying lifeless on that stretcher. She flew through the streets of Tel Aviv knowing all emergency personnel would be going to Ramat Gan affording her safe passage.

Dana deeply loved her father, and especially since the death of her mother, he had been a hero of hers. They had sustained each other over the years through love and a well nurtured, mutual respect. She often recalled the times in her impressionable past when she had sat next to her father as he told stories of Israeli heroism.

He would show her pictures like that of a triumphant Ehud Barak standing on the wing of a Sabena airliner wearing the uniform of a maintenance worker and toting an automatic weapon. Barak had been photographed after his assault team liberated the hijacked airliner at Lod Airport in 1972. What her father never realized was that none of the national icons he educated her about held a candle to her "popi" in her eyes. She prayed that she might have more time with him so that she could tell him.

Dana pulled onto Dafna Street behind an ambulance and followed it up to the emergency dock. The area was utter chaos. There were medical workers, IDF, and press everywhere. The press was especially disruptive. Journalists from all over the world had descended on Tel Aviv to get a different perspective on the Gulf War. Most anticipated an Israeli response to Iraqi aggression and some even worked to fuel Israeli ire so that they would have a lead on the story of the decade.

If Israel struck at Iraq, the effect would be global. All of the Arab nations involved in the coalition forces might withdraw support for the conflict, leaving the US with a significantly weaker force. Dana pushed through the crowd forcefully, straight to the back of the ambulance.

As the doors of the ambulance opened, she held her breath. She was mortified at the prospect of seeing her fallen hero. Tears welled up in her eyes as the medics slid out…a woman. She scanned frantically for some sign of her father. She finally figured that he must have beaten her to the hospital. Ramat Gan is closer to Ichilov than the University, and they'd gotten a head start. She eyed what looked like a young doctor standing next to the double doors leading into the emergency ward.

"You there, are you a doctor?"

"Yes, and I'm very busy," the doctor replied rudely, then turned to walk into the hospital past the Israeli police officers who had been posted at the door.

Dana grabbed his arm and firmly spun him around to face her steely, furious blue eyes, contrasted sharply with her jet-black hair.

Her actions caused one of the officers to approach.

"Where did you take Colonel Urit?" she demanded as she withdrew her military ID.

The police officer then gazed at the doctor inquisitively, as if to repeat Dana's question more forcefully. The daughter of such a great man deserved more respect than she was getting. The doctor recognized the fact that she must be important and quickly conceded.

"This way."

He led Dana through the doors to an isolation room on the far side of the emergency ward. As she approached the closed door, her vision focused on nothing else. The portal centered in the steel white door grew closer until she was upon it. She looked in and saw a frenzy of activity. There were dozen or so hospital staff members working around her father in an apparent struggle to save his life.

Blood was everywhere.

Dana thought her father had to be dead judging from the pool on the floor. She reached for the handle of the door.

"You must not go in, he is very critical."

The young doctor wished he could undo his earlier transgression. He would never have been so callous had he known her to be the daughter of this man whom he felt would surely die.

A hand gently touched her right shoulder. She turned slowly, afraid that if she stopped watching her father, he would die.

It was Mikael.

Her eyes filled with tears. The visible pain spoke volumes.

Within minutes, the doctors became very concerned. He had crushed a section of femoral artery in his right leg. On top of a large stab wound caused by a piece of steel concrete reinforcing Rebar. An exploratory saline levage confirmed what his sinking blood pressure told them. He had major internal bleeding.

"Six more units." Dana heard a doctor say as a nurse opened the door to exit.

The pensive looks on the faces of the doctors offered no comfort. The emergency room was quickly becoming inundated with wounded. Soon doctors were being pulled away from the struggle to save Mordechai. Dana and Mikael could do nothing but watch…and pray. Mikael and Dana snapped to attention at the sight of General Yaakobi walking into the emergency room.

"At ease for God's sake, how is he?"

Dana spoke first, struggling to suppress the emotion.

"He's bleeding badly, I'm worried."

"Don't worry child, he will live," the general peered into the room. "He is too stubborn."

The general had known Dana since birth. General Yaakobi walked into the room. The doctors immediately recognized him and offered no protest. Dana heard the general begin speaking before the door closed behind him.

The doctors began pointing at monitors and shaking their heads. One of them lifted a sheet so the general could see the badly damaged leg. Mikael walked over to General Yaakobi's driver. Dana saw them speaking as if they were well acquainted. She had no idea that they had been through officer training together. She turned back when she heard the door open again. The general grabbed her in an embrace and kissed the top of her head.

"He will be fine little Dana," her tears soaked directly into his uniform as she began to cry softly.

At times like this, she still saw him as more like an uncle than as the highest-ranking military officer in Israel. General Samuelson came jogging up to the double doors much to the surprise of everyone standing in the foyer. Though

General Yaakobi was currently at professional odds with the American, he knew how close Samuelson was to Colonel Urit, so he had contacted him upon learning of the accident.

"Excuse me, Dana," General Yaakobi said as he pulled away.

Dana wiped the tears from her eyes and quickly regained her bearing.

"Dana, you OK?" Samuelson asked with an outstretched hand. He needed to confer with General Yaakobi.

"Yes, Sir. I'm OK," she assured him.

He followed the IDF chief down the hallway to find a private room, away from any prying eyes who might take the meeting as more than that of two concerned friends. They found a tiny break room with two young resident doctors in it.

As soon as they saw the generals enter, they sprang from their seats and quickly walked out of the room, leaving their half-eaten lunches behind. General Samuelson closed the door securely.

"How is he?" Samuelson asked, all formalities understandably aside.

"Not good, General, I need a favor."

"Anything."

"The Doctors aren't certain he will make it through the night. They're taking him to surgery right now to stop the major bleeding, but they are not optimistic." Yaakobi took Samuelson's silence as a cue to continue.

"You've got surgeons relatively close, and rehabilitation facilities. If it were found out that Motta is mortally wounded...well..."

Samuelson understood completely. Colonel Urit had been a death mark to Palestinians since the 1982 Peace for Galilee war. The Palestinians, in fact the entire Arab World, would always associate him with the massacre at the Sabra and Shatilla refugee camps.

Those close to the fiasco knew that he had been a victim of politics and the Kahan Commission that had been unjustly implicated him in the killings. Now it appeared that Saddam Hussein had succeeded in killing him. Regardless of the fact that he was not directly involved, the Arab world would view his death as a victory and would begin to sympathize with Saddam.

In order to ensure the cohesion of the coalition, Colonel Urit needed to either survive, or have his death kept a strict secret. Samuelson combed his brain for answers. Fortunately he was a brilliant man and had ascended the military hierarchy by making correct decisions under the most trying circumstances.

"I'll be right back. I need to make a call," he told General Yaakobi.

The Israeli general simply nodded his understanding.

CHAPTER 5

Soft Target: Al Wafra

The effect was hypnotic. As the team separated the necessary equipment for the new mission, Cross leaned his back against the wheel of his Hummer and stared at an oil well flame some 2000 meters away. There were several burning within view below the pitch-black pall of smoke blanketing the sky, but the sheer size of the unbroken flame erupting from this particular well had captured his gaze.

He pondered how something could burn uninterrupted with such ferocity for so long. All things in the universe were finite except space, he thought. What the world would do when the oil ran out was a source of wonderment. Surely that fact had something to do with why he was here.

God, I'm tired, Cross thought, as his eyes began to feel heavy.

He could have stared at the flame's ethereal beauty until he drifted off to sleep. Were it not for the war around him and the tasks at hand, he could have been in a deep sleep in less than a minute. Instead, he wasn't even aware that in the last seventy-two hours, he had only slept about two.

"Cross?" It was Ward. "you ready?"

The team leader broke Cross's trance and brought his aching head back into the present.

"Yeah dude, let's do it."

Cross had just completed a terrain model of the objective. He had done the best he could with the information provided from Intelligence over the digital computer terminal.

The rest of the team gathered around them in a small semi-circle basked in the dull orange glow of the well fires. Ward, who had read the order three times to make sure he wasn't imagining things, would conduct the briefing while Cross highlighted their movement on the terrain map.

"Al Wafra oilfield…you've seen it on the map," Ward began as he pointed to the middle of the terrain model. "Nearly twenty clicks long from east to west by ten clicks north to south. The east side of the oilfield is flanked by a government agricultural area the size of main side Lejeune."

"Main side" was the term applied to the area of any Marine base that housed the base amenities such as the exchange, recreational facilities, etc.

Camp Lejeune, North Carolina had a main side that was the size of a small city.

"Within this area is the housing and storage complex for the field."

"Until a few days ago, the employee housing facilities were the new home to the Iraqi Fifth Infantry Regiment."

The tired team was hanging on every word he spoke, as each member scanned the visible area around them for any movement.

"While they were there, satellites picked up a truck adjacent to a very large building in the southeast portion of the facility. It's normally used as some kind of greenhouse where they grow new shit for the agricultural area."

Ward paused while Cross pointed out the tent-shaped portion of a brown plastic pouch that had previously contained an MRE, the food staple of the team for the last two months. After consumption, the packaging made convenient improvised props for terrain models.

"It's about eighty meters long, made out of sheet metal over a steel skeleton. S2 believes that the truck may have delivered chemical or bio agents."

The team exchanged glances. They had all been thoroughly trained in nuclear, biological, and chemical warfare, and it scared them more than any enemy. Given a choice, any of them would prefer to be riddled with bullets than to slowly and painfully melt to death from the inside after ingesting Ebola virus or anthrax.

"Now that the division has moved off to the east, we're supposed to secure the contents of the truck and evaluate disposal."

"How many guys got left behind to keep an eye on the fort?" LCpl. Mike Huffman asked.

Good question, Cross thought.

"Two platoons," Ward replied.

"That's still a lot," Huffman said.

"These guys are so fucked up by the bombing, they'll probably be drunk on Sidiki and begging for food." Ward's attempt at quelling concerns fell short.

"It'll be like that time we hit that reserve unit in Albuquerque."

Two years ago the team had been called upon to probe the defenses of an Army Reserve unit while attending the US Department of Energy's urban sniper training course at its Central Training Academy. The CTA is a very well-kept secret housed within Kirtland Air Force Base at Albuquerque, NM. The base itself is a vast expanse of desert and mountains ideal for military training.

While at the course, the commander of the Army unit, Maj. George Duffet, approached Ward. Major Duffet had been a Marine infantryman in Vietnam, and had come to expect more from his soldiers than they were accustomed to. After all, they were Motor Transport, not infantrymen.

Duffet's twice weekly golfing partner was an instructor at the CTA, and had led him to Ward's team at the school. The major wanted Ward's team to test the Army unit's defensive capabilities. Duffet had always been a fan of Recon, and remained so even after his commissioning in the Army. He knew if anyone could compromise the security of his unit in order to teach them a valuable lesson, it would be a Marine recon team.

The following weekend, while Team Three was off, Duffet's unit was on maneuvers in the nearby Manzano Mountains for their monthly drill. Team Three borrowed a van from the CTA as well as one of the instructors to drive them, and headed into the Manzanos to conduct the mission. The van dropped them off three kilometers from where the Army unit was laagered for the night, and picked them up two hours later. Team Three then went back to the base for some sleep.

The following morning, Team Three was at the Armed Forces Reserve Center on Wyoming Blvd. Before they'd even reached the rear door to the center, they heard Duffet's yelling.

"This is the single most embarrassing moment of my entire goddamn career!" That brought a half grin to Cross's face, but he quickly shook it off.

"How does it feel to know that over half of you are corpses?" Duffet continued as Team Three walked out the door.

It added to the moment to see that Duffet was wearing nothing but GI green socks on his feet

"We will stay here all night if we have to. Every single speck will be cleaned off of the weapons, equipment, and vehicles! We will be in the field every friggin' month until you get it through your heads that this is not Camp Goddamn Snoopy!"

Duffet made eye contact with Ward.

"And these are the *six* Marines who killed what, twenty-six of you dipshits?" he pointed to Team Three.

Cross and the rest of the team welled up with pride as they stared out at the forty men in front of them. Most of whose uniforms were adorned with of the bumper stickers. They were also shamefully wearing black stripes across their throats from the permanent markers Team Three had carried the night before.

Nearly all of the Army unit's gear and vehicles were wearing one or more Marine Corps bumper stickers. Ward led his team to the front of the formation where Duffet was standing. They came to attention and saluted Duffet, who dutifully returned it.

"Sir, we would like to present you with these." Ward said loud enough for the entire unit to hear.

LCpls. Rueben Ayala and Daniels walked forward and presented Duffet with the combat boots taken from the back of the Hummer in which he had slept the night before, and an M-60E2 Machine Gun. The M-60 was so totally covered with Marine Corps stickers, that there was no visible exposed metal.

The mission was fairly easy for Team Three who had trained so long together that they had become totally silent in their movements, and they had trained to go up against the best in the world.

The men in front of them were far from that.

Most of the members of the Army unit were awestruck. Some were genuinely disturbed by the fact that they had been silently, if only symbolically, murdered in their sleep. No one had heard nor seen a thing.

The six men before them were phantoms.

The main difference with the mission to Al Wafra was that the bad guys had bullets.

"We're gonna board the helos at zero-one, the SF team will be lead. They're going to infiltrate the Headquarters building here."

Ward nodded and Cross pointed to an empty smoked oyster container he had gotten in a care package weeks ago from home. It was about six inches from the MRE wrapper. In reality, the distance would be about 400 meters

"We're gonna fastrope in a thousand meters to the west, behind a line of about a dozen burning wellheads down in a wadi."

Ward looked up.

"Two fast movers will hit the east side of the target area as a diversion."

"Like they'll time it just right," Danno said sarcastically.

Ward shrugged and continued the briefing for another ten minutes. They skipped rehearsals because they were short on time. It was not as if they needed them, but they always followed the team's standard operating procedure. The operations order called for them to approach the target at a low crawl. This meant that they had to slither silently on their bellies for 1000 meters. Many of them had not low-crawled that far since scout sniper school in Quantico.

"There's a trenchline here," Ward said, pointing to a line in the sand.

"There may or may not be sentries patrolling them. We have to assume that there are."

The order called for them to get past the trenches and on to the greenhouse, determine what was inside, and decide on a course of action. The most likely plan was to call in a platoon of NBC specialists to secure it for disposal.

If they came across resistance, then they were supposed to call in an incendiary air strike, but not before they escaped to the extract point. Like all plans, it sounded perfect in theory, but something always went wrong. Whether slightly inconvenient, or catastrophic, something always went wrong.

This would be the first mission Cross had been on that would almost definitely involve close combat, and that scared him. He was sure everyone felt the same, but no one showed it. He felt heat move up the back of his neck as the adrenaline coursed through his veins. He was not merely scared; he was terrified. It took all of his will to finish his preparations for the mission after Ward was done with the operation order.

From the outside, Cross appeared as competent as ever and was glad the team couldn't see his thoughts. Little did he know they all were suppressing the same wrenching terror.

"I'll be right back…head call," Cross told Ward as he scurried to the far side of the Hummer to a spot twenty yards away.

He barely got his trousers down in time.

The mixture of anxiety and fatigue had done a number on his digestive system. When he returned, Ward looked at him and laughed.

"You O.K., dude?"

"I thought you were supposed to puke when you got nervous," Cross said as he grabbed the can of Copenhagen from Ward's outstretched hand.

He took a large pinch and put it in his lip. The snuff burned badly as it touched Cross's shredded inner lip. The constant stress of operating in enemy territory had he and most of the other members of the team up to about two cans a day.

The disgusting habit shredded the inner linings of the lip.

"We got an hour, get some rack ops," Ward told him.

"Like I could fuckin' sleep." Cross slumped down in the passenger seat of his Hummer.

He pushed the nylon sling that draped over the top of the hood out of the way. They had attached slings to both vehicles so they could be airlifted back to the firebase. Cross removed a static discharge wand from deep beneath the team's gear and unraveled the cable.

There were two essential roles in sling loading anything to the bottom of a helicopter: the hook-up man and the static discharge man. Cross was the latter. He would be responsible for hooking the wand to the cargo load beam before Danno touched it with the clevice that would bear the weight of their vehicle.

Helicopter rotors generate fatal amounts of static electricity that would find the least resistant path to the ground. Cross drove the stake end into the ground.

He was ready.

He pulled out a pen and began writing a letter to his mother, believing it would be the last letter he would ever write.

◆   ◆   ◆

General Samuelson had never cashed in so many favors at once, but he could think of no better reason. Dana had no idea what was going on as the ambulance she was riding in with her dying father reached Sde Dov Airbase on the outskirts of Tel Aviv.

At the moment, she really didn't care.

Colonel Urit had been in surgery for four hours and had confounded everyone by refusing to die. His vital signs stabilized during the emergency procedure as the flow of blood from his internal organs diminished.

Dana just squeezed his hand and whispered words of encouragement into his ear. Mikael was more curious about why they had left the hospital on orders from General Yaakobi. No one had told him anything. The colonel's bodyguard strained to see out the front of the ambulance. It appeared that they were headed right for an American C-20 jet parked near a large hangar.

When the ambulance stopped, the back doors were ripped open from the outside. Mikael and Dana were astonished to see General Samuelson reaching in to unlock Colonel Urit's gurney. He was still in his uniform, but had taken the jacket off and rolled up his sleeves.

Another American, this one in civilian clothes, helped the general. Mikael jumped out of the ambulance to help unload the colonel. Samuelson could tell by the dumbfounded look on Mikael's face that he had not been told what was going on. General Samuelson looked up briefly while he locked the legs of the gurney so they could roll Colonel Urit to the plane.

"I have to go to Riyadh," he told Mikael and Dana.

"I contacted a friend who's going to meet us on the way in King Khalid Military City."

"Who?" Mikael asked on instinct, he was nervous.

"A friend," the General barked. "There's a MASH unit there and they can take care of Motta."

"I'm not leaving my father," Dana stated over the dull whine of the jet's engines.

"You're both going, Dana," Samuelson assured her. "General Yaakobi knows."

He gestured to the man in civilian clothes.

"This is Doctor Norris, he'll keep an eye on your father until we get there, and you two are now in the US Army."

Dana and Mikael looked at each other as Doctor Norris began lifting the head of the gurney up the staircase into the jet.

"I've taken care of everything, there's a change of clothes on the plane," the general said.

◆   ◆   ◆

"Helos inbound!" LCpl. Daniels yelled.

They all heard the familiar phut-phut at the same time; Danno had just spoken first.

"Hollywood, this is Alpha-Tango Six, over." the radio squawked to life.

"Tango Six, this is Hollywood, got you five-by-five, and visual." Cross replied as the flight of two HH-60G Pave Hawks made it into view through the shroud of darkness.

The HH-60G is a Special Operations Forces variant of the UH-60 Blackhawk helicopter. It was perfectly suited for this mission.

"We have the Tee." the pilot had spotted the infrared strobe lights embedded in the sand in the shape of a large T, which designated the helicopter landing zone.

The bottom of the T pointed with the wind making the pilots' approach much easier. Both pilots were flying with "NODs," and the Night Optical Devices were the only way to see the infrared light in the dim orange glow of the distant fire. The Hawks flew past the team at 130 knots and vanished behind the gauntlet of flames to the north.

The pilots banked hard to the left, and when they appeared beyond the other side of the flames, Team Three was staring at the tops of the main rotors. They were tilted very close to ninety degrees as they made the turn to land. The pilots leveled the Hawks simultaneously as they came back toward the team and flared together for a perfect landing just 100 meters from a slowly growing lake of crude oil.

Just as the Hawks touched the ground, the huge form of an Air Force MH-53J Pave Low helicopter emerged from the darkness west of their position.

"Hollywood, this is Ridge Runner, have you visual."

"Roger that, Runner," Cross replied.

The man piloting what was the largest and most technologically advanced helicopter in the free world knew the drill. He had infiltrated deep into Panama with a Special Forces A-team during Operation Just Cause. He didn't need the tee on the ground. The 50,000-pound monster he was piloting was equipped with terrain following and avoidance radar, a forward-looking infrared sensor, and a projected map display, which took away the need for any navigational aids.

Colonel "Red" Richardson still had a sectional map strapped to his leg on a kneeboard. He had learned to fly with a slide rule, and firmly believed that if it was not broken, you didn't fix it. He had over time become an expert at the sophisticated avionics, however. If his canopy had been covered with black paint, he would have made it here just as quickly with no one the wiser. The aircraft was capable of jamming any surviving radar system the Iraqis possessed.

The Pave Low's 99½ foot length carried over 15,000 pounds of jet fuel that could be replenished in-flight via the refueling probe sticking out the front and could lift 36,000 pounds. Red would never feel the Hummer slung underneath him. It was an enormous aircraft.

"Flaring." the pilot prepared his crew chief and the two Air Force Pararescuemen.

Red pulled back on the cyclic and up on the collective in a fashion that would never be fathomed by anyone with fewer hours than he. The nose of the huge helicopter lurched skyward as the seven blades of the 79-foot diameter main rotor began to grab more air. Red nearly had the giant bird vertical. The ground shook from the raw power as the behemoth slowed to a hover directly overhead, and began descending.

◆   ◆   ◆

25,000 feet above them and 120 miles away, an E-3 Sentry was on station. The AWACS saw the helicopters maneuvering below it. The radar dome slowly rotating eleven feet above the aircraft had recently been upgraded through the Air Force's fledgling Radar System Improvement Program with Pulse Doppler/ Pulse Compression waveform. It received the upgrade three years ahead of schedule. PDPC exponentially improved the detection ability of the aircraft, so there was no question to the console operator observing the blips as to whose helos these were. Major Ronald Tomlinson looked over the shoulder of Tech Sergeant Brian Greico who stared at his screen,

"Wouldn't wanna be those guys right about now."

Greico shook his head in concurrence.

"Huh-uh."

◆   ◆   ◆

"Go! Go! Go!" Ward screamed over the three howling General Electric T64-GE-416A, 4,300 horsepower turboshaft engines that powered the bird.

A second MH-53J emerged from the darkness, waiting its turn as it came to a hover. The combined noise would have been deafening at a slightly higher pitch, but the low roar was familiar to the team.

It aroused them.

The sound, combined with the smell of jet exhaust, always gave Cross a stomach ache. One of many legacies he carried from Airborne School. The smell was overwhelming as he boarded jump aircraft during his last week of the course, and he had since possessed the olfactory correlation of jet exhaust to life-threatening experiences. The stomach ache was expected.

He shielded his eyes from the rotor wash as he looked up from where he stood on the rear deck of the Hummer. He saw the silhouette of the crew chief leaning as far as he could out of the crew door. The silhouette was backlit in the eerie glow of red light from inside the 53.

Cross took the static discharge wand and held the hook end up. The pilot had brought the aircraft down so low that Cross didn't even fully extend his arm. There was a bright flash as 50,000 volts jumped from the helicopter to the wand. Knowing this signaled safety, Danno slammed the clevice through the keeper on the cargo hook. He then slapped Cross on the head.

Let's get outta here.

Seeing the two Marines exit from underneath the aircraft, the crew chief gave the pilot the signal to liftoff. Cross could not see him do it, but the crew chief saluted the Marines of Team Three out of respect. Neither he nor anyone else on board knew of the mission ahead. The chief thought about it for a minute and decided he really didn't want to know.

The vehicle that now dangled below his aircraft was the closest thing those guys had to home, and he had just taken it away. If anything bad happened, they would only be able to escape as fast as their legs would take them. He was suddenly very grateful for getting convinced by a recruiter to join the Air Force. He grabbed the toggles of his 7.62-millimeter minigun and stared out into the dark.

Good luck guys. He had his own job to do.

Daley and Ayala repeated the procedure with Sgt. Ward's Hummer. Soon both vehicles were gone.

"Let's go!" Ward yelled.

Team Three was already moving.

The passenger seats in the trail HH-60G faced outward. Ward, Ayala, and Daley went to the left side of the aircraft. Cross, Danno, and Huffman went to the right. The doors had been removed, so they jumped up into the aircraft simultaneously and sat in their designated places. The crew doors were also gone, and each one held a 7.62 millimeter minigun. The aircraft's gunners were diligently manning the miniguns. Their eyes were constantly scanning the scorched earth within their fields of fire for any movement.

Team Three settled in, quickly pointing the muzzles of their weapons down between their legs and fastening their five-point harnesses with the unique buckle that had to be turned to release. Cross found no comfort in remembering the Army's nickname for these buckles at Pathfinder School.

Dial-o'-Death, he shrugged it off.

After all, they also called the aircraft he was on the Crashhawk. The military always found humor in morbidity, no doubt as a means of disguising internal fears.

Cross made eye contact with each member of the team to assure they were on board. He looked at Ward and gave a thumbs-up. There were two Heckler and Koch MP-5SD submachine guns lashed to the forward bulkhead with quick-detachable straps.

Cross and Ward retrieved them along with four loaded magazines apiece. They requested the MP-5s in addition to their M-203 equipped M-16A2 rifles. Daley, Danno and Ayala carried standard M-16A2s. Huffman was in charge of the team's M249 Squad Automatic Weapon, or SAW.

Being a championship wrestler from Minnesota, Huffman's short, bulky frame was perfect for humping around the large weapon. The SAW weighs just over twenty-two pounds fully loaded with a 200-round belt of 5.56mm ammunition. Huffman carried three backup drums of ammunition as well. Even after carrying the burden long distances, he was unmatched in his proficiency with the M-249 in accuracy and ammunition conservation.

One aspect of Recon training doctrine that is not shared by their inter-service counterparts is ammunition compatibility. Every weapon normally carried by the team on a mission not only fired the same caliber ammunition, but would universally accept the magazines that carried it. Even the belt-fed SAW was designed to accept the 30-round M-16 magazine in a pinch. At 750 to 1000 rounds per minute, the M-16 magazine expired in about 2 seconds.

The lesson of ammunition compatibility had been painfully learned during the raid of Patilla airfield in Panama during Operation Just Cause. Four members of SEAL Team Four had paid with their lives. The ammunition factor would never have come into play were it not for the stupidity of an officer who had not even been on the mission.

By ignoring three vastly superior plans by his subordinate team leader, he displayed a tragic example of ego defying logic, and good men had paid with their lives.

The MP-5s were usually reserved for hostage rescue and Close Quarter Battle, or CQB, but had been requested for possible sentry neutralization on this mission. The SD variant of the MP-5 was equipped with an integral noise suppressor that nullified any sound from the muzzle when firing a sub-sonic 9mm round. The magazines Cross and Ward had just received were full of them.

The Pave Hawks lifted off simultaneously. After a curt pause they pitched forward, and headed east.

"Radio check." Ward's voice came over the intercom just as Cross got his headset in place.

"Lima Charlie, Recon," a voice replied. Cross noted a slight southern drawl.

"Who do I got?" Ward asked.

"Shingleton, weapons." Staff Sergeant Phil Shingleton was the A-Team's weapons specialist.

"How we lookin'?"

"Fair to Midland, Recon," definitely southern, "we're 'bout one five mikes out."

The tension was building, and Cross felt like he was going to jump out of his skin in anticipation.

"I got Comm-o on the hook?" Cross inquired about the communications specialist of the A-Team.

"Wait one," Shingleton replied.

He removed his headset and passed it to the Communications Officer, Sgt. David Michaels.

"Check, check." It was Michaels.

"Lima Charlie, need to confirm freqs."

"Primary: seven eight decimal four five, break." Michaels continued, "Secondary, six eight decimal three five, over."

"Roger that," Cross replied.

"Tennn minutes!" Captain Mark Brinker, the A-Team leader hollered across the radio.

Everyone with a headset turned to the others, held up ten fingers and loudly repeated the command. Cross's pulse was beginning to race. It was so pronounced that he could actually feel the arteries thumping in his eye sockets. He needed to get control of it. He had work to do.

Cross stared out into the blackness and took a deep breath. He noted the occasional burning wellhead as it passed in the distance. The slight ambient light enabled him to get glimpses of the ground thirty feet below him. At that distance, and at 150 knots, the glimpses were just blurs.

Breathe, he thought to himself.

He closed his eyes and tried to think of home.

The letter! Cross's eyes sprang open as he frantically reached for his breast pocket to assure himself the letter was still there. It was.

He turned to the crew chief and keyed his headset.

"Hey chief!" Cross stretched out his arm, just reaching the soldier's uniform and tugged on it.

The crew chief immediately broke his vigilant stare out into the darkness over his door-mounted weapon. He turned to Cross, who was pulling the headset away from his ear. The crew chief pulled his off too, and leaned over to within inches of Cross's face.

"Yeah?"

The chief saw him pull the letter from his pocket.

"Could you get this to my mom for me? The address is on it."

It was the kind of request that only a fellow combatant could appreciate. The chief looked up at the Marine's steely-blue eyes from behind his camouflaged face and, for an instant, felt all of his fear.

"Stake your life on it Recon." The chief gently took the letter from Cross's hand. "Even if I have to do it myself, brother."

The gunner nodded at Cross, tucked the letter safely away, and returned to his gunner duties.

Cross released the five-point harness and pushed his two slung rifles under his right arm. It was the responsibility of the rappel master, as he was called, to inspect and properly secure the fastrope prior to insertion. Cross did so quickly, running every inch of the large rope through his bare hands as he felt for anomalies.

After assuring there were none, he fastened the fastrope to one of the cargo loops on the deck of the helicopter. He checked and double-checked that it was secure. When he was confident enough in his work to trust the lives of his team to it, he signaled Ward. Cross then sat back down in his seat.

"One minute! Lock and load!" Captain Brinker yelled over the radio.

The order to charge weapons was just tradition. Brinker knew everyone was ready. Ward and Cross held up one finger and repeated the command. The rest of the team did it again to show acknowledgement. Cross closed his eyes and took several deep breaths.

"Thirty seconds!" Brinker said.

It was officially showtime. An anonymous pilot's voice came next.

"Here we go," was all he said.

The teams were in complete focus as the Pave Hawks traversed the final kilometer and a half to the insert point. The helicopters dropped into a twenty-foot wadi that was nearly a mile long-a veritable Grand Canyon for the Arabian Desert. Cross felt the nose of the aircraft begin to rise as it began to bleed off speed, slowly at first. He then felt the aircraft pitch up violently as the darkness turned bright orange.

Two F/A-18s had dropped four M-77 bombs on the target's eastern flank. The combined 3000 pounds of Incindagel, a more recent version of Napalm, made for quite a show.

The g-force created by the deceleration of the helo pushed the team towards the deck.

1A0U

Print# 1539

"Stand by!" the crew chief yelled at Cross.

As the pilot began to settle into a hover, the crew chief pointed at Cross. Cross heaved the fastrope bag out into the night. He looked towards the Iraqi position as the last glow of the napalm fire faded.

He could have sworn he saw…*couldn't be.*

❧   ❧   ❧

Habbas al-Razzaz had more questions than he had answers. The security at Ichilov Hospital was airtight and he had no idea who the IDF colonel was or even whether he was going to live. The Arab reporter had followed the ambulance out to Sde Dov airbase and watched it unload the colonel onto the American plane from beyond the perimeter fencing.

From a concealed area of the fence, al-Razzaz was able to photograph the activity around the beautiful lines of General Samuelson's executive aircraft.

Where were they taking him? Al-Razzaz wondered.

He had to develop the photos and see what he could find out.

This was big.

❧   ❧   ❧

"Go! Go! Go!" before Ward had finished the command, Cross vanished down the fastrope.

He was followed immediately by the rest of the team. By the time Cross had rolled into his position, Ward, who was the last to exit, was on the rope. Within five seconds all six members of Team Three were in the prone position. Their rifles covering all 360 degrees around the dangling rope.

Within two more seconds, the Pave Hawk pitched its nose down, throttled up, and was gone. In the distance, Cross could hear the other Pave Hawk bank as it began its egress. He was impressed that they had beaten the Army to the ground.

For a moment, he marveled at how decades of testing insertion techniques from helicopters had led to this. The fastest, most efficient, and logistically uncomplicated method was sliding down a big fat rope like a fire pole.

It was too dark to see with unaided vision, so the team members donned their AN/PVS-5 night vision goggles. Cross heard the high pitched whirring of his unit warming up. His eyes were soon filled with green light that faded into the familiar dull honeycomb pattern. The forms of his teammates soon materialized.

He turned the power switch past the on position to activate the tiny infrared lamp between the exterior lenses. He then turned it back off. Ward had seen the light as a bright beacon in his own goggles. Had he not been wearing night vision, he would have seen nothing. Once he received the signal from Cross, Ward patted his head with the palm of his left hand. *Headcount.* That was Cross's job as the assistant team leader.

Even though he could see five other figures lying on the desert floor, he still scurried around to make physical contact with each member. This addressed not only accountability but alerted him to any possible injuries during the insertion.

When the headcount was complete, Cross held up his arm in a large circle that terminated at the top of his head. It was the distant diving signal for "O.K." Ward made a sweeping motion with his left hand. *Move out.*

Danno was the point man. Cross, Huffman, Ayala, Ward, and the team's tail-end-Charlie, Daley, followed in that order. The team spread out and moved slowly to the east. Cross navigated for the team with his wrist mounted dive compass. He had set the bezel for the appropriate azimuth before they ever boarded the choppers.

There were seven burning wellheads in the shape of an offset vee that pointed at the team. They would drop to a low crawl when they reached the wellheads. The wells concealed the team's movement until then.

"Alpha-1, this is Romeo-3, radio check, over," Cross whispered into space.

He was wearing an Eagle tactical headset. His whisper was vastly amplified through small, flat, voice-activated pickups running in front of his ears along the jawline. The vibrations conducted through the bones of the jaw were detected by the sensitive pickups. They heard what someone standing directly next to Cross could not.

Michaels heard him perfectly.

"Alpha-1 is up and mobile."

Cross' silence was his acknowledgment. Radio silence and noise discipline were essential. They'd reached the edge of the wadi they had inserted into. Ward pointed to a large level area that was partially encircled by the wall of the wadi and made a circular motion with his hand. This designated the area as the rally point if they became compromised. Ward then passed his hand over his head. Ward, Ayala, and Huffman dropped to a knee as Cross and the others stayed at the ready.

The men kneeling began unfastening the guille suits wrapped around their waists. Once they had their hand-made camouflage body covers in place, each of the three slithered up and over the edge of the wadi, and became part of the desert landscape.

Once Cross was confident that they were in place, he and the remaining Marines below donned their guille suits. After the team had achieved an acceptable level of camouflage, they crested the edge.

Each member of the team switched off their night vision goggles and slid them onto their foreheads to conserve power. They would crawl the 600 meters to the trench using the faint glow of the fires. Cross confirmed their azimuth with his dive compass. Team Three began moving towards their objective at a low crawl. They were now phantoms in the desert night, stalking an unsuspecting prey.

The Special Forces team had moved into the agricultural complex and was able to cover ground faster than Team Three. The cover of the trees enabled them to patrol in a modified crouch, cognizant of every sound and smell in the darkness. One disadvantage to the cover was the inability to yet see the objective. They would have to reach the far side before they could get a good look at it, but that wouldn't be long now. They were beginning to pick out voices in the distance.

◆   ◆   ◆

Cross pulled back the Nomex flight glove on his left hand to reveal his chronograph. The current time put them about fifty meters from where the trench was supposed to be.

Not long now, he thought.

◆   ◆   ◆

Alpha-1 came to the edge of the trees. Capt. Brinker attempted to focus the exterior lenses of his AN-PVS 5s to no avail. He was unable to identify the amorphous shapes in the distance.

"Break out the Predator," he whispered.

Michaels knelt as Shingleton came over to him to remove the optical component of the team's DIM-36 thermal-imaging scope. The team had actually first learned to use the device while it was mounted on a Bradley fighting vehicle. It took two men to man-pack its components tactically in the field.

Troops called it the "Predator" because the image it produced was similar to the vision of the alien hunter in the film of the same name. It recognized the thermal signature of anything warmer than the cold desert air. The information provided by the Predator scope could be vital to the Marine's infiltration of the target.

The responsibility of the scope fell upon Alpha-1 because Team Three had not been to the rear firebase to prepare for the mission. Once Shingleton had the optical unit out, he gently sat it on the ground and set to digging a small hole in the sand with his hands. As he dug, Michaels moved over to Sgt. Javier Nunez, the team demolition expert. Nunez heard him approach, and without averting his gaze into the unknown, knelt down.

Michaels retrieved the power unit to the thermal imaging scope. He secured Nunez's ALICE pack and returned to Shingleton. Phil attached the two cables from the power unit to the optical unit by touch. Once attached, Michaels opened the tripod and placed it next to the hole in the ground. Michaels mounted the optical unit on the tripod and Shingleton placed the power unit in the hole. He stuck his hand under the sound suppressing foam encasing to the power unit and switched on the power. He quickly withdrew his hand as the vacuum pump came to life and shoved the displaced sand from the hole on top of the machine to further suppress the sound of the pump. With the sand squarely in place, the team could not hear the unit. They could feel the vibration in the sand, but they had successfully baffled all sound from it.

Shingleton, content with the ease of the setup process, settled into the prone position where he could sight through the high-tech optics. He aligned his right eye with the rubber eyepiece to ensure a proper seal, then pushed his head forward. The rubber ventricle inside the eyepiece opened up and his eye was filled with a dull, red glow.

❖   ❖   ❖

As he crawled, Cross suddenly felt the ground angle upward significantly. They had reached the trench.

He slid his PVS-5s back over his eyes and turned the switch, *Dweeeee.*

❖   ❖   ❖

Shingleton saw nothing but a blur. He reached up and turned the focus ring around the lens.

Holy shit, he thought.

◆   ◆   ◆

Cross saw the heads of two Iraqi sentries come together ten meters to his right. The soldiers began whispering in Arabic. He looked up the trench to the left and saw nothing. To the right, he saw only the two sentries. He had gotten very lucky on the timing, and the two sentries appeared to be in the middle of a mobile patrol of the trench.

He slowly and silently slid the MP-5 under his right side. The tritium sight on the MP-5 appeared very bright and out of focus to the night vision. He had to look over the rear peep sight and aimed using only the front sight post at the left sentry's head.

Cross gently placed his finger on the trigger and moved the front sight from one head to the other. He did this three times. When the front sight settled into a perfect rhythm between the two, he was ready.

"One, two,…" *thup thup.*

Both silhouettes vanished from view. The two lifeless bodies fell to the ground, their rifles clattering together on impact.

"ya-ha?" Cross heard.

Oh shit.

Cross's heart nearly jumped out of his skin when he heard the voice of a third sentry who had been out of view in the trench.

Cross dropped over the edge into the trench.

Through the green haze of his goggles, he made out the form of a man with a radio handset up to his ear. Cross brought his weapon up. The Iraqi said something in Arabic just as Cross loosed a five-round burst directly into the man's chest. As the body fell, Cross heard the unmistakable squawk of the handset un-keying.

Oh God, no.

"Romeo-3, Romeo-3, this is Alpha-1." Shingleton didn't sound as collected as Cross would have expected.

"Moosecock, moosecock, moosecock." Cross's vision flashed as his blood surged with adrenaline.

Fear swept over him as he heard the abort code. It had been jokingly selected for the practical reason that no one could possibly mistake it. Its use was an indication that some aspect of the mission had gone drastically wrong.

"I have visual on at least three zero Tango seventy-twos. Get the fuck outta there now!"

Team Three was frozen for a moment. They had all heard the call from Shingleton. Suddenly, the radio lying on the ground forty feet away began talking. Their situation had very rapidly gone from bad to worse. They didn't yet know it, but the platoon-sized element of the Iraqi 5th Infantry Regiment they'd been sent up against had been joined by an entire company from the Medina 2nd Republican Guard Armored Division.

Shingleton had seen the business end of at least thirty of the most advanced tanks available to the Iraqi army.

"Let's go," Ward ordered.

FOOM!

It was the unmistakable hollow sound of a mortar tube firing in the distance. The team froze in their tracks. With a subdued pop, the sky came alive with the brilliant, pulsating light of a white phosphorous parachute flare.

"Down!"

The team dropped to the floor of the trench. The squawking from the Soviet-made radio in the corner abruptly stopped. Ward pointed at his eyes with the index and middle finger of his left hand, then pointed to the edge of the trench. Cross nodded and crept towards the edge of the trench that was all that was separating Team Three from the vastly outnumbering Iraqi forces. As his head slowly crested the trench, his eyes grew wide in disbelief.

He saw men, hundreds of them, moving out of fortified positions. They were manning crew-served weapons, mounting vehicles, and climbing into…tanks.

He watched a white Toyota pick-up pull out of the encampment. The truck had probably been "appropriated" from some Bedouin sheepherder who now lay dead in the middle of the Kuwaiti desert. Manned atop a steel pole in the bed was what appeared to be a GRU-3 machine gun. Two armed soldiers were sitting in the bed along with the gunner.

The truck turned right as it exited the outer perimeter of the Iraqi position and came straight for Team Three.

"Incoming," Cross whispered.

"Huffman," was all the command Ward had to give.

Huffman slowly pointed the barrel of his M-249 over the edge of the trench.

"One to Three, SITREP, over." Shingleton had seen the flare and was requesting a situation report.

"We got company, wait one." Cross prayed for the truck to alter its present course.

It didn't. It just grew larger.

FOOM!

Another flare sailed to its apogee above the trench.

Not having seen nor heard from their sentries, the Iraqis had gone defensive. The Toyota-mobile reactionary force had been sent to investigate, and was now 100 meters directly in front of Team Three. They were moments from being compromised…the mark of failure in any Recon mission.

"Bounding over watch to the rally point." Ward confirmed what they all knew and Cross's skin came alive with goose bumps.

A stealth escape was unattainable.

The fight was on.

CHAPTER 6

Little Bighorn

The men of Team Three could feel their hearts pounding as they leaned forward against the wall of the trench. They carefully aimed at the approaching truck, but Huffman would be the only one firing the initial volley. The others would be ready in case the situation called for additional fire support.

The Toyota truck was still coming at them, and had violated the team's cushion of safety.

Ward had given them ample opportunity to alter their fate.

"Now!"

Forty rounds from Huffman's SAW swept through the cab of the truck. The high-powered rounds tore into the vehicle and across the chests of the front passengers. They died instantly in an explosive shower of blood and glass. The rounds penetrated the thin wall of the cab without a substantial loss in velocity and the Iraqi gunner's left kneecap took a direct hit that nearly amputated his leg. Before he fell out of the truck as it reeled out of control, he was hit four more times below the waist.

Both remaining passengers died before reacting to the machine gun fire. In less than three seconds, Huffman had killed 4 men.

The fifth would die within minutes.

The instant Huffman released the trigger; Cross, Daley, and Danno leapt out of the trench and ran. They ran faster than they ever had into what was now a world in slow-motion, clinching their teeth in anticipation of being shot.

The Marines unconsciously pulled their shoulders in to become smaller targets. Cross could feel his Israeli-made commando boots kicking up sand behind him as he pumped his legs.

"I'm up, he sees me, I'm down," he mumbled out loud with labored breath.

Marine infantry training had taught him that it took the best rifleman about three seconds to acquire a moving target and get off a shot. Cross had been taught the phrase he had just uttered along with every other Marine in the Corps. The time it took to say the phrase was theoretically all the time you had to safely move when withdrawing from an armed adversary.

The trio dropped to the prone position as they spun 180 degrees to face the Iraqis. Cross fired a high-explosive round from his M-203 grenade launcher at the Iraqi perimeter. All three men then unleashed a barrage of offset 3-round bursts as Ward's element ran towards them from the trench. Every fifth round they fired carved a red streak through the sky just feet away from their teammates' heads.

When Ward's group was slightly past Cross's, they turned and started firing. As their first round left downrange, Cross's element got up and ran. With the added firepower of Huffman's M249, Ward's half of the team was able to lay down a substantial barrage of suppressive fire.

The bright muzzle flash generated by the T-72's 125mm smoothbore main gun did not even have time to register in Ward's brain before an enormous projectile impacted thirty meters in front of the team. The blast wave from the explosion as it augured into the desert sand sent all three men from his element through the air. They landed unhurt ten feet from where they had stood.

They'd been fortunate that the Iraqi tank crew had fired a high explosive, anti-tank round. Had they fired an anti-personnel flachette round, they would have all been torn to pieces.

As Ward rose to his feet, he tasted blood. The concussion had caused him to bite off the tip of his tongue. The extreme level of adrenaline shrouded his pain.

By now, there was a steady supply of phosphorous parachute flares illuminating the skirmish. Cross watched Ward, Ayala, and Huffman coming towards his element as he fired at the Iraqis. The three looked as if they were running across the field in a crowded stadium while hundreds of spectators fired at them. Compounded by the fact that the groundskeeper had just turned on the stadium lights.

Flashes from between the T-72 tank positions erupted everywhere. Team 3 had successfully escaped the effective range of the AK-47s firing at them in terms of point targeting, but the sheer volume being projected at them narrowed that slim measure of safety. Ward's element passed Cross's

"aaaaah!" Cross turned to see Ayala collapse and tumble to the ground.

He was screaming in agony from the round that had just ripped through his left side. Ward and Huffman completed the rest of their bound and began firing. Ward's instinct as a team leader caused him to make a visual account as he spun around.

Ayala was missing.

Cross jumped to his feet and ran out of his three-man formation towards Ayala. In the short time it took Cross to reach him, Ayala's camouflage blouse had become saturated in blood. Both of his hands clutched the exit wound as he howled in agony.

The phosphorous flares slowly falling to earth under their small parachutes illuminated Ayala's huge, frightened eyes before the shadow of Cross's head circled around to block out the light.

Cross saw his eyes screaming out to him for help. He had never before seen such fear. The three men he had killed never had a chance to look at him and the image of his dying friend's face would forever be in his thoughts. Ayala was suffocating in pain and fear.

A fine line separates heroism from rational behavior. Heroes risk their lives to save strangers. Brothers, such as these were, possess the will to die for one another without question. Cross never thought twice, and would have preferred death to witnessing the look in Ayala's eyes.

"I gotcha man!" Cross reassured him.

Ayala's wailing subsided at the sight of his friend. Cross sat his rifle on the ground and grabbed Ayala between the legs. With his free hand, Cross grabbed Ayala's H-harness load bearing gear and heaved the injured Marine over his left shoulder. Ayala's blood began immediately began flowing down Cross's neck to his back.

God no.

Cross became horrified at the feel of the warm blood streaming down his back. He had never lost a friend so close. He fetched his weapon and turned towards the West.

Dispensing with the immediate action drills, Cross just ran in a straight line towards safety. He found strength he never knew of from the fear that gripped him. He was going to make it to the rally point and get his friend out of danger. His legs strained as he lugged his dying comrade across the last 100 meters to the wadi.

The remaining members of the team escalated their fire to a frenzied pitch in order to cover Cross's escape. In his peripheral vision, Cross could see the incoming rounds impact the sand around him.

Fifty meters.

Intermingled with the sounds of battle, no one noticed the hollow signature of a mortar tube firing from within the Iraqi perimeter.

Twenty-five meters.

"C'mon Recon!" Cross heard through his earpiece.

It was then that Cross saw muzzle flashes erupt from the edge of the wadi and red tracers flying past him. The Green Berets had cut to the wadi undetected at a full sprint. Their super-human physical conditioning had enabled them to make it to the rally point in record time. They now assisted in Team Three's withdrawal.

"Ruuuun!" Shingleton growled as he fired a continuous volley from his M-60E3.

Ten meters.

Cross's vision constricted to a point.

Almost there.

The blast from the high-explosive mortar round was like a baseball bat to the back of Cross's head. Without losing consciousness, he flew through the air. Ayala slipped from his grip as they sailed over the edge of the wadi. Cross landed face first with an impact that knocked all the air from his lungs. He crumpled into a pile on the floor of the wadi, cringing in pain from the concussion.

Cross pushed up onto his knees and looked around. The SF medic, Sgt. Marcus Wafer, slid over beside him to assess his injuries. Before he could, Cross scrambled over to where Ayala lay. His friend was contorted in a position only attainable while unconscious.

Ayala's bloody face staring wide-eyed into the sky struck Cross with the reality of this war. A man he had spent the last four years with in every aspect of life, whose smell he could distinguish from that of others, whose gait he could pick out of fifty men walking at a distance, a brother, was dead.

Cross was no longer scared of battle. Primal fury had instantly replaced his sense of fear. The hunted was now the hunter.

As the ballistic crack of enemy bullets passed overhead, he stood up to the edge of the wadi, and took aim. His eyes scanned the dimly lit battlefield for targets. He started at the left of the flat, expansive horizon. An Iraqi soldier was running towards them at a full sprint. Cross placed the front sight tip of his rifle directly under the man's neck.

Pop!

Cross disassociated and only heard the familiar sound of the M-16's recoil spring in his right ear.

The Iraqi's legs collapsed below him and he fell forward. His head kicked up dirt as his lifeless corpse burrowed into the sand. Cross's sight picture shifted right.

There were Iraqis everywhere.

It looked as if the entire Iraqi army was trying to reach the trench for cover. As they moved, they wailed with a war cry reminiscent of ancient Celtic battle-fields. Cross leveled on the next man and fired. The man had not yet fallen before he shifted to the next target. He did not care whether the enemy troops were dying or not. He just had to stop as many of them as he could.

"Zulu-six niner, zulu-six niner, this is Alpha-one actual, Moosecock, Moosecock, Moosecock!" Captain Brinker had switched to the emergency extract frequency to hurry their escape.

♦   ♦   ♦

On board the E-3 AWACS, Major Tomlinson did not bother to authenticate. He knew that the operators on the ground needed the cavalry. By the sound of Brinker's voice, it sounded like they needed it five minutes ago.

Tomlinson reached over a shocked Tech Sergeant Grieco's shoulder and flipped a switch that automatically relayed the transmission to the on-station close air support. These were the aircraft orbiting the battle for the contingency no one hoped would come.

It had.

♦   ♦   ♦

"Grid four two six, five three four. Troops and Tango seven twos in the open. Danger close, we are west six zero zero meters. Expedite!" Brinker squeezed the handset harder as he spoke, as if to transmit the peril of their situation to the pilots.

♦ ♦ ♦

The closest aircraft were two OA-10 Thunderbolt IIs. Lovingly called "Warthogs" by their pilots. The A-10 is essentially a flying tank. Surrounded by a protective titanium chassis that can withstand a direct hit from a 23mm armor-piercing round is the heart of the Warthog. Protruding unattractively from the nose of the A-10 is a GAU-8/A 30mm Gatling gun. The gun fires depleted uranium, armor-piercing bullets at 3900 rounds per minute. In addition, the "Hog" carries 16,000 pounds of mixed ordinance. The slow, ugly aircraft was the scourge of Iraqi armor units. The two answering the call for help were one minute out.

♦ ♦ ♦

The men in the wadi continued targeting enemy infantry troops. All exceptionally gifted marksmen, they picked out single targets and fired single shots. Their ammunition supply was dwindling, and they had not heard from the extract bird.

♦ ♦ ♦

"Red" Richardson was listening. His re-fueled and fully armed MH-53J Pave Low was burning a swath through the black desert air. Staff Sergeant Wills, the crew chief, manned a 7.62mm minigun from the right crew door. With his years of experience, he could "feel" how low they were.

The reverberation of the rotor wash from the ground gives seasoned helicopter operators a feeling of depth. He had never heard a 53's engines fired up this high. He knew that at this speed, he had to trust the old man. Red loosely held the controls as the TFTA radar kept the beast from slamming into the occasional sand dune at 150 knots.

"Three minutes." his Co-pilot told him over the intercom.

"Son-of-a-bitch." was the frustrated reply.

Entire wars were won and lost in three minutes, Red thought to himself. He leaned forward in an unconscious effort to make the aircraft fly faster.

◆   ◆   ◆

The four Pararescuemen on the Pave-Low had been fully briefed on the extract procedures. They would provide cover fire and remain on board unless the teams on the ground required assistance due to injury. TSgt. James J. Kerwin was the P.J. Team Leader. His heart was pounding as he sat on the bench against the right side of the aircraft. He stared at the aluminum deck bathed in red nautical light and blinked hard. The adrenaline caused his senses to switch into overdrive. Unfortunately, it also caused time to virtually stand still.

They were originally supposed to pick the two teams up three hours from now.

Jesus. Reality struck him.

Going in this early meant that shit had hit the fan.

◆   ◆   ◆

Major Hugh Smyth crested the horizon in his A-10. He saw the faint signature of a tank come into view on his Low Altitude Safety and Targeting Enhancement system. The LASTE then picked up the flashes of small arms fire being exchanged between the Iraqis and the teams.

"Nightlight, this is Thunder-four. They got a mess, expedite Strike two, over."

"They're inbound, Thunder four." The AWACS mission specialist had already scrambled the flight of eight AH-64D Apache Longbow "tank killer" helicopters. They would be on station within one minute.

The cavalry was coming.

◆   ◆   ◆

"Take that, fucker."

Smyth loosed a volley from his 30mm cannon. The aircraft shook as the gun sent 500 rounds into the two closest tanks. The wave of emotion that swept over the teams in the wadi was palpable.

Salvation was at hand.

They shouted in emotional release at the sight of the 30mm rounds ripping through the pair of tanks. Every Iraqi infantryman cowered to the ground. The weeks of continuous bombing had conditioned them to fear the sound of jet aircraft.

The Fairchild A-10 produced 18,000 pounds combined thrust from its two engines. At an altitude of 30 feet, the roar paralyzed the Iraqis with fear.

Death from above was a completely different feeling from a firefight. In a firefight, you knew where death would come from and had a chance to suppress it. With artillery or air strikes, you only heard it.

Team Three had been shelled for the first time while in garrison south of the Saudi-Kuwaiti border. The invisible, yet audible incoming rounds had left a very deep impression on them. The low, buzzing noise caused by the pressure wave compressing at the nose of the projectile can only be heard from in front of the round as it comes towards you.

The old myth about never hearing the one that hits you is just that. Cross had a piece of Iraqi shrapnel to prove it. The piece had careened off of his Kevlar helmet and he kept it as a souvenir. Team Three would prefer a straight fight any day.

The Iraqi soldiers lying on the ground strained their eyes shut as they tried to become invisible to falling projectiles that were indiscriminate. The strike bought Team Three some time. All of the firing from the Iraqi line halted as the trail warthog made its run.

The Americans in the wadi methodically reloaded. The motion was practically unconscious since they had practiced countless times. Another high-explosive mortar round impacted a few meters in front of the wadi, showering the Americans with debris.

The Iraqis were walking the mortars in on their position. A few more adjustments and the mortars would find their target. The teams were running out of time.

♦   ♦   ♦

Colonel Richardson spotted them first.

"Bingo." He muttered in a tone that successfully shrouded his anxiety.

The panorama that unfolded before him as he approached took his breath away. The sight of this small band of Special Operations troops offering significant resistance against the sheer volume of fire directed at them was inspirational. Red's heart skipped a beat as he quickly took it in.

"Coming right!" He told the crew.

"Jay" Kerwin barely had time to grab a bulkhead cargo strap as the aircraft violently banked to the right, rousing him from his pre-insert trance. He saw the starboard gunner traverse his minigun as Red made the turn directly over the heads of Team Three.

The minigun came to life with a loud *whirr* as it spit forth an unbroken spray of 7.62mm rounds. The gunner's teeth were clenched as tightly as he could manage while he directed the tracers onto the dark shapes that lay prone on the desert floor. He quickly surmised the peril Team Three was in and desperately wanted to kill the men shooting at them.

Pink, pink, pink.

Enemy rounds deflected off of the titanium belly of the mammoth aircraft as the Iraqis tried in vain to drop it from the sky. The men in the wadi felt the rotor wash from the MH-53J immediately after it passed overhead.

Thank God. As the aircraft came around behind the teams to flare for landing, the A-10s came by for another pass.

"Recon, get your man and go! We'll cover!" Brinker ordered.

"Roger that." Ward acknowledged.

The 53 flared and came to rest 100 meters behind the teams. The top of the enormous bird was below the line of sight of the Iraqi troops and safe from small arms fire for the moment. Red would have preferred landing closer, but this was the closest spot to the teams that remotely resembled level terrain.

"Let's go!" Red yelled over the open HF radio net.

Cross turned to Ayala.

He grabbed his dead friend and threw him over his shoulder. He trudged at a jog to the 53 as the Green Berets came closer to running out of ammunition.

"Ridge Runner, this is Longbow Lead, I have you visual. Keep it on the deck, Sir, flight of three coming overhead at eleven o'clock."

The transmission ended at the same instant Red saw the three Apaches spread out from behind a large dune directly off his front at 1500 meters. They opened fire simultaneously and six Hellfire missiles tore through the black sky over the heads of the men in the wadi.

The horizon behind the running team erupted in a yellow flash, helping to illuminate their path. The Apaches then let loose with their full compliment of 2.75 inch aerial rockets, seventy-six apiece. The effect was awesome.

Team Three reached the aircraft and turned to cover the escape of the Green Berets. Cross was the last of Team Three to reach the extract. He swung wide of the giant tail rotor and carried Ayala's body up the ramp into the back of the aircraft. Cross's legs were like Jell-O from hefting his 200-pound friend to the chopper. He made his way to the front of the cargo area and laid Ayala down on the deck.

One of the PJs cradled his head as it settled against the deck. He then went to work on his first combat casualty.

"He's dead!" Cross shouted over the aircraft noise.

The PJ looked down at Ayala and went limp.

Air Force Pararescuemen distinguish themselves not through the taking of lives, but through the saving of them under impossible circumstances. Once you remove their ability to save, they become helpless.

Cross had always admired them. Every member of this elite band undergoes training that parallels that of the rest of the Special Operations community.

The training pages within the service record books of Navy SEALS, Green Berets, Reconnaissance Marines, and Pararescuemen read fundamentally the same. Members of every branch often attend the same schools. What sets PJs apart is the purpose for which they are trained. Rather than facilitate the taking of lives, their primary function is the preservation of life.

That was the spirit of Pararescue.

By dying, Ayala had stripped that spirit from the young PJ hoping to save his life.

The rest of the Recon Marines entered the rear of the aircraft as the Green Berets covering them began their movement to the extract bird. Cross stood up and moved to the starboard crew door. He grabbed a headset off a hook on the bulkhead. As he slipped it on, he heard an Apache pilot yelling over the radio.

"C'mon! Gotta go! Gotta go! Get the hell outta there!"

"I don't have my men!" Red barked back.

"They're about to breach the crest Ridge Runner, you're out of time." a calmer Apache pilot tried to reason with the HH-53 commander.

The Apaches were laying down a steady barrage of cover fire, but the small force of Americans was severely outnumbered. The minigun next to Cross erupted as a constant cone of fire spewed from the barrels. The Iraqis had reached the edge of the wadi.

"Move, Move, Move!" Captain Brinker yelled.

Only Red and Cross's team were on the correct frequency to hear Brinker. Cross and the aircrew were now on the intercom and could not hear what the Green Berets were saying. Conversely, neither the Green Berets nor Cross's team could hear the crew talking to one another.

Cross watched as the Green Berets sprinted for the helicopter, never looking back. The deep sand hampered them, but they were motivated by the thought of death and moved swiftly.

One Green Beret remained behind to cover their escape. Cross saw by the rate of fire that he was firing an M-60. Only the weapons specialist carried an M-60.

"Shingleton." He muttered to himself.

"Go man, let's go!" Cross was becoming more concerned with every moment that passed.

Phil's team was almost to the Helo, and he hadn't yet left his position.

The margin had become unsafe.

As the first of the Green Berets rounded the rear of the aircraft, Shingleton broke contact and started running for the bird. The heavy black weapon he carried contrasted sharply with his uniform in the white phosphorous luminescence of the desert. It bounced up and down as he ran for his life. Cross aimed his M-16 out the crew door next to the minigun.

As the gunner fired a continuous burst across the edge of the wadi, Cross selected single targets for elimination. The blue static discharge from the tips of the rotor blades clearly marked the top of their field of fire. Because they were down in the wadi, they were firing up at the Iraqis. Damaging the blades this late in the game would prove fatal.

Suddenly, to Cross's horror, Shingleton went down about forty meters from the aircraft as an enemy round ripped through his left knee.

"We got one down, we got one down!" the crew chief exclaimed.

Brinker was counting his team onto the aircraft and had not seen his weapons man fall. Before anyone could react, Cross acted on instinct. He ripped the headset off and bolted for the exit at the rear. He passed Brinker just as the Captain realized he was one man short. Cross cleared the tail rotor and ran straight for Shingleton. Brinker followed, dropping to a kneeling position just outside the swath of the main rotor to cover him. Two other Green Berets ran out of the helo and joined Brinker in suppressing enemy fire.

"Ridge Runner, you need to di-di-mao brother." the lead Apache pilot further pleaded with Red.

"Not yet, still short."

Red wasn't going anywhere without all of his men. Since they were going to ride on his bird, they were *his* men. He would have been willing to fight it out hand-to-hand with the Iraqis if need be, but no one got left behind. Cross didn't see any of the tracers streaking inches away from him in both directions.

It didn't concern him.

Without consciously thinking about it, he knew that he would rather die trying to get a man out than live with the suicidal guilt that would haunt him should he choose to save his own life. Death really did come before dishonor for the young Marine.

He just ran. Live or die, he just ran.

He reached Shingleton who was clawing his way through the sand towards the chopper. Cross dove on top of him and quickly removed his pack and weapon. Shingleton had already lost a significant amount of blood. The shock drained his energy and he submitted to the assistance.

"I gotcha, I gotcha buddy." Cross tried to reassure the soldier.

"Get me out of here, man, don't let those fuckers get me." Shingleton's voice broke.

It wasn't fear, but exhaustion that brought out emotions at times like this.

"Never, let's go."

He heaved Phil over his shoulder. The Green Beret let out a shriek as his mangled leg swung down and hit Cross in the back. Cross turned and ran for the aircraft. Having another man's life in his hands amplified the rush of adrenaline in his system. This made him move faster, but didn't dull the impact of a round penetrating his right lung. His vision flashed white from the pain. *Oh no.*

As the round exited his body, it ripped through Shingleton's right forearm, causing him to yell out. Cross stopped for an instant. He knew he had been hit, but was able to remain on his feet and continue towards the helicopter.

Within a few steps, he became short of breath. His lung had collapsed, reducing his oxygen intake by half. Foamy blood welled up in his throat and filled his mouth.

God No, I'm almost there.

As he crossed the last few feet, one of the Green Berets ran forward to assist him. Cross slowed from his injury. As Phil's teammate, Nunez, relieved Cross of his burden, an enemy round ripped through the side of Cross's neck.

The impact threw him forward and he didn't have the energy to lift his hands before impacting the ground with his face. The other soldiers grabbed him by his harness and dragged him up the ramp into the MH-53. Cross felt dizzy as blood rushed out his gaping mouth onto the aircraft deck. He was dying.

"Go, go, go!" Brinker screamed towards the front of the aircraft.

Before the words were out of his mouth, the giant bird lurched, tilting forward. Brinker and the two other Green Berets lost balance from the sudden shift and fell to the deck. Brinker fell on top of Cross, who made no sound.

"Medic!" The Special Forces Team Leader screamed.

Red banked hard left as a high-explosive mortar round impacted where the cockpit had been just seconds before.

Plink plink. Rounds and shrapnel ricocheted off of the fuselage.

The men on board instinctively pulled their arms over their heads and lifted their legs up. As if assuming the fetal position would stop bullets.

Within a few seconds, the aircraft had escaped small arms range. Before they settled into level flight, Jay Kerwin came to the rear and went to work on Cross. He took his shears and sliced up the middle of Cross's camouflage blouse, exposing both of his wounds.

Through the blood, he made out a small rose tattoo on the Marine's right pectoral.

Kerwin froze.

With a single stroke of the shears, he sliced open the right leg of Cross's trousers, exposing his calf. He pulled the sock down to reveal a large tattoo of a recon diver riding a shark.

Jesus no.

He was there when Cross had gotten branded with the calling card of a Marine recon diver. It had been years since that drunken stupor at a tattoo shop in Waikiki the night before graduation from Navy Dive School at Pearl Harbor, Hawaii.

The PJ's blood ran cold as the rescue took on new meaning. His blood soaked hand reached up to key his intercom.

"Move it Colonel!"

The words enraged Red. Not for their candor, but for confirming what he had assumed, they had not gotten out in one piece.

Red set a direct course for the aid station at Al Jubail…and leaned forward.

CHAPTER 7

Trauma

Anne Crossley was cold. The chills that sometimes struck occurred with more frequency as of late. The Gulf War had aged her five years in the last three weeks and she continually prayed for strength. Her husband was at work, and Mike, her middle son had just left. The pictures of her youngest, Len, stared at her from atop the TV in the living room. They were adorned with yellow ribbons awaiting the safe return she sometimes doubted would come. All mothers go through struggles in the course of their child's lives, but this was by far the greatest.

She had flown to North Carolina just prior to Cross's deployment to the Persian Gulf and gone out with Team Three the night before they left. It was a celebration for the warriors who had been called to an eminent battle they were eager to join.

For Anne, it was nothing but a final moment with her baby. A moment of sharing and dancing, of drinking ritual shots of tequila with the men her son called family before they went to war. She knew what line of work they were in, and it scared her.

She hadn't cried until Cross saw her off the next day at the airport. She cried for the entire flight back to California. The young man whose teammates saw him as a cunning killer, she still pictured grasping his baby blanket smiling from ear to ear at the sight of her. She saw her gentle son with aspirations of military greatness.

Anne began sobbing in the silence of her empty home as she stood and walked to his room. She had not heard from him since the war started and knew he was probably either in Iraq or occupied Kuwait. What she did not know was whether he was still alive.

Through the tears, she found his small closet and embraced his hanging clothes.

She still smelled him in the fabric, only a mother can do that. Anne collapsed to the floor of the closet, dragging an armful of clothes from their hangers as her sobs grew louder. She hoped God could feel her anguish, for hers was a pain no one should ever have to feel. The knowledge that her son was twelve thousand miles away and there was an entire army trying to kill him.

♦   ♦   ♦

TSgt. Brian Greico in the E-3 AWACS coordinated the MH-53's egress towards Al-Jubail and notified the aid station that they were on the way. His screen did not cover enough area to pick up the C-20 exiting southern Jordan from the west.

♦   ♦   ♦

"Gimme another one!" Kerwin yelled as a PJ near the front of the aircraft brought him another unit of Lactated Ringers solution.

Cross was stable for the moment, and had been set on a stretcher, but his blood pressure was dropping. He was losing blood quickly.

The exit hole from his collapsed lung was bubbling pink blood as the air Cross breathed in seeped out the wound. Kerwin cut the plastic wrapper from a sterile pressure dressing bandage into a five-inch square while another PJ, Lance Ulrich, cut away the rest of Cross's uniform and swabbed the wound with iodine. Kerwin rinsed the plastic square with alcohol and placed it over the wound to form an airtight seal before securing the pressure dressing over it. Ulrich helped Kerwin lift Cross to get the bandage straps around his back. He felt the vibration of Cross's body as he let out an unconscious groan from the pain.

Team Three watched in horror, knowing they were powerless to help. The excitement of combat was beginning to lift as they got closer to Al-Jubail, and their emotions shifted to their dead brother and dying Assistant Team Leader. The wash of emotions choked most of them up.

Danno didn't know which way was up as the anxiety of losing one third of his team struck home. He had survived an incredible battle, but wondered at what cost. He stared down at Cross. His breath broke in his chest as his eyes filled with involuntary tears.

"C'mon, Hollywood." Danno mumbled to himself.

The war had exacted a heavy enough toll through the scars that had been indelibly etched on the souls of these young men and he did not want to lose Cross on top of it. Danno leaned back against the bulkhead and looked up at the top of the aircraft. He let out a sigh as the tears carved through the camouflage face paint on his cheeks.

Sudden movement in his peripheral vision caused him to instinctively sit upright. The PJs were scrambling around Cross on the deck of the helicopter. Kerwin straddled Cross's chest.

God, no. Danno thought to himself as Kerwin began chest compressions.

Cross's heart had stopped.

Shingleton had been given enough Morphine to control the pain in his leg and leaned up to watch the PJs work on Cross. His heart sank. The survivor's guilt that he felt easily overpowered any residual pain he might have had.

"How far we out, Colonel?"

Red could tell by Kerwin's voice that a life was in the balance, and he was not about to let anyone die on his aircraft.

"Almost there."

The MH-53 was at full speed in a straight approach to the aid station at Al-Jubail harbor. Red could have cared less had there been other air traffic, neither could the air traffic controllers who cleared his way in.

Kerwin began fumbling with the chain around Cross's neck in search of his dog tags.

"A-positive!" Danno yelled before Kerwin found them.

The team knew each other's blood types, Social Security Numbers, and home addresses by heart.

"Colonel, tell Aid he needs A-pos bad." Kerwin said to the pilot.

"Aid-4, this is Ridge Runner, my medic says we need beaucoup A-positive ready when we land."

"Roger that, Ridge Runner." The faceless voice of salvation replied.

◆   ◆   ◆

The medical staff was waiting at the pad as the MH-53 flared to land. The aircraft's ramp was lowering before the landing gear touched the ground.

Five minutes ago, the medical staff had learned that a Marine Recon team had gotten shot up. Since then, each of the staff members had imagined what type of mission it must have been. Visions of elite units blasting their way across the movie screens of bygone youth flashed through their minds. A couple of them were nervous, not because of the trauma alert, but because they had never met, let alone seen, any members of Special Operations. The 9-to-5 military did not see normally come across Operators in the course of their mundane routine.

Most of the staff here were reservists working off their student loans. The citizen-soldiers of the aid station medical staff had much more experience with real trauma than their full-time counterparts, but this felt different.

This was war.

The situation closely equated to the anxiety of waiting for an injured police officer to arrive at the emergency room of any big city hospital. In this venue, the anxiety was just happening on a potentially massive scale.

It was a sobering feeling.

The air of secrecy and elitism that surrounds Special Operations is what had drawn Cross to Recon. Through hard work and sheer zeal, he finally attained the position he had always dreamed of. All he had to do now was survive to revel in the fleeting glory of war.

Kerwin and Ulrich trotted out of the aircraft with Cross's stretcher while the aid staff brought a gurney around the rear to meet them. Kerwin flopped Cross's stretcher onto the gurney, pushing one of the Army nurses out of the way with his elbow. He turned the gurney towards the Emergency Room tent entrance and took off at a jog as Ulrich assisted with steering.

"Hey!" One of the nurses yelled in protest as he reached for the gurney that had been his responsibility.

"Fuck off!" The nurse stopped in his tracks, his mouth agape.

Kerwin's intention had not been to insult the young medical officer, but he was out of time. He fully understood the urgency of the situation since he had been there from the onset and couldn't trust that anyone else would. Sergeant Ward ran after Kerwin, never losing sight of the gurney.

Shingleton pushed away assistance and insisted that he be allowed to hop down the ramp of the helicopter on his good leg. When he got to the bottom, he sat on a collapsed gurney, then laid down with a loud grunt. The pain in his leg was incredible, but his thoughts were with the Marine who had saved his life and he felt shame in having to be rescued. A Marine was probably going to die because of him, a thought that was already ripping him apart. In the back of his mind, he understood.

The men of the black arts were trained to be completely autonomous. Situations like the one they had just been in had taught them over time that the only people they could trust with their survival were each other. Had the tables been turned, he would have done the same for Cross. Unfortunately for Shingleton, they had not.

He laid his healthy arm across his eyes as the staff began rolling him away. While he pondered the sound of the rubber gurney castors rolling across the tarmac, the Scud warning sirens began blaring. Everyone around him went into panic mode and began running about in a frenzy of activity. Phil simply moved his arm to look up at the stars through the dull yellow haze of the camp's generator run lights, hoping in vain to see the Scud coming right for him.

◆   ◆   ◆

"Goddamn Scuds!"

Captain Cecil Brockman was really not in the mood for another Scud alert, especially since he had to break scrub to don his protective gear. No one questioned the procedure since a Scud had impacted a barracks two blocks from the temporary aid station only a week ago.

"Shit."

He walked towards the scrub room to undress. They were about to roll in a shot up Marine who wasn't going to wait for the all clear to sound.

◆   ◆   ◆

"Start two units, now." Kerwin ordered as he entered the triage room, which was in a tent adjacent to the surgical tent.

The Army personnel looked at him with puzzlement as they began scrambling for their protective MOPP gear. An attractive female nurse stepped in front of him, putting her hand on his chest in a show of authority.

"Can I help you?" She asked.

"That's my man." Kerwin told her.

He assumed responsibility for his old dive buddy's health, and until he was out of danger, Jay owned him.

"You'll have to wait outside. We have to get into MOPP gear first."

She pushed on Kerwin's chest. With a fluidity that only accompanies end-less practice, Kerwin's hands came up and grasped the nurse's. He bent her hand backwards and sent her reeling to the floor. She reached out with her other hand, knocking over a surgical tray.

"Aaah!" The nurse let out a surprised yelp.

She was not in much pain, but knew any resistance would alter that fact.

"He doesn't have time to wait, ma'am." Kerwin growled through clinched teeth.

Dr. Brockman had heard the tray fall and entered from the scrub room.

"Hey!" he said at the sight of his nurse on her knees, "What the hell do you think you're doing."

Kerwin stepped past the kneeling nurse with a hard look, releasing his grasp on her hand. She quickly stood, unhurt, saying nothing. She and the Doctor suddenly noticed that Kerwin, and especially Ward, were dressed differently from the soldiers they were used to seeing. These men were covered in strange equipment and had a frightening, empty look in their eyes.

"I'm a PJ. This man needs surgery, now." Kerwin said.

He had qualified his statement to the doctor, who knew very well what a PJ was.

"Is he stable?" The Doctor asked.

"Not yet, he's lost too much blood. I think there's a nick in his carotid."

The doctor saw the frustration in Kerwin's face, and fed the airman's sense of competence.

"I can't put my people at risk, can you prep him real quick?"

Kerwin nodded and began stripping off his fatigue top. The nurse just looked confused.

"I just want to stitch him up to stop the bleeding, then we can send him out to the Comfort."

"OK" Kerwin said. He turned to Sergeant Ward, "I got it, dude."

There was nothing more Ward could do. With a parting glance at his fallen teammate, he turned to leave. Before he reached the exit, Danno stuck his head in the tent.

"Ward, they're here."

Ward grabbed Kerwin's shoulder and looked directly into the PJ's dark brown eyes.

"Don't leave his side."

The question really did not have to be asked.

"I won't." Kerwin assured him.

♦   ♦   ♦

Ward followed Danno out of the tent. When they emerged, he saw Lieutenant Park and the Delta Company Commander, Capt. Warren Ford. Standing behind them was the Company First Sergeant Eugene McPeet, and a civilian whom Ward did not recognize.

"This is James Schaeffer, he's with CIA." McPeet told them.

Schaeffer still worked for the Operations Directorate of the Central Intelligence Agency, but had not been in the field for seven years. The additional requirements of the Gulf War had found it necessary to bring assets out from behind desks.

None of the men wore protective gear for the Scud alert. Having operated so close to the front, they'd learned to ignore the Scud warnings.

It had been the experience of the forward echelon troops that the Iraqis could not hit water if falling from of a boat when it came to long-range artillery. Since the Marines were in the center of a major target, they knew it would never receive a direct hit.

"This way Sergeant." Lieutenant Park said, pointing to a general purpose tent that had several Marines standing around it.

"Cross isn't doing so good, and Ayala's dead, incase you were wondering," the team leader told Park.

Ward had never liked Park, but after the last few days' events, his dislike for the man had turned into a nauseating hatred.

Park looked dumbfounded at Ward as if he had something to say, but said nothing. Ward and Danno entered the tent together, where they joined the rest of the team. The overpowering canvas smell told the weary Marines that sleep was within reach. They were only ever in tents when they were safely in the rear, getting rest.

Debriefs of a highly sensitive nature were normally conducted on the men separately, but with such limited resources, the team would be debriefed as a whole. Gunny McPeet gestured towards Schaeffer.

"He'll be joining us."

Ward nodded at the CIA man as an uneasy silence descended on the tent. Ward assessed the skinny, pasty white-skinned man and concluded he looked like the typical office spook who probably did not know a thing about real-world military operations. Gunny McPeet broke the silence abruptly.

"What the hell happened out there?"

His tone was accusatory, and Ward's blood boiled at the very thought of blame being placed on his team.

"Gunny, why don't you tell me so we'll both know," Ward leaned forward in an aggressive posture.

"Watch your tone, Sergeant."

Ward took his seat in a small folding chair behind a brown card table in the middle of the tent. The dull, yellow glow of three evenly spaced sixty-watt light bulbs illuminated the meeting. Danno, Huffman, and Daley sat next to their team leader.

All of the Marines slouched in one form or another now that the adrenaline sustaining them was gone. They desperately needed sleep. The officers all took their seats opposite Team Three except Schaeffer, who remained standing. A laminated topographic map stared up at the team from the card table, and several flip-chart maps on wooden easels stood behind the officers.

"How did you get compromised?" Lt. Park asked.

"Maybe because we inserted against a whole company, but I dunno," Ward replied sarcastically.

"Bullshit," Schaeffer quipped. "That's impossible."

His condescending inflection infuriated Ward, whose temper was short on a good day.

"I personally counted seventeen T-72s and a company-sized support element," Ward told him, "we never had a prayer. How old was the intel you gave us, anyway."

"Well we had to verify…" Schaeffer began fishing for an answer, which only egged Ward on.

"How old?" Ward demanded.

"Three days," Schaeffer said as he averted direct eye contact with Ward.

The answer surprised everyone in the room. Sheffield had sent updated Lacrosse photos to General Hampton, but Schaeffer never contacted the General for the newer photos. He had incorrectly assumed that the Iraqis would abandon the position and did not take into account the need for reinforcements to protect the truck.

"What?" Gunny McPeet could not believe his own ears.

"You mean you fragged us with three day old Intel?" Ward was losing it quickly.

"We had no reason to believe they…" Schaeffer had not finished his statement before Ward was over the table.

The sergeant leapt past the seated officers and grabbed the CIA man by the head. In the same motion, he slammed his forehead into Schaeffer's nose, shattering it. Schaeffer was sent sprawling into the map boards and through the side flap of the tent. The flap dropped back down and only Schaeffer's feet were visible from the inside of the tent. Ward grabbed his ankles and began pulling him back inside. Park and McPeet grabbed the team leader and pushed him around the table to his seat. Ward held up his hands in surrender and sat down.

"Settle down, damn it!" the gunny yelled.

He could tell that they would get nowhere tonight. The team was just spent. Park stood in all his indecisive glory while McPeet ran things as usual, knowing it was pointless to continue the debrief. Captain Ford was the ranking man, and fortunately was a very capable leader.

"Go gear down, wash up, and get some rest. We'll finish this later," the captain ordered.

He and McPeet then sat and watched as Ward stood, storming out of the tent. His exhausted teammates gathered themselves and followed Ward outside.

Schaeffer was just getting to his feet when the team left. He stood up from a heap on the ground, holding his badly broken nose. When he removed his hand to grab a rag from the dry-erase board, blood flowed freely. Schaeffer grasped his nose with the rag to stem the flow and let out a moan. He had been beaten up plenty in his lifetime, mostly because of his unimposing stature and irritating superiority complex, but he had never been hit this hard before. His head throbbed and he knew it would hurt for days.

"What do you intend to do about this, Captain?" Schaeffer asked in a comically nasal voice.

"Be glad he didn't kill you. I suggest you eat it as a learning experience," McPeet said before Ford could figure out a conciliatory answer.

Knowing Schaeffer could not see them because his face was covered with the rag, the senior Marines looked at each other and smiled.

❖   ❖   ❖

"Before y'all rack out, make sure you turn in all your ordinance at the armory and get me a count."

Park had followed the team outside to seize the opportunity to issue an order of his own. He often found the need to issue any order, no matter how inconsequential, in a vain attempt to retain some level of authority with the team's men.

"They have an armory set up at the Harbormaster's building, over that way."

Park pointed towards the center of the docks.

"Yes, sir," Ward replied as he walked away.

It made no difference that the team had not slept in five days, Park just wanted his orders carried out. That way no one questioned who the boss was in Third Platoon. This lapse in logic would be the last command decision he would ever make.

♦   ♦   ♦

Team three slung the dusty rucks over their shoulders and meandered slowly to the makeshift armory. They appeared beaten, and plodded along like zombies. The Harbormaster's building had been selected as the armory because of its distance from any others. In the event it incurred a direct hit and ignited the ammunition magazines, there would be minimal damage to any surrounding buildings. The closest building was about fifty meters away on dock fourteen, the main dock at Al-Jubail.

The men reached the north side of the building facing a large berthing area where cargo was stored after coming in from, or going out to, the large ships that passed daily. The men slumped down in a semi-circle and began removing any unused ordinance they still possessed.

"This is bullshit," Daley observed.

"Let's just get it over with so we can hit the rack," Ward told him.

It was normal procedure to secure any unexpended ordinance at the end of an operation before standing down. A team that has been engaged for as long as they had customarily received well rested troops to take the administrative burden off the their shoulders.

Ward was as tired as anyone else and his vision pulsated from the extreme fatigue. The depression, frustration, and overwhelming sense of exhaustion that accompanies prolonged sleep deprivation descended on the entire team. Every movement was a struggle.

Compounded by the emotional drain of losing a dear friend, the men were in a mental fog as they began sliding fragmentary grenades that had been "hot fused" for use as booby traps from their cardboard containers. The spoons that activated the zero-delay fuses had been taped to avoid any inadvertent detonations during transport.

Before the men could turn the grenades in to the armory for precious accountability, the fuses had to be switched back to the delay fuses intended for use with them.

"I'm gonna make a head call," Ward said.

He stood from a crouch behind his ruck and walked around the corner of the building in search of a restroom, or the dark side of a tent.

"Wait up," Danno stood and caught up to Ward.

Huffman's eyes struggled to stay open as he began unraveling the green rigger's tape from around one of the grenades. He held it in his lap as he sat cross-legged on the pavement.

I wonder if we'll get real racks, or cots, he thought.

His concentration faltered as the last bit of tape released its hold on the side of the grenade body. His fingers, weak from fatigue, did not contain the grenade as the force he applied to counter the tape's adhesive sent it slipping from his grasp.

In a fraction of a second, just enough time for the spoon to extend, Huffman reacted the only way he could in such a short time by slouching over to suppress the inevitable explosion.

◆   ◆   ◆

Ward jumped and instinctively came down in a crouch with his weapon at the ready upon hearing the detonation. The flash had lit up the entire dock. His mind quickly processed the data and he ran towards his men.

"No, no, no!" He growled as he ran.

When he turned the corner to where they had been sitting, he heard Daley screaming in pain.

"Medic! Medic!" Ward screamed at the top of his lungs towards the medical tents.

Danno ran over to Daley, who was crawling away from Huffman. Huffman was lying back over his ruck, with smoke still rising from his lap. Ward ran over to Huffman and knew instantly that he was dead.

His body was devastated from the explosion. Both of his arms had been blown completely off, as well as his right leg. His torso was severed almost completely in half and there was blood everywhere. Ward looked down at Mike's face. It had been completely untouched by the blast and he stared calmly up at the star-filled sky. Ward could see the ground through where Mike's abdomen should have been and realized he had died before the echo faded.

"Meeeedic!" Ward screamed again as he ran over to Daley.

Danno rolled Daley onto his back and tried to calm him down. Daley's back and all of his appendages were shredded from the shrapnel. He had not gotten his ruck off completely when the grenade went off, which had saved his life. He was bleeding badly, but everything looked superficial.

"Hold on dude, it ain't that bad. You'll be ok," Ward assured Daley, who struggled to turn his screams into growls.

Before becoming a Marine, Daley had ridden bulls all the way to the National Finals Rodeo in Las Vegas. He was an interesting mix of African-American and Santa Domingo Pueblo Indian. Between his heritage and his cowboy upbringing, he was a proud man. Too proud to yell out in pain. Several Army medics and a doctor came running up.

"Move!" one of them yelled as he pushed Ward out of the way.

The tired team leader stood up, covered in his friends' blood. All sound stopped as he backed away from the frenzy of activity. His emotional capacities had just reached the breaking point.

The lack of rest, battle fatigue, and emotional tension that follows one disaster after another had taken their toll. No human can become desensitized to what the last four days had brought him. He backed into the wall of the harbormaster's building as he watched a medic reach though Huffman's mangled throat to retrieve his dog tags.

Ward slowly sank to the ground. He pulled his knees up to his chest and crossed his bloody arms to hold them in place. He stared out at the medics working on Daley and saw Danno just sitting on his knees in shock. Ward began sobbing uncontrollably.

He would not have been able to suppress the emotions even if he had tried. His body and mind could take no more and required release. He covered his head and just cried.

✦   ✦   ✦

The CH-60 Sea Hawk helicopter, a naval variant of the Blackhawk, had barely touched down as Kerwin helped load Cross into one of the litter stations onboard. They had been in surgery for just thirty minutes. Enough time for the very apt army doctor to stick a couple of stitches in Cross's carotid artery.

The regular nurses hadn't even gotten into scrubs after the "all clear" before Kerwin brought Cross out of the tent for his trip to the Comfort.

Kerwin climbed in and signaled the pilot to lift off, never hearing the blast from the docks. The pilot took off and banked east over the Persian Gulf. Kerwin looked out at the dim lights of Al-Jubail, a city whose size had quadrupled by the arrival of the coalition. He did not particularly care for Saudi Arabia, and after making sure his unconscious dive buddy was still stable, his thoughts drifted to home.

CHAPTER 8

An Island of Angels

The USNS Comfort (T-AH 20) is a converted San Clemente class super tanker. The Comfort and her sister ship USNS Mercy (T-AH 19) are floating, fully functioning hospitals. They each contain twelve fully-equipped operating rooms, 1000 hospital beds, labs, radiological facilities, and all the other requirements of a land-based medical center in any large city.

The Geneva Convention prohibits engaging these vessels, but wars had long since ignored the Convention, so no chances were taken. The ships' positions constantly changed to avoid enemy contact. The Comfort was the closer of the two ships to Al-Jubail on this particular night.

Both ships had been activated for the conflict and staffed with some of the best medical personnel in the US. Each fulfilling his or her obligation to Uncle Sam for paying their way through nursing or medical school. Practicing medicine in the peacetime military is tantamount to professional suicide, and consequently most young doctors stuck fulfilling their obligation wore rank with as much pride as a cheap Christmas necktie.

This was war, however, and with it came many older doctors who remained in the reserves for just such an opportunity. They gladly rolled up their million dollar-a-year private practices to get a piece of combat surgery. It gave their lives purpose, and unlike Vietnam, the country was very supportive of the Gulf War effort. Any physician knew they would be well-served to capitalize on the lasting benefits to their civilian careers the war experience would give them.

It was not unusual for the directors of major hospital staffs to be veterans of wars past. It was a very exclusive fraternity, and initiation opportunities were rare. They would be sharing center stage in the play that was the axis of the world's current affairs. The ninety percent pay cut they were taking was insignificant compared to the exposure they would be getting in the home papers.

Dr. Bart Cowen could care less about the money. He had over six million dollars invested in mutual funds and assorted equities back in Massachusetts. At fifty-eight, he could have easily retired years ago, but he loved trauma surgery. It was the ultimate game of strategy and logic. He would never admit it openly, but that's what it was to him.

He made no light of the fact that lives were the stake. He just never lost a game if it was at all winnable. The thrill is what kept him at it far past the professional life expectancy of a trauma surgeon. The salt and pepper haired physician could think of no better place to hone his craft than a war. He had patched up six Marines during the battle of Khafji, saving their lives while subordinate doctors looked on. He performed surgery for 31 hours straight, far outlasting doctors 15 years his junior. The good doctor still had it and had proven it to everyone on board the Comfort. He grinned as he looked down at the white sea spray churning off the Comfort's hull in the Arabian moonlight. He loved the lulling sound of the waves breaking off of "his" hospital.

"Trauma alert, trauma alert, trauma alert," the soft, female voice of one of his nurses said over the intercom system.

Captain Cowen heard the aircraft's rotors growing louder in the distance as he walked back inside to triage.

"Lift One on final, Comfort," the pilot of the Sea Hawk said as he began to bleed off speed for his landing on the ship's helicopter deck.

With his NODs, he could easily see the three red crosses placed equidistant along the side of the 894-foot ship. These identified it as non-combatant.

As he began to flare, the pilot saw medical personnel scampering out of a dull yellow doorway leading to the forward superstructure. He gently set the aircraft down and feathered the main rotor. The Comfort's medical team began unlashing Cross, but was pushed aside by Kerwin. He knew where every quick-release was and did not want any time to be wasted searching.

The nurses looked at Kerwin with contempt. They had little idea of how the combat arm of the military functioned and were ignorant to the fact that the pararescueman would just as soon slit their throats as look at them to save his charge. He helped load Cross onto a gurney and rolled him through the open doorway into the ship.

Kerwin saw the nurses begin rolling Cross towards triage, and he stuck his foot under one of the castors, grinding the gurney to a halt.

"Let me save you the trip. He goes to surgery, now. He has a punctured lung and a lacerated Carotid that's barely stitched together. Where's the OR?" Kerwin said with convincing authority.

The triage nurses turned around and pushed Cross in the direction of operating room four. The surgical team was already assembled in anticipation and the charge nurse stepped across the entry hatch to the OR.

"It's sterile in here," she said as she held her hand up at Jay.

He knew that going in to the sterile environment could do Cross more harm than good.

"Where do I scrub?" he asked the charge nurse.

"I'm afraid you'll just have to wait out here."

Kerwin walked to the next hatch. He knew his way around enough hospitals to know where the scrub room was.

"Wait, now you can't go in there," the nurse yelled after him.

Kerwin pushed through the hatch. It opened into a small anteroom with lockers affixed to the bulkhead for surgical personnel to place their uniforms before surgery. There was a bench bolted to the deck in front of the lockers. Kerwin sat down and began unbuttoning his shirt.

"You'll have to wait outside," the nurse repeated as she followed Jay into the locker room.

This is getting old, he thought as he pretended not to hear her.

The commotion had caught the attention of Captain Cowen. He had just begun scrubbing up when he decided to investigate the ruckus. He swung open the door to the locker room.

"What's going on in here?" he said with obvious authority, "who are you?"

"Jay Kerwin, Air Force Pararescue," he replied succinctly as he continued to disrobe.

"Well, I'm Captain Cowen and I'm in charge of the medical staff on this tub. Why are you pissing off my nurse?"

Kerwin was getting tired, and chose to adopt a more submissive approach than that which he had been using most of the night.

"Sir, we just came in from a very nasty little battle. That Recon Marine in there got shot up pulling two guys out of the mouth of the dragon," his tired eyes pleaded with the captain, "I've managed to keep him alive this long...I just want to see it through."

The doctor stared at the airman for a moment and remembered stories he had heard as a rear echelon hospital medic in Saigon. He'd never seen combat, only its effects. He had learned, however, that a medic who survived just one combat mission knew more than a nurse with two years of classroom study under her belt.

He also knew that to become a PJ, you had to know basic surgery.

"C'mon," the older man said as he turned to finish scrubbing with Kerwin close behind.

The charge nurse just stood in disbelief with her mouth wide open.

✦   ✦   ✦

Daley's growling subsided as the medics injected him with morphine. Ward and Danno had accompanied the litter to the ER tent where the doctors on duty set to stitching him back up. Behind them, two medics hauled in a stretcher with Huffman on it. The attending physician gave him one look and yelled.

"Get him outside and bag him for Christ's sake!"

Though procedure calls for an official pronouncement of death, the doctor was amazed at the lack of common sense displayed by his obedient troops. If a man is cut in half, he's dead. No one will usually fault you for making that call even if you aren't a physician. Ward watched as they reversed to take him outside, he grabbed the stretcher and stopped it.

"Hold on. Where's his other tag?" He asked the medics.

"We didn't get that one yet, but we need both of them for Graves Registration."

Ward's look was enough to discourage any further protest from the medics as he retrieved Huffman's second dog tag from his mangled neck. The feeling of blood and tissue did not repulse Ward. Men this close feel their blood is interchangeable, not something to be wary of. He took the bloody tag and slipped it into his breast pocket as another tear rolled down his cheek.

The scene disturbed the medics. It was an image they never thought they would see in the rear echelon with their TVs and football. They shrugged it off and took Huffman away.

"Doc, he gonna be ok?" Ward asked as Daley slipped under anesthesia.

"Yeah buddy, he's not too bad."

There was nothing more Ward or Danno could do, so they left the ER to explain to base investigators why they had been dismantling hot-fused grenades after five days of no sleep. This would certainly lead to questions about why they possessed them in the first place, and without a choice in the matter, Ward would be able to lead them to Lieutenant Park.

♦   ♦   ♦

Lt. Col. Ron Beckham was confused by the order, but the intrigue surrounding its delivery was enough to keep him from questioning it. It was not that much of an inconvenience since it was only another hour before he woke up anyway.

Beckham commanded the 86th Evacuation Hospital that had been established at King Khalid Military City Hospital. He had a very capable staff, so he wondered why he was ordered to grab a nurse, drive an ambulance out to the airbase, park at the end of the only closed taxiway, and wait. He struggled to see the reasoning for why he was here as he looked east into the growing twilight of morning.

What confounded him more than anything was the fact that the General had told him which nurse to take by name. That made him very suspicious. He was beginning to think that they were being made the butt of a good prank.

Was that really a General? he thought.

His merry band of reservist Kentucky doctors were certainly not above sending his tired butt out to the middle of nowhere for a laugh.

I'll get 'em good if this is a joke, he thought with a smile as he leaned his head back and closed his eyes.

It did not immediately occur to him that the nurse, Lt. Stephanie Ingram, held a Q clearance with her civilian job at the Department of energy. She still performed occasional radiation incident analysis for Oak Ridge National Laboratories in Kentucky, which made her the only person in the unit besides himself that held a Top Secret clearance. The sound of aircraft taking off on the open runways running perpendicular to them was constant, so neither took note when the C-20 carrying Colonel Urit landed.

"I think we've been had, Sir," Ingram said.

Beckham smiled while he stretched his arms over the dashboard.

"I think you're right, Lieutenant," he said with a yawn.

He was about to order the nurse to drive them back to the hospital when he noticed a jet taxiing towards them.

"Well well, the plot doth thicken," he said.

The two medical professionals looked at each other and became uncomfortably anxious at the prospect of this being for real.

The sleek military version of the Gulfstream V slid up to the ambulance and stopped. Beckham and Ingram got out and walked around to the front of the ambulance. The door to the jet opened and General Samuelson immediately came down the stairs. Even without sleep, the general had managed to clean himself up enough on the flight to look presentable. Beckham and his lieutenant quickly saluted as Samuelson approached. He returned the salute and extended his hand to the doctor.

"Colonel Beckham, Tom Samuelson."

"General," the men shook hands. Beckham tilted his head towards the nurse.

"This is Lieutenant.." Samuelson cut him off.

"Ingram. How are you Lieutenant?" the general said as he shook her hand.

The stunningly beautiful African-American lieutenant was noticeably taken aback by the general's familiarity.

One advantage of the cavernous C-20 was its advanced communications suite that allowed General Samuelson to put together a plan via secure channels while in flight. He was able to research the personnel files of the 86th Evac and find a suitable nurse for the task, all within the hour and a half flight from Tel Aviv.

"Fine General," she replied.

The general could feel how curious the two were, so he dispensed with further pleasantries.

"Colonel, I've got a patient who needs surgery pretty badly. Thing is, this has to be kept completely confidential."

The colonel nodded, but Samuelson did not think he fully understood the gravity of his request.

"When I say confidential, I mean no one can know any details about his injuries, his condition, nothing. You're the C.O., so I leave it up to you to take the necessary protective measures."

"Yes, Sir," Colonel Beckham said.

"If you absolutely have to, you can bring in help, but use very strict discretion. I can't stress enough how sensitive this is."

"I understand, General," Beckham assured him.

Doctor Norris backed out of the aircraft holding the foot of Colonel Urit's stretcher. As Norris backed down the steps, Mikael ducked out holding the head of the litter. Dana came down directly behind the IDF Lieutenant holding a pint of blood up in the air that was connected to her father.

Colonel Beckham and Lieutenant Ingram went to the back of the ambulance to open the double doors as Doctor Norris and Mikael walked towards them. General Samuelson did the introductions while everyone assisted in putting Colonel Urit inside and securing him.

"This is Doctor Norris, Lieutenant Jones, and Lieutenant Smith," he said as he pointed to each of them in turn.

Colonel Beckham looked at the general in a way that obviously criticized his originality.

"I'm afraid that will have to do, Colonel."

"Good enough, General." the colonel said.

He knew that he could call the two Israelis anything he wanted to, because he was never going to find out who the hell they really were. When they had Colonel Urit securely fastened and his blood supply hanging from a hook on the ceiling, Samuelson motioned for Colonel Beckham to join him as he walked back to the plane.

"What I will tell you is that that man is a very dear friend of mine. Whatever you need, you just name it. I'm going to be here until he's out of the woods."

"We'll take good care of him General," Beckham assured him. "You know where we'll be."

The men saluted each other and went their separate ways. Samuelson climbed back into the jet. The engines roared the jet into motion before the hydraulic door had completed closing. Samuelson wanted to clear the area before they drew any undue attention. Beckham yelled to Ingram over the noise of the huge Rolls-Royce turbofans.

"You drive and I'll get briefed by Doctor Norris here."

"Yes, Sir," she said as she hopped down out of the back of the ambulance.

Beckham jumped up into the ambulance, as did Dana. Mikael saw how cramped it was and opted to ride up front with Lieutenant Ingram once they had secured the rear doors.

"OK, what have we got?" Beckham asked the doctor who accompanied Colonel Urit as the ambulance started moving.

"He's got a displaced fracture of the femur with a complete transection of the superficial femoral artery and vein," the doctor began.

"Eeesh." Beckham quipped.

"The saphenous nerve appears intact. They were able to partially repair the artery, but it only returned a very weak popliteal and pedal pulse. He needs the femur set and an arterial graft."

"Who's 'they'?" Beckham asked as he lifted the dressing to look at the wound on Colonel Urit's leg.

He realized his faux pas when he got no immediate answer.

"Riiight. Nevermind," he said, much to the relief of Doctor Norris.

"Can you at least tell me how long it's been?"

"About four or five hours," Norris told him.

"We can do that," Beckham assured him.

That got half a smile from Dana.

✦   ✦   ✦

"You think you can close him solo?" Cowen asked Kerwin.

They had been operating for almost three hours. The procedure itself was not very difficult, but since Cross was the only surgical patient right now, Cowen brought all of his available assets to bear and did a very thorough job. He also took the time to explain every move in the minutest detail to Kerwin, who had proven to be an incredibly apt pupil. Cowen enjoyed teaching the impressive young man as much as Jay enjoyed learning.

"Sure, I think so," the PJ replied.

"Shellie can help you."

Cowen's head nurse Shellie McLean had also found the tall pararescueman very impressive, even attractive. At thirty-two, she was relatively young for a head surgical nurse. The age factor may have been what made her more conscious to such a foreign aspect under the circumstances, but whatever the reason, she noticed.

Her fiancée back in Baltimore had written her a "dear Jane" letter two weeks ago confirming her assumptions that his insecurities would be the end of their relationship. He simply could not take her at her word that she could be cooped up on a ship for so long and not get involved with another man. The letter had depressed her some, but she loved her work and was too preoccupied to dwell on it.

She stood by and watched Kerwin assist Doctor Cowen. The handsome combatant made no mistakes and was very polite. Two months at sea with no romantic contact were starting to take their toll and she felt her cheeks flush when he looked directly at her. She was excited that they would be finishing the operation together. Cowen finished the last internal suture and placed his instruments on the tray next to him.

"You kids got it?" he asked.

"Sure," they answered at the same time as they looked uncomfortably up at the doctor.

Under his mask, Cowen smiled. You could cut the sexual tension between the two with a knife. Cowen just shook his head and exited to the scrub room.

The tension continued building for about ten more minutes until Shellie finally mustered up the courage to break the ice.

"So, where you from Jay?"

Doctor Cowen had gotten them on a first name basis during the operation.

"Hasbrouk Heights, New Jersey, You?"

"Baltimore, born and raised."

"You an Orioles fan?"

Kerwin made his best attempt at small talk.

"Not really, I just never found the time."

"Pretty pathetic assuming everyone in Baltimore has been to Camden Yards," he said.

Shellie smiled in polite agreement.

"I've been meaning to ask you…" she said without either of them looking up from their patient, "…what exactly do you do?"

She was, after all, a reservist who had very limited knowledge about the military outside the nurse corps.

"Well, we go in and rescue our boys who get caught in bad guy land."

"Behind enemy lines?" She looked up.

"Yeah."

"Isn't that dangerous?"

She immediately realized the stupidity of the question. "Never mind, of course it is."

She blushed, but had become genuinely intrigued by Kerwin's vocation. Unlike the majority of women serving in the Armed Forces, she was completely turned on by the feats of bravery that men like Jay performed.

"I love it. I get to save lives *and* jump out of perfectly good airplanes."

She could see his cheeks raise up as he smiled under his mask.

"You're nuts," she giggled at his ability to make light of his job. "Do you always treat your patients with such dedication?" she asked.

"No, but this meathead is kinda special to me," she raised a queried eyebrow at him.

"Somewhere, I'm sure I have a picture of us together drunk and half naked at the Wave in Waikiki," Shellie's looked turned to one of total confusion, "he was my dive buddy in Navy Dive School at Pearl Harbor."

"No way, really? Did you know that when you went to rescue him?"

"Had no idea," Kerwin pulled the sheet back, exposing the tattoo on Cross' right leg, "I was there when he got that, had no idea who it was 'til I saw that…his face was covered in blood."

"God, that's like something out of the Twilight Zone. Where did you find him?"

"I probably can't say for sure, but he was in pretty deep." Shellie nodded, she understood operational security.

"What does *he* do?" she asked, making no apologies for her candor.

"Recon, Marine Reconnaissance."

"What's that?"

"You're not very shy, are you?" Kerwin laughed.

"I'm sorry."

"No no, don't be, he sneaks around and finds the bad guys."

He hoped that his juvenile explanations were not coming across as condescending. Judging by her apparent interest, they weren't.

"Jeez, well now he'll remember you every time he looks in the mirror," she gestured at the suture line Kerwin was pulling together on his neck.

"Yeah, I could probably name a few dozen people who would have loved to carve on this idiot."

That brought laughs from most of the OR staff. Once Kerwin had finished closing Cross's neck and chest, one of the subordinate nurses began dressing the wounds. Kerwin removed a rubber glove and gently placed his right hand on Cross' chest.

"You get better, shithead," he smiled, "you owe me."

Shellie had never seen a man who could so deeply and openly care for another man. Not in the military anyway.

Shellie followed Jay to the locker room where he stripped off his gown and surgical mask. For the first time, She really looked at the whole package.

She liked it a lot.

Kerwin had the typical lean, athletic body of a special ops soldier. Compared to what she had seen on the Comfort, Shellie saw total perfection. The sight made her face flush.

Kerwin was a military professional to the core and even though he couldn't help but take notice of Shellie's curves, the thought was forced from his conscious mind. She was a colleague, and real military professionals do not think that way about colleagues.

Shellie, on the other hand, was a civilian twenty-eight days out of the month and happened to be very liberated. When she saw something she wanted, enlisted or not, she very consciously thought about, and even pursued it.

To hell with military regulations, she often thought, *we all put our pants on the same way.*

"You want a drink?" she asked.

Kerwin had not seen a drop of alcohol in three months.

"You have no idea, ma'am."

"It's Shellie, you call me ma'am and it makes me feel sixty."

"OK Shellie, where to?" Jay asked as he sat on the bench to remove the scrub pants covering his uniform.

He was very tired and really wanted sleep, but figured one drink wouldn't kill him.

"My quarters," she said directly.

Kerwin jerked upright and looked surprisingly at the lieutenant.

Ok, Kerwin thought, *one drink just might.*

"Sure."

For the first time, he entertained impure thoughts about the beautiful nurse. It had, after all, been five months since he had kept the company of a woman.

As Shellie led them out of the locker room, Jay could not help but notice the way her camouflage pants so perfectly cupped her very athletic butt.

His face flushed, *damned testosterone.*

Shellie's cabin was modest, but constituted deluxe accommodations for a naval vessel. There was a single rack on the bulkhead on one side of the small room, and a desk that folded out of the other wall. Next to the desk were her wall locker and a hatch that led to a common head she shared with another female officer. Under the desk was a small dorm refrigerator. Shellie reached in to the fridge and pulled out a bottle of Bacardi Light Rum. She began to grab a Coke, but Kerwin stopped her

"Straight is fine," he told her.

Shellie unscrewed the top and took a long pull on the bottle. She handed it to Jay. As he tilted the bottle back into his mouth, Shellie reached up and put her hand on his neck. Her touch was warm and gentle. The absence of physical contact and a preoccupation with the war had viciously subdued his feelings of arousal. With one touch of Shellie's hand, all of the cached feelings came flooding out. He felt like his skin was suddenly on fire and he could hardly breathe.

As he brought the bottle down, she pulled him to her and kissed him deeply with a hunger that only ridiculously prolonged abstinence can bring. The kisses quickly grew in ferocity as they stared into each other's eyes.

Without a word, they sensed a passion in each other that few ever saw in their entire lifetime. They began fumbling with the buttons on their blouses as their bodies rubbed together trying to get closer. Before they were completely undressed, Kerwin hoisted Shellie onto the small desk, knocking everything on it to the floor.

Guided by sheer instinct, she deftly slid him into her. Able to get no closer, she dug her fingernails into his shoulders as she let out a moan of pleasure mixed with a tinge of pain from her body's reaction to something she had gone so long without. The desk collapsed and they fell to the floor.

As if it had never happened, they continued making love with minimal movement. The contractions of their muscular bodies completing the task while clutched in a firm embrace that neither would yield.

They made love several times that night like two fairytale passions that had been separated by vast voids of time and space to be finally reunited. They shared an intimacy traditionally reserved for people who have known each other for years. It came naturally to these two. It was passion with no uncomfortable uncertainties.

It was absolutely perfect.

CHAPTER 9

The Hunter

The pictures turned out perfectly, but Habbas still wasn't sure who the injured IDF colonel was. The Jerusalem Post made no mention of him in the report about the Scud attack.

Colonel Urit had faded from the public view over the last eight years and was not readily recognized on sight by the young journalist's generation, but Habbas was educated enough to know whom to ask. A Muslim scholar named bin Siraj, whom he had met through the newspaper, lived thirty miles away in Ramallah. Habbas had stayed up to develop the pictures and decided to make the journey to Ramallah at first light. He would blend in with the morning traffic and pay a visit to the old man. Surely he would have some answers.

         ♦   ♦   ♦

Four cars behind him, Chalil Davra followed in a dirty blue coup. Davra was a former team leader from the Israeli Navy Shayetet thirteen's famous Haposhtim Palga hostage rescue team, better known as Team four. Shayetet, or Flotilla, thirteen is the naval special warfare branch of the Israeli Navy.

Navy SEALs, Israeli style.

The Israelis boasted that Shayetet thirteen was better than the American counterpart, just as any country boasts of the capabilities of its respective special operations forces. Shayetet thirteen conducts an average of twelve missions a year, mostly along the southern Lebanon front with Israel. That level of operational activity alone more than sets them apart from their worldwide counterparts.

Davra was one of the finest operators in the unit's history, but it was a young man's unit and the A'man had been actively recruiting him for years. It was a natural progression that he eventually accepted and which led him to Metsada. Shayetet thirteen is a unit of amphibious monsters that requires being in fanatical physical shape and Davra managed to leave the unit while he was still on top of his game.

Since applying for a work permit to stay in Tel Aviv, al-Razzaz had been assigned the Mossad operative to shadow his every move. Davra hated the assignment, but it enabled the smoke to clear from his last real mission. He was still assigned to Metsada, the special operations division of the Mossad, but for a few months he would be assisting the Collections Department on low-key assignments in support of the IDF defending Israel from the madman in Baghdad.

There had been a level of international outrage when Davra dispatched Canadian weapons designer Gerald Bull outside his Brussels apartment during his last assignment. It wasn't as if the scientist had not been given every opportunity to abandon his development of Iraq's long range "supergun" and spare his own life. Davra broke into Bull's apartment twice in the weeks preceding the order for his assassination and left obvious signs of intrusion, but the scientist was too deeply committed to his beloved Project Babylon to leave it.

Iraq could only have one purpose for a large bore gun capable of delivering a 600-kilogram chemical projectile 1000 kilometers; and that was to attack Israel. It was no secret, since Saddam had declared that Israel would be his target once he had a deployable arsenal of weapons capable of mass destruction. So the decision had been made to eliminate Bull, and Davra waited in the darkness outside the gun designer's apartment for him to arrive.

As Bull stuck his key in the door, Davra shot him in the back of the head twice with his trademark 22 pistol. It had not been his first. His colleagues had taken to calling him Tsayid, which means hunter in Hebrew. It had become his official moniker at some point; he wasn't exactly sure when.

Tsayid was prolific enough that had become used to the mandatory down time after completing an assassination. He had no idea that this benign surveillance job was going to draw him into a national crisis, but that was his typical luck.

By the time they had reached the outskirts of Ramallah, Tsayid began to assume where his subject was going. Every young Palestinian he had observed went to see the old cleric, bin Siraj, and as soon as Habbas pulled to a stop just south of the center of town, Tsayid's instincts were confirmed. He continued driving past the cleric's home and turned back towards the North along Road 455.

Almost exactly between Ramallah and Ayn Qiniya, he pulled up to a tiny Israeli Police checkpoint, grabbed a pen and paper, and went inside. He presented his identification to the young Israeli officer manning the small desk in the two-room station that amounted to little more than a shack.

"Thank you, sir," the young officer said as Tsayid walked past and grabbed the door handle to the windowless office in the corner.

He looked back at the officer who, after a cautious sweep of the area for anyone watching, reached under his desk and pushed a button. A very faint click announced to Tsayid that the electromagnetic lock on the door had been deactivated and he turned the knob. Inside the office, he pulled up an iron door on the floor that uncovered a short stairwell leading to a room under the station.

This small room housed the receiver for the various listening devices the Mossad had planted in the Palestinian-occupied areas of Ramallah to monitor terrorist activities. With a swipe of his hand, he cleared the dust off of the only chair and sat down. He had worked with this particular receiver many times and knew all of the frequencies he was looking for by heart, so he began dialing them in.

◆   ◆   ◆

Bin Siraj could tell by the pall on the young man's face that he was very distraught. Before Habbas could speak, the old cleric held up his hand.

"Come with me," he said as he arose from his cup of tea.

The elder was a man well educated in the ways of the region, so he led the young man two doors down to a small market. Inside, the proprietor hardly gave a look as the old man and his pupil walked to the back of the store. Bin Siraj sat at a tiny table and gestured for the reporter to do the same.

"The walls of my world have Zionist ears," he explained to Habbas.

The younger Palestinian immediately understood and was thankful to the old man for lending guidance. He was so nervous, he would never have considered the possibility. Unfortunately for them, the trim on the wall that their table rested against contained a tiny microphone. It had been there for months and the ones in the cleric's small home had been long since deactivated. The old man had fallen victim to his own routine.

"What seems to be troubling you, my young friend," Bin Siraj asked the reporter.

"Did you hear about the explosion last night?"

"Yes, another strike against the Jews, Allah be praised."

"There was an IDF colonel there, where the rocket hit."

Habbas was struggling to put words together while he routed around in his bag for the photos.

"What do you mean he was there?" the Cleric asked.

"He ran into a building to rescue a small girl and the building fell on him."

"I saw nothing about that in the papers."

"I know, that's why I came to you. They are handling this as if he were someone very important, but I don't know who he is."

Habbas placed a picture of Colonel Urit taken before he ran into the building on the table. Bin Siraj picked up the photo and Habbas noticed the old man sit up in his chair.

"What else did you find out?" he asked Habbas.

"I tried to find out more from the hospital, but they acted like I was crazy," the young man continued, "I waited around the outside for hours hoping to get closer, but security was very tight around him."

"Is he still there?" Bin Siraj asked.

"No, they took him to the airport and put him on an American jet."

"You're sure it was him."

"Yes, I'm sure."

"Was he dead or alive?"

Habbas knew the colonel must be important to warrant all of these questions.

"He looked dead when they took him to Ichilov, but I'm not certain."

Habbas finally mustered the nerve to ask the burning question.

"Who is he?" he asked.

"He is the Butcher of Shatilla, he is Mordechi Urit."

Habbas's blood ran cold at the mere mention of the name. He had only heard of the man, but that was enough. Colonel Urit shared the company of about five men who, more than any others, were wanted dead or alive by the Palestinians for their allegiance to Ariel Sharon.

"You must tell no one about this, do you understand me? No one," the cleric ordered.

"Sure," Habbas agreed.

"Give me the photos, they will not be safe with you."

Bin Siraj held out his hand. Habbas gave him the remaining four pictures. The elder man noticed Habbas's look of reluctance.

"You have done a great service to the Jihad, Allah be praised for bringing you to me. Notify me of anything else you learn. You will be rewarded."

With that, the young reporter left to return to Tel Aviv.

♦   ♦   ♦

"Hmmm," Tsayid quipped aloud.

He was fluent in Arabic, which allowed him to analyze audio immediately rather than waiting for the tapes to be interpreted. He was learning about this for the first time. If the kid was right, Israel *was* keeping a tight seal on the information. If that were the case, he could only report this to the one man who was sure to know. He hoped the kid was hallucinating though.

Colonel Urit was a great man, and Tsayid did not want to confront the fact that he might be dead. He shook the thought from his mind and returned to the job at hand. He listened for several minutes to the miscellaneous noises that punctuated the small market before hearing bin Siraj speak.

"Fax," Tsayid heard him say in Arabic.

"Go ahead," another voice, that of the shopkeeper, said in the distance.

The main reason that the Mossad had bugged this particular shop was that the owner had one of the only fax machines in the Arab part of Ramalla. The fax machine used the only phone line from the shop and for the time being, the Mossad was only able to track the numbers dialed and any conversation. They didn't have the assets in place to decipher faxes yet simply because bin Siraj had, up until recently, only been involved in Palestinian propaganda. He was not considered a major terrorist threat, and therefore had not warranted the additional assets.

On two occasions in the last three weeks, he tried to send faxes to a number in Baghdad, undoubtedly to relay information about the locations of Scud impacts, but had been unsuccessful. All of the phone lines into the Iraqi capitol had been disabled.

As the old man dialed the number on the fax machine's keypad, it read out on a touch tone decoder next to Tsayid. The Israeli agent looked at the number.

"Medina?" he mumbled aloud.

The fact that Tsayid could not immediately formulate a logical explanation alerted his seasoned intelligence instincts to the probability that something very big was in the works. He needed to find out what was going on from the Israeli side.

♦   ♦   ♦

As General Samuelson and his pilot walked towards the flight operations building at King Khalid, the sun was beginning to peak over the horizon. He stopped and turned to look at the C-20 parked in front of a row of F-15 Eagles.

"Sticks out like a turd in a punchbowl," he commented, keeping true to his southern roots.

The pilot turned and looked.

"Yes, Sir, it does," he agreed.

"See if you can procure a piece of hanger for us," the general ordered.

The key to his success was low visibility. Not only to keep the secret from the Arab world, but also because his career was on the line for an old friend.

"Yes, Sir."

♦   ♦   ♦

Tsayid had gotten out of the habit of calling ahead, much to the dismay of his superiors. He had a certain level of paranoia about using any form of communication other than face-to-face. It came from his ability to intercept electronic means himself. So he sat in the lone chair outside Brigadier General David Yoshom's office, flipping a pen around the fingers of his hand with outlandish dexterity to pass the time. The head of the Metsada Division was surprised to see anyone but security personnel in the offices this early. Tsayid stood immediately upon seeing the general.

"Good morning, General."

"What brings you into civilization, Tsayid," the general joked.

It was widely known that Tsayid harbored a foul taste in his mouth for administration. He was strictly a field agent, and was at peace operating totally alone. The Mossad accepted his idiosyncrasies simply because he was their moneymaker, and one of the best.

"I have something you need to hear, Sir," Tsayid told the general.

Yoshom could tell he was very serious and thought perhaps it was a personal issue since he knew the benign nature of Tsayid's latest assignment. That, in addition to his coming in person, meant that it must be very serious indeed.

"Come in," the general ordered as he opened the door to his fairly simple office.

The Mossad was an agency that thrived because of its anonymity and that carried over into everyday life.

"Please, sit," the senior man motioned towards a chair in front of his desk.

Tsayid closed the door behind him.

"General, I have a tape from my mark during a visit this morning to Ramallah," Tsayid held up the cassette he recorded from the listening post, "he went to see bin Siraj."

That came as no surprise to the General. The cleric was a common attraction in Ramallah for Palestinians.

"Yes?" General Yoshom said as he sat down in his own chair behind the desk, never breaking eye contact with Tsayid.

"He apparently had pictures of Colonel Motta Urit being buried in a building collapse."

The general looked down at his desk and tapped on it several times while he sat up.

"Yes, yes," he said.

Not as a concession to the validity of the statement, but more as a method of pausing the conversation while he dialed the telephone. He leaned back in his chair with the receiver to his ear. Tsayid wondered why the general had not shown more surprise at the revelation.

"This is Yoshom, is General Yaakobi in yet?" he asked. "Very good…General? Yoshom here, would you come to my office please, Sir? It is quite urgent. Yes, Sir."

He hung up the telephone and looked at his confused operative.

"I'm afraid what you heard is correct, Tsayid, Colonel Urit may not live through his injuries."

The statement brought chills to Tsayid. He was among the many who knew the true character of Colonel Urit and he admired him for it. The colonel had been Tsayid's first commander when he worked for A'man, Israeli Military Intelligence.

"I just found out myself early this morning, I want General Yaakobi here before we discuss the issue further. This is extremely sensitive."

The general leaned forward and rested his arms on the desk, still trying to absorb the bad news himself.

"You did the right thing by coming here. I don't think more than six people even know."

General Yaakobi's office happened to be on the same side of the Kirya complex as Yoshom's and it was not long before he entered the office, breaking the uneasy silence in the room.

Both Mossad men stood up, but General Yaakobi motioned for them to sit back down.

"General, you know Davra?" Yoshom asked, pointing to Tsayid.

"Yes, of course," he gave a cursory nod to the assassin.

The IDF chief's time was very valuable, so they took immediately to the business at hand.

"The Palestinians know about Motta."

General Yaakobi's face turned red as he began to assume that Yoshom had informed an agent about something so sensitive.

"He's the one who recorded the tape," Yoshom said with a tilt of his head in Tsayid's direction.

"Tape? What did you hear Tsayid?" Yaakobi showed respect by referring to agent Davra with his codename.

It also signaled that Yoshom was off the hook.

"Well, Sir, the man on the tape is a chel'ah Palestinian journalist. He took photos of the Scud hit in Ramat Gan," Tsayid hesitated for a moment, wondering how deeply involved he wanted to be in this.

"He showed them to bin Siraj and bin Siraj swears that they're images of Colonel Urit getting killed or at least badly injured, he wasn't sure."

With that, Yaakobi sat in the chair next to Tsayid.

"He's not dead, not yet anyway," he said to Tsayid, "you're officially cleared for this now Tsayid. I don't have to tell you what that means."

"Of course General," the agent replied.

"Where are the pictures now? With the journalist?" Yoshom asked.

"No, he left them with bin Siraj."

"We must get those pictures back and contain this immediately," Yaakobi ordered, "since you are the only operative who knows about this, I want you in charge of any operations," he told Tsayid. Yoshom nodded his approval.

"Yes, Sir," Tsayid continued cautiously, "General, bin Siraj sent a fax to a number in Medina. I can only assume that it was one of the photos."

"Give me the number." Yoshom ordered.

Tsayid ripped a leaf of paper from his small notebook and handed it to the general. The agent did not have time to run the number through the Mossad computer database

"Damn," General Yaakobi growled, "Yafai."

"You say they don't know he's dead?" Yaakobi asked Tsayid.

"That's correct, Sir. He wasn't able to find out. He apparently has pictures of Colonel Urit being loaded onto an American plane at Dov,"

General Yaakobi did not acknowledge the last part.

"I thought Yafai was in Jeddah," Tsayid offered.

Both of the senior men were impressed with the young agent. He did his homework.

"He is," Yoshom said.

That was the end of it. Tsayid knew he would not get an answer to the Medina connection. It also was not necessary to tell Tsayid where Urit was, and the fewer who knew the better.

"That will buy us *some* time. Get me this journalist and the old man, Tsayid."

"Done," the Hunter replied as he turned to leave.

◆   ◆   ◆

Colonel Wahid came up empty handed in the morning hours. He had been unable to locate any of his American colleagues, so he took a break from the search to go see his younger brother at the hospital. He was proud of his brother for becoming a prominent surgeon. Not just proud, but a bit envious. What prestige he thought his brother must have for being so brilliant. His brother in turn harbored his own envy for the colonel. Any man with a nurtured sense of masculinity reaches a point in his life where he dreams of being a soldier in some form or fashion. Colonel Wahid's brother was no different.

The elder Wahid exited the National Guard officer's housing and drove along the inside of the base fencing towards the airbase when something out of place caught his eye. The white and gray paint scheme of the big C-20 sharply contrasted against the green and gray aircraft that populated every free spot on the tarmac. The luxurious executive jet had not been there last night when he drove by. He would have noticed something like that.

All of the diplomats are in Riyadh, he thought.

He made a mental note of it and looked at his watch. He would be at the hospital just in time to surprise his brother for lunch.

Doctor Ahmed Wahid stepped off the staff elevator on the third floor of King Khalid Military City Hospital to a very unfamiliar and certainly unwelcome sight. This particular elevator exited facing two sets of stainless steel double doors that lead to the two operating suites on this end of the third floor.

Two armed and very serious looking US Army military policemen stood in front of the doors leading to surgical suite two.

"What is this?" he asked.

Neither soldier said anything.

They weren't being rude, they just were not expecting anyone to come to the back door of the surgical suite. Each suite consisted of a locker room, scrub room, supply room, and an operating room. The MPs were guarding the doors that allowed staff members access to the locker room for suite two. Doctor Wahid was actually going to suite one to retrieve his favorite pen from the locker he'd left it in after a surgical demonstration the day before. The soldiers had just caught him off guard.

"What are you doing here?" he asked the soldiers.

Specialist Fist Class Allan Weaverton took the initiative and spoke up first, assuming he was the more articulate of the two.

"Orders from Lieutenant Colonel Beckham, Sir, No one is allowed in here."

"Like hell I'm not. Do you know who I am?" Doctor Wahid said in his best forceful, broken English.

"A Doctor?" Weaverton said, looking at Wahid's white lab coat.

The smart remark infuriated the Doctor.

"What is your name, soldier?" Doctor Wahid asked.

It was the universal question asked by someone wanting to impress his superiority upon another in the military and the desert camouflage battle dress uniforms the Soldiers had been issued did not have name tapes sewn onto them yet.

"Weaverton, Sir," the MP said with all the insolence that he could muster, never averting his stare into Wahid's eyes.

"Well where is Colonel Beckham?" Wahid asked.

"I'm not at liberty to say, Sir," Weaverton said.

He knew that Beckham was inside the operating room, but the young soldier had, at that very moment, grown tired of the Saudi Doctor's company and decided he had nothing more to say. Doctor Wahid picked up on it and stormed back to the elevator. He pushed the button to go down and the doors opened immediately.

Wahid looked once more at the smart-mouthed soldier and walked into the elevator. He pushed the button for the ground floor and turned to glare at the insolent MP as the doors closed in front of him.

"Damn!" he exclaimed to the empty elevator car, he'd forgotten his pen.

Dr. Wahid could think of no reason why the Americans would need to use *his* hospital for surgery. The 86th had seven operating tables available to them in their own hospital arrangement adjacent to the KKMC Hospital. He had seen them himself. The Army operating rooms were configured within sterile, connectable containers that were transportable. The Saudi Doctor actually found the entire American operation quite impressive, but could think of no good reason why they wouldn't use them instead of the main hospital.

His anger grew with every step as he searched for Lieutenant Colonel Beckham. His pride had been ruffled, and that is a very big deal to a Saudi. He stormed over to the office on the first floor where the 86th Evac maintained their command offices and computer systems.

Since their arrival in Saudi Arabia, the 86th was issued all the hardware necessary to access the Theater Army Medical Information System, or TAMMIS. The system was used to draw upon the entire medical network of the US military. Its primary function at the 86th was to coordinate the Patient Administration Division to keep track of the massive influx of wounded soldiers they expected from the inevitable ground war. Doctor Wahid was briefed on the system and knew that he would be able to research some questions he had before finding Beckham.

Doctor Wahid walked into the office and found one of the nurses pulling a printout from the Teletype system against the back wall.

"Lieutenant, I need to know about one of your patients," he told the nurse.

Lieutenant Carlos Mendoza turned around with a trail of paper in his hand. The noise of the Teletype kept him from hearing the request.

"What's that Doctor?" he asked.

"You have a patient in one of my operating rooms, who is it?"

Mendoza pensively cocked his head and squinted.

"I don't think so, Doctor, no one's been to surgery."

The bulk of the medical cases currently being handled by the hospital were sprains and bruises acquired during training exercises. The most interesting case they had was an acute alcohol poisoning from a soldier trying to distill his own illicit spirits in the alcohol-free country.

"I'm telling you, there is someone in OR Two, and there are guards posted," Doctor Wahid said with a slightly elevated voice while pointing at the ceiling behind him.

Mendoza looked up instinctively, as if he could see the MPs two floors up.

"Hold on, Doctor," Mendoza said while taking a seat at the computer terminal on his desk, "let me check TAMMIS."

Doctor Wahid deflated somewhat at the prospect of getting some assistance in his quest. The episode with the MP had rattled his cage pretty well. He stood quietly by while Mendoza checked the system. He would have blown Wahid off in the name of operational security if he'd even known about Colonel Urit, but he was as much in the dark as the Saudi Doctor was.

"Nothing. No one is scheduled for surgery Doctor," Mendoza told him.

"There has to be!" Doctor Wahid said with growing frustration as he came around the desk to look at the computer screen.

Mendoza rotated the terminal towards Doctor Wahid.

"See for yourself," Mendoza said.

"Have you seen Colonel Beckham?" Doctor Wahid asked.

"No, Sir."

"See if you can find him. Tell him I wish to speak with him immediately," Dr. Wahid ordered.

"Yes, Sir."

Doctor Wahid left the office to resume his search for Lieutenant Beckham when the paging system beeped softly to alert the staff to a page.

"Doctor Wahid, please report to the nurse's station in reception"

"What now?" He mumbled as he turned around to go in the opposite direction.

He walked at an accelerated pace on the assumption that the faster he walked, the faster he could put whatever issue this was to rest so he could get back to finding Beckham. He smacked the silver pressure switch on the wall that opened the doors leading out to reception and he was able to see his brother standing there.

"Brother!" the Doctor said in Arabic as he raised his arms to embrace the colonel.

"You look well, brother," Colonel Wahid said, "have you eaten?"

"No, come with me, we'll eat in the American mess tent." Doctor Wahid said.

The colonel stopped dead in his tracks. His brother reached back and pulled on his arm, knowing full well the colonel's dislike of the Americans.

"Come, the food is better. They will not disturb us," the Doctor said, pulling Colonel Wahid through the doors into the passageway.

It led down a corridor that exited directly towards the American compound. Colonel Wahid became visibly uncomfortable when they found the mess tent and spoke not a word to his brother. Doctor Wahid gave the obligatory acknowledgment when familiar Americans greeted him. Colonel Wahid just stoically followed him around until they had made their selections and were seated in a secluded corner of the tent.

"I know why I am uncomfortable here, because I hate these scum, but what is troubling you brother?" the Colonel said, confident of the fact that any American who may have heard him did not speak Arabic.

"Nothing, really," the Doctor began, "they have a patient upstairs in surgery with armed guards, and no one told me about it."

"Why would they need guards?" the colonel asked.

"That's what I'm trying to find out, but the commander is nowhere to be found."

"That is curious, but I'm here to see you and I don't have very long, so enough of business."

"You're right, my brother," the Doctor agreed as they went to work on the plates of GI slop that they both found so pleasing to the palate, undoubtedly due to the novelty of the dish.

◆   ◆   ◆

"IP inbound," the pilot of the A6-E Intruder said calmly into the oxygen mask fastened securely to his flight helmet.

His helmet was not the traditional gray color of a carrier-based pilot. His was covered in camouflage fabric, the exclusive trademark of a Marine aviator.

The Intruder carved downward in the light of the Kuwaiti sun. The Iraqi soldiers remaining in Al-Wafra oilfield would never see him approaching from the south through the dark smoke.

"In the POP," the pilot said as he angled the Intruder's nose skyward and slightly to the side to allow his bombardier to confirm the target.

"In sight," the bombardier sitting next to the pilot affirmed.

The soldiers standing around the truck from Abu Ghurayb saw the Marine fighter-bomber level out an instant after it emerged from the towering clouds of smoke, and ran for their bunkers.

They would never make it.

"Away," the bombardier said upon the release of the weapon.

A single CBU-72/B released from the underwing hard point and fell towards the truck. At 100 feet, the CBU-72/B separated into three submunitions, each containing seventy-five pounds of ethylene oxide.

At thirty feet, each of the submunitions air burst into explosive clouds of the fuel. The clouds were sixty feet in diameter and eight feet thick. They were placed perfectly around the truck and the soldiers running for their lives, but the Iraqis would not have time to register the feeling of liquid touching their skin.

When the secondary fuse ignited, the clouds exploded in a ball of flame that starved for air to feed the reaction. It took the air from everywhere. For the men who were not vaporized by the heat or ripped to pieces by the overpressure the FAE created, they died by having their lungs literally ripped from their bodies in the reaction's hunger for air.

By the time the sound of the Intruder could no longer be heard, the truck was gone. Whatever tool of horror it carried from Project 600 vaporized in the fireball that rose towards the sky.

CHAPTER 10

Revelation

Tsayid didn't expect Razzaz to offer any relative level of resistance, but considering what was at stake, the Metsada operator took no chances. He called in two fellow agents with whom he had worked extensively. They were with him in Brussels, and were just as glad as Tsayid to be back on a real operation. They knew nothing about the details of the assignment, they simply did what Tsayid told them to. That was their job.

Like Tsayid, they had both come from the Paratrooper Regiments to A'man, and from there were recruited to the special Mossad division. Luck was the primary reason they worked together in the beginning, now it was just assumed they were a team.

Both men maintained a very high level of fitness and sported the lean frames that went along with it. They were equals in most respects to their particular brand of clandestine service, but had one thing setting them apart from one another. The men's height contrast was profound to the point of ridicule.

The taller agent stood nearly six-feet, four inches, and the shorter of the two was five-five. Since their days in the Paratrooper regiments, the two had been called "Tom and Jerry" respectively. The nicknames stuck, and they now carried the monikers as codenames. Through nothing more than chance, Tom and Jerry served together in every unit to which they were assigned including Metsada.

Tom stood behind Tsayid on the stairwell landing on the north end of the brightly lit corridor running along Razzaz's apartment door. The mismatched pair joined Tsayid shortly after his meeting with General Yaakobi, and the three operatives were fortunate enough to find the journalist's car parked on the street in front of his apartment building.

Tsayid was correct in assuming that Razzaz's early morning excursion to Ramallah would require him to catch up on some sleep. Tsayid cracked the stairway access door just enough to offer him a view of the entire length of the hallway. There was no movement in the deserted passage, and it was completely silent. Most of the residents were still out of the city in the hotels, too afraid of the Scuds to return. Razzaz's apartment door was the third from where the Mossad man stood, and the agent had an unobstructed view of it.

Tsayid slowly and silently pushed the door open and slipped out onto the filthy beige carpeting covering the hallway floor in the old building. He began creeping silently down the passage as Jerry shadowed him by inches. Both men slipped the silenced Ruger MK-II pistols from the waistband paddle holsters in the smalls of their backs as if on cue. They knew it was likely they wouldn't need the weapons, and that Razzaz had to be taken alive, but they were not about to take a chance at being surprised.

Tsayid pulled out a duplicate key to Razzaz's apartment that he had made they same day he was assigned to the journalist. The agent was very adept at picking locks, but experience had long since given way to logic and he always made a key in order to access low-risk target residences.

The agents quickly reached the door and Tsayid slipped the key into the lock with nothing more than the most imperceptible sound. He pressed his ear to the white, solid-core door and listened for any sound from within the apartment. He heard a faint hum, *probably a space heater,* he thought.

It was just enough sound to cover the agents' entry.

Tsayid smoothly turned the key until the doorknob throw disengaged the jam, allowing Tsayid to push the door open. He swung it open swiftly, but without a sound. Jerry followed him inside and shut the door behind them.

With a swiftness only acquired through years of practice, the two agents moved through the small apartment. Tsayid looked forward and Jerry looked to the men's back, covering any possible threats to their safety. There was enough daylight entering the apartment from the edges of the blankets draped over the windows that the agents had no need for the small flashlights they carried. Tsayid led them directly to the bedroom where they found Razzaz, still asleep and fully clothed, except for his shoes.

Tsayid grabbed the Palestinian's right arm and spun him over onto his back. Razzaz's eyes sprang open and Tsayid silenced the inevitable scream that was to follow with a punch directly to the journalist's larynx. Razzaz's mouth opened wide in the body's natural, futile tracheal spasm to draw deficient oxygen from the air. The instant it flew open, Jerry squeezed a tennis ball into the horrified man's mouth.

Tsayid held down Razzaz's flailing arms and legs while Jerry secured the gag with two wraps of duct tape around their quarry's head. Tsayid rolled him over and secured his hands with a nylon tie-wrap. Razzaz finally caught his breath and let out a scream through the flared nostrils that were his only route for drawing air in. Tsayid again brought silence by jabbing him in the solar plexus with the barrel of his pistol. Razzaz found himself again gasping for air through flared nostrils.

"Silence, or you will die," Tsayid whispered in flawless Arabic.

Razzaz suddenly became very quiet and lost control of his bladder, soiling his American slacks. His eyes reflected sheer horror to the two Israeli agents.

Jerry took the lead as Tsayid stood the journalist upright and led him to the door. Jerry looked into the hallway, and upon seeing nothing, nodded to Tsayid. Tsayid pushed Razzaz into the hallway past Jerry and headed straight for the stairs. Jerry locked the apartment door and followed his partner.

"Silence," Tsayid again whispered into the ear of his prisoner as he took him through the stairwell door.

Once inside, Jerry again took the point, leading the men down the stairs. They reached the ground floor where a door led out to the alleyway adjacent to the apartment building. Jerry nonchalantly opened the door to assure Tom was waiting with the team's van. He stepped outside and pulled open the rear door of the van. He nodded to Tsayid.

Tsayid pushed the Palestinian through the door and heaved him into the back of the van, climbing in after him. Jerry closed the van door and walked around the passenger side. He got in and Tom pulled out of the alley, blending into traffic like any other van.

❧   ❧   ❧

Colonel Wahid was in a genuinely good mood; he had not seen his brother in months. The distance wasn't the main factor, though. If his brother lived across town, he wouldn't have seen any more of him. The hectic schedule he designed his life around just didn't allow for attention to his personal obligations. For that he knew he was wrong, but made no effort to change. He allowed a tinge of envy to occupy his thoughts about his brother the surgeon.

He smiled. Allah had chosen their paths, and he knew envy was a waste of energy.

As he drove back to his room on the airbase, he looked over towards the tarmac and a row of large hangers. They weren't reinforced hangers, just thick, tan sheet metal to protect expensive aircraft from the ravages of desert weather. All but one of the hanger doors was closed. One had been left open to accommodate the tail of the...*C-20.*

Wahid stepped on the brake pedal harder than he intended. Luckily there were no other vehicles on the small access road around the outside of the airbase fence. The realization hit him like a brick. Whoever was in surgery had arrived on the C-20.

Wahid's first instinct was to flip the car around and storm back to the hospital, but he figured that his chances of finding out what was going on would be no greater than his brother's. He continued to his quarters and placed a call to the prince's assistant, Nasir al-Hamal. The slimy little man had better connections than the king, and had to know something.

"Nasir, my friend, I need some information," Wahid asked.

"What is it?"

The prince had placed a very high measure of priority on Wahid's mission, so al-Hamal took the colonel's calls no matter what he was doing at the time.

"There is an American Air Force executive jet at the airbase here. Do you know who's it is?"

"I can find out."

"Please, and my brother told me that the Americans performed surgery on someone and won't say on whom. I think the two may be related."

"I'm sure I can find something out, is that all?"

"Yes, for now. What news of the war?"

"Soon, very soon." was all he said.

"Very well," Wahid said, then hung up the telephone.

It was time to make another attempt at contacting his colleagues in the US Army.

◆   ◆   ◆

As General Samuelson walked out of the operating room, carefully listening to Colonel Beckham's explanation of the procedure he'd just observed, a young captain was waiting to pass along a message.

"General Samuelson?" the captain asked.

No one could have known he was here so quickly.

"Yes?" he answered cautiously.

"I have a message."

The captain held out a small piece of paper ripped from a yellow legal pad. General Samuelson grabbed the folded note with his hand, which had become pasty white from being inside a latex glove for several hours. He looked the message over quickly and stuffed it into his pocket.

"You never saw me Captain, do you understand?" Samuelson said with brute force in his voice as he stared directly into the young officer's eyes.

"Absolutely, General."

"Dismissed."

Without a word, the captain vanished down the corridor. Colonel Beckham stood by, as if waiting for an explanation as to why one of his staff now knew of the General's presence.

"I need a secure land line out of here," the general told the evac hospital's skipper.

"Come with me, we've got one set up in the building."

"Outside would be better." the general said.

The note simply said *Yaakobi*, and listed a number. he was not about to call Israel from a Saudi building, even if it was a secure line.

"Got that too. C'mon," Beckham told him.

The men walked out of the building to the portable modules. Beckham led them to his office, where he had a secure line set up for calls to and from Riyadh. The phone was capable of calling anywhere, however, and utilized exclusively American satellites for its encrypted transmissions. Beckham pointed to the telephone and began to walk outside, knowing the general would want his privacy.

"I'm going to go get some chow if you need me."

"Thanks," General Samuelson said as he reached into his pocket for the number.

Beckham left and locked the door behind him. He was the only one with the key. Samuelson dialed the phone and waited for the encryption algorithms from his phone and that of General Yaakobi to coordinate. Once they did, he heard a beep indicating the phone on the other end was ringing.

"Yaakobi."

"It's Samuelson."

"Yes, General, I have some information for you. We intercepted a fax transmission from Ramallah to Medina that showed pictures of Motta being loaded onto your jet at Dov."

Samuelson's face turned red, not only from anger at being compromised, but from the frustration associated with becoming a target, which he was sure he had.

"Where the hell did they come from?" he asked angrily.

"A Palestinian journalist, we have him. I think it would be safe to assume that that your trip is no longer a secret."

"Who do you think it is?"

"Yafai, you have to bring him back for his own safety General," Yaakobi said.

"I have to go to Riyadh for a briefing, there's no way I can fly back. Let me see what I can do, I still think he'll be safer here."

"I must implore you to reconsider, General."

"Let me see what I can do and get back to you, sir."

"Very well," the line went dead.

General Samuelson thought for a moment then pulled a small, olive green memo pad from his left breast pocket. He looked up the secure number for the Deputy Commander-in-Chief, Central Command in Riyadh and dialed it. He hoped to get some feel for the timeline he had to work with.

"Brazleton."

Samuelson was pleased to hear the familiar voice of Brigadier General Mitchell Brazleton. Brazleton actually had his own command, but was helping augment the added requirements put upon CENTCOM by the conflict. He was assigned as a senior planner for the Deputy Commander-in-Chief. That was just fine with Samuelson, who had been classmates with Brazleton at West Point.

"Mitch, it's Tom Samuelson."

"How are you? And *where* are you?" General Brazleton asked.

"On my way. What kind of time are we looking at Mitch."

Everything that made mention to a time frame among the military leadership of the coalition was referring to one thing, the ground invasion. The planning for a ground offensive had begun the day Saddam invaded Kuwait.

CINCCENT had most of the tactics drawn up a year prior to the invasion when he developed a battle plan for just such a contingency. The Bear was a military genius, as he was preparing to show the world. Very few people would know when the ground war was to start, but Brazleton was certainly one of them.

"Your one-star derriere needs to be in the war room no later than fourteen hundred hours tomorrow, if that's what you mean General," his old classmate said jovially while conveying the necessary urgency.

"I'll be there," Samuelson assured him.

Without actually being told, he knew that the breech would take place within the next two weeks, that's when the "brass tacks" planning normally begun. There would be no time to get Colonel Urit back to Tel Aviv.

He sat down in Colonel Beckham's chair and leaned forward, resting his elbows on the desk. As he exhaled into his intertwined hands, staring into nowhere, he hoped for a flash of brilliance that would result in the perfect plan. He had run out of influential friends with whom he could continue to perpetrate his clandestine act of friendship. There was no way to avoid the fact that he needed help.

He rose from behind the desk and went to look for Colonel Beckham. He found him just outside, still speaking to one of his medical staff. Both soldiers stopped talking as the general approached. The nurse that Beckham was talking to came to attention and saluted.

"Can we take a walk, Colonel?" Samuelson asked as he returned the junior man's salute.

"Sure, yessir," Beckham agreed.

The men walked beyond the tents in silence, along the sidewalk towards the concentric green domes of the hospital's mosque. When he was comfortable that there was no one interested in their conversation, nor anyone close enough to hear it, the general laid out his cards.

"I need a favor, Ron," Samuelson began as he looked at the sidewalk.

"Anything General."

"Well, you might want to hear what I have to say first," he said with a smile.

"That guy we operated on,"

"Yeah?"

"He's a very close friend of mine."

"I gathered that, General."

"He's an IDF Colonel."

Samuelson expected the statement to stop Beckham in his tracks, but he did not even flinch.

"He's an awful long way from home," Beckham commented.

"Yes, he is, and the Saudis would not be too tickled to find out he's here."

"Why *is* he here? They have great doctors in Israel"

"Well, they didn't think he would actually make it."

"Now I'm really confused," Beckham admitted.

"Let's just say that he's not very popular with the Palestinians."

"Show me an Israeli who is."

"If he were to be confirmed dead, it could sway the coalition in the direction of our pal to the North."

"I get it," Beckham told him, "still, seems like a lot of effort for a containment."

General Samuelson stopped and looked up at Beckham. Beckham knew something was coming and turned to face the general eye-to-eye.

"He's a very dear friend of mine, like a brother to me."

Beckham was among the small, yet very fortunate group of people in this world who can actually grasp the true meaning of such a statement. Beckham let out a snort and turned to start walking again.

"Why didn't you just tell me that in the first place?" he asked, to the great relief of the general, "what do you need, General?"

Samuelson knew he had found the right person to confide in.

"I have to be in Riyadh tomorrow, and I've received information that the true fate of the colonel may not be such a secret anymore. They may even know he's here if anyone saw my jet."

"He's not out of the woods yet, either. It's going to be a while."

"Exactly," the general agreed, "now Colonel, any involvement on your part is strictly a personal request. My ass could very well be retired for this, and so could yours if it ever gets out that you helped me."

"You say he's one of the good guys?" Beckham asked.

"The best."

"Tonight?" Beckham asked.

"As soon as we can, I don't know who they have here," the general referred to the Palestinians.

"'nuff said, General, I'm in. I'll come up with something."

◆   ◆   ◆

Where it not for his sloppy involvement and lack of tactical intellect in the 1979 siege of the Grand Mosque in Mecca, Marwan Yafai would be where his brother, Muta', now was. His ideals ran parallel to those of Muta', and he was a champion for the same cause, but he was simply not intelligent enough to pull it off.

At the time of the Mecca uprising, Marwan was the Mecca chief for his father's construction company. The small army of fundamentalists that took over the mosque had been smuggled into the city, weapons and all, concealed in Yafai Construction trucks. No one could have implemented this method without the knowledge of Marwan Yafai. He had actually taken part in the planning of the operation, but failed to adequately distance himself from the fiasco.

After the uprising was quelled, Marwan was immediately implicated and jailed by King Fahd for his obvious involvement. He was later released through the boundless influence of the Yafai family with the monarchy, on the condition that he be relegated to a menial and very subdued role within the Kingdom. That is how he ended up in Medina.

After realizing how close he came to being publicly beheaded with the uprising's leader Juhaiman al Utaiba and sixty-two of his followers, he was very thankful for that.

Occasionally, he was allowed to stay indirectly involved in the work of the cause by relaying correspondence to Muta', who was now the pivotal figure in the swelling tide of Islamic fundamentalism throughout the region. His involvement was far enough removed from actual events and operations that he rarely knew exactly what he was dealing with, but he knew it was always important.

He combed over the photographs sent by Habbas. The fact that they somehow involved the infidel occupying American Army was in and of itself reason to excite Marwan. The accompanying explanation was vague, almost cryptic:

The butcher of Shatilla has fallen, and the infidels have him.

He picked up the telephone and called his brother's compound in Jeddeh.

"It is Marwan, where is my brother?" he told whichever member of Muta's security entourage had answered the telephone.

Marwan hated going through the entire hassle, but he understood. He sat down on the couch in front of the desk in his office and waited for what seemed like an eternity before Muta' was on the line.

"Marwan," was all Muta' said.

"Allah be praised my brother, I have something for you."

"What is it."

"Pictures from Palestine. Of a man being put on an American plane."

"That tells me nothing brother."

"It says the butcher of Shatilla has fallen and the Americans have him."

"Send it immediately," Muta' ordered, not knowing himself exactly what it meant.

◆   ◆   ◆

Dana was a little surprised at the request. General Samuelson had asked she and Mikael to come to a small meeting that Colonel Beckham had called. The two Israelis felt about as uncomfortable as they had their entire lives as they walked through the corridors of the Saudi hospital behind an M.P. escort. They were in American uniforms and none of the Saudi staff knew better, but they felt as if everyone knew who they were.

It was torture for Dana to be pulled away from her father's bedside, but had she resisted the American soldier might have caught on. The MP led them outside to Beckham's portable office. He stopped at the bottom of the steps leading to the trailer door and gestured for Dana and Mikael to go into the office. The two looked at one another then ascended the five steps into the office where they saw Samuelson, Beckham, and Lieutenant Ingram.

"Close the door please, Dana," General Samuelson said.

Dana's heart nearly jumped out of her chest and she froze in her tracks. Samuelson had used her real name.

"It's OK, please," Samuelson told her.

She closed the door behind her and stepped into the small modular office. The only one sitting was Colonel Beckham, who was perched on the front of his desk with one foot on the floor.

Samuelson spoke first.

"Colonel Beckham and Lieutenant Ingram here know about your father."

"But…" Mikael began.

General Samuelson could tell by his sudden change in posture that he was not very pleased to hear that.

"I had to Mikael," he assured the giant Israeli lieutenant, "I have to go to Riyadh, and word of your father has gotten out…Colonel Beckham has an idea. I think you should here it out."

"Yes, General," Mikael said.

The issue was out in the open and it would not do any good to express his anger.

"Have either of you heard of the hospital ship Comfort." Colonel Beckham asked.

Dana and Mikael shook their heads like school children.

"Well, it's just what it sounds like, a floating hospital out in the Persian Gulf. Now, if the General's information is correct, and I believe it is, the Saudi's may very well know he's here."

"Then we must take him back to Tel Aviv," Mikael said succinctly, as if there were no room for further discussion.

"Now Mikael, there are several reasons why that's a bad Idea, but the number one reason is I have to leave for Riyadh tonight. It's not like we can just order up a bird to fly him out there, Your cover only works when I'm around."

Mikael nodded his understanding as Dana just soaked it all in, waiting for the rest of the plan.

"That's where Lieutenant Ingram comes in. The general is going to fly you and your father to Al Jubail. From there, a helo will take you out to the Comfort. He'll be safe out there. I know the XO, he's someone we can trust."

Colonel Beckham saw that he was successfully selling the idea to the Israelis and continued.

"Lieutenant Ingram here is going along to handle all of the military interactions for you. She knows how our medical system works and'll keep folks from getting suspicious."

Lieutenant Ingram pursed her lips in a cursory grin and nodded her head.

"Not only will they be able to start Motta's rehabilitation, but it takes an act of congress just to get out to that tub. He'll be safe even in the event someone found out where he was, and that's a stretch," General Samuelson assured them.

The room fell silent as everyone anticipated some sort of reaction from Mikael on the matter. To everyone's surprise, Dana broke the silence.

"When do we go," she asked.

The sooner she got off Saudi soil, the better.

"Right now," Samuelson said as he walked towards the door.

◆   ◆   ◆

Nasir al-Hamal was just getting up from his desk to walk out of the palace for a much-needed break. Not only had he spent the day assisting the prince with the tactical operations of the National Guard, he had also been working the telephone trying to find a contact that knew anything about the C-20 at KKMC airbase.

As he began to leave, his private line rang. He exhaled in frustration, having fallen victim to what American's call Murphy's Law.

"Yes," he barked into the telephone.

"It is Muta'."

The very sound of his voice made al-Hamal stand straighter. He had a deep respect for the eccentric millionaire and shared a passion for his cause. It was a very rare occasion indeed that Muta' called for his assistance, but even Muta' knew that the prince's aide was the most well connected man in the Kingdom.

"Allah be praised, how can I serve you?"

"An aircraft left Tel Aviv within the last several days, an American Air Force jet."

Even with no more than that to go by, Al-Hamal's blood ran cold. There was just no way that there could be this much interest in more than one aircraft.

"What sort of plane? A fighter?" he asked.

"No a Gulfstream."

The Yafai Corporation owned four of the civilian versions of General Samuelson's jet, so Muta' knew what he was looking at.

"Yes, yes, there was one in King Khalid City. One of my men saw it there."

"It brought a pig Zionist colonel who was struck down by the will of Allah, It is the Butcher of Shatilla," Muta' let the last statement sink in, "get him. Get him now. The infidels have proven that they will spit on the holy places."

"I will, we will get him and expose the Infidels."

Al-Hamal was excited, almost beside himself at the prospect. He was also furious. The Americans had chosen to desecrate the kingdom with the blood of a dog.

"I do not trust them, they are everywhere in the kingdom and in the house of Fahd. Bring him to me."

"It will be done."

The telephone went dead. Al-Hamal quickly found the number for Wahid's room at KKMC and dialed it. The urgency of the call made it seem like forever before he was connected.

"Yes?" Wahid answered.

"It is Nasir, you must find the person that came in the jet. It is an Israeli colonel, Mordechi Urit."

Wahid jumped out of the couch he was sitting on.

"What?" he yelled, "no!"

Al-Hamal's anger was amplified ten times in the Saudi colonel.

"You must bring him to Muta'."

Without a word, Wahid slammed the telephone down, grabbed his uniform jacket and bolted out the door. He had called the local detachment Headquarters of the National Guard to inquire about the plane. They knew nothing, but he still had the number written in his notebook. He fumbled through the bag on the passenger's seat of his car while he spun the tires in reverse to pull out of his space. He found the number and dialed quickly before slamming the car into drive and speeding out of the lot.

The wind was such that aircraft were taking off from the opposite end of the field from Wahid's quarters. He would never see the jet that was getting ready to leave.

"This is Colonel Wahid," he yelled when the soldier on the other line answered, "I need six men, armed, to meet me at the hospital. Now!"

♦   ♦   ♦

General Samuelson was pleased to see that his pilot had already taxied to the end of the runway and had completed his pre-flight as his driver turned in the gate. He was riding in an MP Humvee in front of Colonel Urit's ambulance. Lieutenant Ingram rode with him so that he could go over some of the final details of the operation. It seemed, on the surface, to be a very easy plan to institute, but Samuelson was a student of a thousand perfect plans going to hell at a moment's notice.

"Here!" General Samuelson yelled over the rumble of the Hummer's turbo diesel engine that resonated throughout the entire non-soundproofed, bare aluminum chassis of the vehicle.

He turned and handed a small sheet of paper from his notebook to Ingram. She took it and looked up at the General, not knowing what to do with it.

"That's a number to General Brazleton at CINCCENT. If you need anything, I will never be very far from him."

"Yessir. Does he know...."

"No," Samuelson cut her off, "no one does."

♦   ♦   ♦

Colonel Wahid was livid by the time he pulled to an abrupt halt outside the entrance to the hospital. He leapt from his Mercedes and stormed around to the entrance door when he heard the sound of a Hummer coming into the medical compound. He stopped when he realized that his men had yet to arrive. He turned and saw the vehicle pulling in behind his.

The rifle-wielding Saudi guardsmen in the back of the open-bed Hummer jumped out before it stopped. Each man with his eyes wide open, wondering what was the matter. A lieutenant got out of the front and walked over to Wahid.

"Follow me," Wahid ordered forcefully.

He stormed into the hospital with the men in tow. He stomped past the reception area that was entirely staffed by Saudi medical workers. They stood up from behind the station, but did nothing. It was obvious that something huge was happening.

"Page Doctor Wahid immediately and tell him he is needed in the ICU." Wahid barked in Arabic without missing a step.

He burst through the first set of double doors leading in the direction of the Intensive Care Unit and saw an American soldier walking in the distance with an IV bag in his hand.

"You there!" Wahid yelled.

He made the US serviceman jump and spin around. All he saw was a squad of angry looking, and heavily armed Saudis walking towards him. His adrenaline started pumping as he responded.

"Yes, Sir."

"Where is the Commanding Officer?"

"Have you tried his office?"

The soldier's tone came across as insolent to Wahid, and with good reason, the American had intended it to. He was not a soldier in the classical sense. He was a medical professional and was not used to being yelled at. Wahid was furious. He walked directly up to the American and stopped uncomfortably close.

"Go find him, now," Wahid ordered as his gaze burned into the young man's eyes.

The inconvenience of a reprimand, more than intimidation, subjugated the American.

"Yes, Sir," he said as he walked away, without the sense of urgency Wahid had expected.

He hated these Americans. As he continued on towards the ICU, he heard the page for his brother over the intercom. He would need the support of someone within the hospital.

"Colonel?" the National Guard Lieutenant asked when the group entered an empty hallway.

"Yes?" Wahid answered without looking back.

"What is this about?"

Wahid stopped and turned around to face him. The other troops stopped in a semi-circle around their lieutenant to hear the answer.

"We are going to take someone prisoner. You're job is to simply make sure it happens at all costs, understood?"

The lieutenant stood upright, understanding the magnitude of what was going on.

"Yes, Sir."

Wahid turned and continued down the corridor, with the others close behind. Rather than take the elevator, he opted for the stairs. He was too impatient to wait for the elevator, and the run upstairs would keep his fury fresh. He burst onto the third floor and walked directly to the doors leading to the unit.

Wahid noticed immediately the absence of any guards and prayed it was an oversight on the part of the Americans. His hopes were dashed when he saw that the ward was completely deserted. The lights were even off to conserved power.

"Check it," he told the lieutenant with a sweep of his arm.

The men fanned out to check every room on the ward. Colonel Wahid spun around when he heard the automatic door opener engage and part the double doors leading into the unit from the waiting area. It was his brother, with a look of utter confusion on his face. He scanned the room and took in the image of armed men searching his hospital.

"What is it, Faisal?" the doctor asked.

"Where is the man they had in here?"

"I have no idea, they would tell me nothing. It was very discreet."

Suddenly a sound began to resonate through the walls of the hospital, an unmistakable sound. It was a large jet aircraft taking off from the adjoining airbase two kilometers away. Colonel Wahid looked at the wall between he and the aircraft, as if looking right through it at General Samuelson's C-20.

"Damn."

He turned and ran out of the ICU.

♦   ♦   ♦

The whole experience had just about taken its toll on Dana. The fear of losing her father, the risk to keep him safe, and the feeling of solitude in this hostile place congealed into one massive feeling of despair. She was exhausted. She just sat and stared at her father as he slept. Lieutenant Ingram saw Dana's blank stare and felt strong empathy for her. Now that she knew what the young Israeli had been through, she wanted to help in any way she could.

"He's fine," she told Dana.

Dana jumped when Ingram spoke and broke her empty trance.

"I didn't mean to startle you. Why don't you try to get some sleep on the way," Ingram told her.

She had never met Dana before today, but knew that the girl looked like hell from the ordeal.

"I'm OK, really, thank you," Dana told her.

She was not very convincing. To Dana's surprise, the American nurse grabbed her arm and lifted her out of the seat next to Colonel Urit. Ingram began leading her towards the rear of the plane.

"Really, I'm fine," Dana told her, but offered no resistance.

She simply didn't have it in her.

"I'll watch your dad, I promise," Ingram assured her.

The flight would only be about thirty minutes, but it would be thirty more minutes of sleep than Dana had seen in two days. General Samuelson sat on a small couch on one side of the cabin, looking through some papers from his meetings in Tel Aviv. He took off the reading glasses he despised when he saw the two women approaching.

"Can she wreck out here, General?" Ingram asked as she guided Dana onto the couch across from Samuelson.

"I insist," he told them as he gathered up his papers and flicked off the reading light.

"I'm sorry…" Dana began.

"Uh uh. You get some sleep or I'll kick your butt," He told her, speaking as the uncle he practically was.

Dana smiled and laid down, curling her legs up onto the couch. Ingram turned to get her a blanket and General Samuelson walked towards the front of the plane. When Ingram turned around to cover Dana, she was already asleep.

◆　　　◆　　　◆

As Lieutenant Colonel Beckham walked through the gate leading from the parking lot to the Hospital, he saw Wahid and his posse of infantrymen stomping towards him down the walkway. He was unstirred from the display, but somewhat surprised to see that the Saudis were so close on the tail of General Samuelson and his charge.

"Colonel, where did that man go?" Wahid demanded as he walked up to Beckham.

"Man? What man?" Beckham said, making no attempt at sincerity.

"You will tell me immediately, Colonel."

Really? Beckham thought.

The tactless display of the Saudi Colonel in the presence of subordinates told Beckham everything he needed to know about the man.

"Can I speak to you over here for a second?" he asked Wahid in the nicest demeanor he could muster.

He was a man of very mild temperament, but Wahid had crossed the line. The two men stepped far enough away to be out of easy earshot.

The two American soldiers who drove Samuelson's entourage to the C-20 just smirked at the squad of Saudis. They knew Beckham, and they liked him. He was their Commanding Officer, and they knew what was coming next.

"Colonel?" Samuelson prodded.

"Wahid."

"Colonel Wahid, now what can I do for you?" Beckham asked politely, effectively slapping Wahid in the face with his show of class.

"I need to know where you sent the man who was operated on yesterday."

"You do, huh?"

Wahid was confused by the response. He was used to people following his every whim without question. His arrogance had never been matched…until now.

"Well, let me tell you that there was no man operated on and I don't know what you are referring to."

Samuelson looked directly into Wahid's eyes and saw the anger brewing. He loved it.

"Colonel, this is outrageous. You will tell me what I need to know."

Wahid's voice elevated to the point that it attracted the attention of the other men standing twenty feet away. Beckham had had enough of this.

"Colonel," he said as he leaned forward.

He was a good four inches taller than Wahid, and knew that was a factor could be used effectively in this culture.

"If the truth be known, I don't have to tell you a single goddamn thing."

Wahid's eyes opened wide. No one had spoken to him that way his entire life.

"The next time you require information from someone, may I suggest you change your approach. Good day, Colonel."

Wahid was flabbergasted, almost speechless.

"You will pay for your insolence, Colonel."

"Then I suggest you drag your ass back to Riyadh and complain to my boss."

Beckham walked nonchalantly away knowing there was very little the Saudi Colonel could or would do considering the situation. Even if so, Beckham really didn't care.

CHAPTER 11

Shell Game

The situation had become unacceptable for Elon Yaakobi. He decided, with the concurrence of General Yoshom, that a contingency plan had to be implemented immediately. General Samuelson called Yaakobi before he left for Al-Jubail and brought the IDF commander up to speed on the plan so far. All the update served to tell Yaakobi was that his friend was now farther away from his homeland.

The Israelis where famous for having backup plans anytime they were required to put their collective national trust in any non-Israeli power. They had never expected anyone else to rescue nor protect their own. It was an undisputed fact that they were the best in the world at doing what had to be done to protect their interests.

Yaakobi's phone rang.

"General, It's Agent Davra," his aide told him.

"Send him in."

Tsayid came into the office with his usual air of quiet professionalism and stood before the two generals.

"Please, sit," Yaakobi told him.

Tsayid took a seat next to Yoshom.

"Colonel Urit has been taken to an American hospital ship in the Persian Gulf," Yaakobi explained.

Tsayid nodded.

"He should be safe there."

"For now, at least," Yoshom added.

"We need you to come up with a plan incase his safety is compromised," Yaakobi told Tsayid.

"A plan?"

"Yes, General Samuelson isn't even with him any longer. Now, Motta swears by the man's character, but I don't know him."

Yaakobi didn't have to add that he trusted nobody outside of Israel.

"Yes, sir," Tsayid agreed.

"Something that can go at a moment's notice. Into Saudi Arabia if necessary."

Tsayid got excited when he heard that, but he didn't even appear to bat an eye.

"If he were to fall into Saudi hands, it would be disastrous. They would turn it into a spectacle."

"If they find him, they will kill him. We must be ready to act upon that without hesitation. Before it gets out of hand," Yoshom interjected.

"We will immediately know if they find him," Yaakobi said.

That told Tsayid that Mossad had someone connected to the intelligence network within Saudi Arabia. That was a comfort.

"Yes, sir, I can select a team. Can I clear anyone for this?"

"No one, not yet. If we have to implement it, clearance will be at your discretion," Yoshom told him.

"Understood General."

Team selection was really all he could do without a clear objective. Once he had the right men, they could begin training for possible scenarios. It was getting the right personnel that was always the tricky part, but he knew exactly where to go. He rose and left the office. The Generals had known him long enough to know that he would keep them abreast of his progress without having to be reminded.

♦   ♦   ♦

Though Colonel Wahid had the temperament of a six-year-old at times, he was not void of intellect. He knew exactly what course to take in his search for Motta Urit. After his dialog with Lieutenant Beckham, he went directly to the control tower of the airfield to hunt down the tower chief.

Any logistical military flight would have to be filed in the tower chief's log. As far as Wahid knew, the tower was still under the control of the Saudi Air Force.

On the short drive over, he also cooled off and decided to change his approach for trying to gather information. The brazen insubordination of Beckham had knocked his ego down about six full pegs. He was going to have to resort to charisma, something he was not considered the resident expert at.

Wahid pulled up to the rear of the building that constituted the ground control tower for the airbase. It was actually a one-story structure with few windows. All movement of aircraft was controlled by computer coordinated radar. Airmen on the tarmac handled any visual requirements.

The Hummer full of guardsman pulled in next to him and men began to jump out of the back.

"Stay here. I don't need you," Colonel Wahid told them.

They all deflated and just stood staring as Wahid went into the offices. He went in and walked towards the control room. As he approached the controlled access door leading into the main control room, he realized that he did not have the necessary identification badge to get through the door. Although he fully rated it, he never acquired one when he arrived in KKMC.

A Saudi Airman exited the control room just as Wahid approached. The Airman was not used to seeing a Colonel of the National Guard in the building and immediately came to attention. Wahid saw his opportunity to distract his subordinate from noticing the absence of proper identification.

"I need the acting tower chief," Wahid said in an uncharacteristically gentle tone.

"Right over there, Sir."

The airman pointed to a US Air Force captain. Wahid knew he was probably not going to be able to find out anything.

"Thank you," Wahid said as he walked in past the star struck airman.

Colonel Wahid stayed in character despite knowing his persistence was probably futile.

"Captain?" he said to the American, who was leaning over the shoulder of a seated US airman manning a radar screen.

"Yes, Colonel, what can I do for you?" the captain said after deciphering the rank insignia on Wahid's epaulettes.

"There was a C-20 that departed a short time ago, do you know where it was going?"

The captain looked suspiciously at Wahid. The question was too direct.

Wahid thought quickly.

"I trained under the General at Ft. Benning, I just missed him at the hospital, and wanted to try and catch up to him."

Wahid prayed that the captain would not ask for the general's name. He had no idea, it was a complete shot in the dark. He just assumed that only a general would fly in such luxury. After a brief pause, the captain grabbed the logbook off the desk next to the air traffic controller. He flipped it open and Colonel Wahid got excited. His ruse may have actually paid off.

"Riyadh," the captain told him.

"Riyadh?" Wahid said in disbelief.

The general was taking a Jew to the capitol city of the kingdom. Wahid was furious.

"Yes, sir, Where else you figure a General would be going?"

"Good point, thank you Captain."

Wahid turned and quickly left. He wanted to call Nasir Al-Hamal from his quarters, so he had to move quickly. Samuelson's C-20 would be in Riyadh shortly and with the assets he had in Riyadh, Wahid knew that he would have his prey shortly.

◆   ◆   ◆

"Lieutenant Urit?" Ingram said softly as she gently, and reluctantly, rocked Dana from her short slumber.

"Yeah," Dana said as she sprang upright from a near coma.

"Let's go," Ingram told her.

Dana looked towards the cockpit and saw nothing but the open passenger door. She noticed that the C-20s engines were still running and heard all of the noise coming from the outside. Ingram noticed the look of horror on the young Israeli's face.

"It's OK, we're here. You're father is already on the helicopter."

"Helicopter?"

"To take us out to the Comfort, the ship."

Dana rubbed her eyes and stood up.

"Oh yes, of course."

Dana strode wobbily down the aisle to the exit door. When she reached the steps, she was suddenly wide-awake. There was a US Navy CH-60 about fifty meters away from the jet, sitting in the pitch darkness of the Arabian night. The lights of the helicopter were out and the only thing she saw was the dull red glow of the interior lights in the passenger area.

Dana stepped onto the top of the stairs and looked around. There was nothing. The sudden dramatic contrast in lighting frightened her and she was immediately very much awake. She looked to the east and barely made out the lights of some buildings that were perhaps half a mile away. Ingram walked up behind her and yelled over the noise of the two aircraft.

"Let's go!"

Ingram pointed to the CH-60 and nudged Dana down the stairs. General Samuelson was walking towards the jet from the CH-60. The three met directly between the two aircraft. He grabbed Dana by the shoulders in a paternal gesture of reassurance.

"Dana, he will be fine, I promise. Where you're going is the safest place with the best facilities for him to get better."

Dana nodded, trying to appear as confident as she could. Samuelson recognized her fear and gave her a very powerful hug.

"I'll be there just as soon as this is all over, I promise. Now go on."

Dana looked at the General. Her eyes pleaded with him to keep his word, although she new there was no chance in the world that he would not. Dana began walking to the CH-60 and Lieutenant Ingram began to follow her. Samuelson grabbed her arm and turned her around to face him.

"Whatever you need Lieutenant, anything. Just take care of them for me."

Ingram was struck by the general's genuine love for his friends. She knew that he risked everything to get them this far.

"They'll be fine General, go fight the war."

Samuelson smiled as Ingram jogged away.

"I'm going to make you a Major for this!" he yelled.

Ingram turned around with a huge grin on her face.

"Damn right you will, sir!" Ingram yelled with the inflection of her sassy, urban African-American roots.

Samuelson laughed and climbed up the stairs to his C-20, turning to look one last time. The inner conflict he felt at leaving his friend's side was nearly crippling. The CH-60 wavered slightly as the pilot added power and began to lift off. Within a few more seconds, the helicopter lurched into the air and dropped its nose.

Samuelson watched as it disappeared into the blackness on its way to the Comfort and stepped into the jet. His friend was now in the hands of fate and the US Navy.

◆   ◆   ◆

"It is Faisal," Wahid told Al-Hamal when he answered the telephone.

He had been anticipating Wahid's call.

"Yes?" the prince's aid replied, expecting to hear news of Urit's capture.

"He is on his way to Riyadh, send Asim," Wahid ordered.

"Right away," Al-Hamal assured him.

♦   ♦   ♦

The basic realization that he didn't know where he was ignited Cross's flight instinct as he tried to claw through the effects of the anesthesia and into consciousness. The glare from the lights in the passageway overloaded his vision and hurt his eyes. He snapped his head to the side and could barely discern the red glow of the fluorescent lights reflecting off of the red painted deck of the ship and onto the walls.

"Easy Marine, easy. It's OK," he heard a man's voice say.

His brain quickly told him that the voice was in English and that he hurt like hell. He was alive and in American hands.

"You're going to be fine, we're just going to take some x-rays," the same faceless voice trailed off and was replaced with a dull, but very powerful humming noise that resonated throughout the hull of the ship.

The sound of the approaching helicopter brought comfort to Cross. Military hardware was the sound of freedom to the young Marine and he drifted back to sleep to the growing din of the rotors.

♦   ♦   ♦

Captain Cowen was on the helo deck to meet Colonel Urit's entourage as they touched down. Two Navy nurses stood next to him with a gurney. As the main rotor of the CH-60 feathered, they quickly scurried to the helicopter.

Lieutenant Ingram was already standing on the deck of the Comfort unstrapping her patient, while Dana and Mikael began fumbling with the harness dials to reluctantly step down onto this strange new temporary home. Of all the people who had been made privy to the real identity of Colonel Urit, Captain Cowen probably held the highest security clearance after General Samuelson.

Networking was practically invented in the military and plays out nicely when it can be accomplished with men of such high standards of honor. Cowen had done his residency with none other than Ron Beckham. Cowen told his medical staff that Urit was simply a patient transfer from the aid station at Al-Jubail. His leg had been crushed in a construction accident at the base in Dhahran.

No one gave it a second thought since these things happen on a regular basis. They don't happen very often to colonels, but this was a war and people's acceptance of the unlikely was much more liberal.

Cowen ran directly to Dana as she got down from the Ch-60. His staff went to assist Ingram with the transfer of Colonel Urit. Mikael saw Cowen coming towards them and instinctively stepped between he and Dana. Dana looked across to her father and did not even notice. Cowen slowed to a walk and came over to Mikael. He leaned towards the massive Israeli and grabbed his shoulder.

"It's all right, come with me!" Cowen yelled over the engine noise.

Mikael and Dana followed Cowen to the front of the helicopter where they met up with Colonel Urit's gurney. Cowen got Lieutenant Ingram's attention and motioned for her to join them. She reluctantly left the side of her patient for a brief instant.

"Yes, Sir?" Ingram yelled over the noise.

"I'm Captain Bart Cowen, come with me please!" he yelled to all three of his new guests.

"Let me find out where they're taking him first!" Ingram protested.

"He'll be fine Lieutenant Ingram, you can trust me!"

His look was very sincere, but Ingram was still reluctant to leave Colonel Urit. As Captain Cowen turned to lead them off the helicopter deck, Ingram opted to follow him, along with Dana and Mikael. As soon as they passed two hatches into the ship, it was quiet enough to speak.

Cowen made note of Ingram's apprehension and thought it best to set her at ease. He turned around and found the tense trio right on his heels.

"I just want to meet real quick in my quarters, then you can go see him, OK?" the captain said with a comforting grin.

Cowen led them through the passages of the ship until they came to his stateroom. He unlocked the door and invited his visitors in. There was a single chair and a small loveseat next to a tiny desk. Beyond them was a rack that folded up into the wall. His was the second largest living quarters on the ship, but was still very small.

"Sit, please," he told them.

Dana and Mikael took the loveseat, while Ingram continued her assertive role as the essential liaison to the little operation by sitting before the captain. He sat down in his chair behind the desk.

"Relax Lieutenant, please. I'm a friend of Ron Beckham's," he assured her.

He actually saw her exhale in relief when he said that.

"I just wanted to introduce myself and let you know that you have a run of the ship. I'd like for you to meet my head nurse when you get a chance. I've pretty much assigned her to you full-time," he looked over to Dana, "you're father is the most serious case we have on this ship, so he will be getting all the attention he needs, I promise."

"Thank you, sir," Dana said sincerely.

"Captain? I was wondering about security," Mikael said.

Ingram and the staff of the ship were here to protect Colonel Urit from a medical fate, Mikael's job was still to cover any other threats.

"Well, besides being in the middle of a carrier group, you just let me know what you need and I'll get it for you. Captain Gerald has been briefed entirely and is also available."

Mikael nodded his thanks. Captain Cowen made a good point. They would be safe out here.

"I am available twenty-four seven. Whatever you need, Shellie will get me directly; and you, Lieutenant, will have unlimited access to the colonel during the touchy days here," he told Ingram.

Colonel Urit was in a great hospital, but he was far from out of the woods. The next few days would determine whether he would even survive the injuries.

"Thank you Captain, thank you very much," Ingram said.

Cowen smiled and picked up the ship's intercom. He dialed Shellie McLean's quarters.

"Hey Lieutenant, it's Bart, would you come down here please? Thank you," he replaced the handset and looked up, "I've briefed her on the colonel's injuries, so she knows you're here, but that's all she knows. He was injured in a construction accident at Dhahran."

"Will I be able to report to General Samuelson?" Ingram asked.

"Absolutely, we have several secure satellite link-ups and STS with Riyadh. Just let me know."

"STS?" Mikael asked.

"Ship-to-shore radio."

Mikael nodded.

"Thank you Captain," Ingram said again.

Cowen was being exceptionally accommodating. She hoped he was as sincere as he sounded.

There was a rap on the stateroom door.

"Come!" Cowen yelled.

Shellie McLean opened the door and smiled, nodding her greetings to the seated trio.

"This is Lieutenant McLean," Cowen introduced her.

"Shellie. How do you do?" the nurse corrected him.

Ingram stood up and extended her hand. It was as much a cover gesture for the other two than a genuine introduction.

"Hi, Stephanie Ingram."

The two nurses shook hands. Ingram turned around.

"Lieutenant Smith and Lieutenant Jones," she said as she pointed Dana and Mikael.

Shellie had been told not to be too concerned about anything that seemed odd about the visitors. She accepted that and suppressed her desire to know otherwise.

"Can we go see him?" Dana asked.

Shellie could tell there was more here than met the eye.

"Sure, come on," she said as she led them out of the captain's quarters.

◆   ◆   ◆

General Samuelson stepped out onto the stairs of the C-20 with his attaché in hand expecting to be met by a staff driver. He was very surprised to look out and see two Hummers flanked by Saudi Soldiers sitting on the tarmac next to his plane.

They're closer than I thought.

He knew exactly what was going on. A Saudi Officer walked up to the general with a very callous look on his face.

"General, I am Major Asim, I am here for Colonel Urit," he told the general. It was business between the Saudis and Israel, he had no intention of disrespecting an American General.

"Colonel who?" Samuelson asked.

"Colonel Mordechi Urit. I know he is with you."

"I'm afraid I have no idea what you're talking about Major. I don't know who Colonel, Urit is it?, is, but I flew here alone."

The look on Asim's face was priceless. He suddenly looked very confused.

"Do you mind, General?" Asim asked as he motioned towards the plane.

"Knock yourself out Major."

Asim walked very quickly over to the plane and began climbing the stairs. He reached the top as the pilot was coming out and squeezed past him in his haste to search the plane. The Air Force pilot stood at the top of the stairs and looked at the general in puzzlement. Samuelson just shrugged as if in total oblivion.

Major Asim emerged from the jet looking as if he had just seen a ghost. He had come just short of accusing a general of wrongdoing and fell on his face. He was very humble and devoid of any suspicion. He walked over to Samuelson, completely defeated, and came to attention before the general.

"General, there has been a dreadful mistake. I apologize."

"That's quite alright, Major. Tell you what, give me a lift over to operations and we'll call it even. How's that?"

"Yes, Sir. Right away sir," Asim said as he scurried with renewed energy at being spared censure.

Samuelson turned to his discreetly smirking pilot and winked.

CHAPTER 12

Orders

"What do you mean he wasn't there?" Wahid barked at the junior officer.

"I searched the plane myself, There was no sign of him." Major Asim assured him.

Nasir Al-Hamal smiled from his side of the desk. Wahid's emotions were overriding his ability to analyze the possibilities. The colonel just didn't understand how Urit could have vanished. The sight of the prince's assistant smiling at just made him angry.

"What is funny about this?" Wahid asked him.

"They are just very good, but we will still find him. It is Allah's will," Al-Hamal proclaimed.

"He had to be on that plane," Wahid said.

He was certain he had not made such a blatant error as to miss Urit in King Khalid Military City.

"I'm sure he was, they just took him somewhere else."

Al-Hamal stood from behind his desk and looked around at his office.

"What time did he leave King Khalid City?" he asked Wahid.

"Right at eight-o-clock."

"And when did you see him land, Asim?"

"After nine."

Wahid and Asim looked at each other in revelation. The flight had taken twice as long as it should have and both men felt like morons for not realizing it.

"There you have it. I would guess Dhahran or the Hospital at al-Jubail."

That is why he was so powerful. He could pluck reason and simplicity from chaos in any given situation.

"I don't have anyone there. Can you see what you can find out?" Wahid asked Al-Hamal.

"Certainly."

The telephone buzzed on the desk. Al-Hamal walked over and picked it up.

"Yes, your Highness," he hung up.

"His Highness would like to see you now Colonel Wahid."

Wahid stood and walked through the common door into Crown Prince Abdallah's office.

"Come in Colonel, sit," the prince ordered him.

"Yes, your Highness."

"All of my senior officers are being called here. You must report to the American command center."

"What is it?" Wahid asked.

"I can only assume that the time for the invasion is at hand," he told Wahid.

"But, your Highness."

"Whatever else you are doing is secondary I'm afraid. It will have to wait."

"Yes, sir. Is that all your Highness?"

"Yes."

Colonel Wahid stood to leave. Infuriated at the fact that his pursuit of Colonel Urit was being put on the back burner in the interest of the American war with Saddam.

◆   ◆   ◆

Malik Abbas never wondered about the weekly job that Prince Nayaf bin Abd-al-Aziz's nephew Kamal had given him. Kamal took care of the prince's land interests around Jeddah and seldom asked anything of the local laborers. What the extra work meant for Malik was a significant supplementation to his meager earnings. He knew better than to ask, in fear it may jeopardize the opportunity for helping his family by doing something so menial.

Once a week he climbed to the rooftop of a market in Jeddah and switched several tiny memory chips in a small box there. He took the old chips from their slots, put them in a small, metallic pink plastic Faraday cage, and waited for one of Kamal's associates to pick them up the next day. As he closed the white box that blended in nicely to the rooftop on the moonlit night, he relished at how fortunate he was to have been blessed with such an easy and lucrative task as this.

Allah be praised, he thought with a smile as he tucked away the old chips and scurried off the roof to the street.

◆   ◆   ◆

Colonel Urit appeared to be resting comfortably when Dana and Mikael finally made it back to his side. The relationship between a woman and her father is one of enchantment that is replicated nowhere else in the human experience. Lieutenant Ingram had such a relationship with her father and was perceptive of the fact that Dana did as well. As they entered the Colonel's room, a wave of emotion swept over Dana. Ingram cued on it and decided to divert Shellie's attention so she would not become suspicious.

"You want to go over his chart real quick?" Ingram asked.

She stepped back outside the room.

"Sure," Shellie told her.

The two stepped away from the room. Just beyond earshot. Mikael stood by the doorway to afford Dana some privacy with the father she so adored.

Dana did not attempt to shroud her emotions. They were best friends since the death of her mother. Colonel Urit was widely regarded throughout Israel as a particularly ingenious tactician and a lethal soldier, but to Dana he was a gentle giant who kept her safe from all harm.

She put her hand gently on her father's arm as a tear cut a path down her cheek. She felt more alone than she ever had. If her father did not survive, that is exactly what she would be. She leaned down until her face was next to her father's.

"Popi? I love you Popi."

Mikael became very uncomfortable as he looked on. It was the first time Dana was able to grieve, and as awkward as it was, he was glad she had the opportunity.

The medical file that Lieutenant Ingram brought for Colonel Urit was a fabricated work of art. It represented the comprehensive medical history of a 22-year officer in the US Army. To anyone who bothered to delve into the Colonel's past medical history, it looked very ordinary. Up to the reports of his current trauma, the file was a fictional account of a hundred benign and unremarkable ailments.

Shellie looked up from the chart when she saw Jay Kerwin approaching. Her smile lit up the entire ship. Lieutenant Ingram could not help but notice and turned to see what caused her colleague to suddenly lose all concentration.

"Would you excuse me for a second?" Shellie asked.

She already started walking away. Ingram smiled.

"You bet."

"Hi. Sorry, am I bothering you?" Kerwin asked Shellie.

"Never. Not at all."

"I wanted to check on Cross," he said.

"OK. Hold on," Shellie turned back to Ingram, "Lieutenant?"

"Yeah?" Ingram responded.

"I'll be right back."

"No problem," Ingram said with a broad, implicating smile.

Shellie was embarrassed by the implied suggestion, but shrugged it off.

◆　　　◆　　　◆

The sensation was dreamlike. Cross slowly opened his eyes in the dim room and tried to focus. He realized that he was safe and his immediate fear subsided for the moment. When he drew his first conscious breath, the pain jolted his body. The bullet that tore through his lung also shattered several ribs. Even in the haze of a steady flow of morphine, the pain was enough to sober Cross and wake him right up.

As his eyes adjusted to the low light, he made out the shadowy figure of someone in his room.

"Hey Aqua-Mouth."

It was Jay Kerwin. Cross's first thought was that it was one of his old SEAL instructors from Navy Dive School. They were the ones who pinned the name on him.

"Huh?" he grumbled.

The attempt to speak pulled at the sutures in his neck. He really was in a lot of pain. Kerwin stepped closer and Cross recognized him immediately.

"Jay? Where am I?" Cross mumbled softly.

He was swept with a feeling of relief. It was very comforting to see a friendly face.

"You're on the Comfort."

"Hospital boat?" Cross asked.

"Yep."

Cross noticed another form in the room step towards him. It was Shellie.

"How are you feeling?" She asked her patient.

"Who are you?" Cross asked.

The sight of a stranger threw him back into the fear of the unknown.

"It's your nurse dude, Shellie," Kerwin assured him.

"Nurse Shellie. Hmmm, I hurt everywhere." Jay and Shellie laughed.

"What are you doing here Jay? Somebody hurt?" Cross asked.

Kerwin knew he was asking about a fellow pararescueman.

"No. I saved your sorry ass, you owe me."

Cross was stunned. He was above all a man of honor and if what Jay said was true, he owed him a life-debt.

"What happened? I...I don't remember?" Cross asked as he looked at the ceiling.

He could not remember anything after the insertion into Al-Wafra.

"I'm not sure, but you guys got all shot up," Kerwin told him.

He could tell by the look on Cross's face that the news was not welcome. By using the plural, Kerwin insinuated that others had been hurt.

"Who else?" Cross asked.

Jay and Cross were cut from the same mold. It was understood that you held nothing back, no matter how bad the news.

"At least one."

"Who?"

"I'm not sure dude," Kerwin looked at the floor unconsciously, "he didn't make it."

Cross leaned his head back and looked at the ceiling again. He hated being out of the loop. He knew nothing. He couldn't remember what had happened and was swept by an incredible wave of depression. Undoubtedly compounded by the regular supply of morphine and his body's natural healing requirements. Cross faded back to sleep.

"He looks like shit," Kerwin stated into the empty air of the hospital room.

Shellie reached up to grab Kerwin's shoulder.

"You'd have to know him, Shell, he isn't supposed to be like this."

Jay balled up a corner of the bed sheet near Cross's arm. It was killing him inside to see his friend in so much pain. Shellie pulled him away from Cross and led him out of the room. They walked outside to get some fresh sea air near a railing.

Jason took a deep breath and quickly regained his composure while their eyes adjusted to the darkness. Shellie saw the opportunity not only to allow this man she was quickly falling for to vent, but to learn more about her patient. She wondered why he revered Cross so much.

"When did you two go to dive school together?" she asked.

"9." Kerwin grinned as he remembered, "we were the outcasts from the first day. Me because I was the only Air Force guy, and Cross because he talked so much shit."

That brought a funny look from Shellie. Jay went on.

"He explained why to me later, but at the time, he just kept telling the SEAL instructors that they couldn't hurt him come hell week. For three weeks he told the instructors that if he made it 'til hell week, they would never hurt him."

Shellie was always amazed by the stories she heard out of what she considered the "real" military.

"Anyway, he makes it to hell week and everyone discovers that the shithead has a three-and-a-half minute breath hold. No matter what they threw at him, he would lie on the bottom of the pool and scream insults, like blah, blah, blah," Kerwin mimicked the muffled sound of inaudible underwater speech. "They took to calling him Aqua-Mouth."

"I was wondering what that was all about," Shellie said.

"Well, that's where."

"Three-and-a-half minutes? Is that long?"

Shellie had never considered having to hold her breath underwater as a matter of life and death.

"Take a deep breath."

She did, and Jay looked at the luminous tritium hands of his dive watch as he reached out to pinch her cute little nose.

"Now hold it."

Shellie did so for about twenty seconds as her cheeks bulged out in an attempt to prolong the exercise.

"Pheeeew!" She gasped as Jay looked at his watch.

"Twenty-five seconds, darlin."

Shellie was shocked, she would have sworn that it had been a minute. She immediately gained an appreciation for Cross's ability.

"It takes a lot of practice and discipline," Kerwin assured her, "in his case, going through three weeks of pre-Scuba school in Albuquerque didn't hurt either."

"Why's that?" she asked.

"The elevation is like a mile, so the air is way thin. He got up to two minutes at Albuquerque. Take him to sea level and you got three and a half."

Jason was already feeling better talking about past times with his old friend. The fact had not escaped him that it had been Shellie who had made it so.

He wasn't falling for her, he'd smacked bottom long ago.

He had been in love with her from their first embrace. The protocol of modern romance had been all that kept him from fumbling over her like a schoolboy.

What he was too afraid to hope for, but was in fact the case, was that she too was crazy about him. She was a little surer of herself though. She did not care what the outcome of the impending war was. If they were still alive, she was going to spend the rest of her life with him, whether he liked it or not.

"What are you grinning at?" Jay asked Shellie as they walked back inside.

"Nothing."

◆   ◆   ◆

Dana needed the tears. It was the release she had been as yet unable to express. She was not prone to emotional release, being such a warrior in her own right, and the purge thoroughly exhausted her.

"These are yours ladies," Shellie said as she opened the door to one of the adjoining officer's staterooms that would be shared by Dana and Lieutenant Ingram.

The first room was next door to Mikael.

"Thank you, Shellie," Ingram said.

She looked at Dana.

"You take this one, Dana."

Ingram wanted her to be closer to Mikael. She thought it would put her at ease somewhat.

"OK," Dana said, she looked at Shellie.

"Please get me if anything changes."

"I promise," Shellie assured her with a smile.

Dana went inside and closed the door behind her. She sat on the small rack and leaned over to take her right boot off. She always started with the right. She leaned back for just a moment and closed her eyes.

The left boot never came off.

◆   ◆   ◆

They are called the Bat Men. Shayetet thirteen are the Naval Special Warfare unit of the Israeli Navy. A very elite unit of amphibious commandos who have distinguished themselves since performing harassment raids on British naval vessels while smuggling Jews into Israel after World War Two. S-13 operators are highly trained in all aspects of special operations and hold the primary responsibility of conducting maritime raids outside the borders of Israel.

As Tsayid pulled into the small naval base at Atlit, south of Haifa on the Mediterranean coast, he felt a sense of nostalgia for his endless months of grueling training to become one of the Bat Men. He saw the old Crusader Fortress that he had run around countless times with his class. He smiled.

He enjoyed the life he led now, but the fondest times in his past were with the men at S-13. He was still very close to all of them and knew he could trust them for anything.

He arrived at the base early in the morning from Tel Aviv, knowing that the teams would all be completing their morning physical training. The students undergoing the rigors of the selection process were somewhere out in the chilling waters of the Mediterranean, performing exercises compounded with sleep deprivation and hypothermia. The cold and fatigue broke down even the strongest athlete and made survival a matter of mental fortitude. Tsayid remembered the endless sessions of torture in the surf zone at three in the morning. Side by side with his fellow students, shivering uncontrollably and fighting the urge to quit. He would have died before he ever seriously considered dropping out of the course. He smiled thinking about the fresh young faces that were turning blue somewhere off a nearby beach.

The men he was there to see were all seasoned operators long removed from the commando course. The Hostage-Rescue element of Flotilla thirteen was Team Four. The current team leader was brand new to the teams when Tsayid was their leader. He recruited Tsayid from the Haposhtime Palga, or Raid Teams, shortly after his selection to S-13. Neri Cohen was one of the best then, and obviously still was. The leader of Team Four was simply the best operator of Shayetet thirteen.

The Commanding Officer of S-13 was Commander Shai Ben-Moshe. He was Tsayid's Team Leader in the Haposhtime Palga and one of his dearest friends. The rest of Shayetet thirteen considered Ben-Moshe to be a salty "old-school" operator, having matriculated under Commander Shaoul Ziv in the 1970s.

Tsayid pulled up to small administrative building and went inside. There was a solitary member of one of the training teams sitting at a desk with his injured leg up on a chair. He looked at Tsayid, and not recognizing him, offered assistance.

"Yes?" the young recruit said.

"I'm looking for Commander Ben-Moshe," the agent told him.

"He's at PT."

Tsayid looked at his watch. The teams were due to return any moment now.

"I'll wait," Tsayid told the young injured prospect.

Tsayid walked back outside just as a team was cresting the road from the other side of Atlit Harbor. They were dressed uniformly in gray t-shirts embroidered with the batwing crest of Shayetet thirteen on the chest. It was Team Four, and the unit's Commanding Officer was at the lead.

Tough old man, Tsayid thought with a smile.

He watched in reverence as the team completed their run.

As the team ran past Tsayid, Commander Ben-Moshe saw his old protégé standing by the office and dropped out of the formation to greet him. For a man his age, Ben-Moshe had hardly broken a sweat.

"Not bad my friend. How far?" the Metsada agent asked.

"About ten kilometers is all." the CO told him, hardly out of breath.

Is all? Tsayid hoped he could do one kilometer when he was Shai's age.

"Got a minute?" Tsayid asked.

"Of course, can I shower first?"

"Please do, I'd rather not smell you."

"Aaah," Ben-Moshe waved him off and walked into the building.

It had only been about ten minutes when Ben-Moshe came into his office wearing a fresh set of fatigues. Tsayid was seated in front of the commander's desk holding a picture of their old team that had been proudly displayed there, facing outward for all to see.

"What can I do for you, my friend?" Commander Ben-Moshe asked.

"I need to put together a team," there was a pause while he waited for the CO to register the request.

"For?"

"Rescue mission maybe. Not real certain just yet."

"You're not helping me very much Tsayid."

"I want our guys, but it's a little different this time," Tsayid told him.

"How so?"

"If it goes, we may have to go into Saudi Arabia."

"Really...Hmph, that is interesting. I need more information to do any good, you know that."

"Well I don't have any right now. I just need, with your help of course, to select a team that could handle going into Saudi Arabia for a snatch," that drew a look of disbelief from Ben-Moshe.

"Snatching hostile or friendly?"

"Israeli," Tsayid conceded.

Ben-Moshe raised an eyebrow.

An Israeli in Saudi Arabia, he thought.

Tsayid could have told Ben-Moshe every classified detail and been confident of his discretion, but he was a soldier, and followed orders. The fact that it involved an Israeli national brought new meaning to the mission. It removed any apprehension about going.

"Very well, how soon do you need them?" the commander asked.

"I'd like to have them selected within the next few days," Tsayid said reluctantly.

"You're staying then?"

"Naturally," Tsayid assured his old boss with a grin.

"What kind of training do we need?"

"I don't even know just yet," Tsayid told him.

The fact was he really didn't have any idea what the mission would entail. Both of them knew that an unknown mission was of very little consequence to the men of S-13.

"Let's get to work," Ben-Moshe ordered.

◆　　　◆　　　◆

There were seven brothers born of the same mother in the Saudi Royal Family. Collectively, they were known as the Seven Sidieris. The Sidieri brothers shared a sense of elitism regarding their standing in the affairs of the kingdom which had served to alienate them from the rest of the princes.

It did not matter to a great extent, because the Sidieris held some of the most important cabinet positions in the Fahd regime. They also held the same contempt for the west, as did most of the Saudi government. One marked difference, however, was the Fact that Crown Prince Abdallah's mother was of the

Shammar tribe, and he was not a Sidieri. That was the only factor that facilitated any cooperation between the Sidieri's and the United States.

King Fahd was a friend of the US, but Prince Abdallah was not. Therefore, when Kamal Abd al Aziz was approached by a CIA operative working in concert with Saudi Intelligence, he was eager to assist. One of the Sidieri brothers just happened to be the head of Saudi Intelligence and Kamal was his nephew. He knew that Prince Abdallah held sympathy for Muta' Yafai.

The US wanted all the information on Yafai that they could acquire. Assuming that the information gained could inhibit Abdallah's ascension to the throne held by King Fahd, Kamal eagerly monitored the wiretap post atop the old building in Jeddah.

Kamal picked up the digital memory chip module from Malik Abbas and took it to the normal drop off where he met Joe Fogan. He liked the American CIA man. Joe had a universal sense of humor that fit any culture and was able to put anyone at ease, even while surrounded by the stress of the business. Abbas walked into the small café eager to hear Fogan's latest witticism.

Fogan was seated, as usual, at a small table at the rear of the room with a Saudi newspaper in front of his face as if he were aloofly awaiting his lover in a Paris cafe.

"Look at you. You look like Humphrey Bogart sitting there." Abbas said in Arabic.

"I, sir, am much prettier," Fogan said in perfect Arabic without moving the newspaper.

After a brief pause, he lowered it so he could see his colleague.

"Whose house did you take today?" Fogan asked.

Abbas was the enforcer for his father's real estate holdings in and around Jeddah.

"Aaaah, you portray me as a monster," Abbas protested.

"Well, you are an effective monster."

Abbas grinned at that. "Why, thank you."

With the initial pleasantries aside, Abbas handed Fogan the module from the wiretap listening post. Fogan slid it into his lap and raised the newspaper again. He would take the module back to the house he was staying in and analyze them before filing three reports.

The first would be to the CIA and would contain every scrap of pertinent information coming from the telephone conversations originating from the Yafai Palace. The second report would be an edited version to placate Saudi Intelligence and make them believe they were involved. The third would be dispatched to General David Yoshom of Mossad. Only two people would know about the third report, Fogan and Yoshom.

"We invade Iraq soon, yes?" Fogan asked his companion.

"It looks that way, I'm afraid."

CHAPTER 13

Healing

Dana could hardly contain her happiness and practically bounced everywhere she walked. Her father's recovery was coming along better than anyone had anticipated. She should have assumed as much, her father was very stubborn and had entirely too much fight left in him to submit to his injuries. Not to lessen their extent, but he had successfully made it out of the woods in record time. The recovery would still be tedious and painful, but he was going to live.

"Nurse?"

Dana was so deeply entrenched in the thoughts of her father that she was startled by the voice coming out of the room next to the colonel's. She turned to see a young patient looking directly at her. It took her a moment to collect herself and realize that he was talking to her.

"Yes?" she replied.

Cross forgot what he was going to say. This was the first time Dana had come to visit her father during the hours that Cross spent awake. He'd never seen her before and was awestruck. Dana was empirically very beautiful.

"I, uh, your not Shellie."

"No, sir, I'm Lieutenant Smith, um, Dana."

"I'm just a corporal, ma'am."

"Excuse me?"

"I'm just a corporal, ma'am, you don't have to call me sir."

"And I am Dana, you don't have to call me ma'am."

"Yes, ma'am." Cross blushed.

Any attempt he made to disguise his minor infatuation just went down in flames. Dana laughed.

"Did you need something Corporal."

"Huh? Oh yeah, I was just hungry. I would get it myself, but Shellie gets kinda steamed when I get out of the rack."

Dana knew it would be best if she played along to protect her cover identity.

"She should, what would you like?"

Cross was suddenly embarrassed. Standing before him was the most beautiful woman he had seen in years. The last thing he wanted to do to look cool was ask her to wait on him. His fragile male Marine ego was taking a beating.

"It's OK, I'll live. I can get something later."

"You need to eat, Corporal, now what would you like?" Dana said as she put her hand on her hips and smiled.

Cross was enchanted.

"Well, how about an omelet with everything."

"That's it?"

Dana didn't think Cross looked like a Marine was supposed to. Two weeks of liquid food had withered him away and she figured a real nurse would encourage eating.

Cross smiled.

"and some pancakes?"

They were smiling together now.

"Sure," Dana turned to leave.

"Dana?"

She turned back around to face her new patient.

"You can call me Cross."

"Cross?"

"Everyone calls me Cross."

"OK Cross."

Dana smiled and left the room. She walked next door and peeked in at her father. She saw Mikael sitting in his chair next to the colonel. Dana could see from the doorway that her father was asleep, so she headed for the galley to get Cross's omelet and pancakes. She was actually looking forward to it.

♦   ♦   ♦

It was a rare occurrence indeed that Nasir al-Hamal was at a loss. After using every means at his disposal, he had been unable to locate the Israeli. The

TAMMIS system listed no unidentified medical cases that would fit Urit's injuries. Even the Saudi medical personnel under his thumb had been unable to produce any leads. Al-Hamal was frustrated with himself in his inability to produce results for Muta'.

Wahid had not done any better, but that was not out of the ordinary. Wahid was the enforcer of most projects undertaken by the National Guard and was only expected to fulfill that role. Al-Hamal was the brains behind the operations. Al-Hamal told Wahid to abandon the search on his end for the time being and concentrate on his logistical planning for the impending invasion by the coalition.

That is what brought Wahid to Al-Jubail. He was tasked with coordinating air transport for his battalion. Even though the invasion was a mere week away, Colonel Wahid had no idea. He, along with a significant portion of the coalition commanders, was kept in the dark to curtail the risk of leaks due to Iraqi sympathy among the Arab nations.

Wahid quickly lost interest in the discussion between his counterpart from the 1st Marine Division and the air liaison officer whose responsibility it was to assign aircraft. Wahid began looking around the large operations office and noticed that the crux of the activity in the room revolved around a large plotting board that took up six tables in the middle of the room. He walked over and blended seamlessly with the buzz of activity surrounding what was affectionately called the "Ouija board".

The board got its name from a similar looking and identically functioning device onboard aircraft carriers. The board showed the paths of what were deemed regular flights for various reasons throughout the region. It also allowed air controllers to move model airplanes around to give a large, real-time image of the skies above the Kuwaiti theater of operations below the high altitude fighters and bombers. Almost all of the traffic on the board was rotary wing aircraft.

Wahid noticed that there were paths leading from within enemy occupied territory to Al-Jubail, Dhahran, and KKMC. These paths were drawn out on the giant map in red, they were the only red paths on the board.

"What are those?" Wahid asked over the shoulder of an airman who was diligently taking notes from the board.

"What's what?" the airman mumbled, not looking up from his work.

He turned when he was done writing and saw the colonel standing there waiting for his answer.

"I'm sorry, sir, what were you asking?" the now frightened airman said.

His eyes darted from side to side to make certain none of his superiors saw his transgression.

"Those, the red lines. What are those?" Wahid asked, pointing to the board.

"Oh, um those are medivac routes."

"I see."

Wahid went back to surveying the board. The airman assumed he was out of the woods and turned to continue taking his notes.

Then something caught Wahid's eye. There was a red medivac path leading from Al-Jubail out into the Gulf. At the end of the path was a small plastic ship painted white. He tapped the airman on the shoulder.

"And that? What is that?" he said, pointing to the ship.

"That's the Comfort."

"The Comfort?" Wahid asked.

"A hospital ship."

To his credit, Wahid did not always require concrete facts to hit him square in the forehead to register. He immediately knew how Colonel Urit could have disappeared into thin air. With the resources they had brought to bear in the fruitless search, it was the only logical explanation.

◆   ◆   ◆

It had been some time since Tsayid was so close to a detonating incendiary distraction device, so when it went off, it affected the old veteran like it would an unsuspecting terrorist. Before the glow from the concussion grenade, or "flash-bang", faded, four black figures swept into the room at the end of brilliant beams of white light and began firing.

Through his earplugs, Tsayid heard the crack of the muzzles and the impacts of the rounds into the wooden targets surrounding him. After a brief three seconds of firing, the room fell silent except for the pinging sound of the last few brass shell casings hitting the floor.

Tsayid smiled. He missed the sounds and the smells of action.

"Clear!" a muffled voice yelled through the confines of a gas mask.

"Clear!" three other voices responded.

The selection had been easier than Tsayid expected. He knew the men he required for the task would be in his old unit, but fate had arranged them to all be on the same team as well. Four members of Shayetet-13 Team Four spoke fluent Arabic in addition to being the best operators in the unit. One of them was Neri Cohen, the team's leader. They would be perfect.

Tsayid and Commander Ben-Moshe were very confident in the team. The four men had been segregated from the rest of Team Four and given a very vague briefing. Tsayid drew up a medley of exercises for the men to perform as the smaller four-man unit. They performed flawlessly. Tsayid walked over to the door and turned on the light.

One by one he checked the targets that were designed to resemble Saudi members of Yafai's inner circle of fundamentalist fighters. Each target had several bullet holes beginning at the center of the body's mass and leading to the head. Kill shots all. The two targets resembling friendlies did not have so much as a scratch on them.

"Nice work Neri," he said to the team's leader.

Cohen just nodded his head in acknowledgement.

"Go get cleaned up," Tsayid told him.

Without a word, the team exited the building.

♦   ♦   ♦

Stephanie Ingram walked into Colonel Urit's room.

"How are you doing, Colonel?" she asked.

"Not bad today. When do we start the torture session?"

"Right after lunch," she assured him.

Ingram was relentless with his rehabilitation. Colonel Urit knew he would be grateful in the end. The mobility he had already displayed was a testament to his tenacity.

Jay Kerwin peeked into the Colonel's room with a rap on the doorway.

"Knock knock," he said, "sorry Colonel," Kerwin apologized for the interruption, "Steph, have you seen Shellie?"

"I saw her at breakfast, did you check next door?"

"Was about to, thanks," he said as he retreated from the room.

"What's next door?" Colonel Urit asked.

Before anyone could open his or her mouth to answer, Dana spoke.

"A Marine Corporal," she said, slightly eluding to the happiness she felt at making at new friend.

"Who is it, Dana?" The colonel asked. Dana was not normally very social.

"There's an injured Marine corporal next door," she said.

"Do we know anything about him?" Colonel Urit asked to anyone in the room who might offer an answer.

"Well, the Marine's name is Crossley, he's recovering from battle wounds," Mikael told him.

It was his job to know about anyone in close proximity to the colonel.

"Where was he injured?" the colonel asked.

"Don't know that. No one seems to know," Mikael told him.

"Dana?" Colonel Urit asked.

She shrugged.

"The guy who stuck his head in here does. He's an Air Force pararescueman. He saved the Marine," Ingram told Colonel Urit.

She and Shellie had grown as close as was practical and Ingram was the depository of Shellie's angst about Jay.

"What did *he* say then?" Colonel Urit asked.

"He's not saying anything, but Cross is in Recon, so you know how that goes," Ingram told him.

"Recon? Hmph," Colonel Urit was impressed, and that explained the secrecy behind the mission, "what's he like?"

"Very nice, good looking too," Ingram told him with a sassy, instigating grin.

That drew a scowl from the Colonel.

"I mean for a white man," Ingram laughed.

"That's just wonderful, what do you know Mikael?" Urit asked.

"Not much, Stephanie here knows more than I do."

Colonel Urit looked at Dana, "Daughter?"

"We just spoke briefly father, he's nice."

"That doesn't help."

Colonel Urit looked at Mikael, "You told me the commander has been very helpful, right?" he asked.

"Yes, Sir."

"See what he knows, call it a security check or something. I'm just curious."

"I'll get what I can Colonel," Mikael assured him.

"Any chance I could meet him?" the colonel asked Ingram.

"I don't see why not, he's almost ambulatory anyway. I'll check with Shellie." Urit nodded his agreement.

❖   ❖   ❖

Jay knew the effect the news would have on Cross and wasn't looking forward to telling him. Cross was a warrior and would take it as hard as Jay would were the roles reversed. Cross could tell by his friend's demeanor what was coming.

"It's time, isn't it?" Cross asked.

Jay nodded and pursed his lips in a vain attempt to smile.

"Yeah man."

"Hey, you gotta go dude. You have a job to do and it ain't me."

"I know," Kerwin agreed.

"You told Shellie yet?"

"I just found out myself. I haven't seen her."

"When are you leaving?" Cross asked him.

"On the next bird."

There were regularly scheduled flights out to the Comfort from Dhahran and Al-Jubail in addition to medivac flights.

"Well go find her dude. What are you doing *here*?" Cross told him.

"I just wanted to tell you goodbye."

"Go dude."

Jay nodded and turned to leave. Cross was swept with a feeling of loneliness and despair. The only person he knew out on this ship was leaving to fight a war he would be left out of. It was as if someone had just ripped his heart out of his chest. He would be completely isolated from a family that included Jay Kerwin.

"Hey Jay?"

Kerwin turned around just outside the door.

"Yeah?"

"Thanks, I owe you big time. Don't get your ass shot off." Kerwin smiled.

"I intend to collect, bitch."

Cross flipped his old friend off in a gesture that equates to blowing a kiss in the Marine Corps. Kerwin smiled and disappeared down the passageway. Cross forced a smile as a tear ran down his cheek, much to his dismay. He wiped it away and looked up at the ceiling.

"Take care of that idiot, will you?"

♦   ♦   ♦

General Yoshom was in Yaakobi's office this time. Yoshom had just received the latest report from Joe Fogan in Saudi Arabia telling them that Yafai did not yet know where Colonel Urit was, but that the search was continuing. Both of the generals were uncomfortable with how close the Saudis were coming to discovering the whereabouts of their quarry.

"Do you think they will find him?" Yaakobi asked his counterpart from the Mossad.

"Yes, I do."

"And then what?" Yaakobi asked.

Yoshom had the intelligence assets to better predict a move by the Saudis.

"I don't think the would dare kill him right away. They need to make a spectacle of his capture to sway the king."

"They can't do that from an American ship," Yaakobi observed.

"No they can't," Yoshom stood from his chair and began pacing in reflection, "I think they will take him to Yafai."

"Why?" Yaakobi asked.

"The Americans will take our side, obviously. They will try to influence the king into giving Motta back to us."

"And if they succeed, Yafai loses his prize," Yaakobi observed.

"Precisely, they will take him to Jeddah. Yafai is not allowed to leave the city."

"How certain are you?"

"It is the most viable scenario. Tsayid agrees with me. We want to move the team to Eilat."

Plans had already been made to move the S-13 rescue team to the port city of Eilat at the southernmost point of Israel. That addressed several issues, foremost of which was its proximity to the Red Sea.

"The only other possibility is if Yafai gets out of Jeddah," Yoshom added.

"Where would he go?" Yaakobi asked.

"He would go to South Yemen, but I think he will stay in Jeddah until this plays out," Yoshom concluded, "either way, we need to stage from Eilat."

Yaakobi nodded his concurrence.

Since the rescue plan included assets of the IDF in addition to the Metsada, it was officially an IDF operation. General Yaakobi would have to give his approval to any operational changes. As soon as the operation was put into effect, approval would be required by the Prime Minister of Israel.

"Very well," Yaakobi trusted Yoshom's assessment. He had never been wrong.

Yoshom stood and left the office.

◆   ◆   ◆

Camp Fifteen was one of the countless personnel facilities built by the Araamco Corporation for their Turkish and Saudi oilfield workers to live. Essentially a small town within white walls, Camp Fifteen, and many others like it, were vacated to be used by the occupying coalition troops.

The headquarters for Second Marine Division under the command of General Morton Creisher, pronounced *Crusher*, was based at Camp Fifteen just west of Al-Jubail. Near the center of the camp was an unmarked administrative building for Araamco containing a conference room used for high-level meetings for Second Marine Division. The entire building was swept daily for listening recovery systems and was totally secure.

When the Second Air-Naval Gunfire Liaison Company was overrun at Observation Post Six, the resulting crypto compromise necessitated the rewriting of all of the allied codes. The interim allowed for two weeks of investigations into the Al-Wafra fiasco and the death of Huffman at the Al-Jubail armory. The board of inquiry, overseen by General Creisher himself, had come to a conclusion.

General Creisher had earned each of his four stars through merit and valor. He never stood for subordinates who tried to ascend the chain of command through favor instead of hard work. He called them "ass-kissers" just as the enlisted men did.

Creisher never really took notice of Lieutenant Colonel Jeff McKlowsky since he had been appointed to head Second Recon Battalion before Creisher's taking over the Division. Creisher was kicking himself now for not reviewing the relatively unimpressive record of the man who commanded his favorite Battalion. The General was personally ashamed that the first he'd heard of the man is when he learned that two of his twenty-eight combat fatalities thus far had come from McKlowsky's negligence.

With his trademark booming, deep voice, General Creisher published the findings of the inquiry to McKlowsky.

"Lieutenant Colonel McKlowsky, it is the finding of this board of inquiry that the firefight at Al-Wafra was the result of poor intelligence supplied to the S-2 section of your Battalion by Central Intelligence. The Battalion S-2 officer notified you of the lapse in time and you ignored his recommendation to abort the mission and sent Sergeant Ward's deep reconnaissance team into a scenario that was essentially suicide."

The highest-ranking officer in Second Marine Division was slowly turning red as he turned the page and looked up glaringly at Colonel McKlowsky.

"For this, I hold you personally responsible. You allowed your personal ambitions to override any logic you may have and it got a Marine killed. One of *my* Marines, Colonel."

Colonel McKlowsky was ashen by now. General Creisher looked down at the report.

"And then to lose another over grenade accountability? I pray the stupidity of that now speaks for itself." The general then pronounced his sentence. "Lieutenant Colonel McKlowsky, I am immediately relieving you of command of Second Reconnaissance Battalion. You are ordered to report to Headquarters Marine Corps within seventy-two hours where I will allow you to tender your intent to retire to the Commandant."

Colonel McKlowsky was now white as a sheet. His career had just come to a screeching halt, and he was being sidelined just before the Super Bowl.

He would have preferred a firing squad.

He had partially expected this after Lieutenant Park was sent stateside a week ago. Within a month, they would both be civilians. Colonel McKlowsky came to attention and stomped out of the room, professionally ruined.

Ward and Danno were standing in the hallway outside the conference room when McKlowsky stormed out and exited the building. Ward's pulse was racing. He had a thousand things he wanted to say as the voice of his dead teammates and consciously fought to suppress the intimidation that is innate when about to face a four-star general. He was going to speak his mind about the injustice, four stars or not.

"Sergeant Ward," a major stuck his head out of the room and called for the two beleaguered Marines.

Drawing upon each other's strength, the last two healthy members of Team Three marched defiantly into the room and came to attention directly in front of General Creisher.

"At ease, gentlemen," the general ordered.

Ward and Danno came to parade rest, which was as close to "at ease" as a recon Marine ever came.

"I know you probably have an earful for me, but I want you to bear with me for a moment."

The general stood and walked around the long table as he continued to speak with the caring and poignancy of a grandfather.

"I have reviewed the last five days that you were operational in southern Kuwait in great detail. Let me first apologize personally for the negligence of the officers in your chain of command."

Ward began to feel some relief, maybe there was justice in the world.

"You are only as good as the men you lead, in which case my performance is unsatisfactory. My own officers have shamed me."

The general stopped directly in front of Ward.

"But that's not what bothers me."

It was then that Ward noticed for the first time the gold master parachutist wings and silver scuba pin that adorned the general's chest. At some point in his career, he had been an operator, which made him family.

"What bothers me is that two of your brothers are dead and I can't bring them back."

A lump rose in Ward's throat when the general reminded him of his loss.

"There are men in this very room who will give thirty years to the Corps and never know what you feel."

A genuine pain reflected in the general's voice. He cleared his throat and continued.

"I lost a whole team in Cambodia in '67 and I have never recovered. Two of my children are named after men that died."

He looked directly into Ward's eyes.

"Your team performed exceptionally. You distinguished yourselves in the finest tradition of the Marine Corps and your nation will always owe you a debt of gratitude."

"I am returning you to operational status without further delay," the general assured them.

"You deserve a ticker-tape parade in Times Square, but the mission is classified indefinitely."

Both men expected that, and did not mind a bit. The general turned back to the table for a second then faced Ward and Danno.

"I'm headed out to the Comfort in a few days to see Corporal Crossley, I'll give him your best."

Ward nodded. The general stood ramrod straight before concluding.

"Gentlemen, you *are* the Marine Corps. I ask you not to judge all of your leadership by the events of late. We have the finest officers in the world, please don't lose faith in us."

With that, Creisher walked up to Ward and embraced him. At six-foot six inches tall and weighing two hundred forty pounds, it was a hug Ward would not soon forget. He then did the same to Danno who was struggling to hold in a torrent of emotions. Both of the Marines looked completely exhausted.

"You're dismissed gentlemen, and if you ever need anything at all, you come to me personally."

They both knew the general was not kidding. Then the commanding general of Second Marine Division, Fleet Marine Force came to attention before his two Marines. Had it been the Army, he would have saluted them, but Marines never salute indoors unless armed.

"Semper Fi," he stated succinctly.

That said it all and sent a chill up the spines of the Recon Marines. They came to attention simultaneously, performed an about face, and left the room. General Creisher turned to his staff.

"I hope you all learned from this fucking mess. It should haunt us for the rest of our lives," he angrily snatched his notebook and cover from the desk where he was sitting, "our lack of quality control in command cost exactly two Marines. Sleep tight gentlemen."

Creisher turned and walked out of the room. The officers at the table sat speechless and watched the "old man" leave.

♦   ♦   ♦

Shellie froze when she opened her cabin door. All of Jay's things were neatly packed into a duffel bag she'd procured for him. He had made the bunk and tidied up everything so that the cabin was spotless. Atop the duffel bag was his cherished maroon beret.

She knew what it all meant and was mortified. Her breathing quickened and she placed her hand on the bulkhead to steady herself. She was unsure of the emotion she was feeling because it was just so alien to her. In reality, it was a collage of emotions overrunning her system. She didn't know what to do.

"Shell?"

It was Jay. He slowly pushed open her ajar door and stepped into the cabin. Shellie turned and grabbed him in an embrace as if it was the last they would ever have. She burst into tears.

"Not now! Not now!" she sobbed, "I just found you."

"Hey, hey," Jay sniffled.

Shellie's display was more than he expected and it was hurting him not only to leave, but to put her through this as well.

"Baby, I'll be back. I promise."

Shellie's sobbing became loud enough that Jay reached back to close the door. Not because he was embarrassed by the display, but to preserve the dignity of the woman he was in love with. It was the first time in his life anyone had felt this way about him and he was completely ignorant as to what would help the situation. He just hugged her as hard as he could and rocked her back and forth.

Shellie gathered her composure and lifted her head.

"When are you going?" she asked.

"Right now. I looked for you…"

"I had to do something for Doctor Cowen, I'm sorry," she sniffled.

"Don't apologize honey. I just found out and I'm on the next bird out of here. It's waiting for me."

There was nothing she could do to change the situation in her favor and Shellie knew it. What she needed to do right now is assure Jay that she would be alright. Where he was going required his total focus.

She pulled away and wiped her face.

"You go baby," she said as she wiped the wet spot on his chest from her tears, "I'll be fine here. Just promise me you'll come back."

"I promise," he said as he cradled her cheek in his hand, "I love you Shellie."

Shellie closed her eyes and leaned her face into his hand. "I love you," her eyes opened and she smiled, "now go."

Jay kissed her deeply, then grabbed his bag and left without another word. Shellie closed the door behind him and turned to face her cabin. She stood in silence for a moment using every ounce of strength she could muster to keep from losing it again.

She walked over to the bunk and sat down. Her thoughts drifted between fear and the fond memories of what she and Jay had shared in such a short time. It was as if they had compressed a lifetime of love into two short weeks. She was beginning to get a grip of her emotions when the sound of Jay's departing helicopter beat out a growing tempo on the hull of the ship. The sound grew louder and Shellie covered her ears in an attempt to escape the audible manifestation of her loneliness.

It did not work.

She collapsed to the bed, sobbing uncontrollably.

◆   ◆   ◆

"Colonel?" Mikael said softly from the doorway.

He didn't realize that the Colonel was asleep.

"Yes, yes. Come in Mikael," Colonel Urit groaned.

He was continually embarrassed by his body's need for rest to recover from such traumatic wounds. He viewed his naps as a sign of weakness.

"I'm sorry, Sir. I didn't know you were asleep. I just saw Captain Cowen."

"No, no. I wasn't asleep," the colonel lied, "what can you tell me about the young Marine?"

Mikael reached into the briefcase that never left his side and retrieved a legal folder.

"He's actually rather impressive," Mikael began.

"Electronics school, amphibious reconnaissance school at Fort Story, Virginia, Army airborne, pathfinder, and ranger schools, Navy dive school, sniper instructor's course at Quantico. The list goes on."

"And he's still just a corporal?"

"Yes, sir, he even has a Baccalaureate in Psychology from the University of New Mexico, and has scored 160 or better on several IQ tests," Mikael added, looking at his notes, "his ASVAB score was off the chart."

"I don't understand…"

"Why he isn't an officer?" Mikael finished the Colonel's sentence.

"Yes."

"I don't know for sure, Sir. It does mention that he has a history of incongruity with most officers he's served under. He has a tendency to point out flaws in command decisions."

"I would too if I were smarter than everyone I worked for." the colonel scoffed, "but I can see where that sort of attitude wouldn't exactly win approval in the Marine Corps."

"Yes, Sir."

"He sounds like an interesting young man. When he's up to it bring him over here would you?"

"Certainly, sir."

◆   ◆   ◆

The two men from Lotar Eilat, IDF Unit 7707, walked right up to Tsayid on the tarmac of Ouvda airbase without the seasoned Metsada man even knowing who they were.

"Been waiting long?" one of the men asked.

Tsayid was shocked. The men both looked scruffy and out of shape. The disheveled rabble before him looked to be a far cry from the talented hostage rescue operators they actually were.

That is why he knew they would be perfect.

"Not really, let's go," Tsayid told them as he grabbed his bag.

He climbed into the first of two vans. The rest of the S-13 team got into the second one. As soon as they exited the airbase northwest of Eilat, the vans spilt up. Tsayid was being taken to the port while the team was taken to a safe house. The Lotar Eilat operators drove in circles for several minutes to identify any unlikely surveillance the mission may have drawn.

Tsayid appreciated the gesture, but knew the mission was the most closely guarded secret in Israel. Not even the Lotar Eilat operators knew why they were escorting someone out to the docks.

While they drove around, no one spoke a word. They were all quiet professionals and knew that if anything needed to be said, it would. They approached a gate on the north side of the harbor and another member of the reserve hostage rescue unit who could easily pass for a Palestinian youth on the streets of Gaza waved them through. They passed several cargo docks and came to yet another gate and another rough looking young Israeli. This one made little attempt to conceal the Galil assault rifle slung underneath his jacket.

The van the men were riding in pulled up to a large concrete slip housing that blended in well with the surrounding docks, but was actually one of the most secure structures in the entire city. An older operator approached the van and slid the side door open to let Tsayid out.

"I'm Amitai," he said simply, extending his hand.

Tsayid shook it firmly. Everyone involved shared a common purpose and dispensed with any inter-unit rivalries.

"Davra. Is it ready?" he asked the Unit 7707 Commander.

"It's always ready." he assured Tsayid as he unlocked the door to the slip hangar and gestured Tsayid inside.

The other operators remained outside and unconsciously spread out for security reasons.

Amitai turned a switch and the giant hangar became awash with the fluorescent yellow glow of the lights warming up. Tsayid saw the dull black sheen from the hull of a Zaharon fast attack boat sitting securely on a hydraulic rack five feet above the surface of the water. It appeared to be in immaculate shape.

"Nice touch," Tsayid remarked.

The boats of S13 were typically olive drab in color. The black would be a better color for their mission.

"Yes, and it's been fitted with auxiliary tanks. I think we can get almost six hundred nautical miles out of it if we run conservatively," Amitai had no idea where the mission would be taking his men, but had a few hunches.

Tsayid knew that would be plenty to make it back from Jeddah, but not nearly enough to get back from Yemen. He would worry about that later.

"Excellent," he told Amitai.

CHAPTER 14

Preparations

Ward smiled. As the MC-130E Combat Talon began controlled depressuriza-tion for the jump, his ears popped. He and Danno pinched their noses in the Valsalva maneuver, normally associated with SCUBA diving, to clear their Eus-tachian tubes. What made Ward smile was the accompanying adrenaline rush that came without fail every time he did a HALO jump.

"Off Comm," Ward told the pilot over the aircraft's intercom.

"Good luck Recon," the pilot responded.

Ward said nothing as he and Danno slipped on their Gentex helmets and snapped the oxygen masks over their faces. The diminishing pressure within the cargo area of the Hercules variant made both men's goggles fog up instantly. In a unison that only comes with experience, they simultaneously activated the bailout oxygen canisters at their sides.

The flow of dry oxygen supplied to the Marines to counter the effects of hypoxia also cleared the condensation from the inside of their goggles and allowed their eyes to re-acquire the red glow of the tactical interior lighting. They were cruising on a jump run at 26,000 feet. If they jumped without oxy-gen, the thin air of this altitude would most likely result in their being rendered unconscious in freefall.

Ward checked the LED display on the global positioning system receiver strapped to his chest to check the heading and position of the Combat Talon. He turned to the crew chief, who was on supplementary oxygen along with the rest of the aircrew, and gave a thumbs-up. They were right on course. He looked at Danno and held up one finger signaling that they were about one minute out from the drop point.

The Crew Chief, secured to the deck of the aircraft by a gunner's belt, stepped up the side of the rear ramp and threw the lever to begin lowering it. As the top portion of the ramp opened inward, the bottom opened outward into the pitch-blackness of the hostile skies above Kuwait.

The mouth of the dragon, Ward thought.

He smiled defiantly at the sight as a roar of cold, rushing air assaulted the interior of the plane. There was no other sound in the world like that of an open ramp at the rear of a C-130 on jump run. The hollow, ear-plugging whine of the massive turboprops coming in the open back door was comforting to any operator. The C-130 and all of its variants were the stand-by workhorses of special operations. They rarely failed their passengers.

Ward stuck the thumb of his right hand into the grip of his left and pulled the thumb out. It was Danno's signal to remove the safety on his pyrotechnic automatic activation device. Ward did the same. They stuck the safety pins in their pockets.

The AAD barometrically determined their velocity and altitude during the descent. If either of the Marines were to become incapacitated in freefall and passed through nine hundred feet traveling faster than one hundred feet per second, the AAD would fire a charge severing the reserve canopy closing loop. The men could very well die during the jump, but the AAD insured that death would not be a result of impact with a rapidly rising Earth.

Ward looked back down at his GPS receiver. They were still riding a perfect vector to the drop point. He held up two fingers close together towards Danno. They were very close. Ward ran his Nomex glove-laden hand along the length of the weapon case strapped to his side. It was still secure, as he knew it would be. He reached over to Danno and flipped on his partner's infrared strobe light. He then turned and allowed Danno to do the same to his. The strobes would allow them to find each other with night vision goggles.

Ward saw the crew chief saying something as he turned towards the front of the plane. The team leader knew what he said without having heard it. The crew chief looked directly at the two Marines and rendered a perfect salute. The Marines nodded and grabbed each others harness with one arm.

They stared into the black mouth of the dragon that had bitten them so badly the last time they were here. In a brief instant that seemed like an eternity, the light at the side of the exit ramp turned from red to green and into the mouth they dove.

◆   ◆   ◆

The groan startled Cross. He was returning to bed from a nocturnal and very unauthorized trip to the galley when he heard the sound coming from Colonel Urit's room. It had been nothing more complicated than bad luck that had kept him from yet meeting the Colonel. Cross's condition had improved dramatically and he had helped Shellie McLean through the anxiety she was feeling with Jay's returning to his unit.

Colonel Urit had been progressing as well, but he had gone back to surgery two days ago to remove an abscess in his hip. It was an unfortunate setback. Cross also noticed that he had been seeing a lot less of that nurse, Dana, with whom he had been so impressed. Shellie had not gone into detail with Cross, but had told him a little about the old colonel, and he really wanted to meet him. Cross's improving condition was highlighting his stark boredom.

"Colonel?" Cross whispered into the room.

The colonel let out another groan and Cross could tell he was in a lot of pain. Cross looked around and saw no one within earshot.

"Shit."

He had no idea what to do, but there was no way he was going to stand by and just let the guy suffer. It went against every moral he knew.

Cross walked over to the Colonel's bedside and put down his midnight snack. Colonel Urit was writhing in obvious pain.

"Colonel? Colonel?"

Cross grabbed the Israeli's arm and shook him gently. Maybe if he were awake, the colonel would be able to tell him what was wrong.

"Mmmmph!" Colonel Urit exhaled as he woke.

His groaning subsided once his conscious ability to suppress pain took over. Cross saw the colonel's eyes open in the faint glow supplied by the corridor lighting.

"What is it Colonel?" Cross asked him.

Colonel Urit's eyes shifted to the side to see the Marine standing next to him. A tear involuntarily ran from the colonel's eye. Cross knew he was in unimaginable pain. Colonel Urit did not recognize Cross, but needed relief from whoever would offer.

"I don't know," Colonel Urit barely got the words out through the agony he felt.

"Hold on Colonel, I'll be right back," Cross assured him.

"No."

Colonel Urit was beyond the superhuman pain threshold he possessed. Whatever was hurting him was also quickly breaking him.

"Just hold on. I'll be right back."

Cross was scared. There was not a colonel alive who should be in that much pain. Cross stepped out into the passageway.

"Hey!" his booming voice echoed down the hallway.

The shout hurt his damaged lung, but damaged or not, the yell would have made his Drill Instructors proud.

Mikael was returning from his cabin and heard Cross just out of sight. His blood ran cold and he bolted down the last few feet until he could turn down the colonel's passageway. He saw Cross leaning out of Colonel Urit's room. His first instinct was to perceive Cross as a threat, but Cross did not give him an opportunity to react.

"You! Go get a nurse, now!" Cross ordered.

His command presence threw Mikael off and immediately drew obedience from the Israeli.

"OK!" Mikael yelled back, turning and running towards the galley, where he knew the shift nurses would be.

He got to the galley and saw that Shellie was already getting up to investigate the yelling. She looked at Mikael for an answer when she saw him.

"It's the colonel," he told her simply.

She ran past him and down the passageway. She turned the corner and saw the look on Cross's face. Cross never looked scared like this.

"What's wrong?" she asked Cross.

"You're the nurse, I have no idea. He's just hurting real bad."

Shellie stepped over to the colonel and felt his forehead like a mother would check a sick child. He was shifting uncontrollably in an attempt to alleviate the pain that was riddling his body.

"Ooooo-K. He's burning up."

She pulled a syringe out of her fanny pack and stuck it in the Colonel's IV drip. It was Morphine. Within a matter of seconds, the colonel's writhing had stopped. Soon after, his groans too subsided.

"I need to go get him some antibiotics. Stay with him for a second," she said.

"OK," both men answered in unison.

"You get back in bed mister!" she yelled at Cross as she left.

He thought he had gotten away with it.

"Thank you corporal," Mikael said genuinely.

He was suddenly feeling very remiss in his duties.

"No sweat, I hate to see him hurting like that."

"Well I appreciate it."

"Don't mention it," Cross told him.

He turned and looked at the snack he left at the colonel's bedside.

"Have at it, I lost my appetite," he said as he left the room.

Mikael smiled and shook his head.

"Thanks," he liked the Marine.

◆   ◆   ◆

The 150-knot blast of air was like an old friend to the recon marines as they exited the Combat Talon over Kuwait. They dove downward and arched their backs to keep from tumbling in the relative wind that came from being thrown forward with the speed of the aircraft. As their forward speed slowed and they began to flatten out on "the hill", the arc carved through the sky during the transition from forward to downward flight, the Marines grasped arms and settled into their five-minute freefall.

This jump was not for enjoyment, although they enjoyed each one. They simply held onto each other until it was time to separate and open. To lose each other on the mission would mean almost certain death. The darkness through which they fell was not the same absolute darkness they saw the last time they were in Kuwait. Ward was able to make out the lights of oil well fires in all directions. The wind was virtually still tonight, so the smoke plumes would hit them at about 10,000 feet.

Ward craned his head down to see past his oxygen mask to the luminous dial on his chest-mounted altimeter as it approached the milepost altitude. He looked up at the shadowy outline of his teammate and watched it disappear before his eyes.

Were it not for the fact that he was holding onto Danno's arms, he would not have known he was there. He shook Danno's arm briskly to check on him. Danno shook back. He was fine. They continued falling.

Ward checked his altimeter again as it approached 1500 feet. Right on cue, the Dytter audible altimeter he was wearing in a cutout pocket inside of his helmet began beeping. It was time to break off. He reached out with his right hand and slapped Danno on the helmet. Danno let go of his grip and turned to track away from his teammate.

The Marines only tracked for three seconds. That barely allowed an adequate distance to insure they did not collide during the violent opening sequence, but it was all they were willing to do. Out of habit, Ward waved off to warn higher jumpers and pulled his main handle. The opening was thankfully uneventful and as soon as he unlocked his toggles, he looked down at the compass next to his altimeter. He'd taped the bezel in place during preparations so that he could concentrate on lining up the tritium north-seeking arrow.

He flew perfectly along the azimuth into the gentle wind. As hard as he tried, however, he could make out nothing of form in his field of view. He saw nothing but absolute blackness.

As the altimeter dial slowly moved counter-clockwise with the decreasing altitude, Ward hoped it was right on. He knew it was not though. Most altimeters are intrinsically off by 50 feet or so. That was more than enough to facilitate a rough landing. He just pulled his legs together and assumed a proper parachute landing fall position. The very same position that anyone who has ever been through the wood shaving pits at Fort Benning, GA can do in his or her sleep.

No mental preparation can spare a jumper from an invisible ground coming up to meet them and Ward knew it. Therefore, when the impact did come, he was not surprised that it scared the hell out of him. He burned into the desert floor without flaring the canopy and stuck like a lawn dart. Fortunately for him, he landed in soft sand.

As he rolled into a heap on the desert floor, he did not move a muscle. He became so instantly silent, that he heard the F-111 nylon canopy rustle to the ground in front of him. He just lay in total silence, listening. He heard nothing in the still desert night. The impromptu listening halt seemed to Ward to last forever, although it had been a mere few seconds. It was time to go to work.

Ward slowly and deliberately unfastened the ALICE pack between his legs and turned it over. He retrieved his night vision goggles from the pack and stowed his Gentex helmet in its place. He slid the goggles over his head and turned them on. After scanning only about forty-five degrees of the horizon, he spotted the flash from Danno's infrared strobe. Ward switched the radio on the back of his tactical vest on and pulled his headset from inside his blouse.

"Danno," he whispered into the bone-conductive microphone pick-ups.

"Good," Danno replied.

He was unhurt from the jump.

"I'm one hundred at two seven zero," Ward told him.

Danno turned to look at that heading.

"Roger that. Moving."

Ward slowly rolled up his canopy and crawled towards Danno. There was no rush, so the two men moved in a calculated, sloth-like motion towards one another. When they met up, Danno handed Ward his CAR-15 rifle and began digging the hole to bury the cumbersome MCXX freefall rigs. Ward scanned the horizon for any threats. There was nothing but black. It was as if they were lost at sea.

After the two Marines had cached the rigs, they donned guille suits and slithered away from the disturbed sand covering the hole. One at a time, Ward and Danno burrowed out belly hides to conceal them for the night. It would be stupid to move and Ward was not going to check the GPS until daylight. They vanished into the desert floor and waited for the dawn.

✦   ✦   ✦

The news would have normally upset Wahid, but his attention was elsewhere. His company would be relegated to a meaningless support role in the impending invasion. They would serve as the occupying Muslim forces after the Infidels had driven out Saddam's Army.

That was fine with the Colonel. If they were going to leave him out of the main event, he would continue on the mission he knew would bring him greatness. He knew the butcher was out on that hospital ship. He could be nowhere else. It was time to go out there and get him.

✦   ✦   ✦

"Excuse me, Corporal?" Mikael asked Cross as he entered the room.

He had committed himself before realizing that Cross was just staring at the ceiling in thought and did not appear to want any interruptions. Cross sat upright.

"Hey, what's going on? How's the Colonel?" Cross asked.

"Much better thanks to you. He was wondering if you would come next door so he could thank you in person."

"That's not necessary, really."

"I'm afraid he insists, Corporal," Mikael said with a smirk.

"Well then."

Cross smiled and hopped down from the bed that had become a prison to him.

Cross followed Mikael to the colonel's room and saw Colonel Urit sitting up as best he could. Cross could see right away that the colonel was a proud man. He was not about to receive anyone lying flat on his back.

"Corporal Crossley isn't it?" Colonel Urit said.

"Yes, Sir. How are you feeling?" Cross asked as he stepped over to Colonel Urit's bed to shake his hand.

"Better, thank you. Mordechi Urit."

Cross raised an eyebrow. The colonel had a very thick accent, but Cross did not peg him for Israeli. The thought never entered his mind considering the circumstances surrounding the conflict.

Mikael was wearing US Army BDUs, so Cross assumed that the colonel must also be American. It just did not fit in his mind though.

"Well good. You gave us a bit of a scare," Cross said.

"I know I have you to thank for getting me help."

"No problem Colonel. If you want to thank me, get me back to my unit," Cross laughed.

Colonel Urit knew he was very serious though.

"What happened to you?" Colonel Urit asked.

"That's a good question Colonel, I don't remember much. Just a lot of bad guys."

Colonel Urit nodded.

"Recon, right?" Colonel Urit asked him.

Cross raised another eyebrow.

"Yes, sir."

"I was with the paratroopers once. Great men."

Paratroopers, Cross thought.

No one called them the paratroopers anymore, and the colonel was not that old. Something was fishy.

"Hundred and first, or eighty-second?" Cross asked.

This should tell him something.

"Israel son," the colonel said bluntly.

Mikael nearly gave birth when Colonel Urit blurted out his nationality. He stepped to the door and shot his head out into the passageway to see if anyone heard him.

Cross saw his reaction and smiled.

"Ah-ha!" he said with a huge grin, "you Colonel, are what we call a no-no," the Marine said.

Cross was one of a handful of enlisted Marines who cared to understand the full ramifications of an Israeli anywhere near the Arab coalition.

"Baah," Colonel Urit waved his hand, "I am who I am."

Cross liked the old man. He had balls of pure brass.

"Well, your secret's safe with me, sir," Cross assured both of the men.

Dana walked into the room and froze in her tracks at the sight of Cross standing next to her father.

"Dana!" Cross blurted out, "there you are."

"Hi Corp, I mean Cross," she replied.

"You here to check on the Colonel?" Cross asked. He leaned over to Colonel Urit. "She never checks on me anymore," he said, feigning a whisper.

Dana reveled in the Marine's insistence to tread somewhere he surely would regret and took her leave before it got ugly.

"I'll come back," she said as she left the room.

"That is absolutely the most beautiful nurse I have ever seen," Cross said, trying to make small talk with the colonel.

"Yes, she is," Colonel Urit agreed with a smile.

Captain Cowen peeked into the room next. The colonel's humble little recovery room was beginning to resemble Grand Central Station.

"Corporal Crossley, there you are," he said.

Cross was surprised.

"Yes, sir?"

"I'm Captain Cowen, got a sec?"

"Yes, sir," Cross agreed.

Cowen stepped back, away from the door. Cross looked at Colonel Urit and shrugged. He followed Cowen out into the passageway.

"You're having a visitor this afternoon Corporal," Cowen told him.

"Who Sir?"

"General Creisher," Cowen said with a look of concern on his face.

Cross felt his heart fall out of his body and onto the floor.

"Oh shit," he quietly exhaled.

Cowen pursed his lips and patted Cross on the shoulder. He had no idea why Creisher was coming out, but by the way Cross reacted, he felt sorry for him.

"Thought you would want a heads-up," Cowen told Cross as he walked past him down the passageway.

Cross simply nodded and looked at the deck. He was horrified. The only thing he knew without question about the battle of Al-Wafra was that he had been shot. That alone told him that the mission had failed.

Unless they are conducting a direct action mission, Recon never engages the enemy. A firefight, while great for stories to the grandkids, is the mark of failure. Cross was sure that General Creisher was coming out to the Comfort to eat him alive.

That's why there was no debriefing, he thought to himself.

He had no idea what he was going to tell the highest ranking officer in the second Marine division. He could not remember what happened out there in the desert.

"Cross?" Dana's voice broke his anxious trance.

Cross looked up and saw that Dana looked concerned. He didn't realize that he was exuding fear like a bright light. Dana also had never seen him deflated like this before. Rather than the huge smile she was used to greeting her, she was met by a blank stare.

"Dana, hi."

"Is everything OK?" she asked sincerely.

"Yeah, yeah. Would you tell the colonel that I will see him later?"

"Sure," she told him as he walked past her and into his room.

Dana walked into her father's room and turned to look back into the passageway, as if to convince herself that she had just seen Cross looking like that.

"What is it Dana?" Colonel Urit asked her.

"What was wrong with Corporal Crossley? Did you yell at him father?"

"Not at all, Captain Cowen was here to see him. Why?"

"He just looked very upset, that's all," Dana said with a glance towards the door again.

"Go talk to him then. See what is the matter," Colonel Urit told her, "he doesn't seem like the type who upsets easily."

"Maybe in a while. How are you feeling today Father?" she quickly changed the subject.

◆   ◆   ◆

The four men Colonel Wahid selected were the best of his company. At least three of them were. The fourth did not fit the profile that the other three did. He was only in Wahid's company because of his relation to a senior cabinet minister.

Ahmed Zaoudi was the furthest thing from a career soldier. He was undisciplined and had no tactical skills whatsoever. He was also the only one in the room besides Wahid who was not acting surprised that he was even in the same room with the rest of the team. In Zaoudi's mind, it was about time he was selected for a premium mission.

"When the breech begins, you will all be in my vehicle, is that clear?" he asked the men. They all nodded.

Wahid looked at Zaoudi.

"This is your chance to prove me wrong about you, Zaoudi. Do not fail me."

Zaoudi looked at Wahid with the same aloof contempt he always had.

What an insult, he thought, *I am as good as anyone.*

"Yes, sir," he replied defiantly.

The other men looked at each other in disgust to protect the ruse.

"Dismissed," Colonel Wahid told the team.

They all stood and remained until Zaoudi exited the office. The three other team members followed behind him. The last one to leave looked at Wahid as he pulled the door shut and nodded.

Wahid nodded back.

❧   ❧   ❧

Tsayid was a little surprised at how well the men worked together. The selected operators from Lotar Eilat had all participated in undercover missions in Gaza and the West Bank with Sayeret Shimshom during the last two years. That made them perfect for assimilating into any Arab culture.

Lotar Eilat's ability to get the S-13 raid team into place would be the key to the entire operation. It was an added bonus that should the need arise, which was a distinct possibility, they were also very adept at hostage rescue.

Tsayid watched approvingly as the teams took turns at the firing line. What made it so interesting was that the men from Eilat firing were not dressed in the black Nomex jump suits that the S-13 Team was. The Lotar Eilat team were firing CAR 15s drawn from under their dishdashahs, the traditional white Arab dress worn by all men of age in Saudi Arabia, and their shot placement was very comparable to their amphibious counterparts. When they were done firing, the CAR 15s disappeared below the robes without a trace.

The S-13 team gave them their due praise, a gesture out of character for inter-service units. The reservists from Eilat were good. They were also ready. Tsayid would notify Yoshom in the morning.

♦   ♦   ♦

"What are you doing Corporal?" Dana asked.

She was shocked to see Cross, without his sling, squirming into a set of desert fatigues. He was bright red and sweat was pouring from his brow. It was obvious he was in a lot of pain. He didn't answer her and continued with his self-torment.

"Here," Dana said as she walked over and helped him get his arm into the sleeve.

Cross exhaled and looked to Dana like he was going to pass out.

"What are you doing?" she asked him again as he reached with his good arm to pull his trousers over his hips.

"There's a general coming out to see me, I have to get dressed."

Dana smirked in resignation and reached down to pull up Cross's trousers. With a tug, she pulled them over his hips and shoved his tee shirt down inside the waistband. Cross nearly swallowed his tongue when her hand came uncomfortably close to his groin.

She buttoned his trousers and went to buttoning up his blouse.

"There," she said when she was finished.

Cross was fire engine red when she looked up at him. Dana smiled.

Cross sat on the edge of his bed and rested his injured arm in his lap. His arm was actually just fine, but the damage to the muscles surrounding the injury to his torso made any movement on that side excruciating.

"Whew," he let out an exhale of relief.

"Now what has you so shaken about this visit?" Dana asked.

"Nothing, It's nothing," he lied.

How would a nurse understand my situation?

"Well, the colonel would like to finish your conversation."

Cross thought about it for a second and decided it would be good to keep his mind off the impending visit from General Creisher.

"Yeah, OK," he said as he stood.

He followed Dana next door. When they walked in, Mikael got out of his chair and left the room with Dana. Cross watched them leave.

"Who is that lieutenant anyway, Colonel?"

"He watches after me."

Cross nodded, "oh, gotcha."

Colonel Urit would normally not have cared about the situation some Marine had gotten himself into, but the colonel genuinely liked him.

"What has you so troubled Marine?" he asked Cross in his fatherly tone.

Cross looked at the deck of the room and shook his head.

"I just don't know what happened out there," he said. Colonel Urit could see that Cross really had no idea.

"There's a Marine general coming out here for a debrief and I just have no idea what to tell him."

"Tell him the truth then," Colonel Urit offered.

"What if *I* was the problem? What if *I* was the reason things went wrong? They obviously did, or my broke ass wouldn't be here, I'd be with my team."

Colonel Urit sympathized with the Marine more than he knew.

"Then son, you face your judgment like a man and move on," the colonel offered simply.

The remark stunned Cross like a slap to the face. He was acting like a child. If he did something wrong, there was nothing he could do about it. War offered no mulligans. Cross nodded his agreement.

"It could ruin me, I'm a good operator," Cross said with resignation.

Colonel Urit laughed.

"Can I tell you a little about ruined?" he asked.

"Sure," Cross said.

He sat down in Mikael's chair to listen to the colonel's lesson in humility. It was one he would not soon forget.

"Have you ever heard of the Sabra and Shatilla massacre?"

Cross shook his head.

"No, sir."

"Sabra and Shatilla are refugee camps in the south of Lebanon. They were being used by terrorists as refuge and for weapons storage. Many attacks against Israel were launched from there."

Cross just nodded. He was listening with total intensity to what the colonel was telling him.

"When we invaded Lebanon to stop the attacks being launched from there, well, we enlisted the aid of some of the Lebanese as a political move. We had reason to believe that after the main invasion, many of the terrorists fled to these two camps. That is where a very grave mistake was made."

Cross nodded again. He began to wonder why the colonel would be divulging something so apparently sensitive.

"Rather than clear the camps ourselves, we allowed a militia, the Christian Phalanges, to do it in our stead."

"What's the difference? Does it matter who gets them?" Cross asked.

"Well, I received intelligence that most of the men we were looking for fled the camps prior to our sending in the Phalanges. I tried to call it off."

Colonel Urit looked away from Cross in apparent shame. It made Cross uncomfortable. Colonel Urit looked back at the Marine.

"Anyway, I was overruled and the raid commenced. Even *I* was certain that if they found no one that would be the end of it."

The room fell silent. Cross wondered if Colonel Urit wanted to continue.

"What happened Colonel?" Cross offered to give the colonel the release he seemed to be pursuing.

Colonel Urit had mentioned massacre. The word is rarely used lightly.

"They found people in the camps. Women, children, old men."

Cross closed his eyes. He knew what was coming.

"They used bayonets and knives so that we wouldn't hear them slaughtering all of the people in the camps," the colonel looked down, "we didn't know."

He shook his head, "cowards...cowards."

Cross sat silently, not knowing what to say.

"There was an investigation launched by the Knesset called the Kahan Commission. Somehow my name was one of a very few mentioned as being in authority at the time of the massacre."

"Didn't you just tell them you tried to call it off?" Cross asked.

Colonel Urit scoffed.

"I said nothing, that would have meant dishonoring good men. So I said nothing," he looked at Cross, "I took my judgment like a man."

Cross nodded his understanding to the colonel.

"There are actually my own countrymen who believe I ordered the killings," he shook his head.

"Well, Colonel, it was war. I'm sure they were collaborating with the terrorists at some point."

"Corporal, there is never an excuse for murdering children. That is without honor. That is disgraceful. Neither myself, nor General Sharon for that matter, would ever condone such an act."

The colonel was growling at the thought of being associated with such a cowardly episode.

Cross felt stupid for making such a weak attempt at comforting the colonel.

"I do know enough to know that there are plenty of Palestinians who would wipe out an entire city of Israeli women and children. They strap bombs to themselves for God's sake." Cross offered.

"That is why we draw a distinction Corporal. The entire world does. That sort of cowardice is not expected of Israel, ever. It is one thing to be viewed as a criminal to the Palestinians, it is quite another to be viewed as a coward by the world as a whole."

"You've never said anything?" Cross asked.

"Those who matter know the truth, but it will never go away. That, my young friend, is your lesson in dishonor and ruin."

Cross was staggered by the revelation and by the colonel's general candor.

"Now, go face your judgment," the colonel began.

"Like a man," Cross finished as he stood up straight.

Colonel Urit smiled and nodded.

◆   ◆   ◆

"How they treating you Marine?" the booming voice of General Creisher echoed down the passageway as he strode into Cross's room, closely followed by a Marine colonel. Cross leapt from his bed and nervously came to attention.

"At ease, Son, you don't need to be bouncing around like that," General Creisher laughed.

"Yes, General," Cross said as he tried to assume parade rest. The pain was enough to cause his forehead to sweat.

"You proved that you can piss fire Marine, so sit down."

Cross was not about to argue with a four-star general. He sat on the edge of his bed.

In the next room, Colonel Urit heard the general arrive and motioned for Mikael to try and eavesdrop. The colonel wanted to know what was going on incase it became necessary to console his young friend.

"How are you feeling?" General Creisher asked Cross.

"I just want to get back to my team General."

An uncomfortable realization suddenly struck the general. "Has anyone been out here to see you son?"

"No General, no one," Cross told him.

"Well, shit," Creisher said.

The comment caught Cross off guard and he realized why the general made it.

"Who General?" Cross asked with all the strength he could summon.

"Ayala and Huffman," Creisher told him, "I'm sorry son."

Cross put his hand over his eyes and pinched his brow.

"Jesus, Mike, I was the Godfather to his son."

"I don't know what to say, son. I thought you knew."

"What about the rest?" Cross asked.

"Daley was injured, he's in Dhahran. Ward and Daniels are still operational."

Cross just shook his head. It would be a while before his loss sank in.

"I had another reason for coming out here, son. I wish it was the only reason."

General Creisher motioned the colonel to come forward. He opened a familiar-looking red folder.

"This is the part you stand up for," Creisher told Cross.

Cross stood up like a robot. He was still in shock.

"To all who shall see these presents greetings," the colonel began, "know ye the reposing special trust and the confidence in the abilities of Len Crossley, I do hereby appoint this Marine a Sergeant, meritoriously, in the United States Marine Corps."

Cross stood silently as the colonel read the rest of the warrant. Any of the Marines in the room could have recited it from memory, but Cross could not even hear the words. He was oblivious to them as he struggled to keep his bearing.

When the colonel finished, he stepped forward and pinned sergeant chevrons on Cross's collar tips. The utilities had belonged to Jay, so Cross had cut off all Air Force markings and Jay's name tag. The colonel noticed, and admired the Marine for making the effort just to be in uniform. He stepped back and shook Cross's hand firmly. General Creisher grabbed a small blue box from the stack left by the colonel on Cross's bedside table as the colonel grabbed another folder, blue this time.

The colonel handed the folder to General Creisher. Creisher stuffed the box under his arm and opened the folder.

"For conspicuous gallantry in combat with the enemy, Corporal Len Crossley is hereby awarded the Navy Cross and accompanying valor device."

General Creisher pulled the box out from under his arm and opened it.

Cross looked down and saw the magnificent decoration. His eyes began to fill with tears from the wave of confusion, guilt, and pride, but he suppressed his emotions in front of the general.

"I would pin it on you, but you can't be sporting this around just yet. The citation has been archived indefinitely."

Creisher closed the box and handed it to Cross. He took the young Marine's hand and shook it firmly, then looked directly into his eyes.

"Thank you son."

CHAPTER 15

100 hours

The spot Ward and Danno had spent the last two days crawling to was perfect. From atop the slight rise in the desert topography, they had an unobstructed view of the entire length of Ahmed al-Jaber airbase in southern Kuwait.

Through his spotting scope, Danno could see most of the Iraqi infantry positions and began committing them to memory. He also made note of the locations of those men carrying themselves like officers. It was not hard to do considering the officers' primary function had switched from coordinating defenses to discouraging desertion.

The two Marines were invisible on the desert horizon. The only anomalies on the surface of the sand covering them were the small openings through which they looked. They lay motionless and observed. This would be their last position before the beginning of the ground war. Night was beginning to fall, and by morning, it will have begun.

♦   ♦   ♦

Colonel Wahid's team sat in silence during the drive to the assembly point for the First Marine Division. The men were going over the mission in their minds, as was Colonel Wahid. Zaoudi was thinking of a mission too, but what he was contemplating involved the assault into Kuwait. He just assumed that the others were thinking about the same thing. He grinned and reveled in his newfound glory as a member of the elite.

◆   ◆   ◆

"We are ready General," Tsayid told Yoshom over the secure telephone line, "it is loaded and we are staged."

The attack boat had been loaded into the submersible stern of a maritime repair ship. A floating dry dock of sorts, whose public purpose was to repair the flotilla of Israeli fishing trawlers in the Red Sea, but unofficially most of the trawlers it repaired were surveillance ships.

"Very good," Yoshom agreed, "proceed and stand by," Tsayid hung up the telephone. He was a little surprised that the mission was actually proceeding this far. It excited him. As soon as they put to sea, he would be able to tell the men of the rescue team what this was all about. He walked out of his room and down the hallway of the safe house.

The rest of the team were in the basement packing the last of their mission essentials when they stopped to see Tsayid walk down the stairs. The team leader simply nodded his head and went back up. The operation was on. The members of the rescue team went back to packing without a word.

"It's the best we can do Elon," Yoshom said to General Yaakobi. He rose from his chair in Yaakobi's office. "Samuelson is probably right and we will never need to use Tsayid."

"I hope so David, I hope so."

◆   ◆   ◆

Dawn came to the airbase with an unremarkable dullness that obscured the transition from the dark of night to the depressing khaki that heralded day. Ward looked at his watch and elbowed Danno. They locked eyes, and in the telepathic way that only silent warriors know, told each other the same thing.

The ground war is on its way.

If the battle went well, they would be in the company of their brother Marines within the first day. If not, then they were, as they were accustomed to, completely on their own in an environment of unimaginable hostility.

Ward's white teeth contrasted sharply with the loam and brown face paint that rendered him invisible to the enemy.

Danno smiled back.

♦   ♦   ♦

"They've invaded Kuwait," the deep voice of Colonel Urit came softly out of the tinny darkness of the room and startled Cross from a restless sleep.

"Huh?"

Cross heard the colonel, but was groggy in the haze of waking up. He looked up and was amazed to see Colonel Urit in a wheelchair. He did not bother to consider how difficult it must have been for the colonel to get into it.

"The breech has begun," the colonel spoke with cautious words.

He knew that this was expected news, but it would certainly be unwelcome to his young friend. Cross was a warrior, perhaps even a little anachronistic in what was still his youth, but he was different from the rank-and-file military in that his life had only one purpose…combat. He was not in it for job experience, travel, or college money. He was in it to fight battles. Any climb and place, as the hymn went. The colonel had sensed this immediately when he met the young Marine, and admired him for it. That factor alone meant that he and the old IDF commander had a common bond that was very uncommon in nature.

Knowing this, the colonel also knew that it was like telling Babe Ruth to take a seat for game seven of the World Series. The news would bring Cross pain, and the colonel felt a strange obligation to comfort the young hero.

"You feel like taking a walk?" the colonel asked from his wheelchair next to Cross's bed.

"Yessir."

Cross squinted as the lights in the room came on. When his eyes had fully adjusted to the light in the room, he noticed that the colonel was alone. Cross slid out of bed while the colonel tried to turn around. His wheelchair banged into Cross's bed.

"Damn it," the colonel was getting frustrated with his struggle.

Cross got up and helped the colonel turn around, then pulled on his clothes. It was never easy for men of action to witness peers at their most vulnerable, and with these two, it went both ways. They were both about as useless as they could be from a combat-readiness standpoint and found comfort in helping each other preserve what shards of dignity they had left.

"Let's go," the colonel said.

♦   ♦   ♦

"Is that Swanson?" Sergeant Foy asked his assistant, Cpl. Sean Doran.

Doran steadied his hands and strained to see through his binoculars. He smiled, then laughed out loud.

In the distance, the first of Second Recon Battalion's teams was coming up from the south along the path mapped out by Foy's team through the Iraqi minefield. The lead vehicle was a hummer whose .50 gunner was Lcpl. Mike Swanson. Swanson had fashioned two massive horns from an MRE carton and affixed them to his Kevlar helmet with duct tape to make himself look like a conquering Viking warrior. The six-and-a-half foot tall Marine stood defiantly above anything else in view.

The vehicle approached the position Foy's team had taken up days before, and to a man, the Marines began rolling with laughter. There were no Iraqis around to hear them anyway.

To the men of Recon, leading the unstoppable Second Marine Division juggernaut, the war had become a joke.

♦   ♦   ♦

"You cannot be in every battle," colonel Urit spoke towards the television monitor.

"I know," Cross was barely able to speak.

The mixture of anger, fear, and shame made it impossible to speak without coming apart. He just remained quiet, and looked up to the monitors.

"Besides, I don't think there is much fight left in them." the colonel assured him.

Cross's unit had been briefed by intelligence to expect heavy resistance once the ground war started. He had seen quite a bit himself before the breech, but had noticed that the Iraqis had been surrendering by exponentially greater numbers in the last few weeks.

Maybe the colonel was right, he thought, and he was not missing all that much. The two men sat in silence with their Navy counterparts as images of Multiple Launch Rocket Systems streaked trails of white light into the night sky for the CNN cameras.

◆   ◆   ◆

Even Colonel Wahid was amazed at the swiftness by which the coalition forces were advancing through the Iraqi defenses. Although he was familiar with the tactics and training of his American counterparts, he realized after the first twelve hours of combat that he had vastly underestimated the abilities of the infidels.

He looked at his watch. The time for the initiation of their own mission was at hand, but he was much deeper into Kuwait than he had originally anticipated. That would be of little consequence to the mission's success, however.

Within another few hours, the First Marine Division would be approaching the perimeter defenses of Ahmed al-Jaber airbase. In the flurry of conspiracy that was occupying his every thought, Wahid realized that the airbase would be the perfect setting. Everything was coming together according to Allah's divine plan.

◆   ◆   ◆

"Cross? Cross?" Dana's very soothing, even alluring voice brought Cross back from the horror of his latest nocturnal visit to Al-Wafra.

His eyes shot open and he gasped for air. To Dana's surprise, he reached out and firmly grasped her arm, almost hurting it. The look in his eyes frightened her. He held on for a moment until he caught his breath, then looked around the room in an attempt to escape the grip of his nightmare.

Dana saw his chest jump from the desperate, rapid beating of his heart.

"It's OK, It's Dana," she told him as she squeezed his hand.

A tear ran down Cross's cheek. Dana could not imagine what could be so horrifying.

"Dana. Oh God," Cross sighed as he finally realized he was not back in the battle that almost killed him.

He closed his eyes and exhaled, "oh my God."

"You're fine, Cross. You're OK," she assured him. He just nodded.

"I heard you yelling," she told him.

"Was I?" he said, embarrassed by what he saw as an inability to cope.

Cross and the colonel had succumbed to fatigue and gone straight to bed from watching the war on television. The images of battle undoubtedly had refreshed Cross's own memories of the chaos.

"Did I miss breakfast?" he asked, changing the subject and veiling his embarrassment, "I was supposed to have breakfast with the colonel."

"I was just about to go get him," she said.

"OK," Cross exhaled again, still trying to catch his breath, "I'll go with you."

Dana smiled. She waited for Cross to get out of his bed and drape his blouse over his shoulder. She led them next door to Colonel Urit's room where they found him already sitting up in bed, trying to wiggle into the wheelchair Mikael held for him.

"Good morning father," Dana said.

It took a second for the phrase to register in Cross's groggy head.

"Father?" he said, stopping in his tracks.

Colonel Urit laughed through the pain of trying to get into the wheelchair.

"Yes, father." he grumbled with an accompanying look of feigned disapproval.

"Uuugh."

Cross was suddenly very uncomfortable. He put his hand on his forehead to think of something to say, but came up speechless.

"It's OK Cross, you had no way of knowing," Dana said.

"You can make it up to me later, let's go eat," Colonel Urit said.

He wheeled himself out into the passageway, followed closely by Dana and Mikael.

Cross, incredibly humbled, slithered out behind them. His day was off to a poor start.

♦   ♦   ♦

"Looks like we got a maverick," Danno whispered to Ward.

They were about five hundred meters from the northwest corner of the airbase. The Iraqi Air Force occupied the airstrip since the occupation, but the only objects even remotely resembling aircraft remaining at the base were the gutted skeletons of Migs. Their pilots had been too afraid of death to attempt an egress to Iran. Those who had attempted the trip, or to make it back to Iraq, were blown from the sky by the impenetrable safety net of the allied air forces.

The Iraqi high command still deemed it necessary to hold this useless piece of real estate for some reason. Ward had been offered an entire team of replacements and several more missions, but realized it would be suicide to go back into combat with men he had not trained with. He convinced the company commander that he and Danno would be more effective as a sniper team in support of the main invasion force. After jumping in two nights ago, they moved into position and lied in wait at the edge of the airbase. The two Marines were now an invisible and very efficient tool of death.

Ward and Danno had heard the opening volleys of the airbase assault about twenty minutes ago, as the advancing division overran the first lines of Iraqi defense. The Iraqis heard it too, and were in the process of determining their fate.

Danno watched through the spotting scope as the debilitated force of defenders near the largest hanger pondered surrender. One of the Iraqis, apparently an officer, was attempting to quash the wave of sedition sweeping throughout his ranks of conscripts. Through the scope, Danno began patterning the movements of the officer and could predict what was happening. His years of sniper training gave him the ability to surmise the dialog between people from their body movements.

One soldier, who had apparently had enough, was confronting the officer before the entire gathered unit. He was holding a white flag and by the way he was shaking it in the officer's face, looked fully prepared to use it. Another soldier wearing a regular Iraqi Army uniform ran up to the apparent leader of the mutiny and leveled him with a butt stroke from an AK-47. No one came to his aid. The officer pulled out his Takarev service pistol and was about to make a very strong argument to the men against surrender.

"Range me," Ward whispered to Danno, who had already calculated the range to the center of the officer's chest.

"Eight seventy-two, no wind," Danno immediately said.

Without breaking his gaze through the Halor coated lenses, Ward reached up and put two and a half more clicks of elevation on the Unertyl scope.

Eight hundred and seventy two meters was routine for someone as well trained as Ward. The Remington M-77 Ro-Bar converted rifle he was aiming was fully capable of half minute of angle shooting. At this distance, Ward could group five shots within an area the size of a regular playing card.

Ward breathed in as the officer began yelling something at the rest of his men. When he stopped to raise the pistol at the kneeling soldier, Ward fired. The 7.62-millimeter round was not NATO issue, but was from Ward's private stock of precision reloads. The soft-tipped round hit the Iraqi officer in the center of his sternum and left an exit hole the size of a coffee can lid.

The man fell straight down on legs that had turned to oatmeal. About half a second later, the report of the rifle reached the soldiers. They immediately began running towards the trenches surrounding the hanger. The Iraqi regular

Army soldier just stayed in the fetal position a few feet away from the defiant conscript, who was still kneeling.

Amidst the confusion, the single soldier who had defied the dead officer stood up. He turned in Ward and Danno's direction, and with unimaginable confidence in the face of what he had just witnessed, pulled a blue baseball cap out of his leg pocket and put it on. He slowly raised his white flag. He was obviously horrified, but willing to take his chances appealing to the sniper's sense of humanity.

The two Marines were overcome with feelings of empathy.

They could not fully understand what forces could cause someone to face certain death to avoid another, more certain death.

"Dude, holy shit," Danno squinted to convince his brain that his eyes were indeed working. "He's wearing a Cubs cap."

Ward had been sweeping the other troops, assessing the threat, and had not seen the soldier put it on. He brought the crosshairs of the rifle to rest on the orange emblem on the man's cap.

It doesn't get any more American than that, Ward thought.

This war was already over, and that single resolute symbol standing in the middle of the airfield was the only one who really knew it.

"I'll be damned," Ward said.

♦   ♦   ♦

Sweat poured down the face of Sergeant Rafik Nassim as he waited for the bullet to strike his chest while he waved the white sheet.

It never did.

He had not been this scared since the Iraqi Army had come to his ailing mother's house in Baghdad and dragged him into a truck bound for the front. The entire time he yelled at them in Arabic and English that he was an American citizen. Since the third day of his visit from the states to see his mother, his life had been a nightmare, as it had for most of the conscripts near the front.

One by one, members of his company began getting up from where they had been lying. As they realized that the gesture of surrender was being heeded, they began waving their arms in the direction of the mysterious American sniper. Within moments, there were over a hundred men waving their arms and anything white they could get their hands on. Then they began walking towards an empty horizon, not knowing to whom they were gesturing. They were walking right towards Ward and Danno.

"Uh, what the fuck we gonna do with all these prisoners?" Danno asked.

Their very rational tactical fear was that they were grossly outnumbered. If the Iraqis were so inclined, they could coordinate an attack that would eventually defeat the two Marines. They barely had enough ammo to spare one bullet per man. The two surviving members of Team Three were good, but not that good.

"I dunno, but iiit's gonna be close," Ward joked like a baseball announcer.

He then stood in his guille suit as the Iraqis got within two hundred meters. They all froze at the sight of this apparition that just materialized out of the desert sand. With his long rifle, Ward made a motion as if he was setting it on the ground. The enemy troops got the message and all dropped their weapons to the ground. They then began the waving of arms again, this time it accompanied blown kisses, bows, and kneeling prayers.

"I don't believe this shit," Ward said as a smile grew across his invisible face.

He then made an exaggerated motion with his rifle towards the south. The troops turned and started walking in that direction, all of them.

"No one will ever believe us," Danno said, never taking his aim off the group from where he was still lying.

"Fuck it," Ward laughed.

❧   ❧   ❧

Colonel Urit comforted Cross to the point that they were able to escape to an exterior causeway on their deck. Cross leaned against the railing and gathered the rest of his composure. The two warriors silently watched the warships in the distance across the dancing blue waters of the Persian Gulf.

The colonel had grown very fond of Cross and felt that the young warrior was the kind of man who was worthy of enlightenment by own philosophies. One in particular, he hoped, would shape the rest of Cross's life.

"You need to know something about what you've become a part of," the colonel began, "those men on your team, the loyalty they give you and expect in return from you is something that you will never see again."

Both men continued staring out into the Gulf as the colonel sighed.

"I'm not sure what you mean sir," Cross said softly.

"You are very young. The future holds countless changes for you and for your team, collectively and as individuals. There will be very hard times for you, as there are for all men, but you must know that men you speak of as your team are different from the rest of society. You will find no one else in any aspect of life with whom you can place such trust."

Cross looked over at the colonel, absorbing every word that came out of his mouth.

"Do you know why you are here?" the colonel asked.

The question seemed silly, but Cross thought carefully before formulating an answer.

"Oil?"

"Yes, but it's more complicated than that. Hussein is an animal. It wouldn't be so bad for one person to control that much oil, but just not *that* person, and I assure you, this is also a liberation. The people of Kuwait will die by the hoards under Saddam," the colonel continued, "never question the cause, sergeant, combat is combat regardless of the underlying motivation. There are some political motivations that may obscure the cause and there are some causes that are noble beyond scrutiny."

"Like Entebbe?" Cross said, using his knowledge of historical events to try and appeal to the colonel's sense of nationalism.

"Certainly, but even if it had been a fiasco, bonds are created that are for life. We will always look out for each other."

Colonel Urit's response drew an inquisitive look from Cross.

The Colonel grinned slightly, "Yes, I was there."

"No shit?" Cross said.

He was immediately embarrassed by his choice of words, "I mean that operation is doctrine in Recon. You pulled that off with only one casualty."

"One too many," Colonel Urit said.

"Did you know him personally, the guy who died, I mean?"

Colonel Urit looked down at the table, "His name was Colonel Jonathan Netanyahu...he was my best friend. We all watched him die on the deck of that plane."

"I'm sorry, sir."

"He was one of a very close family to me, we were born of battle."

"Like my men?" Cross asked.

The colonel looked up and grinned.

"Exactly," he said.

Cross had heard for the first time someone state what he had already assumed. He and his team shared special bonds even before they had been in combat. Combat and the fear associated with it had served only to temper those bonds. The thought of shouldering the responsibility of total trust from these men excited him.

As a young man, Cross had fantasized about secret societies of dark figures that came out of the shadows to stand by each other's side in times of turmoil. Now he knew not only that they existed, but that he was a part of them. Cross began nodding his head unconsciously. He understood. The colonel looked over at his young protégé.

"It is called honor. It rarely exists in its pure form anymore, but you have it. You must live by it for the rest of your life. To betray it is worse than death."

"Death before dishonor," Cross recited the age-old adage.

"Yes, but it is much more than a stupid tattoo you get across your chest on a drunken liberty. Men will try to betray you and sabotage you for the rest of your life, no matter what you end up doing for a living. It's even worse in the civilian world, I've seen it. They know nothing of honor. When those times come, remember the men who live by the code."

"Yes sir."

♦   ♦   ♦

Colonel Wahid motioned his driver to stop at a spot several hundred meters away from the American command vehicles. The position would be close enough to his American counterparts that they would not question him, yet far enough that they wouldn't see anything.

Night was falling and the assault on the Ahmed al-Jaber airbase was underway. As had been the case with every pocket of resistance they had come across, Wahid and his team were expected to stay back and watch from a distance. His relegation to such an ancillary role would normally have driven him to protest, but it worked in his favor for the real mission at hand.

The Hummer came to a stop on a small rise overlooking the base and the men all stepped out. Zaoudi looked like an excited child as he grabbed the only set of binoculars from Wahid's seat and ran to the front of the vehicle to observe the battle for the airbase. Wahid exhaled in disgust at Zaoudi's typical unprofessional behavior.

The other three men of the team took Zaoudi's lack of attention to their actions as an opportunity to look at Colonel Wahid for guidance. Wahid gazed over in the direction of the Americans and saw that all of the officers congregating around the division commander's light armored vehicle were on the opposite side from he and his men. He looked at his watch.

It was time.

Zaoudi carried himself as a self-righteous, elitist Officer to the Americans, and they had long since abandoned trying to entertain he and the rest of the team. The Americans had come to ignore them and let them do their own thing. Wahid looked at his men and nodded.

The next senior man in the team below Wahid, Sergeant Anwar Sabir, passed the other two members of the team as they walked to Colonel Wahid's side of the Humvee. Colonel Wahid led all three of them away from the Hummer in the opposite direction from where Zaoudi stood leaning over the hood.

Sabir walked up behind Zaoudi and bumped him as he reached into the front seat of the vehicle. Zaoudi turned from what he was doing and gave the sergeant a scowl for interrupting his observations. Sabir shrugged him off in defiance and Zaoudi went back to his binoculars. Zaoudi did not hear Sabir slip the pin out of the grenade he withdrew from the front floorboard. Sabir stood up and latched the Humvee door.

Zaoudi's arrogance became his undoing as he ignored the sound of the grenade landing in the sand at his feet. Sabir walked to the rear of the Hummer and turned the corner. As soon as he was sure Zaoudi would not see him, he began running after the other members of his team.

The blast was very pronounced in the relative quiet atop the rise. Colonel Wahid and his team switched into surprise mode and ran around to where Zaoudi lay screaming next to the vehicle. It had worked perfectly. Zaoudi's injuries were horrendous, but he was still alive. Both of his legs were almost completely severed at the knees and he was soaked in blood.

Sergeant Sabir began working feverishly, if only symbolically, to stem the flow of blood from Zaoudi's mangled appendages. Wahid looked around the rear of the Hummer and saw several Americans running their way.

"Medic! Medic!" Wahid yelled in his best urgent voice.

The order was relayed to the command vehicles and a Navy corpsman came running over. He began assisting Sabir with first aid.

"What happened?" an unidentified Marine major yelled to the group standing around Zaoudi.

"Grenade," Colonel Wahid said in feigned terrible English.

The deception worked. The major saw no use in trying to get more information from the Saudi colonel.

"We need a Medivac!" the major yelled to one of the approaching Americans.

"Roger that!" the Marine yelled as he turned and ran back to the vehicles.

The corpsman attending to Zaoudi worked fanatically to tamp the endless supply of blood running from the Saudi's legs. Zaoudi's screams soon subsided as his body surrendered to the shock of such massive blood loss. He fell unconscious, which made the corpsman work faster. Wahid admired the young sailor for his zeal, but harbored no guilt at subjecting him to the emotional trauma of working in vain to save an injured ally.

Within minutes, the unmistakable *thup thup* of a Marine UH-1 Huey could be heard over the sounds of the battlefield. It approached very low to avoid being hit by the Iraqi defensive fire in the distance. A Marine staff sergeant ran down the rise about twenty-five meters and began terminal guidance to bring the Medivac chopper in to the closest practical landing zone. The pilot ignored the signals of the flashlight-wielding Marine and slid the Huey to a perfect landing directly in front of him.

"Go!" Wahid yelled at his men in Arabic over the sound of the Huey.

They ran down the hill to the Huey and retrieved a stretcher from the two medics who were excitedly exiting the helicopter. The Saudis brought the stretcher up the hill and assisted the corpsman who had been working so diligently on their comrade to load Zaoudi onto it. As they began towards the Medivac bird, Wahid turned to the Marine major.

"I go!" he yelled.

The major assumed that Wahid wanted to go with his man to the aid station. He had no problem with that. The Saudi was just in the way.

"Yeah! You Go!" he yelled to Wahid.

Wahid followed his men to the helicopter and watched them strap in Zaoudi. When he was secure, the entire team of Saudis got in.

"Hey! What are you doing?" the crew chief yelled at Wahid, who appeared to any casual observer to be the man in charge.

Wahid motioned angrily with his arm for the helicopter to lift off. The crew chief did not know a word of Arabic and was not about to try his hand at it. He simply nodded and keyed his intercom.

"Let's go sir," he told the pilot, "they're all coming."

"Whatever blows their hair back," the pilot responded as the Huey lifted off and banked sharply for Al-Jubail.

✦   ✦   ✦

"Conn, sonar," Petty Officer Antonio Rosario said from the sonar room of the USS Chicago.

"Conn, aye," Commander J.D. LaFosse answered.

"New contact bearing one nine five out of Eilat."

"What is it?" LaFosse asked.

"Israeli surveillance tub."

"Conn, aye, start a track."

"Sonar, aye."

◆   ◆   ◆

Wahid's Saudi pilot had been sitting on the helipad at Al-Jubail twelve minutes longer than he was supposed to and was wondering what had gone wrong. He knew the American ground controllers would be getting suspicious of his simply sitting on the pad with his helicopter under full power.

It had been a whole twenty-five seconds since he last had, so he looked at his watch again. He saw an American soldier walking towards the helicopter signaling him to exit the aircraft. The Saudi looked at his co-pilot and ignored the American. To his relief, he heard the pilot of Colonel Wahid's Medivac helicopter report that he was within sight of the base.

The Saudi pilot looked up and saw the Huey approaching. The interruption of the landing helicopter distracted the soldier who had been trying to get his attention. That elicited a sigh from the Saudi.

As soon as the Huey touched down, there were several members of the Army medical staff began running towards it with a gurney to collect Zaoudi and run him into triage. As they arrived at the Saudi helicopter, they were pushed aside by the members of Wahid's team.

Wahid stepped from the helicopter and motioned the American medics to back away. He grabbed his bag from the crew compartment and walked directly to the Saudi bird. He never paid a look in the direction of Zaoudi before he climbed in and sat down.

The Americans stood by impotently and watched in amazement while the Saudi Soldiers unloaded their injured man and put him on another helicopter. It was obvious that the man was severely injured, but his comrades did not seem to be too concerned. Although aid was just feet away, they took the man. It simply made no sense.

As soon as Wahid's men had Zaoudi strapped in, the pilot lifted off and banked out over the Persian Gulf. In the fading sound of the rotors, the Americans looked at each other.

"Where the Hell are they taking him?" One of them asked.

"God knows. Fucking Saudis just do their own thing," his fellow soldier responded.

The two men turned around and went back inside. Within hours, they would have forgotten all about the bizarre episode.

Not a word was said over the intercom of the Saudi Blackhawk. The pilot simply set a heading for the last known position of the Comfort. A position which had been supplied directly to the pilot by Nasir al-Hamal himself.

CHAPTER 16

A Silent Jihad

The Silent Professionals.

The motto of the United States Special Operations Command, but it is a description universally applied to operators the world over. The members of the Israeli rescue team had not discussed their suspicions about the operation that was to come. Each man had his own scenario for what they seemed to be about to face, but kept it to themselves. Experience had taught them that speculation is counterproductive.

It was the first time they had assembled for a briefing other than for training. They were out to sea and knew that all of the questions they had formulated were about to be answered.

When the team was assembled in the large galley of the repair ship, Tsayid walked in with a flight crew bag full of maps and diagrams of Jeddah and South Yemen. The crew of the ship was told to report to their quarters or duty stations and none were allowed within close proximity to the galley. The crew consisted entirely of Mossad agents and knew the routine.

"You all know Motta Urit," Tsayid began.

He knew that they all did.

"He was almost killed several weeks ago saving a young girl's life in Ramat Gan after a Scud strike. A building fell on him."

Some of the men looked at each other. They had no idea.

"For reasons of state security, he was taken to a US hospital ship in the Persian Gulf for treatment."

The room was silent. They knew the implications of that fact alone.

"The Palestinians know where he is. Which is why we are all here. We have assurances from the Americans about his safety, but felt it necessary to implement a contingency plan."

Tsayid pointed to the team.

"You're it."

    ◆   ◆   ◆

It had been a very trying day for Cross. The emotional toll exacted by having to confront so many demons was significant. He was already in a deep sleep when the hull of the Comfort began humming to the distant sound of an approaching helicopter. As it grew louder, his sleep grew deeper. It would land without him knowing.

    ◆   ◆   ◆

"This is a Royal Saudi Air Force helicopter. I have an injured man onboard. I must land," Wahid's pilot continued to plead with the Fleet Air Defense air traffic controller.

"Negative, you must divert back to Al-Jubail sir," the voice of a young man repeated across the radio.

Wahid was beginning to sense failure in the mission as the pilot was forced to enter a hover 5000 meters from the Comfort's helicopter deck. Two battle group F-14 Tomcats on anti-surface warfare patrol already had the helicopter locked. If the pilot flinched towards any of the ships of the group without clearance, they would blow him from the sky without hesitation.

Wahid had underestimated the amount of security involved in landing aboard the ship. He had one more chance to get on the ship or they would have to abort the mission. He looked towards Zaoudi and keyed his intercom.

"Is he still alive?" he asked Sergeant Sabir.

"Barely," he said.

Wahid switched to the Battle Group fleet air defense net.

"This is Colonel Faisal Wahid of the Royal Saudi Ground Forces. I have an injured captain who is a member of the Royal Family. We were sent from Al-Jubail and must be permitted to land."

He let the statement sink in, which it obviously had judging from the silence he heard. It was several seconds before there was a response.

"You are cleared to approach the Comfort. Medical staff has been notified," a voice different from that of the controller answered.

"Very well, thank you," Wahid told him in his best frustrated voice.

The pilot pitched forward and made a quick approach to the Comfort. He flared without synchronizing with the pitch of the ship and landed hard on the Comfort's deck. The misjudgment served to project a sense of urgency to the awaiting medical staff and actually worked in the Saudis' favor.

Wahid had anticipated having to let the helicopter leave but quickly thought of an alternative plan. He leaned forward and grabbed the pilot's shoulder.

"Tell them you have a problem with the landing gear. I need one hour," he said over the intercom.

"Yes, Colonel," the pilot assured him.

This time, the team members allowed the American medical staff to unload Zaoudi without any assistance. The team got out in twos and stood behind the medical workers. When they had Zaoudi loaded onto a gurney and rolling towards the hatch leading into the ship, the team members fell in behind them.

As soon as they entered the ship, several doctors and nurses appeared to aid in the assessment of Zaoudi. His injuries appeared mortal, but the American trauma staff still found a pulse. That meant that they were a very long way from giving up.

In the calamity surrounding Zaoudi, Sergeant Sabir and one of the men turned right and disappeared down a passageway. None of the Americans noticed, and if they had, most likely would not have cared. Wahid took the other member of the team and went left. As soon as they were out of sight of the Americans, Wahid slid on a headset and turned on the radio under his coat.

"Sabir?" he said quietly.

"Here Colonel," Sergeant Sabir replied.

He had stopped to study a grainy photo of Colonel Urit while he waited for the radio check.

Satisfied with the communications, Wahid then unsnapped the holster on his belt holding a Beretta M9 pistol and began searching for the butcher of Shatilla. It would not take long.

❖   ❖   ❖

"Captain, could you come up here please?" the watch officer asked a sleepy Bart Cowen on his direct line to the bridge.

"Yeah, what is it?"

"We had a Saudi medivac land and it looks like the gear got all dicked up. We may have a problem getting the deck cleared."

"Shit, we'll just push it over if we have to. I'll be right there," Cowen said as he got up to get dressed.

♦   ♦   ♦

Wahid was just settling into a rhythm when he turned the corner opposite the galley and saw a woman coming out of one of the rooms. He slowed ever so slightly to assess the woman when she looked up and made eye contact with him.

Colonel Wahid had few gifts, but one he did possess was the ability to interpret facial expressions accurately. The woman he was looking at froze in her tracks. She was suddenly very frightened and he knew it. He sensed her fear like a wild predator does that of its prey. Before the woman walked into the next room in an attempt to veil her fear, he knew he had found the colonel.

♦   ♦   ♦

There weren't supposed to be any Saudis on the ship. The sight of the two coming her way was terrifying. Dana froze reflexively, almost inperceptively. The man leading the pair noticed, she just knew it. She walked quickly into her father's room to warn them…it was her only defense.

Mikael looked up and immediately knew something was wrong. He had never seen Dana so frightened.

"What?" Mikael said as he stood.

"Arab soldiers coming down the hallway," She whispered through clinched teeth.

Dana was visibly shaking and her father knew she was scared. Mikael was immediately in defensive mode and stepped to the door just as Colonel Wahid approached.

♦   ♦   ♦

"They are here."

Sergeant Sabir froze at the words from Colonel Wahid on the radio.

"Where," he asked.

"Deck two, corridor Hotel."

Sabir was running before the colonel finished giving him the location.

♦   ♦   ♦

When Wahid saw Mikael step to the doorway and peer out, he pulled his pistol from its holster. From Mikael's American uniform, Wahid took him to be part of the ship's security detachment. This would complicate things, but it was too late to turn back now.

Wahid barely got the gun out when Mikael lunged towards him and grabbed the wrist of his pistol hand. With a single fluid motion, the IDF commando pulled Colonel Wahid towards him with a furious tug. As the colonel's momentum carried him into Mikael, the Israeli brought his right elbow across in a violent swing. Mikael's elbow impacted Wahid's left temple with such force that it opened a four-inch laceration on the Saudi's eyebrow.

The preemptive strike had caught Colonel Wahid dreadfully off guard. He crumpled to the floor, nearly unconscious from the blow to the head. The other man, a Saudi corporal, came at Mikael with his hands since he had not had time to withdraw his pistol from its holster. Mikael was not back into a fighting stance from downing Colonel Wahid, but saw the Corporal coming and struck him in the side with both fists as the Saudi attacked.

The redirection of the corporal's momentum sent him sprawling into Colonel Wahid's room. Without hesitation, Dana reared back and kicked the lying soldier in the face as soon as he came to rest on the deck. The impact sent his head jerking back and blood flew from his shattered mouth. Guided now by fear, which is much more lethal than fury in a fight, Dana jumped on the man's back and grabbed his hair.

With a look of possession in her eyes and saliva flying from her locked teeth as she panted, Dana slammed the Saudi corporal's face into the deck of the room repeatedly. She saw blood splatter in a fan pattern from underneath his face with every impact. It caused her to increase the ferocity with which she assaulted the corporal. She had no intention of stopping until the man's body became flaccid from lifelessness.

Colonel Urit looked on helplessly, unable to move from his bed.

"Kill him Dana!" he yelled.

Urit knew why the men were here. If they survived, he and Dana would certainly die as a result.

Colonel Wahid was able to shake off the blow in an instant and bring the Beretta around towards Mikael. The Israeli saw him turning and dropped to bring all of his significant weight down on Wahid with one knee. The unmistakable sound of three ribs snapping under the pressure was only exceeded by the colonel's shriek of pain. Mikael reached for the pistol, but in the struggle simply sent it sliding out of reach down the corridor.

The scream rousted Cross from his sleep, but had faded before he could process what it actually was. As he began to wake, his pulse started racing. His body had recognized the familiar sounds of battle before he had.

Colonel Wahid could barely breathe and was now in survival mode. That gave him greater strength to resist Mikael, but he would never last. Mikael was hitting him with such force, he was sure to surrender to unconsciousness shortly. The Israeli landed a palm-heel strike to Wahid's nose, shattering it. The Saudi was being bested in short order by the superior ability of Mikael.

Sergeant Sabir had much more experience and training than Wahid. He came running down the corridor making little sound, wielding a knife instead of the much less tactically sound pistol. He knew that one shot from a gun on the ship would put an end to the mission immediately. He saw by Mikael's brutality as he closed the distance to the combatants that all bets were off. This was not a fight for intimidation, it was a fight for life.

Mikael made a mistake. He assumed that the two attackers were all there were and focused his attention on them. He had not reserved any of his awareness to proximity warning and never sensed Sabir coming up behind him. His first sign of an attack came when Sabir's knife sank into his throat. Mikael's vision flashed from the trauma to the tissues of his neck. He felt a tugging sensation as Sabir jerked the knife across the side of his throat, severing his carotid artery.

As Mikael turned to face his mysterious adversary, the laceration in his throat separated. The fight had elevated his blood pressure to a point where the opening sent blood spraying onto the bulkhead in unbelievable volume. Neither he nor his attacker noticed the gruesome phenomenon as Sabir drew the knife back for another swing.

Sabir was a knife fighter, which meant he carried the knife with the blade pointed down rather than up. He retracted the knife blade along his right forearm as he prepared for another strike. The strike came as a blinding punching motion that carried with it the razor sharp blade. Mikael barely got his arm up in time to take the impact.

The blade slammed into Mikael's right forearm and slid effortlessly through muscle and nerve tissue until it struck his ulna. Mikael lost the function of his right hand instantly. He was now on the losing end of the struggle. Before he could formulate a defense, Sabir came down with two rapid successive backhands that sank the knife to the hilt in Mikael's right side beneath his armpit.

Mikael was now losing massive amounts of blood and began to feel it. His vision rapidly constricted to a pinpoint of white light as he collapsed onto the floor. He had just hit the deck when Cross stepped out of his room.

The Marine had been involved in enough conflicts to hone his ability to react without hesitation. He instantly assessed the situation and dove for Sabir.

"Motherfucker!" he growled as if a man possessed.

Sabir was still crouched from his assault on Mikael and was at a slight disadvantage. Not only did Cross have a positional edge, but also outweighed the Saudi sergeant by about sixty pounds.

Cross grabbed Sabir's knife arm with one hand and his throat with the other as he drove the smaller man into the deck of the passageway. With both hands occupied, Cross began driving his forehead into Sabir's face with massive force in a flurry of head butts. Sabir punched at Cross with his left hand with no effect. Cross exploded the sergeant's face within seconds of his seemingly psychotic and very effective assault.

The Saudi corporal who had accompanied Sabir kicked at Cross's head, but missed with the first attempt. The Marine's head was moving so quickly as it pummeled Sabir that it made for a difficult target. The second one found home and landed on Cross's ear, breaking his savage rhythm.

Cross looked up briefly, and the corporal was horrified by what he saw. Cross's blue eyes had turned bright gray, almost white, in the fury of combat. Contrasted by the thick coat of Sabir's blood covering his face, he looked like Satan himself.

Cross lunged forward and punched the corporal in the knee, buckling it and sending him to the floor. Sabir moaned from the pain of his shattered nose and maxillary sinus cavity. Cross felt the sergeant's hand loosen the grip it held on the knife. Cross did not hesitate, he grabbed the knife and sunk it into the jugular notch at the base of the Saudi's throat. Sabir began making a disquieting sound that was a combination of choking on blood and gasping for air that would never again come. He would be dead in seconds.

Cross withdrew the knife from Sabir's throat, climbed off and scrambled towards the corporal to dispatch him. Before he made it, Wahid scurried to his feet and retrieved his pistol. He turned back to the melee and slammed the barrel into Cross's head, splitting it open and dazing the Marine enough that Wahid and the corporal were able to overpower him.

Dana quickly beat the other Saudi corporal unconscious and got to her feet. She stepped outside just as Wahid was climbing onto Cross's back, pinning him to the ground. With a growl, she jumped onto Wahid's back and wrapped her arms around his throat.

Summoning all of her strength, she attempted to choke the life from their attacker. Wahid stood and backed viciously into the bulkhead. The impact knocked Dana's breath out and sapped her strength, enabling Wahid to shake her grip loose and turn to face her. He then punched her in the face several times, incapacitating her.

The remaining corporal stood and kicked Cross in the ribs. Unknowingly, he had found the Marine's Achilles' heel and re-broke two of the ribs that had shattered from the rifle round at Al-Wafra. Cross let out a moan of agony and rolled into the fetal position. He was out of the fight. It had lasted every bit of two and a half minutes.

Wahid shoved Dana into Colonel Urit's room and threw her to the deck. He stuck his pistol into the side of her head hard enough for the pressure to hurt.

Cross opened his eyes and saw Mikael's lifeless eyes staring directly at him. In a sudden realization, Cross reached underneath his chest and snapped off his dog tags. Without any rapid movements to draw attention, Cross waited until Wahid was completely inside Colonel Urit's room and draped the tags over the back of Mikael's neck.

"If you move, I will kill all of you," Wahid grumbled.

"Get them," Wahid told Sabir's corporal, motioning out to the hallway.

The Saudi soldier dragged Cross into the room and lay him next to Dana. He then pulled the bodies of Mikael and Sabir into the room as well. Wahid had hoped it would lessen any attention drawn should someone look down the hallway, but he saw that the passageway was awash in blood. They needed to move immediately.

Wahid noticed the tags on Mikael and snatched them up.

"Marine...hmph," he grunted.

◆   ◆   ◆

"Now *who* did they bring?" Cowen asked the watch officer as he took a sip from his coffee cup. He knew he wasn't going back to sleep anytime soon.

"They said he was a prince or something. Anyway, he died in surgery."

"And the Blackhawk?" Cowen asked.

"The pilot says he thinks he damaged the main gear when he splatted that thing into the deck, the non-flying bitch."

"Alright, I'll check it out," Cowen laughed at the comment and left the bridge for the flight deck.

◆   ◆   ◆

"Colonel Mordechi Urit," Wahid said coldly, just staring at his prize.

He walked over to the Israeli colonel and pulled the sheet covering him back. He saw the dressings on Urit's hip covering the various pins and braces affixed for setting his shattered pelvis. Wahid slammed his fist down on Colonel Urit's hip. Urit let out a shriek that chilled Cross's blood.

"Father!" Dana screamed.

That brought a pistol smashing into her face from Sabir's corporal. It cut her just above the eye. Dana ducked her head in pain. Wahid smiled.

Father? he thought.

Colonel Urit winced at the realization that Dana had inadvertently made herself a certain hostage. The unimaginable pain that racked his body compounded with the knowledge that they were defeated made him slump in acquiescence.

"Put him in the wheelchair," Wahid told the Sabir's corporal.

◆   ◆   ◆

"Excuse me, hi there," Captain Cowen said as he approached the Saudi helicopter pilot.

The pilot was kneeling next to his co-pilot, apparently assessing the damage to the landing gear of the Blackhawk. Cowen thought that the gear looked fine. The pilot stood up and saluted Cowen. Cowen returned it.

"I'm Bart Cowen, what seems to be the problem now?" he asked the Saudi.

The pilot spoke near perfect English, but turned to his co-pilot with a look of utter confusion on his face. Cowen recognized the universal gesture of the language barrier.

"Shit," Cowen growled.

Cowen pointed to the wheels and asked again very slowly, as if by saying it slower the man would miraculously understand.

"What is wrong?" he said with exaggerated facial movements.

Immediately as he said it, he realized how stupid he must look.

"Aaaah," the pilot nodded his acknowledgement to Cowen's hand signals, "no good."

"Great," Cowen said.

He was going to get nowhere, so he turned to one of the flight deck crewmen.

"Go find me a translator!" he yelled across the deck.

"Aye Sir!" the sailor responded, turning and running inside the ship.

Cowen could not understand the Arabic that came across the Blackhawk's radio, but the pilot stood up and turned immediately to the skipper.

"Good, we fly," he told Cowen.

Cowen was totally confused. Without touching the helicopter, the pilot judged it airworthy and climbed in to power it up.

"Whatever," Cowen just waved his hands at the pilot and walked into the ship.

✦   ✦   ✦

Wahid called the pilot at just the right time to ensure the Blackhawk was ready to lift off from the Comfort when they arrived. The Saudi corporal that Dana had beaten nearly to death was now standing. They waited for his assurance that he could make it to the flight deck before setting out from Colonel Urit's room.

"Colonel, I assure you that I will kill your daughter at the slightest provocation," Wahid told Colonel Urit in British accented English.

Wahid finished cleaning the remaining blood from his wounds to improve his appearance as best he could.

"You, *yahood*, push him," he said to Cross.

Wahid assumed that since he too was injured, Cross was an Israeli soldier that had been injured in Ramat Gan. There had, afterall, according to bin Saraj, been three Israleis seen getting onto Samuelson's plane. He had called Cross an Arabic insult for Jew, and was happy to have another for Yafai.

Wahid followed closely with his Beretta in Dana's ribcage. Dana's hands were bound behind her with strips fashioned from bed sheets. The two corporals followed last with interlocked arms. Sabir's assistant was helping his groggy teammate walk. He leaned the injured corporal against the bulkhead before going back into the room and propping Sabir's body against the door.

He secured it on the way out, making sure that the sergeant's body came to rest at the base of the door, making it difficult to open.

The battle-weary group slowly made their way through the corridors of the Comfort. The very late hour made their passage free of any interaction with the ship's crew. Wahid looked around every corner before allowing Cross to proceed with Colonel Urit and they soon found themselves behind the final corner that lead out to the flight deck. They could hear the Blackhawk clearly through the bulkhead of the Comfort.

Cross prayed for someone, anyone, to be around the last corner. If he got on the helicopter, he knew they would die. If given the option, however, he was not going to leave Dana and the colonel. Their fates were now one in the same, and he would have it no other way.

Wahid motioned to the healthy corporal to make the corner first and look for anyone from the ship's crew. The corporal leaned his friend against the bulkhead and strode confidently around the corner. The rest of the band stood completely silent in the hypnotic hum of the helicopter noise. The corporal soon reappeared.

"Quickly," he said to Wahid in Arabic.

"Go!" Wahid yelled at Cross.

Cross pushed Wahid around the corner and through the doors leading out to the flight deck. The helicopter was at full power and the pilot looked to everyone to be very eager to leave.

As they approached the side of the Blackhawk, Colonel Wahid waved for the co-pilot to get out and assist them. The frightened co-pilot ripped his headset off and threw it down on the console between he and the pilot. He jumped down and immediately grabbed the wheelchair from Cross.

"Get in!" Wahid screamed at Cross over the roar of the helicopter.

Cross reluctantly climbed aboard and painfully fastened his dial-o'-death five-point harness buckle.

"Go!" Wahid yelled to Dana with a wave of the gun once he saw that Cross was secured.

Dana leaned forward and drew her leg up to get into the Blackhawk. Wahid would not risk cutting her bindings loose, so she lost her balance and fell to the deck of the helicopter. Cross stuck his foot under her arm and helped her roll over. She stood back up and sat next to Cross. She looked at him, not knowing what to do. The look of despair in her eyes devastated Cross.

"It's OK!" he yelled to her.

Dana looked frightened as Cross fastened her harness.

Wahid helped Sabir's corporal load the injured Saudi onto the helicopter. He then turned to Colonel Urit, grabbed him under one arm, and looked at the co-pilot. The co-pilot followed Wahid's lead and grabbed the other. With no regard to his comfort, they hoisted up the Israeli colonel and heaved him onto the deck of the Blackhawk. Dana and Cross could hear Urit scream over the noise of the helicopter.

Wahid motioned with his head for the co-pilot to secure the crew door behind him. Wahid climbed into the Blackhawk as the crew door slid forward and settled into the locking mechanism. The pilot lifted off before the co-pilot was completely inside and banked towards the coast.

Cross looked at Dana. They could read each other's minds and knew that the chances of living through the night were slim. They also understood without a word that whatever they were about to face, they were going to face it together.

♦   ♦   ♦

"Finally," Cowen remarked as he saw the lights of the Saudi Blackhawk sweep past the bridge and head west.

"They take their friends with them?" the watch Officer asked.

Cowen looked at him with puzzlement.

"Huh?"

"There were four other guys who came on with the one who died. I'm assuming they left too right?" he asked Cowen, thinking that the captain saw them get on.

"I have no idea. Where were these other guys?"

"They came on with the casualty. I never saw 'em."

"Where's the Chief of the Watch?" he asked the Watch Officer.

The other officer turned and picked up the intercom.

"Chief of the Watch report to the bridge," he said into the handset.

"I don't like the idea of Saudi regulars running around on my boat," Cowen said.

Then he remembered what implications he could face because of his secret patient. He turned to one of the enlisted crewmen on the bridge.

"Seaman," he said.

The young boy turned, startled by the captain's request.

"Yes, sir."

"Go to Lieutenant McLean's quarters and wake her up. I need her up here," Cowen ordered.

"Aye sir," the young man said, turning to leave.

CHAPTER 17

The Brass Ring

The seaman was too embarrassed to ask Captain Cowen exactly where Shellie's cabin was, so he took nearly twenty minutes to locate it. Shellie fumbled with her clothes when she heard the knocking on her cabin door. She opted for just a robe, hoping in vain that she would be allowed to return to sleep. She opened the door and saw the nervous sailor standing in the corridor.

"Ma'am, Captain Cowen needs you on the bridge."

"Now?" she asked.

"Yes Ma'am, it sounded urgent," he pleaded.

Shellie rubbed her eyes.

"OK, I'll be right there," she assured him as she closed the door to get dressed.

♦   ♦   ♦

The flight seemed to be taking forever, though Cross knew they had only been airborne for a short time. He craned his neck to see out the crew window, but saw only the stark blackness of the Arabian night. He sensed a gain in altitude as the Blackhawk passed over the coast of Saudi Arabia. Were it not for the lights of Al-Jubail harbor to the north, he would never have known they were over land.

He looked at Wahid and saw him saying something into his headset. He then turned to Dana and saw her staring forward into space. Cross reached over and grabbed her arm, squeezing it tightly. Dana turned to Cross and he noticed a tear slip out of her eye and cross the streaks of blood on her face from the cut above on her brow.

Be strong, Cross's expression told her.

Neither of them knew where they going once the lights of Al-Jubail slipped behind them in the distance.

♦   ♦   ♦

"Sorry about this Shell," Cowen told his head surgical nurse.

He could tell she had practically sleepwalked to the bridge.

"Ugh, no problem," she responded in a raspy voice.

She cleared her throat, "what's up?"

"Well, I'm not really sure, but I need you to check on our patient. I can't leave the bridge right now."

Shellie nodded. If there was an issue with Colonel Urit, she was the only one to deal with it, regardless of the hour.

"Yes sir, I'm on it," she said with a yawn.

Shellie left the bridge and descended a flight of stairs, ladder in the Navy, to the deck above Colonel Urit's room. She walked inside the ship took another ladder down to the correct level. The smells of pre-breakfast preparations hit her in the face as soon as she stepped onto the deck. She instantly realized that she was famished.

She turned the corner to Colonel Urit's passageway and knew immediately that something was amiss. The red deck of the ship concealed the pools of blood from this distance, but the walls were white. Even from where she stood, she could see the huge fan created by Mikael's arterial spray.

Shellie ran down the passageway and saw the pools of blood on the floor when she got closer to the scene of the struggle. Her heart raced with fear. She stopped at Cross's room and looked in the open door. She saw that his room was empty and moved towards Colonel Urit's door. Stepping over a large pool of purple, gelatinous blood, she grabbed the door handle.

When she pushed on the door, it opened about an inch and came to a soft halt. She could tell that something was in the way. Shellie leaned on the door with all of her weight and was able to slide Sabir's body a few inches. It was just enough for her to see inside the room.

Wahid had turned off the lights in the room, but there was enough light from the corridor for Shellie to see Mikael's lifeless, bloody body lying against the far wall.

"Colonel?" she yelled into the silent room.

Hearing nothing, she assumed the worst and ran for help. She sprinted into the galley and startled the cooks who were milling around. Shellie grabbed the ship's intercom near the serving line and, not knowing the direct number to the bridge, waited for the switchboard technician to answer.

"The bridge, get me the bridge!" she yelled into the handset.

All of the cooks within earshot stopped what they were doing to surmise what had the lieutenant so upset.

"Get me Captain Cowen," she told the seaman who had come to wake her.

"Cowen," Captain Cowen answered.

"Captain, get down here now sir," Shellie said, looking around at her audience.

"What is it?" he asked.

She opted not to go into detail and to let the Captain handle this one.

"Now sir," her voice broke from the excitement.

"On my way."

Shellie hung up the telephone and attempted to gain her composure. She wanted desperately to get Stephanie Ingram, but knew the captain had to see this first. She left the perplexed cooks to watch her leave. She went back to the passageway and waited for the captain to arrive.

♦   ♦   ♦

Cross was now beginning to worry in earnest. They had traveled long enough to be deep within Saudi Arabia and he knew the deeper they got, the fewer friendly forces there would be. The only place he thought they might stand a chance was Riyadh. He closed his eyes and prayed. He prayed they were going to Riyadh.

♦   ♦   ♦

The two armed members of the Comfort's security response team that accompanied Captain Cowen leaned into Colonel Urit's door with all of their collective weight. The door slowly slid Sergeant Sabir's body along the floor and opened to reveal carnage.

"Jesus Christ," Cowen said for all of them as he surveyed the room.

He looked at the Sailors.

"Seal this corridor. Not a word, Do you understand me? Total security on this," he said with a pointed finger at the two men.

"Yes, sir," they responded in unison.

"Give me that," Cowen said, grabbing one of the men's radios.

"This is Captain Cowen, sound general quarters," he said.

He turned to Shellie.

"Go get Ingram," he ordered, "I need all of the colonel's files."

He looked at his watch as Shellie broke into a run down the corridor.

"Shit."

It had already been an hour since they left, which was only significant if Colonel Urit was on board the Saudi helicopter. In an hour, the Blackhawk could be almost anywhere.

The sound of the alarm was very unfamiliar on board the Comfort. It was normally only heard during drills that were rumored thoroughly in advance.

"All Hands, general quarters, general quarters," the intercom blasted throughout the ship. "man your battle stations."

Cowen started for the Combat Information Center, which on the Comfort was a converted galley below the bridge.

◆   ◆   ◆

"Stephanie!" Shellie yelled while she pounded on Ingram's door.

The door flew open and Ingram squinted to adjust to the light from the corridor. She wasn't angry for the interruption though, she already knew something was very wrong.

"What is it?" she asked Shellie.

"Somebody came on the ship and took the colonel."

"What?" Ingram's eyes opened wide.

"Mikael's been killed and the colonel's missing," Shellie told her.

"Let's go," Ingram told her as she pushed past and ran barefoot down the corridor in her light blue satin pajamas.

"Wait!" Shellie yelled, "Doctor Cowen needs all of his files."

Ingram stopped and turned around.

"Why?"

She was still on a mission.

"Steph, it's over."

Ingram deflated and realized that the ruse was indeed over.

"I'll get them," she said, walking back into her cabin.

♦   ♦   ♦

"Captain on deck!" the petty officer regulating access to the Combat Information Center shouted into the room.

"Carry on," Captain Wes Martin told the assemblage of the Comfort's Officers.

No one had had a chance to stand upon his arrival and he did not care. He needed to get down to business quickly. The Commanding Officer of the Comfort walked directly up to Cowen, who was standing in the middle of several confused Officers.

"What happened Bart?" the skipper asked.

"The colonel's missing, and there's two dead men in his room," Cowen told him.

The other Officers looked at each other in disbelief. They knew this was no drill.

"How? Who?" Captain Martin asked.

"A group of Saudis brought in a casualty. It looks like it was all set up."

"Who cleared them?" Martin asked.

He did not like uninvited guests aboard his boat.

"Fleet," Cowen told him, "he was some kind of prince or something."

"And the dead?" Martin asked.

"The colonel's bodyguard and a Saudi. It looks pretty bad down there."

The other officers stood dumbfounded and looked eager to hear the full explanation. Captain Martin was not going to give it to them.

Martin nodded.

"Are we sure they got off the ship?" he asked.

It was a question that Cowen had pondered himself.

"It looks that way sir, the bird left in an awful hurry," Cowen assured him.

"I want to make sure. Gerald, I want an armed sweep. We're looking for some Saudi regulars and a colonel that can't walk."

"Aye Sir," the excited operations officer said as he walked swiftly towards the door.

"Armed!" Martin reminded him.

"Aye."

Martin shook his head and looked at Cowen.

"This is going to sting Bart," he told his friend.

"Yep," Cowen conceded.

This was no longer a clandestine favor. They were going to have to let the cat out of the bag.

"Get me the Midway on secure comm," Captain Martin ordered.

The United States Naval assets in the Persian Gulf were massive. The Comfort was part of the Persian Gulf Battle Force which was designated Carrier Group Five. Carrier Group Five was additionally comprised of a conglomeration of five separate Carrier Battle Groups. The USS Midway (CV-41), USS Ranger (CV-61), USS Teddy Roosevelt (CV-71), and since early February, the USS America (CVA-66) Battle Groups. Combined with the Battle Group in the Red Sea, it was the largest naval force assembled since World War Two. The Commander of Carrier Group Five, (COMCARGRU)5, ran the naval war from aboard the USS Midway.

"Wes?" Cowen asked.

Captain Martin looked up as he pondered the consequences.

"Yeah."

"The Marine's missing too," Cowen told him.

"Shhhit," Martin breathed and rubbed his forehead.

Captain Martin was about to tell the Commander of every naval vessel in the Persian Gulf, a man very busy with a little thing called the war, that the Comfort had been infiltrated and that there were casualties. To cap it all off, the first recipient of the Navy Cross in this conflict was one of them.

"Where's Ingram with that file?" he asked.

♦   ♦   ♦

The destination was so dark that the pilot had to momentarily turn on his landing light to see the ground. Cross saw nothing on the horizon and caught only a brief glimpse of two civilian cargo trucks at the fringe of the Blackhawk's illumination. As soon as the landing gear touched the ground, the pilot turned off the light and they were all shrouded in complete darkness.

The crew door flew open and by the red tactical lighting illuminating the cabin, Cross saw at least eight armed Saudi soldiers begin grabbing at he and the Urits. Two of the men grabbed Colonel Urit by the armpits and legs and carried him to the first truck. The colonel was still unconscious from the shock of enduring such unimaginable pain.

Cross was thrown to the ground outside the Blackhawk and nearly knocked cold by an M-16 butt to the head. His hands were bound with nylon tie wraps and he was stood up to walk to the second truck. While he walked, he looked all around. There was nothing on the horizon to indicate where he was.

Cross moaned and threw his head back, feigning incoherence from the blow to his head. He looked at the sky and found Polaris, the North Star. The trucks were pointed east. That was the best he could do. He surmised that they must be headed east.

He was thrown in the back along with Dana and several soldiers climbed in with them. Before he sat down, the truck began rocking as the Blackhawk pilot increased power and lifted off. The sound became deafening as he banked over the top of the truck then began to taper off into a shallow, distant hum. Within seconds, the truck Cross was on began rolling.

Colonel Wahid climbed into the cab of the lead truck. Now that the adrenaline had subsided, he realized how sore he was. It angered him to have been so badly surprised and beaten, especially by an infidel Marine. He would sleep it off on the ride to Jeddah.

♦   ♦   ♦

"Yes Admiral, Yes Sir, Ye…yes Sir," Captain Martin said into the secure ship to ship handset.

The officers of the Comfort, along with the pajama-clad Lieutenant Ingram, stood idly by and watched the captain of the ship explain the entire scenario to the battle group commander and assume sole responsibility. What came at the end appeared to be one of the most severe censures any of them had ever seen and it made them incredibly uncomfortable.

"I understand completely Admiral, yes sir," Captain Martin hung up and pursed his lips.

He looked at the other officers, including Captain Cowen.

"Well, two things," he started.

There was silence as the officers awaited a rundown of the conversation.

"It's a damn good thing there's a war on."

The captain stood up from his stool.

"and it's a good thing the Admiral likes the Saudis about as much as anyone."

It was no secret that while the American forces in the Gulf had no reservations about fighting a war for their ally, they really harbored no love for the people as a whole. By the normal standard of the American way of life, the

Saudis were backwards, oppressive, and hateful towards the US anyway. They would die defending them, but would do so without the luxury of approval.

"We need to find them now," Captain Martin said, "That is paramount. The admiral is going to notify CINCCENT, but he thinks the Bear will want to sweep this under the rug as quickly as possible…regardless, we find them first."

Martin thought for a moment, "The Saudis don't have enough balls for this kind of bullshit. It's probably some fringe group."

"Hmm," Captain Cowen remarked with a pensive nod.

Captain Martin glared at Cowen; Bart had never seen his Captain so furious, "No one gets away with this shit on my boat," the senior officer said.

⬥　　　⬥　　　⬥

"Stop it!" Dana growled.

Cross was blindfolded, but easily recognized the sound Dana made as an indication she was about to be sexually assaulted. There was absolutely no way Cross would be able to sit and hear that.

"Dana?" Cross said.

One of the soldiers yelled something in Arabic at Cross. Dana did not answer.

Cross rubbed his head against the wall of the van in an up and down motion until he was able to wiggle the blindfold just far enough out of the way to see Dana. One of the soldiers was leaning over her fondling one of her breasts and attempting to kiss her. She squirmed so much that he was not able to kiss her lips.

Cross became enraged.

The recon Marine had one particular trait that was responsible more than any other for what had become legendary prowess on the field of battle. When he was properly motivated and allowed himself to do so, he could become blind with homicidal rage. It surfaced during the fight on the Comfort and was beginning to burgeon again within the confines of the truck. He had extraordinary control over his moods and could turn them on like a switch. The sight of the cowardly assault occurring to a woman he respected dearly brought that primal fury to the surface in an instant.

The soldiers could not hear Cross's breathing increase, nor did they notice his legs withdraw underneath him. They were so focused on the concept of what they were about to witness that they never saw it coming.

Cross coiled his legs beneath him and was able to slide his wrists under his feet to the front. No one noticed in their thirst for a vicarious sexual thrill.

In a flash, Cross rose and took two steps past his guards in the direction of Dana's assailant. With a mammoth force drawn upon through both anger and years of playing soccer as a child, Cross let loose a kick that landed directly under the chin of the Saudi soldier.

Dana could not see it through her blindfold, but recognized what hit her in the face. The impact sent four of the man's teeth spraying out in a mixture of saliva and blood. She spit, trying to get the blood off her lips. The attacker let out a yell that was muffled quickly from his badly shattered jaw. He crumpled to the floor of the truck in agony. A stream of dark blood flowed freely from his broken face.

Cross turned as the other soldiers sprang into action. He instinctively backed up to Dana to protect her as one of the Saudis rushed him with a rifle butt. Cross leaned quickly to his right as the soldier swung. As the rifle passed Cross's face, he brought his cuffed hands down over the man's arms, pinning them to his side. Cross turned to the left and pulled the man towards him. With perfect timing, the Marine impacted the bridge of the soldier's nose with his forehead. The Saudi's forward momentum amplified the blow and his nose exploded in a spray of blood across his cheeks that looked like a huge red mustache.

The soldier's body crumpled backwards and Cross followed him to the floor of the truck. He landed with his arms across the Saudi's throat and immediately began his trademark fusillade of head butts on the already unconscious soldier.

The blind rage fueling Cross was the only thing that enabled him to resist the first blow to the back of the head.

The second one stunned him.

He never felt the third one.

CHAPTER 18

Operation Hejazi

All accounts of the battle to liberate Kuwait pointed to the war concluding by the end of the day. General Samuelson was very relieved by that fact. He looked forward to getting his old friend back to Israel and to pretending that the entire affair never happened. He was the last to admit the fact that sending Colonel Urit to the Comfort made him very uncomfortable. Too many variables could bring about disaster to the entire operation.

Samuelson finished buttoning his BDU shirt after just two hours of sleep and walked to the door of his quarters. He was "hot-racking" with several of the other staff officers. They rotated through the same bunk every couple of hours to get just enough sleep to keep sharp. At the rate the war had been exploited, they hadn't required much sleep.

He opened his door and was surprised to see a captain standing before him, about to knock.

"General Samuelson?" the captain asked.

"Yes Captain, what can I do for you?"

"General Piatt needs you right away."

Odd, Samuelson thought.

He could not immediately think of a reason why the second highest-ranking man in the coalition would need him. General Harold Piatt worked directly for the Bear. Samuelson considered himself little a fish. He never imagined what the topic of discussion would be.

Samuelson shook off the cobwebs from his nap and strode confidently towards General Piatt's office. When he entered, he sensed immediately that something was wrong. He could read the look on the general's face.

"Samuelson," Piatt said as the door shut behind the brigadier general.

"Yes, General, how are you?"

The two men had never formally met, so Samuelson was just making his normal conversation.

"Well, we have a bit of a problem, I'm afraid," Piatt told him.

"Oh?"

"A group of Saudi soldiers, it's assumed they were Saudi from their uniforms anyway, boarded the Comfort and took your Israeli colonel."

Samuelson's heart was in his throat. He suddenly became flushed with the anxiety that accompanies being discovered doing something very, very bad.

"Sit down, General," Piatt ordered.

Samuelson was relieved by the order, he felt like he was going to pass out. It was then that the true nature of his friendship to Colonel Urit shone through. He was suddenly more concerned about his friend than his career, which was going down in a ball of flames.

"Do we know where he is?" Samuelson asked.

"No, now I need your full candor on this Samuelson. Tell me everything," Piatt ordered with a gaze of unquestionable authority.

"Yes General."

♦   ♦   ♦

Cross awoke in the fetal position on a tile floor in a tiny, cold room. His vision was blurry at first, but soon focused on the dark brown ceramic checkerboard that was sapping the heat from his broken body. The room had a window to the outside and Cross could see daylight shining in. He had no idea where he was and Dana was nowhere in sight. He strained his neck to see the rest of the room, but was in entirely too much pain. He felt like they had beaten him the entire time that he was asleep.

"Dana!" he groaned.

He heard the faint sound of talking outside the room. It grew louder and the door opened. Two men walked in. Cross could only see their legs, but could tell that one of them was a soldier and the other wore a traditional dishdasha.

"What is your name?" one of them asked in broken but understandable English.

"Where are they?" Cross asked.

"Do not concern yourself with them, what is your name?"

Cross realized that the one asking the questions was the man in the robe because the soldier was walking towards him as the question was asked and there was no change in inflection.

"Fuck you," Cross mumbled.

He barely had the strength to be defiant.

The soldier reared back and kicked Cross in the stomach. The Marine let out a grown and rolled over. The kick hurt much worse than it should have. Something was broken on the inside and he knew it. It was clear that the soldiers in the truck must have beaten him badly.

Cross heard the distant whimper of a female voice. In the short time he knew her, he was able to recognize the sound as Dana.

"Dana!" He yelled, much louder this time.

"Cross!" Dana shrieked at the top of her lungs.

Cross could tell she was scared.

"They'll know I'm missing fuckhead. My boys will come looking."

"Humph!" the Saudi scoffed.

A boot crashed down on Cross's head, knocking him out again.

♦   ♦   ♦

"We have him, Allah be praised," Wahid told Nasir al-Hamal.

They were certain that no one would be monitoring their conversation, but they were used to speaking in cryptic brevity.

Al-Hamal smiled.

"Where are you?" Al-Hamal asked.

"With our friend."

"Allah the beneficent has brought you glory, Colonel."

"Say nothing to the prince. The pig may die anyway. He is at the hospital. A doctor there says he has internal bleeding," Wahid said with disappointment.

Victory would still be his, but the political leverage they would have from possessing Colonel Urit would be greatly reduced upon his death.

"They must keep him alive," Al-Hamal said.

"We also have his daughter and another Israeli soldier," Wahid told him.

"Where are they?" Al-Hamal asked.

"The palace." Wahid told him.

"Let me know when the pig colonel improves," Al-Hamal said before hanging up.

❖   ❖   ❖

Malik Abbas ran nervously across the street and scurried up the side of the old market. He had overslept and was about to miss his drop with Kamal Abd al-Azziz. Kamal told him to begin pulling the memory chips every night for the last week. He had no idea why, but was slightly put off by the fact that he was not being paid more. He knew better then to complain however. The aging laborer grabbed the chip and jumped down off the roof. Several people walking by looked at him as if he had just lost his mind.

❖   ❖   ❖

Kamal did not mind the increased activity asked of him by the CIA man Fogan. He liked the ridiculous conversations they had together. They made him feel American.

"Joe, I beat you today," Kamal said as Fogan walked quickly into the shop, swinging his hips around to avoid bumping the seated patrons along his path.

"Yes, I'm sorry my friend. I'm afraid the war has us very busy. I won't be able to stay," Fogan told him.

"Oh, well," Kamal said as he reached into his pocket and retrieved the single memory chip, "perhaps tomorrow."

He handed the chip to Fogan.

"Of course," Fogan said as he left.

❖   ❖   ❖

"Well Tom, you have one shot at this," Piatt said as he entered his office.

He had just told the entire story of Colonel Urit's journey to the Bear in five minutes. That was all CINCCENT would give him.

"Until the war ends," Piatt said, looking at his watch. "Which looks like sometime tonight, this little episode belongs to me."

"Yes General," Samuelson said.

He was amazed that he was being given any latitude whatsoever.

"If news of your colonel gets out, it's going to end up involving the Secretary of State, maybe even the President."

Samuelson nodded.

"At that point, you know your ass is history."

"Yes sir."

"We need to find the colonel and this Marine," Piatt ordered.

"Yes sir," Samuelson said.

He didn't bother telling Piatt that he had no idea where to start.

◆　　　◆　　　◆

"General Yaakobi? Tom Samuelson," Samuelson said with all the humility he could muster.

"Yes General, I've been waiting for your call."

"Sir, there was an attack," Samuelson said.

He heard total silence on the other end.

"Mikael was killed. Motta and Dana are missing. They were taken by what we think were Saudis."

General Yaakobi's blood ran cold. He knew that it was Yafai and his network that were responsible. They had taken the life of an Israeli officer, an act that could not pass without retribution. The lives of 1000 terrorists were not worth one Israeli, and Yaakobi knew the symbolic importance of demonstrating that fact to the world.

"How did they find out?" Yaakobi said.

The IDF commander was furious and trying as hard as he could to maintain an even keel.

"I don't know General. I will find him, I promise you. I don't know what else to say," Samuelson said.

He knew he had destroyed any credibility he held with the Israelis.

"There really isn't anything else *to* say General."

The only thing that kept Yaakobi from ripping into Samuelson was the fact that any measure of restraint on an Israeli reaction was now released, "Keep me apprised."

The telephone went dead.

Yaakobi dialed another number.

"David, get over here right away please," he told the head of Mossad.

◆　　　◆　　　◆

"Yaakobi," Major General Yaakobi answered his telephone.

"The Orphan is in Yemen," the voice on the other end said.

Yaakobi knew it was Fogan. He never called directly, but the situation was very unusual. He told Yaakobi in code that Urit was with Muta' Yafai in Jeddah.

Since Colonel Urit's departure from Israeli soil, he was assigned the code name of Orphan, referring to his reputation among the top echelons of the government as the Orphan of Galilee. The name was a veiled acknowledgement that he had been a patsy to the Kahan Commission after the massacres at Sabra and Shatilla.

Fogan was fully briefed on what a mission to rescue him would entail. He just needed confirmation that it was a go.

"Hejazi," Yaakobi said.

"Hejazi." Fogan repeated before hanging up.

There were two code words for the rescue mission should it be needed. Hejazi, which refered to the predominant tribe in Jeddah, meant that not only was the team of Israeli commandos to rescue Colonel Urit, but the mission would involve comprehensive direct action against Yafai's terrorist network. The rules of engagement were now established.

There were no restrictions.

The State of Israel was about to dictate a very powerful message in a place considered off limits to them by the rest of the world.

♦   ♦   ♦

The radio operator at Eilat Naval Base knew better than to speculate about any of the things he heard. He was a professional and his job was to report and record. So when Tsayid's voice crackled over the unsecured short-wave maritime radio band, he acted as he was trained to.

"At the gate," Tsayid said.

The team was staged off the coast of Jeddah. The radio operator did not know what the code word meant, but he knew how he was to respond.

"Hejazi. Hejazi." He said slowly to avoid confusion.

"Hejazi."

♦   ♦   ♦

Tsayid smiled the smile of a hungry predator that had just been released into the wild. For every hundred missions a special operator prepares, ninety-five of them are aborted before they begin. It is the nature of that particular beast and something men like Tsayid came to tolerate.

Then there was the dream mission. A mission that Israeli legend was made of. The thought never occurred to Tsayid, but what did occur was that he had just been authorized to proceed with a mission he had waited his entire adult life for.

Tsayid left the radio room of the ship and strode towards the crew compartments. He did not realize that the excitement of the mission caused him to walk faster than usual. He reached Neri Cohen's quarters and knocked on the door.

The S-13 team leader opened the door without a word.

"We're on, get Amitai and meet me in my quarters," Tsayid told him.

Cohen nodded, showing no indication that his heart rate jumped twenty beats per minute at the comment.

♦   ♦   ♦

Colonel Urit was dying.

The pain racking his body and the absence of any medication to ease it were slowly overcoming his ability to fight. The human body can endure a finite amount of severe pain and he was reaching his limit.

Like most things involving women in Saudi Arabia, childbirth was kept in the shadows. The act itself was not celebrated as it was in western culture. It was a necessity of the animal kingdom, but nothing to openly view. Once a child is brought into the world, the celebration could begin, but the birth itself was shrouded in obscurity.

The small delivery wing in the basement of the hospital in Jeddah was the best place to keep Colonel Urit out of the path of prying eyes. It was a quiet place devoid of visitors and containing a minimal staff of medical personnel.

He heard no noise as he struggled to focus on the dimly lit room around him. He realized that his only escape from the agony was sleep, so he began to surrender to it and fade back into unconsciousness. Then he heard Arabic voices approaching and struggled to remain awake. The prospect of learning anything about his fate outweighed the incredible pain.

The white wooden door opened and two armed Saudi men entered. They were not soldiers, the colonel noted, but rather appeared to be average Saudi men. The men scanned the room in the same manner that Mikael would for the colonel. They appeared to be some kind of bodyguards.

The next man to enter the room brought a feeling of utter helplessness to Colonel Urit. The tall, slender, gangly form of Muta' Yafai answered the question of his fate. The towering image of hate looked at Colonel Urit with a contempt the Israeli had never seen before. Behind the man who was quickly becoming the subject of reports in every intelligence agency in the free world was a Saudi doctor.

With a look of disgust that caused him to curl his lip, Yafai said something to the doctor in Arabic. The evil Saudi millionaire then walked next to Urit and looked down into the Israeli's eyes. Colonel Urit stared directly into the dark, empty soul of this madman, in what he knew would probably be his final act of defiance.

Yafai turned away as if he had been polluted by the presence of a disease and walked out of the room. Colonel Urit knew he was going to die very soon and was powerless to defend himself. He closed his eyes and tried to block the images of what he knew Dana must have been enduring.

❖   ❖   ❖

Joe Fogan was now on a very strict schedule and had to find out exactly where Colonel Urit was before nightfall. The best he had so far was the entrance of the hospital used by Yafai. That was entirely too general to be of tactical value to him and he had to get better information.

Fogan had followed the entourage to the hospital in hopes it would better reveal the colonel's location. He found a secluded spot to park that discreetly faced the staff entrance to the woman's wing of the hospital and sat with his Nikon SLR camera in his lap.

Fogan was now relying on intelligence provided him by the CIA and Mossad. Yafai was a fanatical Wahabbist Muslim, so there would have to be an extraordinary reason for him to enter the women's wing of the hospital. He was widely known to avert his eyes from the sight of any female.

While the evidence was logically solid, it was not irrefutable. The strike team would require more accurate information before they could proceed with the rescue.

Fogan stared blankly at the entrance to the woman's wing of the hospital pondering his next move when Yafai's bodyguards stepped through the door. Yafai followed them immediately and Fogan saw him talking to the doctor. The Mossad sleeper agent raised his camera above the steering wheel and snapped several close-up photos of the men.

He had gotten his break.

♦   ♦   ♦

"Colonel Beckham, it's Tom Samuelson, you got a minute?"

"Yes, Sir, you bet. Is this my ass chewing?" Beckham said into the telephone. He knew it would come at some point.

"Excuse me?" Samuelson asked.

"Is this about that Saudi colonel I pissed off? I knew he'd bitch to someone. I'm sorry General."

Samuelson was utterly confused by what Beckham was telling him.

"What are you talking about?" the general asked.

"There was a Saudi colonel that came running through here right after you left. I played stupid, but the guy was an exceptional asshole, if you'll pardon the expression."

"What was his name Ron?" the general asked.

Beckham could tell by the tone in the general's voice that something had happened. He wished he would have paid closer attention to what the Saudi said during his tirade.

"Oh shit…umm, Wahad, Wahood. Damn, it was something like that."

"How sure are you?" Samuelson asked in a voice that began to reveal the urgency of the information.

"It was real close to that, I never forget an asshole."

"Thanks Colonel."

"What's going on General?"

"I'll tell you later," Samuelson hung up the telephone.

Beckham shrugged and felt some measure of relief that he had avoided a reprimand for snubbing the Saudi colonel.

Samuelson hit pay dirt and he knew it. The connection between the Palestinians and the Saudis had to be this colonel.

He looked up at General Piatt.

"Who do we have in the Saudi Army?" he asked.

"I'll find out," Piatt assured him as he reached for another telephone.

"We need an ID on the dead Saudi from the Comfort." Samuelson said.

Piatt nodded his understanding. Someone in the Saudi Army would provide them with the information they needed.

♦   ♦   ♦

Fogan developed the pictures of the doctor and was very satisfied. There was a risk he would leave before nightfall, but the risk at this point had to be accepted.

Fogan picked up the telephone and dialed Kamal.

"Kamal, my friend," Fogan said endearingly.

It was time to cash in on his Saudi friend's eagerness to participate in the world of international espionage.

"I need a favor."

♦   ♦   ♦

Tsayid was originally slated to be the coxswain of the Zaharon attack boat. To his relief, he was now going into Jeddah with the team. The repair ship's First Mate was cleared as an alternate Coxswain before the team left Eilat but did not find out until three hours before it was time to leave on the Zaharon. He was excited. He had learned on a Zaharon years ago and was eager to take part in the mission.

Tsayid pulled the straps on his tactical vest tight and slid his Colt Commando assault rifle around to his back. He pulled his Sig Sauer 226 pistol from the drop holster on his right leg and press-checked the slide to ensure there was a round chambered. It was time to go.

He walked down to the hold where the rest of the team was assembled.

The Lotar Eilat team was dressed in traditional Saudi attire and looked like any group of respectable Saudi men ready for a stroll through Jeddah. Their tactical vests and CAR-15 rifles were invisible beneath their dishdasha robes. Concealed beneath their shumags, the men each wore a radio headset.

The S-13 team looked like black clad ninja assassins in their Nomex jump suits and balaclavas. The only visible skin was that beneath their clear Scott goggles.

Tsayid keyed his headset.

"Radio check," he whispered.

Each member of the strike team responded in turn. The enthusiastic Mossad coxswain answered last.

Tsayid nodded to the deck operator who began flooding the rear of the ship. Each of the team members climbed into their assigned spots on the attack boat and waited for it to float. A loud hydraulic whine accompanied the lowering of the ship's rear ramp into the darkening Red Sea. They were right on time, Tsayid thought. The team would be on Saudi soil just after dark.

♦   ♦   ♦

"Conn, sonar!" the excited voice of petty officer Rosario yelled from the Chicago's sonar room.

The tone of his voice startled Captain LaFosse.

"Conn aye," he responded.

"New contact Captain, bearing zero four zero towards the harbor at Jeddah."

"How far out is it?" the captain asked.

"Two zero nautical miles."

The captain sat up straight. The new contact seemed to have materialized out of nowhere.

"Speed?" he asked his sonarman.

"Fifty-two knots."

"Fifty two knots? What the hell is it Rosario?"

"Sir, it says Zulu class Israeli attack boat."

Captain LaFosse stood up and took off his reading glasses. The crew around him froze.

"You're kidding me."

"That's what it says Sir."

"Helm, periscope depth," LaFosse ordered, turning to his Chief of the Boat, "this is not good," he observed.

There was an Israeli attack boat within the twenty-four mile security cushion established for the entire border of Saudi Arabia by the US Navy. No one realistically expected to enforce the buffer zone outside the Persian Gulf, especially against Israel.

"No sir," the COB agreed.

♦   ♦   ♦

"That's it?" Kamal asked Fogan.

"That's it, I really appreciate it Kamal," Fogan assured him.

The American double agent could tell his Saudi helper was disappointed, but there was no time to placate him.

"I'll take it from here, I owe you my friend," Fogan told him.

Kamal nodded and got into the car driven by one of the members of his staff and left. Kamal let Fogan borrow two of the vans from his compound, two white minivans with dark tinted windows that the team would need for the mission.

Fogan was grateful that Kamal did not ask why they parked the vans next to the beach in the middle of nowhere, almost a mile from the city. The agent just sat and tapped his foot nervously.

❖   ❖   ❖

The Commander of Carrier Group Two (COMCARGRU) 2 was stationed aboard the USS John F. Kennedy (CV-67) and was in charge of the Red Sea. Admiral Gary Provenzano's main concern thus far in the conflict had been coordinating the launches of Tomahawk missiles and ensuring a smooth transition of the USS America Carrier Battle Group to the Persian Gulf from under his command. The ground war was essentially over and Provenzano had been able to watch the whole thing unfold without much involvement.

That was about to change.

"Admiral?" The Kennedy Battle Group's Anti-Surface Warfare Officer said as he approached Provenzano.

"Yeah."

"Sir, we just got a report from a Nimrod that there's an Israeli attack boat approaching Jeddah."

The Admiral nearly jumped out of his seat.

"What?" he asked.

"An Israeli fast attack boat," The ASUW repeated.

Another officer walked up and handed the ASUW a slip of paper. He read it quickly.

"The Chicago's tracking it too."

"Intercept it, quietly and quickly. Keep it from the Saudis if you can," COM-CARGRU 2 ordered.

Provenzano turned to his aide.

"What the hell would the Israelis be doing in Jeddah?" he asked.

"I have no idea Admiral, but I doubt it's a good thing."

Admiral Provenzano nodded.

"Get me NAVCENT on the horn, now."

♦   ♦   ♦

Fogan could barely make out the boat as it approached the small fishing dock southwest of the Hay Al-Quarayat section of Jeddah. The matte black paint scheme made the Zaharon nearly invisible in the moonless night of the Arabian West Coast.

The coxswain skillfully drove the boat towards the dock at high speed and reversed the thrusters. As soon as the engines quieted, Tsayid picked up the short-wave transmitter on the Zaharon.

"Crossing Jordan," he said.

The code words were chosen from Operation Thunderball in Entebbe. They referenced the Jordan River, beyond which was hostility towards Israel. Since that operation, the words have meant that Israeli troops were entering a dangerous, foreign land. He was telling Yaakobi that they had arrived.

The boat stopped just as the bow came in contact with the dock and he added slight forward thrust to keep the boat against it. The team members exited the boat swiftly and ran silently up the dock.

The Coxswain turned the boat around and fled out to sea. The entire insertion took less than a minute and the team ran towards the road.

Fogan climbed into the back of the lead van and slid the cargo door open, signaling the team that it was clear for them to proceed. The Lotar Eilat men jumped into Fogan's van while Tsayid's S-13 team got into the trail vehicle. Tsayid clambered into the driver seat and started the van. Once Cohen was certain they were all accounted for, he dove in and closed the door.

Fogan pulled away and Amitai sat down next to him in the passenger seat. Tsayid followed closely with the S-13 team.

"Here," Fogan said, handing Amitai the photos of the doctor.

Amitai pulled out a small red-lens Mag Lite, turned it on, and held it in his teeth while he thumbed through the black and white photos.

"I think the colonel will be in the north wing, but I couldn't confirm it," Fogan told him.

Fogan pointed to the photos in Amitai's hands.

"This Doctor was with Yafai today in the north wing."

Amitai perused the photos silently and passed the copies around to the rest of the team. They studied quickly knowing they were only about five minutes from the hospital.

♦   ♦   ♦

The Bear, as the Commander in Chief for the United States Central Command was known, was thrilled by the swiftness of the ground campaign. He had been confident in his plan from the onset and the success had served as a validation of his storied career. He never thought about it at the time, but his pathetically skewed routing of the mighty Iraqi Army would permanently inscribe his name in history books throughout the world.

He sat at his Command table with the Saudi Ground Forces Commander for what was to be one of the final press photo opportunities of the short ground war. The distraught look on the face of his senior naval officer caught him by surprise as he walked up and leaned down to whisper in his ear.

"General, we have a situation," Admiral Macintosh said succinctly.

"Excuse me General," the Bear told his Saudi colleague.

He stood and walked to the back of the room with the Admiral. Macintosh spoke in a very guarded tone to the coalition Commander.

"General, we intercepted the track of an Israeli attack boat near Jeddah Harbor."

The Bear knew immediately what this involved. He also knew that it could permanently damage the post-war relationship that was sure to blossom from Desert Storm.

"Go straight to General Piatt and tell him exactly what you just told me. Tell him I said to drop everything and take care of this right now. He'll know."

"Yes, Sir."

♦   ♦   ♦

The vans pulled into the staff parking lot off Al-Jadid Street, behind the north wing of the Jeddah hospital. They assimilated nicely into the cars that were parked there and pulled into adjacent spots.

The Lotar Eilat team got out and walked calmly towards the door that Fogan had seen Yafai walk out of. Amitai led them through the door into an empty hallway lined with rooms. At the far end was a nurse's station. He was hoping not to have to walk that deeply into the foreign hospital, but needed to ask one of the nurses about the doctor in the picture.

Before they reached the nurse's station, one of the female nurses looked up in shock to see four men walking down the hallway. She stood and turned towards someone standing out of Amitai's line of sight. From her body language, the Israeli could tell they were not supposed to be there, even as Saudi men.

The doctor from the photos stepped out from behind the nurse's station and walked towards the team.

"What are you doing here?" the doctor asked in Arabic.

"I must speak to you," Amitai responded in perfect Arabic with a western Saudi accent.

He stopped halfway between the exit and the nurse's station, forcing the doctor to continue walking towards them.

"What is it?" the doctor said as he approached.

When the doctor reached the team. Two of the Israelis stepped between he and the Nurse's station, blocking the nurses' view.

"Where is the colonel?" Amitai asked directly.

"What are you talking about?" the doctor asked.

Amitai slid his hand to his rifle and tilted it up until the barrel was in the doctor's ribcage.

"I will murder you right here and find him myself. Now where is he?" Amitai said in a very cold, direct tone.

The doctor was an unwilling pawn in the whole episode. He wanted nothing to do with violence and was suddenly very frightened. For a moment, Amitai thought the Saudi was going to pass out.

"Downstairs, he's downstairs," the doctor stuttered from behind wide eyes.

"Take me there."

"This way," the doctor turned towards the nurse's station.

"No," Amitai said, grabbing the doctor's arm, "the stairs."

The doctor nodded and walked towards the exit door. Just inside was a door leading to the outer stairwell. The nurse at the other end sat back down, assuming everything was fine.

"Is he guarded?" Amitai asked the doctor.

"One guard only. He is badly injured. He can't even walk," the doctor told him.

Without the doctor noticing, Amitai slid the rifle back around his side and pulled out his silenced 22 pistol. The men emerged on the bottom floor and stepped into the unoccupied basement of the north wing. The only light in the hallway came from the colonel's room, which was second on the right from the stairwell.

The doctor stepped into the room and the Saudi guard stood from his chair. Before he even noticed the men behind the doctor, Amitai leveled the 22 over the doctor's shoulder and fired two rounds into the guard's face, killing him instantly.

The doctor jumped at the sight and cowered in the corner behind the fallen terrorist.

"Colonel?" Amitai said in Hebrew as he shook Colonel Urit awake, "Colonel Urit?"

"Yes, yes," the colonel was shocked by the sound of his native language.

"You will be safe now, let's go," Amitai said.

Two of the Lotar Eilat team members grabbed Colonel Urit and arranged him as best they could to carry him up the stairs to the van. Colonel Urit summoned the final reserves of strength he had to suppress the urge to yell out in pain. Salvation was at hand.

The men carrying Colonel Urit were lead out of the room by the forth team member and headed for the stairs. Amitai turned to the doctor who was cowering in the corner and without any emotion, raised his pistol.

The doctor held up his hands in defense, but they failed to slow the two rounds fired at his head. He slumped to the floor, dead.

It was a message.

In all its brutality, the message would dictate in a common language to those who followed that collusion with the enemies of Israel was intolerable.

Amitai swiftly caught up to the rest of the team and covered their escape. The point man looked out the door at the top of the stairs and saw no one at the Nurse's station. The team quickly exited the north wing and walked to the van.

"Dana, where's Dana?" the colonel pleaded.

"We will get her Colonel," Amitai assured him.

As gently as they could, the Lotar Eilat men set Colonel Urit on the floor of the van. Amitai looked up at Fogan.

"Take him to the boat, now."

He then slid the door shut.

Fogan drove off in the direction of the fishing dock and the Lotar Eilat team climbed into Tsayid's van.

"Let's go," Amitai told the mission leader.

♦   ♦   ♦

Fogan pulled up to the dock and flashed his headlights out to sea. The Mossad coxswain saw the signal and accelerated in the direction of the dock. The roar of the Zaharon's powerful engines rose just as the distant sound of the US Navy Frigate would have been audible to him.

"Colonel, can you walk at all?" Fogan asked.

"No, I don't think so."

"OK, hold on," Fogan told him.

The agent ran around the van and opened the door. He could hear the sound of the attack boat growing louder and felt an adequate flow of adrenaline to assure his ability to carry Colonel Urit.

"Alright Colonel, hold on," Fogan told Colonel Urit as he heaved the colonel over his shoulder.

Colonel Urit let out a groan of agony, but knew the ordeal was almost over. Fogan adjusted Colonel Urit into a fireman's carry and began shuffling down the dock just as the Zaharon pulled up to it. The agent got the colonel to the boat and flipped him off of his shoulder onto the bow.

"Aaaah!" Colonel Urit shrieked.

The Coxswain set the throttle and scurried onto the bow to pull the colonel all the way aboard. Fogan jumped onto the boat, and together they wrestled the battered colonel into a seat.

"Let's go!" Fogan yelled at the coxswain.

The Mossad man turned the boat and slowly pushed the throttles to the stops. The boat jumped the surf and jarred the colonel in his seat. With every wave, Colonel Urit let out a groan of pain. He was now in shock and close to falling unconscious. The only thing keeping him awake was the uncertain fate of his beloved daughter.

The spotlight from the frigate was blinding as it hit the coxswain directly in the eyes. He had not been looking at the radar to see the large vessel pull into their path. Fogan squinted through the glaring white light and saw the bow wake of the warship cutting towards them.

"Stop!" Fogan yelled.

"But…"

"They will blow us out of the water. We can't run."

The coxswain throttled back and settled the boat to a crawl.

"Damn!" he exclaimed.

◆   ◆   ◆

When Colonel Wahid came through the door to the room that had become his cell, Cross knew he was about to die. The Saudi Colonel had cleaned himself up somewhat, but would permanently wear scars from the injuries the Marine inflicted upon him. The look on the Saudi's face was one of pure hatred. Cross knew that by not finishing off Wahid, he had sealed his own fate. True to his nature, Cross was going to go out with his head high.

"What the fuck do you want?" Cross barked.

He spit at the Colonel in defiance. Wahid backhanded Cross, who had no way to defend himself. The blow knocked Cross to the floor.

The Marine's laughing infuriated Wahid.

"My mother hits harder than that, bitch," Cross laughed, spitting out blood onto the floor.

He would rather die defiant than as a coward.

◆   ◆   ◆

It would be a fast and very ferocious raid on the compound of Muta' Yafai. The team knew that the inner circle of Yafai's organization viewed all outsiders as enemies of Islam and would react violently. Tsayid wanted to beat them to it.

The vans passed the Emirate compound and turned North on Al Mina-Al Balad Street two blocks from the Khuzam Palace.

"Now," Tsayid said.

Amitai slid open the door and the rest of the rescue team kicked out the tinted windows of the small van to facilitate accurate shooting.

Tsayid turned right onto Al Matar-Al Jami'ah, Yafai's compound was a block away.

"Get ready!" Tsayid ordered.

Two team members leaned out of either side of the van and Amitai grabbed a satchel charge from underneath the middle bench seat. He felt along with his fingers until he found the fuse igniter.

There were two guards at the palace gate and both looked in the direction of the van when they heard its engine whine to near fifty miles an hour. Before they could ascertain the make of the small van, four of the team members fired bursts from their suppressed CAR-15 rifles.

The suppressors only served to muffle the muzzle blast since the assault rifles fired the supersonic 5.56mm NATO round, but they were too far from the house for the ballistic report to alert the residents.

The bodies of the guards jerked from the impacting rounds and they fell dead to the sidewalk.

Tsayid crashed through the iron gate and accelerated down the long drive to the main house. The noise from the gate tumbling out of the path was actually louder than the rifle fire that killed the two sentries.

The team leader was relieved to see that there were no guards standing outside the main house as they pulled up. He stopped the van well short of the door, as Amitai jumped out, ran towards the massive wooden barricade, and pulled the ring on the satchel charge fuse trigger. He pinched the time fuse and waited until he could feel the heat from the smoldering material within it before tossing the satchel at the base of the door.

As the charge slammed into the base of the huge door, the rest of the team fanned out along the periphery of the driveway. The impacting satchel charge served to alert someone on the inside who began opening the door before the fuse reached its end.

The door opened about a foot before the charge exploded. The blast not only removed the door, but also collapsed the entire front of the one-story building.

The team ran for the opening with total fluidity, covering every angle with their weapons as they moved.

◆   ◆   ◆

The blast made Cross jump. His heart began racing as he tried to assess what it was he had heard. Outside his door, people started yelling in Arabic. He swung his feet underneath him and stood, backing to the opposite side of the room from the door. He could tell immediately by the look on Wahid's face that the sound was unexpected.

"Hear that?" Cross asked.

Wahid looked at him and the Marine smiled.

"Those would be my boys. You are a dead man."

◆   ◆   ◆

Dana was also very optimistic about the noises she was hearing. The beatings she had endured after her successful resistance to rape had strengthened her resolve. She knew help was on the way.

"Here!" She screamed.

The yelling hurt her broken ribs, but she had to hope; that was all she had left.

"I'm in here!"

◆   ◆   ◆

The team immediately noticed that Yafai's palace was an exact copy of the shooting house, built using information provided by Joe Fogan, that they practiced in at Ouvda airbase. They split into four two-man elements to begin clearing the u-shaped structure room-to-room.

The S-13 team went to the right and began engaging terrorists immediately. Two team members would remain in the main corridor while the other two cleared a room.

They cleared rooms methodically with tactics learned from the illustrious history of the British SAS.

Tsayid threw a concussion grenade in the first room and rolled away from the door until it detonated. Before the flash faded, he entered the room and exited the "fatal funnel" to the right. There was no one in the room, so he and his partner exited swiftly and crossed the hallway to the side running along the outside of the courtyard.

Tsayid took up a defensive posture while the other two-man element cleared a room in the same fashion. They repeated the process all the way down the hall. He heard yelling from around a turn in the corridor, but saw no one. He began to dread what they would see when the team made the turn, especially since they had yet to see anyone in the rooms they'd cleared.

Tsayid held up a fist when the team cleared the last room before the corner. The team froze.

Tsayid pulled out a tiny mirror on a telescoping rod that resembled the antenna on a portable radio. He positioned the mirror and pushed it slowly around the corner to see what was waiting for them.

He saw six men congregating at the end of the hallway as if trying to decide who was in charge.

Amateurs, he thought, but did not for one second take the terrorists' stupidity for granted.

He touched his index finger to his thumb on his free hand to tell them men that there were six men.

Tsayid made a sweeping motion with the hand telling the men that they would turn the corner together. The three other members of the team stacked up behind Tsayid at the corner and tapped him to signal that they were ready.

Tsayid gave the signal with his finger and the last man in the stack began moving out into the line of fire. The other members of the team timed their departure perfectly so they all became exposed at the same time.

Yafai's henchmen had no time to react before their bodies were riddled with magnificently placed shot groups from the Israeli commandos.

All six died instantly.

As soon as the sound faded, Tsayid heard something. He held a hand to his ear and the team again froze.

"Here!" he heard the distant sound of a female voice and knew it was Dana.

"Let's go," he said over the radio.

The men skipped all the remaining rooms as they slid their feet cautiously and swiftly towards the end and the sound. Two men faced forward and two rearward. They were covered.

"Lieutenant Urit!" Tsayid yelled when they reached the pile of dead Saudis.

"In here!" she yelled from behind the door directly in front of Tsayid.

The team leader kicked the door in and saw Dana standing against the far wall.

"Are you OK?" he asked in Hebrew.

Dana was stunned. She expected her rescuers to be American, not Israeli.

"Yes, where is my father?" she asked.

"Safe, let's move," Tsayid ordered.

"I have her," he said into his microphone.

"Let's go," Amitai responded.

Tsayid led Dana back into the hallway.

"Did you find Cross?" she asked.

"What?" Tsayid asked her.

"The Marine, where is he?"

"There's no Marine, let's go!" Tsayid said forcefully.

Dana became horrified.

"I am not leaving without him, he's here!" she said.

Tsayid turned and glared at the beautiful Israeli officer.

"Let's go!" he growled.

"He saved our lives, we find him or I stay here."

Dana's ultimatum was delivered like ice. There was no debating the issue. Operation Hejazi called for inflicting the maximum amount of damage in the process of the rescue. They hoped to get Muta' Yafai and put to death what the Mossad saw as the threat of the future, but as soon as they had both Urits, the mission was over.

Tsayid gritted his teeth. The longer they remained here, the more chances they had of failing.

They had come too far.

"Two, did you finish clearing?" Tsayid asked Amitai.

Amitai stopped in the middle of the corridor on the opposite end of the palace.

"What? No," he responded.

"Look for one more, a Marine, an American Marine."

"Roger," Amitai agreed.

He did not mind rescuing more people. It offered him the opportunity to kill more terrorists.

Amitai's element heard the order and went back to sweeping the rooms towards the end of the hallway.

♦   ♦   ♦

Cross heard them coming and heard them shooting. Basic reasoning told him that anyone shooting his captors could not be very bad, so he decided to gamble.

"Hey!" he yelled.

Amitai froze in his tracks.

Colonel Wahid drew his pistol and slammed it into Cross's face, silencing him.

"Did you hear something?" Amitai asked his assistant.

"No."

"Hey!" Cross yelled again from the floor.

Amitai and his assistant looked at each other and ran towards the sound. The team leader tried the handle before risking a broken ankle from kicking it in, and it turned. He opened the door.

Wahid stood up Cross and held the Marine in front of him. The Saudi drove the barrel of his pistol into Cross's temple.

When the door opened, a figure dressed as an Arab looked in. Colonel Wahid had barely inhaled to say something when the Arab drew a pistol and put a round directly into his open mouth.

Wahid's legs buckled beneath him as his lifeless body crumpled to the ground.

Cross did not speak a word of Arabic and said the only thing he thought the Saudi liberators would understand.

"American," Cross said, holding up his hands in surrender. "I'm an American."

Amitai smiled as he surveyed the badly beaten Marine.

"We're Israeli, can you walk?"

Cross's inflated at the revelation.

"No shit? Hell yes! I'll crawl if I have to," the ecstatic Marine assured him.

"Let's go," Amitai ordered.

CHAPTER 19

Escape

Tsayid drove as fast as the overloaded van would go towards the coast. The members of the rescue team stayed withdrawn inside the van in the hope that the missing windows would go unnoticed to onlookers. They were far from being safe.

As he made the last turn onto the seaside highway, the right rear tire of the van exploded in a shower of rubber chunks that flew into the shattered windows. Tsayid fought to keep the van from rolling over and managed to slow it down. The short distance they had left to cover seemed to take an eternity.

Tsayid pulled into the parking area of the dock and flashed his lights. The rest of the team began unloading and headed towards the edge of the water. Dana and Cross helped each other walk and refused to be separated in the interest of time. Together, they hobbled down the long dock, surrounded by their armed saviors.

Tsayid brought up the rear and Neri Cohen tapped him as he passed to get a count. Everyone was accounted for.

Tsayid froze.

The boat was nowhere in sight.

"My God," Tsayid whispered as he looked at Cohen.

They knew something had gone drastically wrong.

"Bat 2, Bat 2," Tsayid said into his mouthpiece.

There was no response.

Sirens could be heard in the distance and the men began to get restless. The police had been alerted to the raid on the Yafai palace and were searching the streets for Tsayid's team.

They were running out of time.

"Where is it?" Amitai snarled at the blank sea.

The sound of tires skidding in the distance made all of the team members crouch down.

"There," Cohen whispered, pointing towards the city.

There were two white cars speeding towards them from the city center. Tsayid looked around and knew that they could not make it back to the van in time to escape.

It would not do them any good regardless.

The Saudi Police cars slowed at the sight of the van and Tsayid knew that time had just run out for the rescue team.

"Into the water," Cross growled.

The Marine was worried about their prospects, as were the rest of the team. There was one place that any amphibious operator can find haven and Cross's instincts, his fear of capture, pulled him towards it.

When he graduated from US Navy dive school at Ford Island, Hawaii, Cross was given a certificate that proclaimed him worthy of joining the realm of Neptune. Cross's Navy Diver diploma was signed by the God of the Sea as a declaration of his transformation into a creature that found more comfort in the dark, silent womb of the ocean than on solid ground. When threatened, he always had a home that would shelter him.

That home was the Sea.

"Go!" Tsayid yelled.

The S-13 operators shared Cross's comfort with water and were thinking the same thing.

"Dana, stay with me," Cross told her.

The men slid to the edge of the dock just as the Police cars were pulling alongside the van.

"Go," Cross whispered to Dana.

Dana slid her legs off the edge and let go. The drop was nearly ten feet and she landed slightly askew. The impact knocked her breath out, but she was able to surface and tread water. Cross landed next to her and sank several feet into the blackness. The rumble of the bubbles and the buoyant force of the seawater felt like a massive hand, safely nestling the Marine in its grasp. Cross was safe.

When he surfaced, Cross saw that Dana was having trouble staying afloat due to her injuries. Their utilities were saturated and quickly lost any ability to assist their buoyancy.

Fortunately for the team, there was a constant supply of small waves crashing around them to veil any noises they made. Cross did not have the strength to keep Dana afloat and he knew it.

"Hold on Dana, hold on," Cross said between waves.

The recon Marine let himself slide under the surface of the sea and sink. As he descended, he took off his trousers and tied the cuffs together in a square knot. He tugged on the knot to lock it in place and began slowly, calmly kicking back to the surface.

He surfaced next to Dana, who was about to submit to her injuries and sink below the waves.

"Here!" Cross told her.

He draped the trousers, tied in a loop, around her neck with the waist in front of her face. With scooping motion to draw air underwater, Cross filled the trousers with air. Dana felt the field-expedient life vest inflate around her head and she instinctively draped her arms over it to rest. She was amazed at how well the contraption worked.

When fully inflated, the utility trousers kept her afloat with no effort. She rested and felt better immediately.

"Thank you Cross," she said in a very exhausted voice.

"You OK?" he asked.

"Yes, thank you."

Among the chaos and stress of the situation, Cross became conscious that he was not wearing underwear. As long as Recon spent in the field during combat without bathing, it was a moot point.

Oh well, he thought, *at least the cause is noble.*

As the Saudi policemen searched around the van, the rescue team slowly swam closer to shore. They had no idea what the currents of the Red Sea would be like and had no way of summoning aid should the need arise.

Killing the policemen was a safer option.

Tsayid was swimming next to Neri Cohen and grabbed the S-13 team leader when he saw two additional police cars approaching. Tsayid pointed to the cars. Cohen nodded. Their situation was getting worse by the second.

When the other two cars parked, two men emerged from each. The members of the rescue team were almost to the beach and saw what was beginning to look like the ingredients for a formidable firefight. The Saudis had completed their search of the area and were beginning to spread out to search of the beach. It was go time for the rescue team.

Cross jerked his head around when he heard the sound. He saw nothing for a moment and thought he had imagined it. Then the unmistakable high-frequency rotor chop of a Blackhawk became loud enough to hear over the crashing waves.

The Sea Hawk variant was coming from the south, parallel to the beach and directly over the surf zone. Tsayid looked at the fast-approaching helicopter and then to the Saudi police. They stopped near the van to see what the helicopter was going to do.

The Sea Hawk passed directly over the team at one hundred knots. Cross could not see the markings, but knew it was American. He just felt it. The Navy helicopter banked hard out to sea to bleed off speed and came back in directly towards the Saudis. The pilot swung the helicopter sideways and a brilliant spotlight came to life from the Sea Hawk's left crew door.

The Saudi policemen held hands in front of their faces to shield their eyes from the night sun. They all ducked as the helicopter flared and landed twenty feet from where they were standing.

As the main rotor feathered, Tsayid and the rest of the rescue team could see a man get out of the Sea Hawk and approach the Saudis. The man was not dressed in a military uniform, but rather civilian clothes. He waved his hands in an animated fashion as he spoke and it was obvious he was telling the Saudis something of great import. The Saudis quickly stood up straight and ran to their cars. They sped off in a line, back towards town.

Cross was next to Tsayid and Cohen now. The three were lying on their stomachs as the waves rolled on top of them. With every wave, their bodies would float a few inches and slide up the beach. Then when the wave ran back out, they were drawn into a shallow depression from the water dredging the wet sand from around their bodies. It was soothing to these men of the sea.

The men looked at each other and shrugged. No one knew what was going on.

The man from the Sea Hawk jogged down to the dock and ran out onto it in a frantic search for something. He reached the end of the dock and scanned the horizon. When he saw nothing, he turned around. Tsayid saw his chance to get closer and see who it was, so he came to a crouch and shuffled quickly back towards the dock. When the mystery man finished his search, he turned and ran towards the helicopter.

Tsyaid intercepted his path.

As the man approached in the darkness, Tsayid recognized him.

It was Joe Fogan.

"Here!" Tsayid yelled in a powerful whisper.

Fogan nearly jumped out of his skin.

"My God man!" Fogan yelled, catching his breath, "where are they?"

Tsayid put two fingers in his mouth and whistled very loudly. Within seconds, Fogan could see the team emerging from the surf, running towards the helicopter.

"Let's get the hell out of here," Fogan ordered.

Tsayid ran towards the helicopter and arrived just before the rest of his team. He nervously stood and counted each member in, beginning with Dana and the Marine. In his urgency, he made no notice of the fact that Cross was naked from the waist down.

Once the team was aboard and accounted for, Tsayid gave a thumbs-up to Fogan. The CIA man motioned to the pilot and they lifted off.

Cross leaned back in the relief of having lived through the ordeal and in the knowledge that Dana was safe.

"Here!" Dana said, pulling the saturated trousers over her head to give back to Cross.

She gazed briefly down at Cross's lap and smiled.

"Hey! The water was cold!" the Marine yelled with an embarrassed smirk as he covered himself with his drenched fatigues.

Epilogue

"Colonel, I owe you!" Jay Kerwin yelled over the roar of the Pave Low's engines.

Colonel Red Richardson just laughed as he maneuvered the massive aircraft over the deck of the USNS Comfort.

"Go get her kid!" he yelled to the PJ.

Jay slung his ALICE pack and ran to the back of the helicopter through the huge grins from his fellow pararescuemen. Each of the men slapped him on the back and he tried not to smile.

At the rear of the MH-53J, attached to a bar running over the rear door, was a fastrope. Jay looked back to his team one last time and grabbed it. He slid down the rope to the deck of the ship, several yards from the mass of sailors who were on hand to witness the spectacle.

When he reached the bottom, Shellie McLean ran over to him. In the rotor wash of the departing helicopter, they kissed to the inaudible cheers of his teammates, and the thunderous roar of the Comfort's crew. Shellie's long, blonde hair flailed in the wind, covering their faces.

The kiss seemed to last forever, not that they were in a hurry for it to end.

♦   ♦   ♦

USS John F. Kennedy (CV-67)
Red Sea

"Come!" Colonel Urit turned from his beloved Dana and yelled in response to the rap on the infirmary hatch.

General Tom Samuelson peeked around the door and looked into the nicely appointed, however small, medical room.

"Tom!" Colonel Urit yelled.

Dana let go of her father's hand and walked over to give the general a hug. Samuelson coughed to suppress a slight choking up. He was not expecting a warm reception from the two people he had risked everything to protect.

"What's wrong?" Dana asked the man who was effectively her uncle.

"I'm so sorry," he said softly, fighting back emotion.

"Why? You saved my life," Colonel Urit said.

Samuelson looked confused.

"Tom, they would have gotten me anyway. The surgery saved me," the Colonel smiled, "what you risked, I owe you my life."

"You would have done the same, Motta," Samuelson looked down, "probably better."

"Stop this nonsense, General, we are both alive and thankful to you," Dana said, "now stop it."

"Fair enough," Samuelson agreed.

"Where to, Tom?" Colonel Urit asked.

"Well, let's just say I will have a lot of time to entertain you when you come to Virginia."

Colonel Urit frowned.

"I'm sorry Tom."

"Hey, I'm just glad they're letting me bow out gracefully. No big deal," Samuelson assured him.

There was another knock on the hatch and the general scooted out of the way to facilitate the door opening again into the tiny room.

"Cross!" Dana squealed.

She stepped past the general and hugged the Marine around the neck, nearly cutting off the circulation to his head.

In the days since their escape from Jeddah, Cross had not been allowed contact with the Israelis. From the time he stepped off the Sea Hawk that came to rescue them, he was in debriefings. It was the first time Dana had seen him.

"Dana! Let the man breathe!" Colonel Urit yelled from his bed.

She released Cross from her grip and pulled away, smiling. She wiped her tears and became suddenly embarrassed by the display.

General Samuelson looked at Colonel Urit with confusion.

"Tom, this is Sergeant Crossley, he saved Dana. Hell, he saved all of us."

"General," Cross said with a nod, "I don't know about all that."

Samuelson extended his hand.

"A Navy Cross winner, the pleasure's mine."

Colonel Urit reached over to his bedside and retrieved a small pin.

"I have something for you, son," he said.

"They brought these to me," the colonel said, handing the pin to Cross.

Cross walked past the general and a smiling Dana to the IDF colonel's bedside. The colonel handed him the pin. It was a shield with a set of black wings coming out of either side.

They looked like bat wings.

"Those were mine," the colonel told him, "my S-13 wings."

"Wow," Cross said, handing the crest back.

Colonel Urit held up a hand, "I want you to have them."

Cross was floored. He didn't know what to say.

"Why?" he asked.

"Because you are a man of honor. You risked your life to save ours for no other reason than you saw injustice. You deserve them."

The colonel extended his hand and gave Cross a firm handshake.

"Thank you Cross."

"Anytime, Sir."

Cross turned to Dana.

"I have to leave, they're flying me back to my unit."

"Now?" Dana said, openly disappointed.

Cross nodded.

"Walk with him Dana," Colonel Urit told her, "I'm not going anywhere."

Cross and Dana walked out into the corridor and turned to each other.

"I…" he began.

Cross reached out with his hand and placed it on Dana's cheek.

"I know," Dana stopped him, and gave him a hug.

"Will I ever see you again?" she asked, with an awkwardness that was apparent to both of them.

The emotional barrier they had established out of a professional rapport was beginning to dissolve.

"Absolutely," the Marine said with a sheepish grin.

0-595-28243-1